One Religion Book

Different Paths

By Steven L Williams

One Religion Book

Different Paths

By Steven W.

One Religion Book

Visit our Web site at www.OneReligionBook.com

First Paperback Edition: November 2014

First Hardcover Edition: November 2014

ISBN : 978-0-578-15252-3

Printed in the United States of America

"Within each of us there is a silence, a silence as vast as the universe. And when we experience that silence, we remember who we are."
~ Gunilla Norris ~

Dedication

For my children and the children of the future,

Most people take their ideas to the graveyard and I have faith that you won't make that mistake. If you do all that you've dreamed of doing you will have an outstanding life. One day when I leave this earth I will make sure to have left on empty—not leaving with unanswered dreams or opportunities left untaken. When your day comes to leave this earth, leave knowing that you've accomplished every single thing you've wanted to do. It is only then that I'll know that I got my point across to you.

Acknowledgement

I cannot express enough thanks to my family and friends for their continued support and encouragement through this innovative, amazing journey: Alesia Richmond, Lester Richmond, Octavia Thomas, Patricia Daugherty and Vanessa Cristy Malevski, I offer my sincere appreciation to you.

The completion of this book could not have been accomplished without the support of Jill McKellan, my editor and proof reader. You've definitely earned a trip to Disney!

The people who inspired my interest for this science fictional book are innovative, technology driven, creative, artistic pioneers that have paved the way in our culture and society. I cannot go without recognizing great inspirations such as: Bill Gates, Larry Ellison, Mark Zuckerberg, Larry Page, Sergey Brin, Steve Jobs, Steve Harvey, Pharrell Williams, Shawn Carter, Kanye West, Aubrey Drake Graham, Scott Ramon Seguro Mescudi and Paramahansa Yogananda.

There are many more people who I feel gratitude for and am thankful for their inspiration but time, space, and modesty compel me to stop here.

Finally, my deepest gratitude for this book goes out to Disney. Through the Disney College Program, I've learned some amazing things and I know that anything is possible. The friendships I've made through DCP and the bonds that were built are strong and will never be broken.

Table of Contents

Prologue

Part One

Prologue

"There may be one universe but there are many worlds that exist within it."

The power to change the world, perhaps the entire universe, is in the hands of those who dare to dream for something bigger, something better. Of course, those same individuals can choose destruction if they so desire. In the end, it all gets sorted out.

Staring out the window all he could see was the brightly illuminated surface of the paved parking lot below with cast shadows of street lamps and other buildings around it. Carlisle Lewis's amber eyes seemed to be focused on it but his thoughts were clearly elsewhere—they gave him away. They held a certain light that couldn't be hidden in them. It was the intense look of a warrior but also the deeper reflections of a scholar—a thinker, as they say. In short, Carlisle Elias Lewis was a man who didn't assume anything without a lot of contemplation and research.

Carlisle's attention turned to the door of the room. He watched Aerial Kennedy walk in, wearing a deep gray suit with a dark blue tie, his shoulder length silver hair stayed neatly in place and his peppered beard was neatly trimmed.

"Mr. Lewis, I'm glad to finally have the chance to meet you. You've intrigued me for quite some time."

Carlisle stood up and walked over shaking the man's hand but the suspicion in his eyes couldn't be hidden.

"Ah, you don't trust me. Very wise—not to trust someone you don't know well, *yet.*"

"Yet, Mr. Kennedy?"

"Aerial, please," he said, gesturing toward the chairs for Carlisle to sit back down.

He sat down, crossing his one leg over the other and then ran his hand down his white shirt, which was habit.

The two men assessed each other for just a few seconds, not saying anything but looking for the clues in what was left unsaid. A hint from the body posture. An escaped emotion out of the eye. A nervous habit.

Although he couldn't say for certain why, Carlisle sensed that he liked the man and appreciated him greatly. In part, it was because Aerial Kennedy was one of the most prominent, successful businessmen of the century, making the still relevant Forbes Top Ten Influential Entrepreneur's list—something that he'd aspired to do some day. He was close but he wasn't quite there.

"So, tell me more about O.R.B., Carlisle."

Aerial's piercing blue eyes stared into Carlisle's, showing he was a man who seldom had to wait for answers.

"When it comes to the logistics…" Carlisle was quickly cut off by Aerial, who raised his hand in the air and didn't need to say a single word to stop him in mid-sentence.

"Pardon me for interrupting. I know all the logistics, probably as well as you do. What I don't know is the philosophical aspect behind it. What inspired the One Religion Book, or O.R.B., as it is known by to so many?"

Carlisle smiled. If there was anything he enjoyed discussing, it was his motivation behind the website. In a way, although O.R.B. was a website, it was also the means to define the story of his life.

"I have a feeling you have some ideas but I'll gladly share the philosophical value of O.R.B. with you, Aerial.

"My upbringing wasn't—ideal, let's just say. Is that uncommon? No, not so much. However, I found that I was constantly up against greater adversities than just coming from a lousy, rat trap of a neighborhood, without a sound family structure."

Carlisle glanced over to Aerial, who seemed to be piercing right through him with those lucid blue eyes and tapping into his thoughts. It was unsettling but he sensed these questions were important; that they were leading to something he didn't quite understand. He wanted to be in the know.

"You see, everything from my skin color to the people I associated with down to the way I chose to view life was met with resistance at some point or another. At first, it pissed me off but then something clicked in me one day that made me view it all differently. I was smart enough to see what was happening. I wasn't afraid to work hard to make a change. I even had, and still do, that optimistic feeling that I can change the world by example. Those thoughts swirled around in my mind, kind of marinating, for a long time."

"But you didn't do anything immediately?" Aerial replied. He asked it like a question but it was actually more of a statement.

"No, like most men, I was driven by something."

"The death." Again, a question that came across as a statement.

"Yeah," Carlisle said. That was one subject he didn't want to expand further on.

"You see, Aerial, the website became a place where everyone could go to in order to satisfy their curiosities, ask the questions they had, and find solutions without judging—as much as possible. I'm sure you've noticed the safeguards against such activity on the site. I don't want anyone to be cast away because they are curious by someone who has a stranglehold on some preconceived notion."

"You want everyone to be one," Aerial said, putting his hand under his chin and leaning forward.

"Sure, something like that."

"Do you think that's possible, Carlisle?"

"No, but that's never been my intention. A hope…perhaps but I am a realistic man despite still being a relatively young man."

"I can tell," Aerial said.

"So, what I am interested in is why you've called me here," Carlisle said. "I know you're a busy man and while my story may fascinate you, it hardly warrants such elaborate methods to set up a meeting with me."

"You seem to discredit your success. I'm sure people flock to you for your time."

"People—yes. People like Aerial Kennedy, not so much. I make the connections with those that can help take me places."

Aerial laughed softly and the crease lines around his eyes made him look less intimidating, an easier man to open up to.

"Well spoken, Carlisle. What I want to talk to you about is something that is happening right now, in the world as you know it, that I know you are not aware of."

Carlisle stared at him, not sure how to process what he meant.

"There's another society within the fabric of the one we currently have here on Earth, as well as other places."

Now it was Carlisle who cut off Aerial. "Other places? You mean like outer space?"

3

"Yes but not in the way you may be thinking. It's a society that is forming and striving toward creating a more united universe, not just world."

No one liked to be played for a fool and part of Carlisle's common sense was shouting that he was being taken on some crazy joy ride by an eccentric Aerial Kennedy. It didn't fit the bill of what the man was known for.

"I see the doubt in your eyes. It's quite logical, actually, but here me out, Carlisle. This society is one that's meant to start creating a new world, one in which everyone of value recognizes their role and contributes to something better…something stronger."

"You sound like Hitler with his weeding out the weak deal," Carlisle said suspiciously. The brief description he'd been provided appeared to be the exact opposite of everything he tried to stand for in his life.

"I assure you that is not the case, although I understand your point. Answer me one question. Do you think that everyone in this world will use their gifts, their potential?"

"No, unfortunately."

"Do you think that if they knew they were going to die they'd use their gifts to try and salvage their lives?"

"For a bit of time but if they don't want to embrace them, they're likely to revert back," Carlisle said.

"Exactly. What I am talking about is a world where everyone knows their role and what they are destined to do. There are entrepreneurs, forward minded thinking people such as ourselves that help create the environment we live in. Then there are those who are excellent at implementation and follow-through, while others like to do the busy work, doing what they're told and not really questioning the source of it.

"It's this concept that I am talking of when I tell you about this parallel society which already exists and is growing stronger by the day."

"Like some secret society?"

"It's secretive at this time but such won't always be the case."

"Why tell me without any sort of commitment or at least signing a NDA or something like that?"

"Well, we are friendly and inclusive but I can assure you that you'd have challenges if you tried to sabotage the efforts in any way."

4

"Challenges…like death."

"Well, I don't prefer to think so drably. I was thinking that no one would believe you, you'd lose credibility, and before you knew it, someone would be buying O.R.B. for half its worth just to salvage it and get you out of the picture.

"That's how most 'buy-outs' happen to take place, after all."

"You definitely know about that, Aerial."

"Yes, I definitely do."

"So, what is it you ask of me?"

"Just to hear me out, which you've done. Think about what I've told you, Carlisle. I believe we can be of great value to each other and over time, dare I say, develop a friendship or at least a fond rapport for each other."

"Who else is a part of this?" Carlisle asked.

"People you'll know in due time. Some that you've never heard of before, of course."

Aerial stood up and looked downward, assessing that his suit hadn't wrinkled and then looked at Carlisle casually, almost as if he hadn't just revealed anything of substantial importance at all, and added, "How long would you like to think things over before we meet again?"

Carlisle's instincts had taken him far and he felt them saying that there was no reason to delay the inevitable. "I look forward to hearing the details. Call me when you have specifics available."

"A wise, young man, just like I'd heard."

"And every bit the masterful negotiator, as I've always heard," Carlisle replied.

The two men laughed and Carlisle stood up and walked over to Aerial and shook his hand.

He walked out of Aerial's luxurious penthouse on Wycombe Square, a swarthy part of London without a doubt, and made his way down to the street, where his driver was waiting.

Part One

1

"There is always something more, something better. You just have to find it."

The only light in the room came from the computer monitor as Carlisle stared at it like a bug drawn to light. With an intent look on his face he scrolled down the website, looking at beautiful face after beautiful face. Unlike when he was at his school as one of many "seemingly insignificant" twelfth graders, when he was on the website networking he was considerably more cool, more eloquent. Or at least as eloquent as an eighteen year old guy in high school can get.

"Ah, she's pretty," he mumbled, nodding his head approvingly.

Ding.

Carlisle looked down and saw an emoticon in the bottom corner of his screen with a blue circle around it—someone had sent him a wink and a message. He was immediately curious and couldn't click on it fast enough to see what was happening.

Misz Sunshine: Hi CarmaMax. Noticed your picture. You're cute.

Okay, play this cool, man.

CarmaMax: And you're beautiful. What's happening?

Misz Sunshine: Looking for someone interesting to talk with. Not much else happening.

CarmaMax: Well, I'm interested in talking, too.

Misz Sunshine: You're funny.

CarmaMax: Is that a good thing.

Misz Sunshine: Sure is. What's your name?

CarmaMax: Carlisle.

Misz Sunshine: I like that…strong name to fit that good looking face.

CarmaMax: What's your name?

Misz Sunshine: Nicki.

I can't believe this. I'm actually having a real conversation with a hot girl, assuming she looks like her picture. Go ahead…ask.

CarmaMax: So, how about going out on a real date to talk sometime? Might be more fun than the IM route.

Misz Sunshine: I'd like that Carlisle. Tomorrow?

CarmaMax: Absolutely.

Misz Sunshine: 7:00?

CarmaMax: Perfect.

The two ended their IM and Carlisle stared down at a pad of white paper on his desk. It was definitely a small conquest to have gotten not only the address and telephone number but also a date with this girl. She was older, too, twenty. To an eighteen year old guy without tons of dating experience—okay, practically no dating experience—that was just like striking gold.

Carlisle's phone buzzed and he looked down. It was Ethan.

"What's happening?"

"Not much, just looking online."

"On that site again?"

"Yeah. I got a date tomorrow night."

"Really?" Ethan asked.

"Thanks for the vote of confidence. You've got to have some faith once in awhile, man."

"Hopefully she really shows up. Where you meeting?"

"I got her address. I'm meeting her at her apartment."

"No shit. How you going to get there?"

"Bus, I guess. I sure don't have a car—yet," Carlisle said.

"Man, can't wait to you get some wheels. Life will be so much easier."

"I'm not trying to save up and get them to be your chauffeur. I want to go where I want to go when I want to go. My schedule, no one else's."

"You'd abandon your bro?" Ethan asked. Was he serious? No. Still, there was a tone.

"We've been friends since second grade, through thick and thin, don't play like that."

"Well, I can't wait to hear how the big date turns out, Carlisle. I'll leave you to it. I've got to go study for this algebra test. If I don't pass, I'm screwed. Oh, and this weekend, I get to go do a rap at an amateur festival downtown. It'll be my chance to be found."

"Hope you're right. You got the talent, Ethan. Just need the break."

After the call, Carlisle got ready for bed. He was deep in thought about the following night. In his mind, he could see exactly how he wanted the night to go but the reality was that he wasn't as smooth as he wanted to be and a guy who was practically broke, living with his parents in their extremely shoddy house didn't have a whole lot to offer, aside from charm and being funny—at least he had the funny down according to Nicki.

By the next night, he'd went through a slew of emotions: nervous, excited, composed, and oddly enough, exhilarated. He couldn't explain that one but what did it matter?

The bus dropped him off at the corner in front of the entrance to the Disney Vista apartments. He looked around and they looked great from the outside, meticulously groomed and in good condition. As he approached the entrance to the grounds, he glanced down at the piece of paper with the specific directions on how to get to Nicki's apartment. Sounds of laughter were heard coming from somewhere on the grounds, although he couldn't say where. There was definitely a good time being had by some group of people. Girls screeching. Guys shouting and laughing. Music blaring.

This place is awesome, Carlisle thought. His curiosity immediately grew. It was like a whole different world within Orlando. How come he hadn't heard about it before?

It was easy to find the building but Carlisle still hadn't pinpointed the source of the party going on. He wondered if that was what they were going to do that night. No specific plan had been set. Even in his excitement he didn't want to commit to anything for too long until he knew he liked hanging around this girl—that she was who she seemed to be.

A few minutes later, Carlisle was inside Nicki's building and standing outside her apartment, ready to knock. He drew in a deep breath and paused for a brief period. Then he knocked.

On the second knock, the door opened and Nicki was standing there with a huge smile on her face. She looked just like her picture had: long, black smoothed out hair, muscular and athletic, a bright smile, and sparkling brown eyes. He thought he might be looking at Princess Jasmine herself. Her wedge sandals made her almost as tall as him. He was 5'10" and they were definitely standing eye to eye. Her bright yellow halter dress made her look exotic, yet friendly and energetic. She was nothing short of amazing.

9

"Carlisle?"

"Yeah, it's great to meet you, Nicki."

"Come on in? Were my directions decent?"

"Real easy. The bus schedule was ideal for 7:00."

"Good, I'd thought it would be."

With the door shut and Nicki walking first, Carlisle admired her body and the way she moved. She knew how to use what she had to its maximum potential. Even his limited experience told him that.

"So, what is this place? I've lived in Orlando my entire life and have never known about this."

"Really? It's like a giant party dorm for those of us who are attending DCP."

"DCP. What's that?"

Nicki looked at Carlisle and smiled. "Disney College Program."

"So, you go to college just for Disney?" Maybe she really is trying to be Princess Jasmine.

"No, not at all. It's an internship opportunity. It's pretty cool. Great housing, lots of fun, working for the Disney company in some way."

"What do you do for the program?"

"I'm in hospitality management so I'm working with the reservations program, learning a bit more about how they operate. It's a big corporation; there's a lot to it…a lot to learn."

"So, you just apply?"

"Yeah, it's pretty cool the way the set-up is. There's a bus to take us around, to work and when we're not working we can take the party bus to the clubs to hang out, too, if we want."

"Do you go to the clubs a lot?"

"I like to but I'm trying to save up money so I can't go as often others do. Plus, scamming around really isn't my thing. That's why I liked your profile."

Carlisle had put a great amount of thought into his profile on the website. He wanted to sound serious and smart, but also fun. Ethan had laughed his ass off at him while he was doing it but out of the two, he'd certainly gotten further. Then again, Ethan really didn't need a website to help him out because he wasn't afraid to be bold and take his chances with girls.

"So, how many people live here?" Carlisle asked.

"There's four of us."

"Wow. Must be hard to be alone?"

"Not as bad as you'd think. Two of my roomies have hooked up with some guys and spend a lot of time at their apartment. They don't live in the Vista. The other one works evenings with maintenance in the parks. I got lucky."

"Sounds like it."

<u>She is so beautiful. I want to get lucky.</u>

"Do you want a tour?" Nicki asked.

"Sure."

The tour didn't take too long. Two bedrooms, each with two beds pressed against opposite walls, one walk-in closet with each person taking half, and a bathroom with a shower, toilet, and sink. Then there was a vanity outside of it. Practical, efficient, and mostly like a hotel room or maybe a dorm room, although Carlisle had no clue. He hadn't gotten to that point. There was also a small television in the corner and a white fridge that was as empty as it might be sitting in the store, only it had some scuffs on the front of it.

"Well, that's it. Let's go sit down." Nicki walked over to the couch.

"Is this your couch?" Carlisle asked, sitting down and feeling a spring press against his butt, which made him squirm.

"No way," Nicki said. "They come with the place. Not very comfortable, are they?"

"Definitely not. They probably help a lot of chiropractors make some extra money, though. Does Disney have a chiropractor on site?"

Nicki laughed, which made Carlisle blush slightly.

"No chiropractor but that's not a bad idea."

A loud, giggling screech wafted through the windows from outside. Carlisle looked over, curious about it. Nicki didn't even seem to hear it.

"Where's the party?" he asked, pointing outside.

11

"Oh, that's the pool."

"There's a pool here?"

"Yeah, it gets pretty wild. Want to go take a look?"

"Sure."

Carlisle went down to the pool with Nicki and his eyes just about popped out of his head. He couldn't believe the mix of people he saw and the crazy fun they were having. There were no hindrances, barriers, or anything aside from laughter and fun. Skin of every color, people from all sorts of cultures, and definitely bodies of all shapes and sizes were there. Two Asian girls were hanging on this white guy, giggling at his every word. This super skinny blonde with not a whole lot to fill out her swimsuit top was kissing this big black guy whose bicep looked bigger than her waist. It was amazing…not like Carlisle's neighborhood dynamics or the cliques he saw at his high school. His interest was piqued.

Almost to himself, he said, "So everyone just gets along?"

"Yeah, pretty much. Sometimes there's a few jerks or bitches around but overall…everyone's making the most of their DCP experience."

"That's awesome."

"You should apply."

"I'm not sure what I want to do yet."

"Go to an information meeting then. Should be really easy for you to get to one, Carlisle. Then you can find out a little bit more about all the different things out there. You just never know."

"Do you have to live here?"

"No, but most of us are from different parts of the country; living here is the only choice."

"That's cool."

"So, what do you want to do?" Nicki asked.

Carlisle looked at her and in her eyes he saw that she wanted something a bit more intimate than the all-out, balls to the walls, pool party they were witnessing.

Holy crap.

The two walked back up to the apartment and Carlisle found himself starting to ramble a bit, talking about highly irrelevant things to forget about his increasing heart rate, his sweaty palms, and his growing hard-on, which became more noticeable with each brush against Nicki's arm and each bounce of her rather large breasts. She was incredible and he'd thought she was beautiful when he first saw her. Now, she seemed more like a goddess—a temptress and he was willing to take any bait she threw his way. She had him hook, line, and sinker.

They were back in the apartment.

"Why don't we go hang out in the bedroom. Considerably more comfortable than the couch," Nicki suggested.

"Sure," Carlisle said. She offered her hand and he took it.

The two sat down on the bed and Carlisle realized that he was no veteran at this but he wanted to take control of the situation, do something to be proactive in what he was pretty sure was an offer for more.

Taking a deep breath, he leaned in and kissed Nicki softly, then backed away, wanting to make sure it was okay. She wrapped her hands around his shoulders and pressed him back in. The two kissed softly, then aggressively, and it felt so good. Carlisle had kissed about five other girls before but he could tell that kissing Nicki was different. He was kissing a woman. Those two extra years of life she had made a big difference.

Carlisle's hands began to roam. One thing led to another and before he could even put it into perspective, the two's bodies were tangled up in each other, caramel flesh to olive flesh, and Nicki somehow managed to slide some protection on Carlisle. A few minutes later, he'd lost his virginity and was staring at the beautiful woman with the bright smile that had given him that moment. Yeah, he'd waited a long time. Mostly due to a lack of willing participants, though. Computer hacking smart guys were not prime material for most girls in high school. He'd always thrived on that notion that girls marry the nerds in the end because they are the ones who become filthy rich. That concept was enough to keep him patient, if anything.

"Wow!" Carlisle said.

"That was nice."

Am I supposed to tell her that was my first time?

"Was that your first time?" Nicki asked softly, leaning in to kiss him.

He just shook his head, not actually wanting to say "yes."

"Not bad; it gets better every time."

13

"Well, that felt pretty damn good," Carlisle said.

Then the two laid there for a few minutes talking, got dressed, ordered a pizza and Carlisle put Nicki through the ringer about DCP. He wasn't sure what to make of it but he was as excited about the opportunities with that program as he was about losing his virginity.

Finally, it was time to go home. It wasn't that his parents didn't give him a curfew but it wasn't really a smart idea to be trotting around his neighborhood in the wee hours of the morning. The cops were suspicious of it and the trouble makers hoped for it.

The next day, Carlisle and Ethan were talking in his room.

"So, how did the night go?"

"Good," Carlisle said with a huge, knowing grin.

"That's cool she was there."

Carlisle went on to tell Ethan all about Vista Way and DCP. He was interested but not as much as Carlisle.

"So, are you going to do it with me if I figure everything out? It's a great opportunity...something good for you to do while you're waiting for that big break."

"Sure, maybe," Ethan said, shrugging it off and tapping out a beat on his thigh.

"Oh, and guess what else?" Carlisle added.

"What?"

"It happened last night."

"What happened?"

"You know," Carlisle said. He couldn't just say these sort of things the way other guys did, all crass and direct.

He'd gotten Ethan's full attention. The drumming on his leg stopped.

"No way. You *finally* did it, huh? With a twenty year old. Bullshit."

"I'm not shittin' ya', man."

"Prove it."

"How am I going to prove that, Ethan? I didn't save the condom."

"You took some over?"

"No, she had them."

"Damn, that's hot."

After Carlisle's disclosure it didn't take Ethan long to agree to check out DCP further. Women were a huge motivation for him, just as much as money—and okay, women—were a huge motivation for Carlisle. They were two very different guys but they came from the same background had a good understanding of each other. They were brothers through and through.

2

"You've got to get the skills and be seen with the assets if you want to get ahead."

Carlisle went to work trying to figure out how he could be a part of the DCP. It turned out that he really couldn't but he couldn't get how appealing that aspect of life was to him. He was smart but his grades didn't reflect it. There was no college in his future because he didn't have the money or resources to go. He was a man with no plan...until he decided that socializing with the women who did the DCP would be a good second. They lived in a world that was like its own universe within the crazy tourist trap of Orlando. He wanted to be a part of it and nothing was going to stop him. Ethan was on board for women, if nothing else.

"Hey, I got Nicki's picture," Carlisle said to Ethan, walking up to him at his home.

"I can't wait to see this," Ethan said. He'd been harassing Carlisle that he was probably talking her up.

Carlisle swiped his smart phone and showed her picture.

"Damn, she's hot," Ethan commented appreciatively. "You didn't down load this? You could walk up to this chick and she'd know your name?"

"Yeah, she'd know my name. Maybe her hot roommates will get to know your name," Carlisle added. He decided to leave out the fact that he hadn't met them yet because it might be counterproductive to his incorporation of Ethan, the smooth talker, into his plan.

"When can we go?"

"How about tonight?"

It was technically a school night but neither Carlisle or Ethan had parents that really paid much attention to that. They were either gone or at work. Carlisle had no other siblings to deal with, either, and Ethan's mom would never trust him to taking care of his two younger siblings. So, they basically did as they pleased.

Carlisle and Nicki's relationship continued on and while it was pleasant, it was mostly Sex Ed 101 for Carlisle. He didn't mind and he was growing more confident, learning the right things to say and do all the time. Then, the day came when Nicki told Carlisle that it had been fun but ...

Carlisle was cool with the break-up, knowing that it really didn't have a chance to go anywhere. Nicki had given him a lot to be grateful for and he was going to use it until it ran its course.

Ethan and he had volunteered to take all the girls they could meet around Orlando, showing them the local hot spots and going to high school parties. The girls, although being older, didn't mind because it was cheaper to party at a house compared to a club. In exchange, they just had to act friendly toward them and pay some attention. It was a fair exchange and the two friends found that their popularity skyrocketed the last three months of high school. Add in the fact that they started selling some pot to cover their expenses and things were pretty decent. The pot was also a big factor in their draw for a lot of the college kids in the program.

Through navigating the program and using it to his advantage, Carlisle learned a great many things, including his life philosophy: if you can't beat it, go around it. With each passing day, his confidence started to grow and before he knew it, he was the guy who wasn't the awkward guy any longer. Life was good.

One girl, who'd grown highly suggestive to Ethan, was hinting that she wanted more than to be his party arm candy. He didn't let it ruffle him; instead, he began to ask her questions that made it seem like he was interested despite him not being interested in anything more than her body for that night.

"So, what happens at the end of the semester, babe, when you leave?" he asked.

"Well, another group comes in and I have to return to college for classes."

"So, you'd be leaving?"

"Yeah, but I only have a year left after this. It wouldn't take me long to get back here."

"That's something to think about," Ethan said. Then he leaned in and kissed her, quieting her and somehow, with his suave, she took that as an affirmation that he was seriously considering it. Carlisle was impressed with his skills.

That night, when they were heading back on the bus to their houses, Ethan and Carlisle leaned back on the back benches of the bus on the route as it took them to their destination. There were some drunk people getting on and off as it went past various clubs. In a few weeks time, they'd have their fake IDs so they could get into the clubs, too. Their growing clout would only take them so far. The IDs, combined with the girls and pot, were really their ticket to a better world. A gateway to greater ambitions for both—Ethan with his rapping and Carlisle with his incessant desire to become wealthy and move to that house high on the hill.

"You're pretty smart, man, I've got to hand it to you," Ethan said. "I think this plan is actually going to work. We're both getting what we want and making some strides."

"And what about all the different cultures," Carlisle said. "Food and females. Religions, too. It's fascinating to me."

"You're more philosophical than me but I get your point. If we hadn't ventured out of the little world of our high school, we'd have no clue how diverse people can all get along so well."

"At least for a semester at DCP," Carlisle said.

"You got that." Ethan put his knuckles out and they bumped knuckles and then continued talking.

Ethan continued talking. "That new security guard was one big bad-ass, wasn't he?"

"The one at Chatham? Yeah, he seemed cool, though."

"He knew our game," Ethan said.

"As long as we behave and our guests still stay there, he doesn't care. He doesn't get paid to care about anything aside from following the rules in the apartments."

* * *

With the doors to the balcony open, Carlisle and Ethan, sat there enjoying a rare breeze that wasn't infiltrated with humidity as they waited for their dates to get ready. They'd been in hundreds of apartments in Vista, Chatham and Commons by that time and for the most part, they all remained identical with their white walls, square architecture, and uncomfortable couch. Their running joke was that the couches made for the best excuse to get into the bedroom—if they ever switched them out they'd have to adapt an entirely new approach to getting the ladies into bed.

The two were on the couch, their knees up tall from their height, despite the sunken cushions. Ethan looked over to Carlisle, taking in a huge drag from his joint, held it a few seconds, and then exhaled. Blue smoke immediately assaulted the air and Carlisle waved his hands. "You smoke that shit too much. It's not good business to use your product all the time."

"Don't get righteous on me. It just helps me relax, puts me in the party mood."

Carlisle laughed. Ethan found a way to make everything an excuse to get high. In high school, if he got a good grade on his algebra test, it was a reason to get high. Getting out of school one detention short of not being able to walk across the stage in the ceremony was a

18

reason to get high. Now, that they were living at Vista Way as basically permanent guests of others, being around the beautiful women from across the world with the hot bodies was his reason to get high.

For about the hundredth time, Ethan said, "Man, can you believe how well all this has worked out. We have a hell of a good game going here."

His voice was loud and Carlisle raised his finger to his lip, indicating he should be a bit more quiet.

"A means to an end," Carlisle said, suddenly standing up. "I'm going to go wait outside."

"You just want to scope out that hot, new girl." Ethan leaned back and took another hit, talking while the smoke lingered in his throat. "She's fine. I can't blame ya'."

"You could just play the game until it's all over, couldn't you, Ethan."

"Yup."

"All this," Carlisle began with his arms held out, looking around the room, "is better but I still want more."

"Why don't you live a little first? Stop thinking and calculating so much, kick it a little more."

Carlisle looked at Ethan and the two burst out laughing.

"First of all, we've been living it for nearly three years. I'd be over half done with college by now if I'd gone that route. Second, when have you known me not to calculate?"

"Never. You even calculated when you used to do your mini hack jobs," Ethan said. He tilted his head back for a minute and it landed on the back side of the couch. His hat fell off and he rubbed his hands across his shaven scalp. "Hey...who was that one guy, again?"

Carlisle looked. He knew but he didn't like to relive the glory days of a petty jealousy. Maybe he'll forget about it if I don't respond.

"Justin...no, Jake...no..."

"Jason," Carlisle finally conceded. "No need to relive that story again."

"It's classic, jealous Carlisle, amateur hacker, constantly getting vanilla gift cards and spending them around the city. Love it. They never figured it out—you beat the system."

19

"They suspected but they just couldn't pin it to me. I was lucky. I operate smarter now," Carlisle said.

"And smoother," Ethan said with a loud snort.

Carlisle rolled his eyes.

"Man, those were some pretty desperate times when we first started perusing that "My Spacious" website, hoping some chick from another school would give us the time of day that none of the really hot ones would at ours," Ethan said.

"Can't argue that, brother. Man that website was my addiction for about two years but now it's a business tool, more than anything else. All it took was that one message, *I think you're cute*, to give me hope."

"And look at us now. We can both get a fine piece of ass anytime we want, Carlisle."

"Don't be so crass, Ethan. I don't just want to hop around woman to woman; I want to find someone and settle down with them. Plus, if I wouldn't have met that girl our dumb asses never would have thought of the Disney College Program and all this."

"True but let's get back to what's important, Carlisle. Women. Limiting yourself to hopes of one gives you tunnel vision. You have got to keep your options open."

"At first but not forever, otherwise that's just avoidance."

"Well, you go get all serious with a girl and I'll just take care of all the ladies you're passing by."

"Deal," Carlisle said. He glanced at the wall at the plain white clock with black minute and second hands. "Time to go or we'll miss the bus."

"Okay," Ethan said, taking one last hit from his joint. He offered it to Carlisle.

"Okay, just one," Carlisle said. He walked over and took a hit, feeling the moisture of the paper. It always disgusted him but he couldn't deny that a hit did feel good on occasion. Not as good as it obviously did to Ethan but good.

Ethan grabbed it back and stubbed the end out. He pulled a small tin out of his pocket and tossed the roach in it, along with a few others. It became a part of his stash, waiting to be smoked at a time when he realized that he was running low on his main stash. If Ethan had any travesties in the world that he really dwelled on, it was a shortage of Mary Jane, "his main lady," in his opinion.

"Are you ladies ready?" Carlisle called out.

20

"Yeah, almost," one voice called out.

"The bus will be here shortly."

"We're coming," another voice called out.

"What are their names again?" Ethan whispered.

"Veronica and Mimi."

"Got it."

The women walked out and they were looking good, definitely ready to have a good time and make the rounds in Orlando. Veronica was an Asian beauty and Mimi a southern belle. It was Tuesday night, which meant that it was time for Senor Frogs and a night filled with tequila marinated beauties, body shots, and lively dirty dancing. And, by the end of the night, if Carlisle and Ethan were lucky—which they usually were—they'd watch either their ladies that evening do some body shots off each other or they'd get to do one off them or other willing participants. Anything could happen.

The four rolled out of the apartments, nodding to the security guards on their way, and walked toward the cab. The girls were each hanging on one of their arms. Carlisle looked suave, set to roll with the big league, while Ethan looked more like he was set to go hang out with the crew and rap them a song as they contorted their bodies into some incredible moves. There wasn't a much odder pairing of best friends but the two complimented each other's ambitions quite well. Of course, at that moment, they wanted to hop on the bus and do some clubbing and networking.

3

"A young adults goals are simple: make money, party, and have sex as much as you can."

The "party bus" was really just like any other bus on the outside; however, what happened inside of it was an entirely different story. Connections were made, whether for the night or just the bus ride, and the later it got into the evening the louder the bus became.

Wil the Photographer was the face of the "party bus," but he'd had a bit of inspiration from Ethan from a chance encounter at the House of Blues one night.

Ethan had needed to go have a smoke and walked out to the smoking area. Another guy happened to be out there. It wasn't too crowded yet and they got to talking. Ethan had seen him around before. It was Wil, the guy known for taking the pictures of sexy, sultry, young adults from around the world and capturing the spirit of DCPers and college students in the Orlando area.

"Hey, how are you?" Ethan asked.

"Never a complaint," Wil said.

"You're the guy who does the party bus, right?"

"Yeah, you've been on there?" Wil had asked, assuming Ethan had. He really had no reason to think that any college student in Orlando who was interested in fun would *not* take the bus. Cheaper than a taxi and a hell of a lot more fun, safer than a car if you were lucky enough to have one.

"No, not in college. Got connections to get into Vista but that's an entirely different story."

"Ah, player." Wil nodded his head and took a drag of his cigarette.

"Well, kind of. It's a means to an end, no complaints."

"What's the end?"

"Hopefully a music contract. I'm a rapper."

"Any good?"

"They say I am."

"Let's hear something," Wil offered, extending his hand out.

Ethan, never one to skip a beat, took him up on his offer.

Pretty soon he had a small crowd around him, enjoying what he did and he soaked it all in as much as a tourist soaks in the sunny skies of Florida.

"That was decent," Wil said afterward. "You'd be fun on the party bus."

"It'd be great to be on there but I'm not willing to go to college just to ride it."

"I bet."

"You know, I've heard some of my friends in the DCP talk about the bus and a few have mentioned that it would be decent to have a text message as to what was happening at various places each day of the week. Then they'd know if they wanted to head out."

Wil's eyes lit up. "That's a solid idea. I tell you what, if I try that out and it works, you can ride the bus for free to the clubs—even if you're not a student. What do you say?"

"And my main man, Carlisle?"

"And Carlisle."

That was how Carlisle and Ethan were allowed to be on the party bus without having any college credentials to back them up. It was a great story and one that their dates-of-the-night always liked because it made them feel like they were with high rollers.

Ethan finished telling his story to Veronica and Mimi. As history had often showed, they soaked it in and Veronica, who'd been loosely hanging on his arm, squeezed him in a bit tighter.

They were standing outside of Vista, the second stop on the DCP campus for the party bus, and could hear its loud diesel coming as it rounded the corner. One bus kept going straight, already full, and the other one stopped in front of them and they nodded to the driver, then got on, handing over Veronica and Mimi's tickets.

The driver did the standard safety blurb, stating everyone needed to remain seated, and then took off. Did everyone remain seated? Hell no. They were leaning over, talking to people in the back. Tight, firm backsides were blocking the aisles, only moving when someone goosed them passing by. They'd screech, then smile, sometimes start flirting. It all depended. The one unspoken rule was that no one got offended or acted righteous on the party bus. It was the start and end of a journey of fun to the various clubs. That night was Senor Frogs, but Wednesday through Saturday also had lively destinations on the map, including: Roxy, The Attic, Vice, and Ono.

23

"So, what is it that you do again?" Mimi asked Carlisle, yelling in his ear.

"I work part-time as a timeshare reservation customer service worker."

Carlisle noticed that Mimi's eyes glazed over at that but he didn't mind. It was as dull as a job as what it sounded like but it was decent money and a means to an end. He'd be able to buy a car soon and that would expand his possibilities past the party bus. It was a step in the right direction. Truthfully, the small sideline business of selling pot was considerably more lucrative but that was the money he used for his party fund.

"Do you want a dance or a drink first?"

"Let's dance until they bring around some tequila shots...we can get one of those."

"I knew you were a tequila girl," Carlisle said, smiling coyly.

"And a rum girl, and a beer girl...honey, I can be whatever kind of girl you want me to be."

"I've always been partial to the naughty girls."

Mimi giggled and the two made their way onto the floor just in time for a remix of some highly suggestive words from various songs. The two began to put on their acting skills, doing what each move suggested. It resulted in life performance foreplay. Her hips thrust forward and Carlisle responded. He would run his hands down Mimi's torso and she'd stare at him with wild, I want your sex, eyes.

The song was over and the two walked over to a ledge and leaned against it, waiting for a server to come by. Ethan and Veronica were out on the dance floor, moving their body's wildly to the new beat, a tribal, heart racing sound that was capable of bringing out the animal in anyone.

"So, do you have your own place, Carlisle?" Mimi asked.

He lied. "Yes." There was no way he was going to admit that he was still living at home, that his only responsibility was paying the light bill each month trying to save up his money for a car and an apartment. He wasn't quite there—yet—and he knew that being twenty-one now, he needed to take that next step.

"Maybe we can go back there after this," Mimi offered. "I'd love to see it."

"Tonight's not good. I'm in the middle of remodeling, it's a mess."

"You don't have a girlfriend, do you?"

"No, I'd never cheat on a girlfriend."

Mimi's eyes widened, liking the declaration, and Carlisle felt a bit of an "oh shit," panic. He was saved by the waitress coming over and asking what they'd like to drink.

"A watermelon margarita, crushed," Mimi said.

"Heineken in a bottle," Carlisle added, "and two shots of Petron Silver, salt, and lime."

The waitress nodded and headed toward the bar.

Carlisle turned to Mimi and pressed his hand behind her back, his fingers lingering just above her butt. She was wearing some really short, white shorts, along with a watermelon colored top that made it look like her blonde hair had strawberry highlights. Her bright blue eyes looked at Carlisle with spry curiosity and it was clear that she was waiting to be swept off her feet by some remark he might make.

She is hard to read. Is she out for a good time or to find a guy to be serious with?

"Where are you from again?" Carlisle asked.

"Dothan, Alabama, born and raised."

"I've never heard of it."

"Not many people have. I'm hoping that I can put it on the map."

The waitress was back and handed over the drinks and shots. Carlisle handed her the money and a "big spender" tip, then turned to look at Mimi. She was clearly excited.

"Here," she said, offering her wrist, which already had salt on it.

Carlisle smiled and grabbed the shot of tequila and slammed it down, followed by quickly sucking on the lime wedge and ending with her wrist. He slowly sucked the salt off of it and he felt her body shudder. He'd learned that move from Tina from Brazil and it had been as successful with others as it was with him that first day.

"Wow! I always liked tequila but now I think I love it. Let's go dance."

They went out on the floor for a bit more and the night went on. It ended with Ethan and Carlisle standing there, drinking their beers, while Veronica and Mimi were up on stage dancing and shaking everything they had to the music. They were whispering and giggling, too, pointing to Ethan and Carlisle.

The two walked back over and looked wildly sexy with their sweaty hair and visible intoxication by that point.

"So, we were talking," Veronica said, leaning up against Ethan's shoulder. "We were wondering if you guys wanted to try something new."

"Like what?" Ethan said, definitely loving the innuendo.

"Maybe the four of us can play around together?"

Ethan stopped, surprised by the request. Carlisle, too. The two had one steadfast rule, no mixing their sexual experiences with the other. Neither had any desire to see the other one in live action or their junk for that matter.

"Maybe some other night," Ethan said right away.

Mimi looked to Carlisle, who also shook his head.

Before they knew it, the party bus was outside of Senor Frogs and it was time to head back to Vista and call it a night.

Neither Carlisle nor Ethan had to work until the next afternoon so they extended their guests privilege to overnight. Ethan and Veronica went off into the bedroom and quickly became as loud as the club had been just an hour earlier. As for Carlisle, he looked over at Mimi and saw that she'd definitely enjoyed her tequila too much that evening.

"Excuse me," she said.

She went into the bathroom and the sounds were not pretty.

Carlisle sent Ethan a text message to his phone and took off, taking a cab home.

What an interesting ride home it proved to be, too. He got this Haitian cab driver, something fairly common to see in Orlando. The two got to talking about drugs—for some reason those conversations can flow freely with the right connections. There are times when you just know you can say what's on your mind without any repercussions.

"You have anything for me? Me shift almost done," the guy asked casually in his thick accent. If Carlisle wouldn't have been raised in a neighborhood without a lot of Haitian people he never would have understand the guy. He was obviously quite new to the US.

"Nah, not on me."

"Not any?"

"That's a bold question. How do you know I'm not a cop?"

"I know."

"Why do you want some? Won't you get fired?"

"No, cab drivers make no money. It extra service."

"What?" Carlisle asked. He had a hunch that he knew but he was trying to process things and needed a minute to think.

He continued. "People come into the cab and buy pot from you?"

"Yes. Other things, too."

"How?"

"Code word. We have source. We there source."

Carlisle stayed clear of other things. Hell, he liked to stay clear of marijuana as much as he could, too. That was Ethan's favorite employer, not his. What the driver had to say was very curious, however.

"Oh."

"You call me if you need a ride or want to talk business .I see in your eyes that you're an ambitious man," the driver said. "My name Mannie."

The cab stopped at a light and he slid back a business card through the door. It read the name *Mannie* and had a number.

"Thanks, man, I'll keep this in mind," Carlisle said.

The rest of the ride was relatively silent. <u>This is strange but it's also interesting.</u>

That night, Carlisle couldn't sleep. He'd heard that a lot of Haitian immigrants were eager to make some money and knew how to do it creatively but he'd never have guessed that there would be the potential to do it as a cab driver. It intrigued him.

The next day, Carlisle met up with Ethan to talk about it. He was really hung over when he walked into his bedroom but the guy quickly perked up when he mentioned a possible way for them to make some money. Ethan also subscribed to the path of least resistance. For a poor guy who wanted big things, selling a little pot definitely worked well with that path.

By the end of the conversation, Ethan had Mannie's card in his hand and said, "I'll take it from here, bro. This is a valuable connection."

27

Carlisle let it be.

* * *

It was a Saturday night and Carlisle and Ethan were hanging out at Roxy with two girls that were Disney characters on Main Street Disney. They were fun, sweet, and ready to reveal the side of themselves that they didn't dare show when they were in character. Suffice it to say, the two princesses had a wild side.

Ethan was enjoying their company thoroughly and for some reason, Carlisle was distracted. He couldn't get the thoughts that he'd grown stagnant out of his mind and it was unsettling. Clubbing was fun but after three plus years of doing it several times a week it wasn't as new or exciting as it used to be. Even the people were starting to blend together like they were one person of every race, religion, culture, etc. That sounded like an utopist point of view but it was not a compliment. All of the charm of the bus had started to wear off and something was ticking internally in Carlisle that made him realize he was wasting time in pursuing what he really wanted. Some may say he was growing up but he thought he was getting wiser.

"You want to dance?" the one young lady asked.

"Not quite yet. I'll get your drinks. You guys go dance."

The girl shrugged her shoulders and Ethan began walking away with them but not before turning around and giving Carlisle a *what the hell is the matter with you* look. Carlisle smiled, knowing that his friend was more than capable of handling two women at once.

He motioned to the waitress from the table he was seated at and she came over, looking at him with a sultry smile that would likely fade as the night went on.

"Two cosmopolitans, a Hennessy served straight, and a gin and tonic."

"Sounds good. You want to start a tab? I'll need a card if you do."

"No, I'll just pay cash but I'll tip you good if you don't forget about us."

She smiled—those words were music to a cocktail waitresses ears.

When the drinks came back, Carlisle leaned back and watched everyone dancing. People were filing into the club and some were on the waiting list now, hoping that others would leave. Roxy was one of his favorite clubs to go to. He liked the entertainment, MMA included sometimes, and the overall aesthetics of it. They were pleasing to him, an infusion of bright colors with white and black tones in the lounge areas but when you went down to the floors and the music started, it sounded phenomenal and you couldn't help but get wrapped up in it. Roxy knew how to deliver, making it a constantly happening venue.

Carlisle leaned back on the couch and took in the scenery. As always, his wheels were turning with thoughts of how he could take his skills and talents and convert them into something more meaningful. He was ready to take the next step—a leap into a future with a greater plan. He'd outgrown the one he was currently existing in.

As if they had ESP, the drinks arrived and Ethan and the girls were back by him within a minute, thirsty and ready to enjoy them. They were talking away and Carlisle managed to participate without paying particular attention but his glances kept giving it away that he was looking elsewhere. The company was beautiful, the scene was good, but he had this inexplicable feeling that he was missing something. The last time he'd had it was when he met Nicki and learned about DCP and lost the big V. He trusted his instincts and he was tuned in…curious about what they were indicating.

Everyone finished their drink and went back to the dance floor, leaving Carlisle once again. He felt his phone vibrate and reached down to grab it. A message from some girl he'd been out with a few weeks ago. How had she gotten his number anyway? He didn't give it away freely.

"Is anyone sitting here?" someone asked.

Carlisle looked up and froze. A woman was standing there that was so incredibly enchanting, hazel eyes, silky dark brown hair, and a soft smile that seemed to give away that she had a heart of gold.

"Unfortunately, yes," Carlisle found himself saying, "but please, sit down for awhile. I suspect it'll be a bit of time before they return."

"Not much of a dancer?"

"I like to dance…just not in the mood tonight," he said, thinking that he should have said that better. He'd get up and dance with her in a heartbeat if she wanted him to.

"My name is Carlisle Lewis."

"Joan, Joan Montalvo."

"It's nice to meet you, Joan."

The waitress came back and asked if he wanted another drink. Carlisle turned to Joan first. "I'll have a red wine, merlot preferably."

"And another Hennessy straight up for me," Carlisle said.

"Any others?"

"No, they're on their own."

Carlisle didn't lie either. Ethan came back with the others to the table just in time to see Carlisle and the new woman he was with bidding them adieu. It was rude to just leave that other girl hanging but she didn't look too upset.

Outside the club, Joan asked, "Do you have a car?"

"Yes, but I took a cab tonight just to be safe."

<u>That may be a lie right now but I am going to make it the truth real soon.</u>

And he did, the very next day Carlisle went out and purchased his first car. It was a 2012 black Camero convertible, only a few thousand miles on it, but a better set of wheels than he'd ever driven before in his life. It would be good for business and even better for pleasure.

4

"You know you've found someone special when you'll do anything for them."

Meeting Joan was immediately impactful to Carlisle. She was beautiful—smoking sexy—and also smart and fun. It was an intoxicating combination and Carlisle couldn't have been more excited for his first chance to actually go out on a date with her. It was nice to look at a woman as more than arm candy or an ornament, something he'd been doing for far too long.

He could feel his heart beating rapidly as he stared at her number in his cell phone. Briefly thinking about what he'd say, he rehearsed it in his mind, just like he would a sales presentation for work. Just let me be smooth.

Feeling prepared, his thumb pressed down on his cell phone to send the call. He waited and then he heard it, the silky voice that he had instantly responded to.

"Hello."

"Hi...Joan, this is Carlisle—from Roxy."

"Hi Carlisle. How are you today?" she asked.

"Great. I was wondering if you'd like to get together, hang out a bit. Maybe tonight."

"Tonight's no good. I've got to work."

There was a slight pause. Carlisle quickly tried assessing if this was a kind rejection or a legitimate excuse. He went with the optimistic route. "How about tomorrow?"

"Yeah, tomorrow would be great."

"Where do you live? I'll pick you up."

"I live in Chatham, part of Vista. Do you know where it is?"

Do I ever.

"I know exactly where it is. Why don't you text me your specific address and I'll pick you up at 7:00. The number I called you from is my cell."

"Sounds good. I'm looking forward to it," Joan replied.

"Yeah, me too."

There was a small silence. Carlisle didn't want to be the first one to say goodbye and hang up—cool or not. He wasn't a great game player, anyway.

"Well, then, I'll see you tomorrow, Carlisle."

Click.

The phone went dead and Carlisle was frozen, phone still to his ear, and smiling wildly. Her voice drew him in like she was his sexy fifth grade teacher, Ms. Parker.

Now, it was time for the next call.

"Hey, do you by chance have any opening for some new rims today?" Carlisle asked.

"Yes. Great. Do you have the No.1 Glossy Black Machined Face Chrome Lip by 2Crave?"

"Awesome! And you're the Rent A Wheel on West Colonial Drive...2395...great, sure. I'll see you in an hour."

Things were working out great and Carlisle felt on top of the world. A new car, the rims of his dreams, and possibly a new girl. It felt great and everything felt really aligned at that moment. He was moving forward, no more stagnancy.

It was only his second time driving it but Carlisle was immediately in sync with his new car, so sleek, sexy, and powerful sounding. He loved how heads turned when they looked at it. Some were wondering what the deep rumble was and others simply wanted to appreciate it. It was a stellar car. Really, it was almost surreal how the car of his dreams for now—the one he'd been eying up for quite awhile was suddenly his. It was worth every pretty penny, too.

After this, high end performance Audi, he thought. Then he reminded himself to enjoy what he had for the moment and not already be worried about the next thing. What was that saying his mother had: don't put the cart ahead of the horse. Yeah, that was it.

Carlisle hadn't told Ethan, his mother, or his step-father that he was getting that car. He wanted everyone to be surprised and to have the full impact of the car with the ideal wheels on it. It wasn't that the factory ones were bad, they just weren't "bad."

Pulling out of Rent A Wheel, Carlisle called Ethan through his blue tooth, which he'd hooked up while waiting for his financing to get done. It sounded sweet coming out of the Harman Kardon speaker system in the car—an aftermarket addition.

"Hey, what's up? You at home?"

"Yeah, where are you, man? I've been looking for you," Ethan said, his voice blasting through the speaker.

"Had some errands. I'm coming over if you're at home."

"Give me a half hour. You sound funny. Where you at?"

"Must be the cell service," Carlisle said with a wicked grin. He was already excited to see Ethan's reaction to the wheels. He had wanted a car, too, but didn't have the same knack for saving money that Carlisle did, making his dream car an orange and black Monte Carlo that his cousin had agreed to sell to him when he had the money. It was a good thing his cousin was patient and not in need of money because he'd been waiting awhile.

Carlisle hung up the phone by pressing the telephone button on the dashboard of his Camero and punched down on the gas pedal so he could make it through the yellow stoplight.

Since he had a few minutes to spare, he just drove around waiting for a half hour to pass. He was more than content to stay busy that day and make it go by as quickly as he could. Since Joan couldn't go out that night he'd decided to take on an extra shift to start rebuilding his cash supply. Of course, he'd be spending it the following night on a "guaranteed to impress" first date restaurant.

Finally the next night came and Carlisle headed out, wearing a pair of khaki's and a light blue linen shirt. He was so excited.

When he arrived at Chatham, he smiled at the guard, who simply said, "And how are you tonight, Carlisle?"

"Great, and thank you."

The guards were always more relaxed when it was just Carlisle because he was considerably more subtle than his cohort in Vista invasions, Ethan.

Taking the stairs up to the second floor, Carlisle walked down to the end of the hall and to the last door on the right. He knew he'd been in there before but wasn't sure who he'd gone to visit. It didn't matter because that night it was Joan and he couldn't wait to learn more about her.

It took two knocks on the door for Joan to answer and she looked truly incredible, her long hair down and shiny, her eyes sparkling with just the right amount of smoky eye make-up on, and wearing a black, off the shoulder shirt and a short, black skirt. Her legs were long and tanned and in an instant, Carlisle thought he might just like to find out how they'd feel wrapped around him.

"Right on time," Joan said.

"Always."

"Impressive, come on in."

Carlisle walked in and saw another girl sitting over on the couch, eyeing him curiously and giving a smile that seemed to say, "I know something about you that you don't."

"Carlisle, this is my roommate Megan. Megan, Carlisle."

"It's great to meet you," Carlisle said.

"So, am I dressed okay?" Joan asked. "I wasn't sure what we were doing tonight?"

"Well, if you like sushi I was thinking we could go to Oishi's."

"Damn, he's a keeper, Jojo," Megan said from the couch.

"I do love sushi, in fact, and I'm not just saying that because you're a keeper," Joan said with a mischievous tone.

"Well great, you ready to go?"

"Sure am."

Carlisle opened the door and had Joan walk through first and then followed, shutting it behind him.

"Could you park close?"

"Not bad, just across the street by chance."

Of course, I waited for that spot because there was no way I was parking the car too far away.

34

The two walked out and crossed the street, talking casually.

"Is that your car?" Joan asked.

"Yeah."

"Impressive."

"How long have you had it?"

"Not too long," Carlisle answered. That definitely was the truth.

"You must do good at a timeshare vacation reservation service …or whatever it is."

"That's basically right and, yeah, I do pretty decent. I really like sales."

Carlisle opened the passenger door and Joan got in while they were talking. Then he walked around to the driver's side. The convertible top lending to a steady conversation was a benefit he hadn't thought of until that moment. Another score for the car.

"When you're good at things like that I suppose you do. I don't think I'd be too good at sales."

"Why?" Carlisle asked. He couldn't imagine her not being able to sell anything to anyone.

"First off, I don't care for that sort of thing. Second off, I am not a very high pressure person."

"Well, those are two good reasons. But, you don't have to be high pressure as much as convincing of the benefits."

Carlisle looked over and saw Joan smiling. He realized that he was starting off on a lame conversation and she was being polite.

"Let's go," he said, starting the car and putting it into drive.

There was a break in traffic and he darted out onto the boulevard and accelerated down, getting to the speed limit in about a second flat. Wow, he loved that feeling.

It was easy to see that the conversation flowed immediately and it was honest, down to earth, too. Carlisle confessed that he wasn't the most popular guy in high school and Joan shared how she had ridiculous buck teeth that had taken some serious orthodontic work to eliminate. Carlisle looked at her and tried to imagine her with buck teeth. He couldn't but thought she'd probably still be really attractive even if she did have them.

"Well, here we are," he said, pulling into the strip mall that Oishi's was located on. It was at the end and while the outside may not look very fancy like some restaurants, the sushi they made on the inside was nothing short of divine temptation. Carlisle didn't get to eat there often but every time he had, he'd enjoyed every bite completely.

"I can't wait to try this place. I hear people talk about it but I haven't been here yet."

"I don't come here often, but tonight seems like a perfect night to give it a try," Carlisle said. He smiled and felt a slight bit of heat flush his cheeks, followed by the hairs on his neck standing up. His response to Joan was almost uncomfortable—it was that strong.

Once inside, the two ordered the *sex on the moon* sushi roll for starters. It had fried shrimp, eel, avocado, cream cheese, asparagus, smelt roe topped w/fresh tuna, tempura flake, eel sauce, spicy mayo, scallion and caviar.

"This is so good," Joan said, lifting her shoulders up and licking her bottom lip. "If this is what sex on the moon would make me feel like, I'm all for it."

"You want to go to the moon?" Carlisle asked.

"Sure, why not…it'd be an adventure. Don't you?"

"I'm probably a little too grounded for that type of thing."

"You are kind of serious, aren't you?"

"I prefer focused but I do like to have fun, too. There's just a lot I want to do in life. Places I want to go."

"Just not the moon," Joan said, lifting up her glass of plum wine in salute.

"Just not the moon," Carlisle repeated and lifted up his glass, clanking it.

"Good thing that's really not possible then—in a commercial sense, anyway."

36

"How about Sir Richard Branson and the Virgin Galactic?"

"That's for mega billionaire's or something, isn't it?"

"Definitely not affordable."

"What if you were a mega billionaire? Would you go?"

"If it was a good investment."

Joan paused and smiled. Carlisle could tell it was genuine and that she was having a good night at minimum. As for him, he was having a great night and when it came to an end he was too sad to see it go.

He decided to take things slow, not wanting to blow it by being too aggressive. It was not easy.

One date led to another and before Carlisle knew it, he and Joan had been dating exclusively for over a month. It had been an incredible month at that.

On a beautiful, breezy night, the two were laying on the hood of his car, staring up at shooting stars out near the vast expansion of the Disney empire.

"I'd love to walk on the moon," Joan said. Then she added, "Too bad you're not interested in going to the moon."

Carlisle reached over and grabbed her hand, squeezing it softly, and said, "I'm beginning to reconsider that. With you, I'd do it."

The two turned their heads toward each other and leaned in and kissed softly, feeling the warmth of each other's bodies as they did. Their chemistry was undeniable; their compatibility was easy to see.

As Carlisle's other hand pressed against her back, moving her as close to him as he could he realized that she was someone that he wanted around, not someone who he wanted to leave in a few short weeks.

"I want you to stay here with me," Carlisle said.

"I have school to finish," Joan justified but her argument was weak.

"You have a semester left and most of your classes can be done virtually. You said so."

Thank you, technology!

"Where would we live?"

"Say yes and I'll go and find an apartment first thing tomorrow."

Carlisle watched as Joan contemplated the idea in her mind. He sensed he had her.

"Please jojo . I would never let you down, baby."

Joan smiled. "Okay then. Let's give it a go."

"Yes!" Carlisle shouted out into the night.

In the distance there was a faint reply. "Yes back at ya'!"

The two laughed but it was settled. Joan would be moving down to Orlando to finish school and that meant that Carlisle had one thing left to do—find an apartment.

Throughout the past month, Carlisle had found himself busier with Joan and work, meaning he saw Ethan less. In fact, Ethan hadn't really had a chance to hang out with Joan at all the past month and he'd been harassing Carlisle to stop holding back and let him meet her. "So what if you're whipped. You're not the first one in history and you won't be the last."

Carlisle had agreed that they'd all go out some night, Megan, too. It made sense since he'd gotten an apartment and Joan would be moving into it. He was talking with Ethan and coordinating the details.

"Should we do some ecstasy?" Ethan asked.

"Sure, I think the girls would like that, it'll be fun."

"Great, I'll go to my connection."

A day later, Ethan called and said that his connection had gotten busted the week before. He wasn't happy because it would make his side business of dealing a bit more challenging for a bit but he was relieved to find a temporary "go to" source for his needs.

Two days later, they were all set to go and meet at Attic. There was no party bus this time, as Carlisle preferred driving everywhere now.

"We'll meet in the parking lot and take the thizz. Not smart to carry it in," Carlisle said to Joan on the phone. It was smart to use code words for these types of things because you just never knew who might be listening. After the phone call with Joan, Carlisle called Ethan to inform him of the details.

"Great. Pick me up at 9:00 and we'll go from there," Ethan said.

Joan and Megan took a taxi to Ono, easily spotting where Carlisle had parked.

The four slid the small green pills with a smiley face on one side and went into the club, ready to have some fun.

Ethan immediately liked Megan, thinking her cutting edge style was "Rhianna-like," according to him but she was very petite, yet muscular like a gymnast. They both had an intensity to them that really came out when they were on the dance floor with the music.

Carlisle and Joan, now more comfortable with each other and naturally a bit more reserved, had a great time dancing and then being playful at the table they'd found to sit down at. They'd become intimate but it was clear that night, with the help of a little green pill, drinks and their increasing feelings for each other, that they were ready to get a bit more wild, bust out of their shells a bit and feel the explosive energy of two people that have to have each other.

Not wanting to break away from a hot, inviting kiss from Joan, Carlisle was forced to.

"I'll be right back," he said, getting up from the table and adjusting his pants to hide the hard-on that he was forming.

"Don't take long," Joan said. "Maybe we should go afterward. Leave Ethan and Megan to do their thing."

"I like that idea," Carlisle said.

He went to the bathroom, thinking about how great it felt to be in a relationship with someone who got him, complimented him, and turned him on as much mentally as she did physically. And, although he would never say it out loud yet, he was pretty sure that he did love her. Some things you just realized quickly in life and that was one of them. Why he didn't say it yet? He had no idea but maybe he would later…maybe.

Carlisle walked back to the table and Joan glanced up at him. The look of a sexual animal had left them and it was replaced with the ferocity of an approaching tiger on the hunt.

"Hey, what's wrong?" Carlisle asked, immediately concerned.

"This is what's wrong," Joan said, shoving his cell phone toward him.

Carlisle looked down and saw a text. It was from some woman he'd met last month. He didn't even know it was there but there was a feed of messages back and forth on it.

"What's going on with you two?" Joan asked, not hiding the accusation in her tone.

"Nothing. I didn't even know she texted."

"Obviously," she said. "Mr. Smooth Talker would have just brushed it off or hid it, I suppose."

"Come on. That's not fair. I haven't done anything."

"Never...with her?"

Carlisle had kissed her before he met Joan but there was no way in hell he was disclosing that. It turned out that he didn't have to. He must have had a guilty look.

Joan stood up and said, "I'm out of here."

Carlisle tried to stop her and got up and grabbed her arm. She yanked it away from him and kept walking, not turning back. He knew there was no use in following and suddenly, his amazing buzz had turned into a big disaster.

"Don't go," he whispered.

Joan walked up to Ethan and Megan and talked to them. Carlisle watched as she spoke. She looked so sad and soon, Ethan and Megan were looking over at him.

Megan nodded her head and walked away with Joan.

Ethan walked over to Carlisle. "Man, what the hell did you do? That girl is worse than pissed, she is sad. All teary eyed and shit."

"I didn't do anything," Carlisle said. Then he added, "Fuck!" He slammed his fist on the table and the glasses rattled.

"Calm down, man. Getting kicked out ain't gonna' solve your problems."

"Hey, I'm going. You ready to leave?"

"No, I'll take a taxi man. You should, too. You're in no condition to drive."

Carlisle ignored him. He knew that he had to go see Joan and he couldn't just let what happened remain the way it was. She'd understand if she just let him explain.

<u>Maybe she's still outside waiting for a cab.</u>

Carlisle ran toward the entrance, weaving through the thick crowd and hoping that he'd be in luck. At minimal, if there was a scene at least it would be outside, not inside the club. There would be a few less gawkers.

He burst through the set of doors to the outside and didn't see Joan or Megan.

He turned around to head toward his car and ran into a group of guys.

"Watch it, man."

"Sorry, Bro" Carlisle mumbled and then he walked away.

Once in his car, he sat down and took a few deep breaths in. He was trying to focus and clear his head to drive. The amount he'd had was close to too much but he'd be fine. He'd just open the top and the fresh air would keep him alert and safe.

He took off down Central Boulevard, heading toward the interstate.

Before having a chance to reach it, a group of kids charged out into the street, not looking for oncoming traffic and Carlisle had the sense to swerve to the right and miss them. The group of drunken pedestrians may have been safe from harm but the Camero was not. It slammed into a street lamp and sent it slowly swaying backward until it toppled from the leverage.

Sitting there, stunned, Carlisle stared at the hood of his car, which had an ugly crease in it and saw the kids running away, yelling and laughing. "Holy shit. Did you see that?"

Carlisle tried to back up and drive away but his car was caught up on something and he couldn't move it. A minute later, the police arrived.

Oh, shit!

"Are you alright, sir? Do you need us to call an ambulance?"

"I'm fine."

"Step out of the vehicle, please."

Carlisle got out and looked at the officers, handing over his license and registration.

"Have you been drinking tonight, Mr. Lewis," the one officer said, holding a flashlight down on his license.

"No, sir," Carlisle said, suddenly realizing that a lot more was at stake here than some repairs to his car.

"Would you mind taking a breathalyzer?"

"Yes, I would. I told you I wasn't drinking."

Or doing ecstasy.

"So, you are refusing?"

"Yes," Carlisle said.

"You are under the arrest for suspicion of driving while intoxicated, Mr. Lewis."

The Miranda Rights were read.

Carlisle was taken away and was given the opportunity to make one telephone call. He felt like he was living in some bizarre cop show and he thought about who to call. Would Ethan be too wasted to come and bail him out? He wasn't sure but he knew that he couldn't call his mother or step-father either. That would be a far worse fate—and lecture. So, Ethan it was.

Ethan showed up to bail him out, paying $200.00 in cash through a bails bond agency.

They got out to the parking lot and a taxi was waiting. They got in and then Ethan began talking.

"You ass, I told you not to drive." Then his face got very serious, however, and it was a different type of serious. Carlisle couldn't help but notice it.

"What's wrong?"

"I don't know how to tell you this, Carlisle."

"Just tell me," he said, thinking it was some sort of lecture about what he'd done that evening.

"Something happened to Joan. I got a call from Megan about two hours ago."

"What happened?" Carlisle asked, his thoughts immediately going to someone trying to mug her or hurt her.

"She started having a seizure and there was nothing they could do. When 911 got there, it was too late."

"A seizure…too late." The blurry mind Carlisle had when he'd taken off driving from Ono returned and he kept repeating his words, seemingly not able to process them.

"She's dead. I'm really sorry, man."

"I didn't get to tell her I loved her. I was going to tell her that," Carlisle said. That was all he could think of and he squeezed his eyes shut, trying to stop the tears that were welling up behind them from escaping.

5

"Jesus, have the wheel."

Alone in his new apartment, one that he wouldn't be sharing with anyone, Carlisle stood in front of the mirror, staring at his reflection, and feeling sick to his stomach. All the steam he'd thought he had in his sails just two days ago was gone. It wasn't the car; it was Joan and her death impacted him unlike any other death he'd ever witnessed. She was so good, so innocent, so full of life—someone who'd been destined to contribute great things to this world, not to mention to his quality of life. It was all torn away in a fluke incident—a seizure.

In the back of his mind, Carlisle didn't dare confront the accusations that came from the deepest parts of him. It was those bad drugs. You shouldn't have offered if she wanted to do ecstasy. This is all your fault. Of course, another part of his mind fought back. This is all Ethan's fault. He got the drugs. Blame him, not me.

Did it really matter who was to blame? Joan was dead.

That morning, Carlisle's life would be greatly impacted by Joan's memorial service in Florida before she returned to her family's home in Cleveland for her final resting place. There would be no open casket, her face and flesh distorted from the seizure and efforts to bring her back to the living. All that Carlisle would see, aside from the images in his mind, was a picture of her sitting on a table with some ashes right beside it from her cremation.

It was time to go. He was set with his black suit, black tie, and polished black business shoes. Not having a car, Carlisle's step-father picked him up for the service and would take him there and then to his afternoon appointment, another one he couldn't bear to think about at that moment. Honestly, it hardly seemed significant to him, anyway. He was so distracted with grief.

"Are you ready?" his step-father said in a more compassionate way than he'd ever spoken to Carlisle. James Lewis was a good man but he and Carlisle had been through their share of rocky moments with each other. Today, however, he was there to support.

"Yeah, thanks for driving me," Carlisle said vacantly.

On the way to the Compass Pointe Cremation Services on Futures Drive, Carlisle couldn't help but think of the irony. He was going there to say goodbye to someone with no future—not here on earth, anyway. There would definitely be no trip to the moon with Joan—ever.

Carlisle's stomach was tightened as he walked in through the doors to the service. What would people think of him? Would they blame him the way he was blaming himself? He had no idea but his questions were quickly answered.

Megan walked up to Carlisle and gave him a hug without saying a single word. It was kind and warm, not condemning. Then she separated from him, holding his arms in her hand and looking into his eyes.

"I'm glad to see you." She hugged him tight again and whispered, "It's not your fault. Don't think that way. Joan wouldn't want you to."

"What I wouldn't give to start that night over again. I never got a chance …"

He stopped talking, not able to choke out the words.

"But she knew. We could all tell," Megan offered.

Then the service began. Carlisle didn't cry but he just sat there and listened to the standard words about a woman who was anything other than standard. His step-father was next to him and he sensed his stillness. He glanced over once to see his eyes closed, staring straight ahead and his hands folded in prayer.

Twenty minutes later, the service was over and Carlisle was walking out. He avoided all the looks of people from the DCP, friends' of Joan's. Looking at them would have been torture to his soul. Maybe he was being a coward but at that moment, that's what he felt he had to do.

Once back in the passenger seat of the car, Carlisle breathed a huge sigh of relief.

"You okay?"

"I am. It was just so crazy."

"I know, things like that are never easy, especially when you care about someone."

If there was anything his step-father understood, it was death. He'd had to bury two brothers in the past, one from a drug overdose and another the victim of a violent crime.

45

"I have something I want to give you, Carlisle."

Carlisle looked over and saw him pulling out a long, thin, box from under the driver's seat of the old, 1998 Cadillac Seville that he had driven for the past ten years.

"What is it?" Carlisle asked with intrigue.

He opened up the box and was staring at a gold tie, perfectly folded in the center and looking as luxurious as a gold bar might—not that he'd ever seen one. Instinctually, Carlisle reached his hand up and felt the smooth, soft silk of the tie.

"Thanks," he said, showing he was a bit confused. "It's great."

"That tie is to bring you luck," his step-father began. "You see, there's a legend about gold ties and helping good men who've made some mistakes, men like you, get out of their situations a bit better off than they might otherwise."

Carlisle smiled, the first genuine smile he'd had in a few days. "I could use that. It's occurred to me, however, that even if society gives me a bit of a pass, I still have myself to deal with. That isn't going to be quite as easy."

"It never is but if you're coming from a genuine place it'll happen, Carlisle. I know that and your mother knows that, too."

Carlisle flipped down the passenger side visor and took off his black tie, resting it across his legs. Then he took out the gold tie and put it around his neck, tying it in a perfect Windsor knot, something that his step-father had taught him while saying, "Every man should know how to tie a perfect Windsor knot." At the time, Carlisle thought it was just some *crazy adult thing* but that day he understood it perfectly well. What a way to be forced to grow up.

"Looks good, Carlisle."

"Thanks. It feels good on." Then he glanced at the clock. It was one hour until the court date and they had about a half hour drive to get to the courthouse on Orange Avenue.

The two road in relative silence and Carlisle began to visualize the presentation that he was going to be giving that day to the judge. It would be unlike anything else he'd ever done in his years of vacation activation services. The ideal outcome would be for the judge to say,

"Let's just drop this entire thing." However, even with a fairly optimistic point of view, Carlisle knew that was a foolish aspiration. All he knew for certain was that he didn't want to go to jail—he couldn't. It would ruin everything and make all his goals twice as challenging to achieve, if not impossible.

As the large Cadillac pulled into the parking garage for the courthouse, Carlisle felt his stomach tensing up for the second time that day. The service for Joan didn't seem that real to him, just a formality in saying goodbye, but not comparable to the processes that were going on internally. This courthouse represented something very real, though. It would impact his future, just as it had impacted his present.

Carlisle walked in with his step-father walking slowly behind him, there for support but not to offer any advice of any sort. He was grateful for it and he knew that if his mother had been there, she would have been chatting incessantly, nervous and full of last minute wisdom that would have actually made things worse. Her heart was in the right place but when she was nervous, her mouth seldom was.

"Carlisle Lewis," the court reporter called out.

"Yes, ma'am," Carlisle said, standing up and walking forward.

He could feel the eyes on him and it made his body heat up from the tension. He walked forward and the judge didn't look at him, the man, but looked down at "him on paper."

"You understand what you are being charged with?" the judge asked.

"Yes, your Honor."

"Do you have an attorney present?"

"No, Your Honor."

"Is this because you cannot afford a counsel?"

"Yes, Your Honor."

"Would you like to request one, Mr. Lewis?"

"No, Your Honor."

"Okay then, we shall proceed."

Carlisle was sworn in and took the stand to the right of the judge, where the assistant DA asked him a few basic questions, to which he honestly replied. Flashbacks of being reprimanded in kindergarten for painting on the wall came into his mind. He hadn't thought about that for years. Why now? He quickly found out.

"You shall have your license suspended for a year, twenty hours of community service, three alcohol awareness courses and a small fine. I believe that will give you time to reflect and decide what you want to do with your life, Mr. Lewis, and the choices you want to make," the judge said.

"Thank you, Your Honor," Carlisle said, wanting to grin bigger than a Cheshire cat but not wanting to appear disrespectful.

As if reading his mind, the judge said, "It's okay to smile. I expect great things from you, Mr. Lewis. Don't disappoint me by me seeing you back here again."

"I won't, Your Honor."

"You can go. See the clerk on the way out to pay your fine."

Carlisle got up and didn't turn back. His hand touched the gold tie and he nodded his head softly. It had brought him luck. Then he looked to his step-father, who was sitting in the last row, and he gave Carlisle a thumb up.

Joan was still weighing heavy on his heart but Carlisle felt so grateful for being given a second chance. Not having a license would be a pain in the ass but he didn't even own a car accept for a month so it wasn't like he was used to having to drive everywhere. He could take the bus, taxis, hitch rides from friends, whatever. He'd received a fortunate break and he wasn't going to complain about the details.

* * *

For the next month, Carlisle focused on work and didn't have much of a desire to go out and party or do anything. On the surface, everything was fine but internally, not so much. He still held on to some serious anger about what had happened with Joan and felt that if he allowed himself to move on, he would be dishonoring her memory, as well as that unspoken love for her.

48

"Come on, let's go out. You don't have to worry about driving. You just have to have some fun. It's not healthy to just work and stay cooped up in your apartment so long," Ethan said, staring at Carlisle from the swivel chair in the corner of his apartment. His hands were on his legs and his baseball hat was turned sideways.

"I don't know. I'm not sure…"

Ethan cut him off. "Well, I'm sure and I know you best. We can do a little pot, have some fun, and meet a few ladies."

The drug reference sent Carlisle into a temporary spin.

"It was the drugs you gave that possibly led to Joan's seizure. Doesn't that fuckin' bother you, man?"

"Calm down, Carlisle," Ethan said, jumping up from his seat quickly. "I know you're pissed about that but it was a fluke and you know it. I didn't kill her any more than you did."

"You son of a …"

Now Carlisle jumped up and charged toward him, his fist cocked, and he began to swing but just stopped in mid-air.

"Look, I'm sorry, Ethan. I know it's not your fault but I'm still so pissed off."

"It's okay to have a distraction. No one—and I mean *no one*—wants you to stay up in this apartment doing nothing for the next year or whoever knows how long. You'll end up like one of those freaky people who end up going postal."

"I sure hope not," Carlisle said, having to give a laugh at that. It was a much needed laugh because it diffused the situation immediately, making him think that it may not be such a bad idea to actually go out for a bit.

"What should we do?" Carlisle asked.

"I have just the plan," Ethan said.

"Why am I not surprised?"

"Hey, you plan life and I plan fun. It's what we do best. You're all business and I'm all about the entertainment."

The two headed out in Ethan's wheels, which were still intact, and the car navigated the two toward the old familiar path that led to the Vista.

"These girls are really incredible, I'm telling you. You're going to have a fun time."

"What are their names?"

"Jenna and Monique."

Ethan picked up his phone while driving, something that suddenly disturbed Carlisle. Maybe Ethan had been right when he said he was being a bit too extreme. He had to mellow out and loosen up a bit or else he would drive himself crazy.

"Yeah, we'll meet you at Tier in a half hour. Sounds good?"

Ethan hung up. Then he turned around, heading toward Tier instead of Vista.

They got to the club and the girl's arrived ten minutes later. The four walked in together and Carlisle looked at the two beauties, one with a killer English accent and the other with a hint of Cali slang in it. They were gorgeous and perfect by most standards but they didn't arouse anything in Carlisle the way they would have not so long ago. They were pleasant.

The result of the evening was a "pleasant" evening with some good conversation and no commitment to call and do anything else from Carlisle's end. Ethan always committed to everyone, whether he ever did call them again or not was a different story. He always said he would, though, which led to him having to avoid certain clubs for months at a time until the girls DCP stays were up.

On the way home the two talked casually.

"So, what can we do to get your rap career moving along a bit more quickly?" Carlisle asked. "I have lots of time to do research for you or anything you need to help you out."

"It's a long road to the top," Ethan said. He'd adopted that as his current motto as to why he hadn't made it yet. It was two miles past his deadline.

"Let's think about you. What's been going on? Never a day goes by when you aren't planning some crazy shit for the future, trying to make something happen."

"Well, I've had one idea milling around in my mind. It's pretty huge, though."

"What is it?"

"A website; one where everyone from everywhere can connect and talk, have some real conversations, and hopefully learn a few things."

"Like a dating site?"

"No, more like a...awareness site."

"Are you turning into some sort of spiritual guru on me?"

"No. Even though I am so sick of this Disney College Program game it's helped me learn some pretty cool things. Same for you, we've talked about it."

"Like what?"

"All these different cultures, food, religions, and personalities that we've met over the years through hanging out with the Disney College Program crowd."

"That has been pretty cool, hasn't it? So, you're thinking of making a website that's kind of like a melting pot...you know, how they refer to the US with all the cultures that came here to form it."

Carlisle couldn't believe what he heard. "Ethan, that may very well be the smartest thing you've ever said, man. I knew there was a genius hidden in there somewhere."

Ethan laughed. "Just don't tell anyone, you'll cramp my style. You're the insightful intellect of this group and I'm the charismatic, outgoing one."

"Man, you're nuts. I'm the whole package," Carlisle said.

The two laughed about it and that was the end of the conversation for the night.

51

"So, tomorrow night, we're going out again. Got it?" Ethan said as he dropped Carlisle off.

"What if I say no?"

"I'll pick you up at 8:00."

Apparently no isn't an option, Carlisle thought.

That night, he went to bed tired and exhausted, shoving the website idea to the back of his mind. It was a huge idea, one worthy of a ten year goal, not an immediate one.

6

"The time is always now."

Carlisle walked out to the curb and got into Ethan's car, not particularly excited to be going out again but thankful that it would at least get his friend off his back. He got it—Ethan was worried; everyone was worried. However, Carlisle knew he'd be good in the end and things would sort themselves out. He just had to find a direction—one single direction to stick with for the time being. He didn't want to use his hacking skills because he couldn't risk getting into trouble but there were times when he was surely tempted. Case in point—tapping into the DMV and changing that license status from "revoked" to "active."

"You set for a great night," Ethan said, rapping his words and throwing in an occasional beat box tune.

Carlisle could tell that he was feeling good and it wasn't just a natural euphoria, he was high on something—something quite effective to have it impact him the way it seemed to. Oddly enough, that side of Ethan was often quite appealing because he relaxed about his talk about women and was more likely to dive into his aspirations about being a rapper.

"So, did you go home and start brainstorming a website last night?" Ethan asked.

"No," Carlisle said. "I went to bed."

"You surprise me, man. If I were a betting man, I would have bet you did."

"You are a betting man but I guess you lost that one, brother."

"Carlisle, it's a cool idea. One that we could definitely do. You got the brain power and I got the social finesse."

"In time." Carlisle chose to say nothing more than that.

"Well, it's time for some fun," Ethan said, pulling into a parking lot in Vista, marked "Visitors Only." Technically he was.

Making their way up to the apartment of Ethan's latest temptation, he briefly told Carlisle that she was really hot, from Brazil, and one of the finest looking women he'd ever seen.

53

"And what about her roommate?" Carlisle asked.

"Hot girls always end up by each other, right? She's guaranteed to be hot."

"Guaranteed, huh?" Carlisle laughed, knowing enough to not take any guarantee from Ethan seriously.

The two knocked and the Brazilian beauty let them into the apartment. Sitting there, on the lumpy couch—something that was an ongoing joke among DCPers—was the hot girl's roommate. She definitely was not hot.

Ethan didn't even look at Carlisle after the introduction, not wanting to get one of those *I'm out of here* glances. He took off, immediately latching on to his conquest, and the two began to laugh and giggle, leaving Carlisle to watch the roommate. She was heavy, from some place he couldn't pinpoint—which was rare—and very complacent with the silence.

"So, where you from?" Carlisle finally asked, feeling awkward with the silence.

"Nepal." She offered nothing more. Then she got up and went to her bedroom, leaving Carlisle alone with Ethan and the other girl.

Not knowing what to do, he pulled out his smart phone and began to surf the Internet for something of interest, trying to waste time until it was appropriate to just get out of there and leave.

Ethan, being a fast mover for nearly his entire life, was suddenly walking hand in hand with his Brazilian beauty to her bedroom. He quickly turned around and smiled brightly before shutting the door, leaving Carlisle all alone in the living room. He glanced around, seeing the same old apartment he'd been seeing for many years. Didn't matter what number you were in, they were all the same all the time.

"Fuck this," Carlisle mumbled. He got up to leave, thinking he'd go outside and hail a cab or even hop on the party bus. Anything besides what he was doing.

He heard a small humming noise and turned around. The bedroom door was cracked open to the roomie's bedroom and she was sitting on the floor, surrounded by incense, and her palms were facing upward. She was meditating or something—no she was praying. He'd never seen anything like it. It sounded beautiful and drew him in enough that he sat back down and decided to be a spectator for her ritual.

Carlisle wasn't fascinated by a whole lot but something about watching this woman feel comfortable enough to do what she wanted to do and be who she was, even knowing he was there, was very interesting to him. You didn't meet many people like that.

On occasion, the "Oh God, yes," would come from the bedroom Ethan was in, stopping the trance that Carlisle was in watching the woman pray and it would distract him. Then he'd get back to observing the roommate. He wanted to take a picture but knew that would be rude. He was so curious about it.

Then she stopped. Her eyes opened up and she looked at Carlisle in a way that made his heart skip a beat. It was intense and alluring, making him feel a draw to her despite not thinking of her as anything more than a chubby lady a short while ago.

She walked out.

"That was beautiful. What religion are you?"

"It's called Tantrism."

"I've never heard of it. Is it only in Nepal?"

"It is not very common."

"What's it about?"

"It's hard to explain; something best researched, I think."

"Was that praying?"

"Yes, it's meditation based and has many mantras but it is a call to my goddesses."

"Goddesses?"

"Yes, it focuses on the feminine gods, the female's sexuality."

"So, how does…"

Ethan and his conquest came out of her room, laughing loudly and stopped Carlisle's conversation with the roommate dead in its tracks. He'd never been so disappointed to see Ethan. Now his curiosity was running amuck and he wanted to find out more about Tantrism. He quickly pulled out his phone, making a note of the name so he wouldn't forget.

"Well, baby, I've got to go. Have to work early," Ethan said.

Carlisle looked at him, knowing he was full of shit. What was going on? It certainly couldn't be that he felt guilty about leaving him out there. That had never happened before. Ho's always trumped bro's, unlike the way the saying usually went: bro's before ho's.

Once they were in the car, Carlisle asked.

"I felt bad for leaving you there with her, man. Plus, she started talking all serious, planning out like an entire week of my social life. That's when I knew it was time for me to fly and I knew you wouldn't mind."

"Oddly enough, I wish you would have done your thing a bit longer," Carlisle asked.

"Don't tell me you were getting into the fatty?" Ethan asked, eyes wide.

"She was interesting." Carlisle told Ethan what he'd seen and found out and Ethan was actually intrigued by it, too.

"This is *definitely* a sign that you should be doing that website, Carlisle. You know the path but I know how to do it right, you know?"

"I love the idea but…"

Ethan pressed down his brakes hard, coming to a red light, and Carlisle's body moved forward, stopping him midsentence.

"I don't want to hear any but, Carlisle. I think we need to do this. It's a great idea and the time is right. You just got a signal from whoever, wherever, too. How about we call ourselves the 'Right-Path.' That's a righteous name. What do you say? You take care of your brainiac stuff and I'll take care of the networking. Let's do this."

"I don't know," Carlisle rebutted.

"Seriously, what else do you have to do, anyway? You don't care to go out on the scene the way you used to and you're stuck at home without a license. You have the time."

"Ouch, that stings…but yeah, it's true, I guess. Let's do it, let's see what we can do with this idea," Carlisle said.

Once he said the words out loud he felt freer than he had in a long while and motivation poured into him. Unlike what he'd thought just the night before, there was no better time than the present to see what could become of his idea.

* * *

Carlisle's hacker experience was helpful to the start-up of his website. He got to work developing the outline first, which included creating a: home page, about us page, and many pages with references on many different religions. It was a complicated website platform, one with more technical finesse required than even with Facebook and certainly with the dying My Spacious website.

One thing was for certain, Carlisle would need lots of talent to help develop this website and get it up and running. That meant he needed capital so he began to take on extra shifts, making his life threefold: eat, work, and sleep. He didn't do anything else and he was consumed by it.

Talking with Ethan one day, they were trying to decide on a name. Ethan wanted Right-Path but Carlisle didn't like it. The hyphen made Google searches more challenging and the name implied there was a wrong path. The website was all about unity, satisfying curiosity, and allowing people to celebrate who they were.

"Okay, if not Right-Path, what?" Ethan asked, growing impatient. He didn't like the business details as much as the networking and it showed.

"Let's see. We need to brainstorm this."

"Then I have just the perfect thing to allow the creativity to flow," Ethan said. He pulled a baggie out of his front pocket, along with a pinch hitter, and lighter.

He lit up and took a hit, offering it to Carlisle while he held it in. "No thanks."

"Suit yourself," Ethan managed to get out.

"How about just 'One,'" Ethan offered.

"Taken. Some web host or something like that," Carlisle countered.

"How about Perceive Social, let's look it up and see if that domain name is available."

"Dammit, some smart guy has that too."

Ethan threw out a few more ideas, none of which fit.

"Hey, how about an acronym or something?" Carlisle said, more to himself than Ethan.

"What's that?"

"You know, a series of letters together that stand for something. Just like NBA stands for National Basketball Association."

"Cool. Any ideas?"

Carlisle thought about it. He really liked the thought of 'one' being in the name somehow. Exactly how was the unknown.

He tapped his fingers on the coffee table, hoping it would help him to think. We have religion, we have one, we have a website."

"How about ORW."

Carlisle's eyebrows wrinkled. "What did you say? ORW?"

"Yeah," Ethan said, taking another hit.

"There's no flow to that."

Ethan shrugged. "Suit yourself."

Then, as in all moments of awareness, Carlisle had it. He stood up and said, "O.R.B."

"Orb, what?" Ethan asked, staring at him through glassy eyes.

"O.R.B., One Religion Book."

"That sounds great. O.R.B. it is. Are we done now?"

Carlisle shook his head. "Yeah, we're done."

"Okay, great. Catch ya' later."

Then Carlisle remembered. "I have to find some people to help with this next. Are you still going to be able to contribute some funds to paying them?"

"Sure, yeah, I'm working on it."

"How much? I need to know what to budget."

"I'll let you know in a few days."

Then Ethan left. Not surprisingly, Carlisle discovered that the few days never came. Ethan wanted the website and to network for it but not to actually back it with his own precious capital.

Carlisle took complete control of the project.

Finding the talent to help him with his platform was not too challenging. He hired other guys, not unlike himself, who had skills they hadn't always used for good, and were in need of a little extra money. They did premium work at a fairly minimal price compared to what it would cost to hire a web developing firm.

Each and every day, Carlisle learned new and exciting things. He learned about new religions, new things about web development, and also about marketing. While Ethan was the out-and-about marketing guy, he still needed to know how to develop strong SEO to get people to the website.

Finally, launch day came and it was so exciting, although lackluster in a way. There was no big party or anything like that. Instead, there was monitoring of the site for glitches, comments, and questions. It was labor intensive, to say the least.

Ethan had shown up, out of friendship more than anything else, and after an hour of twiddling his thumbs and not wanting to learn about what he could do technology-wise, he took off to the club, saying he was going to go spread the word.

"Sure," Carlisle said. What else could he say?

Carlisle wanted to have faith that Ethan would do what he said but he knew how easy he got distracted. It had kept him from going the extra mile with his rap talents—which really were stellar—and it couldn't be relied on for O.R.B. to be successful, either.

For once, Carlisle was glad to be proven wrong. Within an hour, people were liking the Facebook page and browsing the website, setting things up. The guy that had developed the app was incredible and people seemed to be navigating the site effortlessly from their smart phones and even their home computers and tablets.

Yes!

That night, Carlisle didn't sleep a wink, as he checked everything out and watched the membership number increase as the night went on. When first light came and he finally went to bed, there were one hundred people signed up. It was four times the amount he'd hoped for and he felt great about exceeding his day one goals.

Within one week, Carlisle felt confident that he could get advertisers for the site and start making some return on his investment. The numbers kept going steadily up over the next months, now spanning cross the world, not just in the Orlando area, then Florida, and the US. He couldn't even believe it some of the times. He'd look at the numbers and blink, wondering if this was really it—if he was onto something huger than he initially guessed.

A few hundred dollars a week started pouring in from pay-per-click advertising and a few solid advertising spots, including Wil the Photographer, as well as a few of the clubs that Ethan and Carlisle had frequented over the years. Those were accounts that Carlisle set up. It had become a self-moving machine now and anything Ethan talked about was more braggadocio than adding actual viewers. After all, he'd tapped the Orlando market.

An unfamiliar local number came up on Carlisle's phone and he answered it. It was a local radio station.

"Hey, are you interested in doing a quick phone interview on O.R.B. for Power 95.3?" someone asked.

"Yes," Carlisle answered. No need to hesitate on that decision. This type of exposure was important to the message of O.R.B. and gaining international attention.

A day later, Carlisle had done that interview, which went decent considering it was his first radio interview ever. He knew he had to be better prepared and from there, he began to read up on public speaking and giving good interviews. He had to be better than good, he had to be great.

Then it was time for an interview on one of the local morning talk shows. Ethan was supposed to be a part of that interview but it was early in the morning and he didn't show up. Internally, Carlisle was grateful because he really couldn't trust how Ethan would act. He wasn't always polished and he knew that in order to take this thing further a polished image was necessary. It wasn't to be mean or diss' his friend. It was a fact of business.

A few weeks later, Carlisle found himself being interviewed by Entrepreneur Magazine and he was starting to think that life couldn't get any better than it had been. When his copies of the magazine came he found himself on the corner of the front cover with the title, "The New Great Uniter." Of course, that had been a term that former President Reagan had been referred to quite often. That was some serious company to keep.

Carlisle was feeling great and had finally broke even from all the investments he'd made into creating O.R.B. Everything now, aside from maintenance and payroll for three employees, was going to be profit. Ethan was feeling like a king pin with the extra income, using it to brag about his success. Many people did believe him because Carlisle was not out at the club scene anymore. He'd grown past it and was more mature, starting to run in different circles.

Then, the phone rang, and a thick English accent asked, "Hello, is this Carlisle Lewis?"

"Yes," Carlisle replied.

"This is Alicia from Mr. Ariel Kennedy's offices in London."

Carlisle froze. He knew who this guy was, always making one Forbes list or another. He was calling for him.

"What can I do for you?" he asked, making his tone more alert and trying to up how professional he sounded.

"Mr. Kennedy would like to fly you to London to have a meeting. Would that be possible in your schedule for this upcoming week?"

"Please hold while I confirm."

Carlisle put his hand over the phone and danced around a bit, grinning in a wildly ridiculous way.

"Yes, I can make that work."

"Wonderful. I will email you the eTickets, itinerary, and some funds for expenses along the way."

She hung up.

Carlisle couldn't believe it. A one minute call had possibly changed his life forever.

He went on the move, getting organized for his first overseas trip. Hell, it was his first trip ever out of Florida. This was big—really fucking big.

Express fees for passports were issued and an itinerary was sent. First class to London. Yeah, Carlisle was already sold hook, line, and sinker on the good life.

7

"It's just business."

Not many things made Carlisle nervous but meeting Mr. Aerial Kennedy was something that did. It was huge—by far the biggest thing that had ever happened to him. What could he want?

He soon found out.

"Mr. Lewis, I'm glad to finally have the chance to meet you. You've intrigued me for quite some time."

Carlisle stood up and walked over shaking the man's hand and suddenly felt suspicious. He couldn't hide it.

"It's nice to meet you, Mr. Kennedy,"

"Aerial, please. Sit back down."

He sat down, crossing his one leg over the other and then ran his hand down his white shirt, which was habit.

The two men assessed each other for just a few seconds.

Although he couldn't say for certain why, Carlisle sensed that he liked the man and appreciated him greatly. In part, it was because Aerial Kennedy was one of the most prominent, successful businessmen of the century, making the still relevant Forbes Top Ten Influential Entrepreneur's list—something that he'd aspired to do some day. He was close but he wasn't quite there.

"So, tell me more about O.R.B., Carlisle."

Aerial's piercing blue eyes stared into Carlisle's, showing he was a man who seldom had to wait for answers.

"When it comes to the logistics…" Carlisle was quickly cut off by Aerial, who raised his hand in the air and didn't need to say a single word to stop him in mid-sentence.

"Pardon me for interrupting. I know all the logistics, probably as well as you do. What I don't know is the philosophical aspect behind it. What inspired the One Religion Book, or O.R.B., as it is known by to so many?"

Carlisle told the story, mastering it from the numerous interviews he'd been doing over the past months. Then, he decided it was time for him to ask a few questions.

"So, what I am interested in is why you've called me here," Carlisle said.

I hope it's not bad to say that O.R.B. is just me, not Ethan, too. After all, I've done all the work and invested all the capital.

"You seem to discredit your success. I'm sure people flock to you for your time."

"People—yes. People like Aerial Kennedy, not so much. I make the connections with those that can help take me places."

Aerial laughed softly and the crease lines around his eyes made him look less intimidating, an easier man to open up to.

"Well spoken, Carlisle. What I want to talk to you about is something that is happening right now, in the world as you know it, that I know you are not aware of."

Carlisle stared at him, not sure how to process what he meant.

"There's another society within the fabric of the one we currently have here on Earth, as well as other places."

Now it was Carlisle who cut off Aerial. "Other places? You mean like outer space?"

Joan, he thought.

"Yes but not in the way you may be thinking. It's a society that is forming and striving toward creating a more united universe, not just world."

No one liked to be played for a fool and part of Carlisle's common sense was shouting that he was being taken on some crazy joy ride by an eccentric Aerial Kennedy. It didn't fit the bill of what the man was known for.

"I see the doubt in your eyes. It's quite logical, actually, but here me out, Carlisle. This society is one that's meant to start creating a new world, one in which everyone of value recognizes their role and contributes to something better…something stronger."

"You sound like Hitler with his weeding out the weak deal," Carlisle said suspiciously. The brief description he'd been provided appeared to be the exact opposite of everything he tried to stand for in his life.

"I assure you that is not the case, although I understand your point. Answer me one question. Do you think that everyone in this world will use their gifts, their potential?"

"No, unfortunately."

"Do you think that if they knew they were going to die they'd use their gifts to try and salvage their lives?"

"For a bit of time but if they don't want to embrace them, they're likely to revert back," Carlisle said.

"Exactly. What I am talking about is a world where everyone knows their role and what they are destined to do. There are entrepreneurs, forward minded thinking people such as ourselves that help create the environment we live in. Then there are those who are excellent at implementation and follow-through, while others like to do the busy work, doing what they're told and not really questioning the source of it.

"It's this concept that I am talking of when I tell you about this parallel society which already exists and is growing stronger by the day."

"Like some secret society?"

"It's secretive at this time but such won't always be the case."

"Why tell me without any sort of commitment or at least signing a NDA or something like that?"

"Well, we are friendly and inclusive but I can assure you that you'd have challenges if you tried to sabotage the efforts in any way."

"Challenges…like death."

"Well, I don't prefer to think so drably. I was thinking that no one would believe you, you'd lose credibility, and before you knew it, someone would be buying O.R.B. for half its worth just to salvage it and get you out of the picture.

"That's how most 'buy-outs' happen to take place, after all."

"You definitely know about that, Aerial."

"Yes, I definitely do."

"So, what is it you ask of me?"

"Just to hear me out, which you've done. Think about what I've told you, Carlisle. I believe we can be of great value to each other and over time, dare I say, develop a friendship or at least a fond rapport for each other."

"Who else is a part of this?" Carlisle asked.

"People you'll know in due time. Some that you've never heard of before, of course."

Aerial stood up and looked downward, assessing that his suit hadn't wrinkled and then looked at Carlisle casually, almost as if he hadn't just revealed anything of substantial importance at all, and added, "How long would you like to think things over before we meet again?"

Carlisle's instincts had taken him far and he felt them saying that there was no reason to delay the inevitable. "I look forward to hearing the details. Call me when you have specifics available."

"A wise, young man, just like I'd heard."

"And every bit the masterful negotiator, as I've always heard," Carlisle replied.

The two men laughed and Carlisle stood up now, walked over to Aerial and shook his hand.

He walked out of Aerial's luxurious penthouse on Wycombe Square, a swarthy part of London without a doubt, and made his way down to the street, where his driver was waiting.

That evening, he received a call to meet with Aerial the following day back at his penthouse. Things were getting interesting.

* * *

The following day, just in the mid-afternoon, Carlisle made his way back to Aerial's penthouse and was greeted by the butler, who acknowledged, "Good afternoon, Mr. Lewis. This way, please," in his thick, polished accent.

Carlisle went into the office and this time he was surprised to find Aerial sitting there with a pleasant smile upon his face and his eyes dancing merrily like he'd just received the best news of his life.

"Right on time. I like punctuality," Aerial said.

66

Carlisle walked over with his hand extended. "Great to see you again."

Naturally, Carlisle had assumed that he was going to get some information on this secret society, something he was definitely interested in finding out about. Just the thought of it drew him in, like a bug to a street light.

"Do you mind if I speak boldly, Carlisle?"

"No, not at all. I assume you're going to share details with me about this secret society."

"In due time, yes, but for now, I'd like to talk business."

"Sure, what business?" Carlisle asked.

"O.R.B. and Kennedy Investments purchasing it."

Carlisle was taken aback. His website was quickly becoming popular and he was proud of that. It didn't seem like it would be Kennedy Investments type of thing, though.

"You want to buy it?"

I must have discovered something more valuable than I've even realized yet, Carlisle thought.

"Yes."

"Why?" Carlisle asked, adding, "Hopefully you don't mind my boldness, as well."

"It is something that aligns very well with certain aspects of my enterprises and that is interesting to me. The way people have responded to it interests me, too."

Aerial leaned over to the polished, black credenza behind him and pulled out a stack of papers.

He continued on. "All of this is comments from people online, articles, etc., about O.R.B. It has everyone talking regardless of how they feel. Some are hostile and that's a good thing—shows that it is very realistic to a great many people."

"You know what they say, 'bad publicity is the best publicity.' Can't say it's any easier to take, though," Carlisle said. He started laughing. Aerial did, too.

"Yes, I've learned that lesson rather well."

Carlisle's curiosity was piqued, wondering what he had discovered and what it was worth. "What did you have in mind?"

"To invest in O.R.B. You could remain as CEO or move on to your next endeavor, whatever you preferred. Or, just enjoy a life of riches for awhile until you figure the next thing out."

That would require a lot of money.

"So, what did you have in mind, Aerial?" Carlisle asked again, trying not to sound too eager—like a junk yard dog salivating for a steak.

Again, Aerial reached to the credenza behind him and this time he offered Carlisle a substantially thinner maroon, glossed manila folder with the Kennedy Investments logo stamped on the front.

Carlisle reached for it and opened it up. He stared down and then blinked. Then he stared again.

One billion dollars. Holy fucking shit!

"I see that the number is satisfactory," Aerial replied.

Carlisle looked up and couldn't hide his 'shock and awe' expression and he didn't care.

"Take a few minutes to read over the details," Aerial added.

It wasn't a full legal contract but it seemed to have all the necessary items listed in the bullet points. A portion of proceeds, remain CEO if he chose, receive a percentage of proceeds, incorporate and sell stock, Aerial would be Chairman of the Board, etc.

He didn't have to think twice about it. "I look forward to working with you."

"And congratulations on becoming the world's next billionaire," Aerial added.

Carlisle smiled and lost his composure for a moment, standing up and pulling back his fist with a whispered, "Yes."

"I love that response and there will likely come a day when you do, too, Carlisle."

"I hope so," he said.

"A scotch to celebrate?"

"Sure, why not," Carlisle said.

He'd never drank scotch before but had no doubts that he was about to start with some of the finest scotch that money could buy. It was perfect.

The two toasted and the crystal lowball glasses clinked together in celebration. When the warm, amber liquid touched Carlisle's lips he smiled, feeling its warmth trickle down his throat and into his stomach. This is unbelievable.

"One thing, Aerial," Carlisle said after the toast.

"What's that?"

"Can we keep this out of the media until I'm home and get a chance to talk to a few people. It will make for a smoother transition, you know."

"I do indeed. One thing you'll find out with money is that those people who've been lifelong friends suddenly get a little…uglier, let's just say."

Does he know about Ethan?

"So I've heard…about people winning the lottery, anyway."

"This far surpasses the lottery, wouldn't you say?"

"I would."

And from that second on, Carlisle felt the bond of friendship between Aerial and him. The man was obviously someone he could learn from but also someone who was driven and well-connected, two things that Carlisle had always strived for.

8

"It's easier to do good when your bank account isn't in the red."

Carlisle got back to his small apartment, not thinking of Joan for the first time when he walked into it since her death. It felt good but he also knew that she had started the series of good fortunes that he'd encountered. Knowing that she'd died for it made him realize that he didn't have the luxury of squandering the opportunity he'd been given by Aerial Kennedy; who was a good and decent guy, aside from being insanely wealthy.

After unpacking from his quick three day journey to London, Carlisle took a shower to unwind and prepared to start making his calls. He couldn't wait to call his step-father and mother, knowing that they'd be completely floored by the news. After that, he'd call Ethan, who might not be so floored—although it shouldn't matter. His claim to fame was talking about the site and he could still do that.

The phone rang.

Carlisle grabbed it without even looking at it, distracted in the amazing thoughts that were now a part of his life.

"Man, where have you been? I was beginning to think you fell off the face of the earth?" Ethan asked, his voice sounding odd. Not anxious, but odd.

"I went to London on a little trip."

"London? What? Why?" The questions kept rolling off his tongue.

Carlisle laughed. "Slow down and I'll tell you. I should tell you in person, though."

"I'll be over in ten."

For nearly the first time in his life, Ethan was on time. He walked right into Carlisle's apartment without saying a single word and went over to the fridge, opened it up, and pulled out a Heineken, cranked it open, and sat down.

"So, what was going on in London? Did you meet some chick?"

"No, no chicks. That would be you that would up and fly to London for a girl."

"True," Ethan said, not bothering to disagree.

"I had a meeting with Aerial Kennedy."

"I think I've heard of him. What about?"

"O.R.B. He wanted to invest in it."

"How come I wasn't invited?"

Carlisle shrugged, not willing to mention that he hadn't even brought up Ethan's name to him.

"I don't know."

"What did you tell him?"

"I said 'yes.'"

"Without talking to me?" Ethan asked, stopping in mid sip of his beer.

"I didn't know what there would be to talk about. It was my capital for the business after all."

Ethan was thinking how to respond. He was clearly shocked and trying to control his temper.

"How much did he invest?" he asked quietly…cautiously.

"A billion."

"What?"

"You heard me."

Ethan jumped up and screamed at the top of his lungs. "We're billionaires!"

"No, not we…me," Carlisle replied.

The air immediately silenced.

"What do you mean?"

"This was my idea, Ethan, not yours, and I'm the one whose invested all the time, energy, and personal resources."

"You're kidding, right?"

Carlisle didn't answer and Ethan could immediately see that it was no joke.

"Well, fuck you!" he shouted with a loud, shaking voice.

"Come on, man, calm down. I think you'll see…"

Ethan cut Carlisle off. "I think I see that my best friend has just shit on me. That's what I see. Well, I don't need you and I don't need to be treated that way. Just fuck off and go take a hike."

The bottle of beer was still in Ethan's hand and he smashed it into the wall above the TV and stormed out of the apartment, slamming that door, too.

Carlisle watched him go and felt bad but Aerial's warning also entered into his mind about how friends could act when they found out another friend had reached a different level. In the back of his mind, he'd never thought that Ethan would do that. He'd never wanted to hurt or undermine him, either. It had just sort of…happened. Remember, you have good reasons.

By the next morning, the headlines in the newspapers said it all: Local Guy Becomes the Youngest Billionaire Ever Overnight. Next to it, was a picture of Carlisle and a huge article, detailing his life, mostly by what he'd told people about during his various interviews.

His phone was ringing off the hook and he eventually had it disconnected, having an attorney put more anonymous measures in place. If he was going to give back to people in some way it would be with what he wanted to do and not what the leaches wanted from him.

One week later, he found out that Ethan hadn't cooled down at all. He'd been served papers that he was being sued for breach of contract. Some lawyer was looking to make some quick bucks. There had never been a contract between Carlisle and Ethan.

Carlisle had an amazing new life to live, which included work with O.R.B. still, as well as doing some other things that he felt were important. He knew that he wanted to give to the Orlando community in some way. As he began to think of ideas, reading the newspaper to find what organizations and charities may be in need, he found some great ideas. He also discovered that he needed to have a beautiful woman—not just any woman either—by his side for the parties, events, and various functions he was expected to be a part of now. He'd taken his mother a few times but that clearly wasn't going to cut it for either of them. She didn't like going to all those 'fancy affairs' any more than he wanted to be known as the 'youngest billionaire who takes his mom everywhere.'

The one thing that Carlisle saw as a sure investment was the Orlando City Soccer Club's new stadium. They were getting a professional team and it wasn't that he'd ever played soccer or could even tell you all the rules. He was at an interview about his substantial investment.

"Why invest in a sport you have no connection to?" the reporter asked, looking at him with doe eyes.

"It's simple, really, Neena. Soccer is a sport that everyone can play, regardless of income levels, and the organization has a strong history of reaching out to underprivileged children and allowing them to be a part of that sport. And that's just the type of activity I want to be associated with because it's good for Orlando…it's good for the way it makes me feel, too."

"This is what happens when local people do good, everyone. We wish you much success in everything you're involved in, Mr. Lewis."

"Carlisle, please."

"Okay, Carlisle. So, where are you off to next?"

"Believe it or not, I'm going backpacking across Europe for a fun adventure."

"With anyone special?"

"Yes, but I'm not going to tell."

"Not even a hint?"

"No hints, Neena, but rest assured, we won't be staying in five star hotels on this trip. The beautiful sights of Europe by bike and foot—that's what we'll be experiencing."

"Sounds romantic."

Carlisle just smiled, leaving everyone speculating. He knew the time for the interview was up and it was a little technique that he'd learned along the way.

Of course, Carlisle was now linked to beautiful and amazing women who were established in their own right but he refused to have a serious relationship with anyone. It wasn't the time to do that. He had too much going on and too many options.

The backpacking was fun for Carlisle, a greater test of his athleticism that's what he'd normally be interested in, but he'd fared decently. However, he was glad to get back and move on to the next thing he'd been thinking of—some stocks to turn his investments into huge successes. He was going to talk with Aerial about that, as his advice and instincts had proven to be quite successful for him.

"So, how diverse are you willing to go?" Aerial asked.

"As long as it's not freaky, pretty diverse. Why? What's out there?"

"Do you have a computer nearby?"

"Yes."

"It's good to diversify, having one 'outside the box' type stock and one that's more technology drive. Make sense?"

"Don't put all your eggs in one basket," Carlisle replied.

"Exactly."

Aerial walked him through a few steps to find the best ones that would work for him and what to look for in trends, as well as performance. Then he left Carlisle with the following words of wisdom. "Start with smaller investments and see where it takes you. Don't over-invest in case it's a wrong call and don't be impatient either, pulling a stock at the first bad day."

Carlisle researched a lot.

He thought a lot.

Finally, he was ready to act. He'd chosen two investments. One was in marijuana stocks and he chose two: CANV and GWP.L. They seemed to be the best fit for him to try at that time. As for technology, he went with the big, well known name because it had always performed decent enough and had a newer division that wasn't over-saturated yet: Lockheed Martin's exoskeleton technology. In short, exoskeleton's are mobile machinery worn by people—very cool! Go LMT.

So much was happening so quickly and with every waking day, Carlisle found himself more energized, fit, and curious about how to maximize everything he touched. This meant he had to take care of himself: body, mind, and soul.

He hired a fitness trainer to come to his new home, which was a substantial upgrade from the old apartment. He had a penthouse on Eola Drive that he was renting until he figured out his final plan. Honestly, Carlisle wasn't sure if it was in Orlando or not. He was starting to get a lot more worldly experience and his adventures seemed to warrant having a few different places to call 'home.'

So much had been happening that Carlisle had completely forgotten about the fact that he was due in court soon for the lawsuit hearing with Ethan. It was a thought he'd had at the TomorrowLand Music Festival that reminded him. He was thinking that Ethan was good enough to be up on that stage with the likes of Avicii, Bassnectar, David Guetta, Dimitri Vegas and Like Mike, Diplo, Kaskade, Martin Garrix, Nicky Romero, Skrillex, Steve Aoki, Tiësto, and Zedd. However, he wasn't. He was too busy being a hater and wasting his talents.

Carlisle was curious to see Ethan because he hadn't run into him for the past eight months. Their schedules were so different and Carlisle didn't frequently go to all those same clubs he had for so many years before.

There were a small slew of reporters outside the courtroom waiting to hear Carlisle's thoughts on the matter. He hadn't spoke about it until that day.

"Obviously, I'm sad that it's come down to this with my childhood friend."

"Did you willingly cut Ethan Bryson out of the O.R.B. website when you took a partnership with Aerial Kennedy?"

"There was no agreement so how could I have willingly done anything wrong?" Carlisle asked.

The reporter didn't know how to answer and another one jumped in.

"What will you do if the court finds in favor of Ethan Bryson?"

"That will be addressed *if* it needs to be."

Carlisle's lawyers had been quiet, surrounding him like bodyguards, but one of them finally spoke up. "If you'll excuse us, Mr. Lewis needs to take his place in court."

With that, Carlisle walked in and Ethan followed behind, receiving only one or two questions.

After a longer than expected six hours, both sides had stated their cases.

The jury received their instructions.

No answer was in by the end of day and they were instructed that they'd be called to make their appearance after the jury came to a decision.

The following morning by 9 a.m. the call came. The jury was in.

At 1 p.m. the court reconvened and Carlisle found out that the charges were dropped and Ethan walked away with nothing, refusing to even walk away with his friendship with Carlisle. It was the end of a long friendship and it made Carlisle sad and distraught. He realized that he only had one true friend now, Aerial.

9

"I won't give up. I made a promise."

Ethan was forced to reflect on everything that had transpired the past eight months. So much had been happening and the anger festered in him. He was angry at so many people around him, thinking they'd failed him. He wasn't ready to admit that he was mad at himself, as well, because it was easier to blame others.

At that moment, losing the lawsuit wasn't as agonizing as going to see his mother. One month ago, she'd been diagnosed with cancer and it was serious, so bad. He went to visit her in the hospital room, feeling disgusted that he couldn't buy her state-of-the-art healthcare or even a private suite in a private hospital to deal with her problems. That had been what he wanted to use the proceeds from the lawsuit on after he'd found out she was sick. Before that, it had been revenge on Carlisle for the way he'd been stabbed in the back but one look at his mother when she told him the news changed his mind. He wanted to give her everything he could. Sadly, it wasn't much.

"I lost the lawsuit, Momma," Ethan said, hanging his head down.

"That's okay, child. It wasn't meant to be."

"There's just so much that you…"

She put her finger up to Ethan's lip, quieting her son down. "I need you to be the best you can be, Ethan. I want you to be happy and use your God given gifts to bring the world joy."

"Just like Carlisle did," Ethan said. He turned his head away, feeling stung by the thought.

"I know you don't like to hear it but Carlisle did use his gifts to create that website and he worked hard. Now, he's using that money to give back to the community and do good things for people. Don't hate against that, son. You're better than that and I hope I raised you to think better than that."

"I know, I know, Momma," Ethan said, looking at her through glassy eyes and squeezing her hand gently. "It's just so hard."

78

"Life isn't meant to always be easy, Ethan."

Ethan looked at his mother, who knew that more than just about anyone. She'd had a rough childhood and certainly not a great adult life with Ethan's dad being a non-existent person and Ethan himself causing her troubles on more than one occasion. He felt so guilty.

"Promise me something."

"Anything, Momma."

"Start making the change you want to see."

"There are just so many things standing in my way."

"Climb over them or go around them. Just do the right thing, son, and you'll be able to do amazing things. I won't get to watch from here but by the grace of God, I'll get to watch from heaven above."

"Don't talk that way."

"It's the truth, Ethan. I'm tired and I'm in pain. I don't want to keep fighting to hold on to those things forever. The only thing I want to use my strength for is to get you to see that you have so much potential that you haven't begun to tap into yet. You're a good rapper and I know that you could do more with that."

"I thought you didn't like rap music?" Ethan asked with a faint smile.

"I don't but I guess I'm one of the few in this world who don't. You'd be a great gospel man, too, but I don't think that's what you want. I think you can really touch people through your music and poetry if you put it out there. 'Keep it real,' as you young people say."

"You're young, too," Ethan replied. His mother now looked frail instead of robust but she was only fifty-five years old.

"But life has worn me down—not that I'm complaining."

"Well, I have to get going to work," Ethan said. "I don't want to go, though."
"You don't worry about me. I'll be just fine," she said, smiling at him. He could see that it hurt her just to smile and that their small conversation had worn her out.

"Is there anything you need before I leave?"

"Just a sip of water," she said.

Ethan held the cup up and slowly tipped it until the water touched her lips, moving more carefully than one would with a newborn baby.

She sipped and gave a little cough as she swallowed it down.

"I'll be back tomorrow, Momma."

"I know."

"I love you," Ethan said.

"I love you, too, baby. As long as your mom loves you, don't you ever put another woman above me."

"Never," Ethan replied. He blew her one last kiss and started to leave the room.

He didn't want to take his eyes off his Momma. His heart felt so heavy and burdened. What had he done? Nothing; that was the problem.

<u>I am going to become more successful than Carlisle. I'm going to do it for Momma and she'll make it through this and see what I've become.</u>

That night, Ethan went to work and in his mind, he was writing a new rap song that he was going to hit the circuit with and get out there—no matter what it took. The first person he was going to perform it for was his mother, though.

The next day, Ethan went to the hospital before work again and saw that she was looking weaker than she had the day before.

"How did you sleep?"

"Good. They gave me something."

"I have something to show you," Ethan said.

"What's that?"

"My new rap song. I want you to be the first to hear it."

"Oh, that's good. Let's hear it then," she said softly, her eyes sparkling against her dulling skin.

Ethan performed the verses of his rap song in acapella and used his hand against his chest as the background music to the rhythm.

Believe /
I never thought I'd see the day /
That you would be proud for the words I say/
Believe/
Ain't a woman alive that could be you momma /
Working two jobs /
Then in the kitchen/
Just to keep away the hunger/
you made sure I never seen a jail cell /
I reminisce on the stress I caused, it was hell /
I wish I could do so much for you /
But lately I don't know what to do /
Be strong/
I'm here but I feel like your all alone /
Let me be the light to bring you back home /
I know you want the best for me /
So I have to ignite my dreams/
To find my destiny/

...

Ethan got into his song and his eyes were shut, feeling the words flow from him in a release that he needed badly and seemed to free him in a way. He was into the words he'd created and they had come from his heart and also had the direction of where he needed to go.

When he was done, Ethan opened his eyes and saw his mother looking at him with a warm smile and tears streaming down her face.

"That was beautiful," she said. "So beautiful." Her voice was so soft that she was whispering and Ethan leaned down over her so he could hear her better.

He heard one last thing. It was a small escape of breath.

In that moment, he was afraid to look up, realizing what it was. His mother had just taken her last breath, using her last words on him and complimenting his song.

Ethan put his head down over her heart, feeling the tubes pressing against his cheek, and he heard nothing coming from within her body. Somehow he knew that she'd transferred her heart into him and expected him to do good with it—by both of them.

It was hard to do but Ethan pressed the button to the nurse's station.

"Yes," a voice said.

"She's passed on," he said.

They came in and he watched in numbness as they went about proclaiming her life had ended in a very sterile and medical way.

"Are you going to collect her possessions and take them now or would you prefer to do it later?" one nurse asked with a compassionate tone.

"I'll do it now."

His Momma didn't have many possessions but he went to the closet and grabbed her purse. In it, he found $4, her bus pass, and her red matte lighter.

Ethan picked the lighter up and held it, rubbing his thumb against its smooth surface. His mother had loved that lighter and it was ironic that it was symbolic of the cancer that had killed her, too. His mother would always be alive in his heart but having that lighter in his pocket all the time would be his way of taking her with him everywhere he went in life.

Sad for loss but optimistic for the future, Ethan left the hospital that day with the sole mission of becoming somebody important to someone other than his mother. He wanted to do something great and would do whatever he had to in order to achieve that success.

* * *

Two months had passed and Ethan was trying to do good by his momma; he really was but it was hard to get anywhere without some capital. Everyone wanted money for everything when it came to pursuing a rap career, even in the underground rap circuits. He was developing a name but he needed more.

Selling drugs was never foreign to Ethan but he'd taken to selling them with some bad ass people, not the harmless DCPers who just wanted to get high and dance the night away during their time at Disney.

The Haitian cab drivers still helped deliver a nice profit but it was those who he met through the underground that knew how to get the big money.

"We're going to try and do a half a million flip from 250g's of coke. You in?" one guy asked Ethan one day. His reputation for doing the extreme for a hefty profit was out there.

"Doesn't seem possible. Is it the drug you're trying to get rid of or lot of green you're trying to bring in?" Ethan asked.

"The green."

"Then you're better off with heroin."

"Know where to get any?"

"You supply the capital and I've got the source," Ethan said.

And so he did. Transactions like that were common place for him and he started earning enough money to find a promoter to get him more rap gigs.

Ethan also had a trademark of sorts, something that was most uncommon for what people would expect from him. Whenever he was counting out grams or kilos or money after a transaction, he'd always play his Frank Sinatra playlist on his iPod. Why? His mother had loved Frank Sinatra and he once gave her a huge tip when she was the cleaning person for one of his hotel rooms. That kindness was all it took and Ethan liked to think that channeling some Frank was good for business.

83

Ethan's promoter, Dante Vanders, was not always great at keeping in touch. It wasn't uncommon but these guys didn't talk just to talk. They networked and that's how they got things done. Needless to say, when the phone rang and it was your promoter, you answered right away.

"Hey, Dante, what's up?" Ethan asked.

"Great news. I think I've got you a deal. Can you make it down to Phantom City Studio for a taping tomorrow, 9 a.m."

He was preparing to say that it was kind of early but wisely shut his mouth. "I'll be there."

Dante gave the address and Ethan knew he was one of a few people that were given the address to that place. It was kept fairly quiet. The irony that he'd driven nearby the place a million times on his way to Vista didn't escape him.

He showed up the next morning and gave it his all. They thanked him and had him leave without any feedback. It annoyed him but he tried to keep his thoughts in the positive.

Dante called the next day. It was definitely positive.

"Thanks, man. This is it! I'm on my way."

"It's a nice deal. Treat it right and it'll treat you right, too."

Life began to get crazy and fast-paced for Ethan, too, making it so he was intrigued with his own success each and every day more than Carlisle's. Things were turning around.

He now had moved on from Dante and had an agent, who he didn't really like but they made things happen. He just wanted to market himself and perform and have lots of sex. He was doing that so he let the new agent do their thing in relative peace.

The agent called. "They'd like you to be on Jimmy Fallon."

"No way? That's dope, man!"

"Would I call if it wasn't?" the agent replied.

Ethan ignored it. He was right, however. He wouldn't.

"When's the taping?"

"Next week. NYC. You'll be there two nights."

The taping got postponed but it wasn't until after Ethan was in NYC. His agent went to quick work and got him a radio interview with Power 105.1 with the Breakfast Club—a real score.

That next morning, the interview was under way and Ethan had found an audience that he felt could really connect with him.

"So, Ethan, what's it like to go from relative obscurity to really becoming a name that everyone knows in the industry?"

"It's surreal, man. At times I feel like I'm waking up in a dream. I'm tired and exhausted but feeling good about doing what I love—what I'm passionate about. Everything I've always wanted is starting to happen and I'm grateful. I wish it had been just a bit earlier."

"What do you mean? You're a young guy," the DJ asked.

"Before my mother passed away. She would have loved to see this," Ethan said. "She always believed in me but now others do, too. It's really surreal."

As was his habit, Ethan took out the red matte lighter and flicked it on, staring at it as if his mother's face was about to appear in it.

"Ah, the lighter we've all heard about. That's a touching story, man, real touching."

"I pay tribute to her in every way I can," Ethan said.

There was a slight pause before the DJ continued. "If you could do a song with any artist out there who has passed away, who would it be?"

"No doubt about it—I'd go with the King of Pop."

"Word has it that you like Sinatra but you'd pick Michael Jackson?"

"Sinatra is a link to my mother but Michael Jackson, he was a revolutionary in the music industry to me and I have crazy respect for his talents."

"We're almost out of time. One last question. What's next for you?"

"I'm actually going international as part of rap tour. Excited about that."

"Well great. What an honor it's been to talk with you and best of luck with everything, Ethan."

"Thanks."

The two bumped knuckles and then Ethan was out of there. He had an interesting feeling inside of him, contentment perhaps, but he wanted more.

10

"Money doesn't buy peace of mind."

Carlisle walked into the luxurious, out of this world entrance of Leeds Castle, just thirty miles south of London. This was where he was going to finally have the introduction to the members of the new society that Aerial had spoken of nearly a year before. He'd proven himself and got enough vote for the invitation. He was nervous but more than anything, he was excited. Just being invited was something so rare and secretive that it was off the radar on Google or any internet searches at all. Of course, it made Carlisle wonder if it was either death or acceptance. He was pretty sure he knew the answer based on the first conversation he'd ever had with Aerial. Yet, the man had become a great friend, as well as a mentor, and he trusted him.

A man that looked to be a tour guide for the castle said, "Welcome," and then bowed slightly.

"No need to escort us," Aerial replied confidently.

The man bowed again and Carlisle looked at him, wondering if he knew what was going on. You certainly had to have reliable people for security and whatnot for these types of societies, he imagined, but the butler didn't look all too lethal, should anyone decide to cause a ruckus.

"Does he know where we're headed?" Carlisle asked.

"Of course."

"Is this entire castle part of this society?"

"No, they do tours and whatnot. He is just highly paid to help us when necessary. There are many people willing to cooperate with us, for money if nothing else."

"I'd imagine so."

Carlisle was in awe as they walked through a formal portrait room and into an old, grand library. There were three floors of books with a widow walk around each level. Each shelf was filled and looked to be meticulous.

Aerial glanced over his shoulder and saw that no one, aside from Carlisle and him, were in there. He went over to one shelf and reached his hand underneath and his fingers moved ever so slightly.

87

"Secret button?" Carlisle asked.

This is just like a Hollywood movie.

"Code, a button could be stumbled upon by happenstance, which we couldn't allow to happen."

Of course not, Carlisle thought. It all seemed so cryptic to him suddenly that it struck him as amusing.

Carlisle stared at the bookshelves, expecting them to move but he was mistaken. Instead, a panel slid across the floor to the left of them and it revealed a set of stairs. Aerial motioned for him to follow and the two walked down the stairs. The top slid closed above them and a series of bright lights came on, making it nearly as bright as if there were natural sunlight flowing into the tunnel.

"This is fascinating," Carlisle said, truly amazed by what he was experiencing. "Is this meeting place underground?"

"No, it's at the top of the tower but it's just a more secretive route to get there. The view is quit stunning. I believe you'll be amazed."

A sound came from behind and Carlisle turned around, seeing a group of four men walking down the stairs.

I never would have guessed something like this could be real.

The end of the tunnel came and there was a door there with a keypad on the right side. Aerial pressed a series of buttons and the door slid open, showing that it was actually an elevator. They stepped in and Carlisle thought Aerial might acknowledge or wait for the other gentlemen but he seemed eager to close the door and have them ascend.

About thirty seconds later, the doors opened again, revealing a gorgeous room full of old world luxury and charm with a view that was beautiful, showing the manmade ponds and gardens of the estate. A huge maze could also be seen below.

"Come," Aerial said.

Carlisle saw that Aerial seemed different, more reserved and less laid back. He wondered if this place was that formal. If it was, it may not be the place for him.

"I want to introduce you to a few key people that are very important to our society and their opinion of you, while favorable now, will need to stay so in order for things to work out the way we have planned."

<u>We?</u>

"You are going to have a private conversation with someone, whom I shall introduce you to shortly. It'll be at their sole discretion to allow you into the society or say it isn't meant to be."

"How will I know?" Carlisle asked, suddenly feeling like that high school kid again who just wanted to be accepted by all the 'cool kids.'

"You'll receive two things; each of them valuable and the lifetime mark of your membership to this society."

"Okay, Aerial. I'm ready."

Carlisle couldn't avoid noticing the intense look that Aerial gave him. He simply replied, "Yes, I believe you are."

As Carlisle followed Aerial around, meeting people and having casual conversation it was all he could do to not have his jaw drop. These were successful men and women, ones he'd read about in magazines for years—the best of the best; the most prestigious.

What a crazy ride! How did I become a part of this group? Carlisle thought.

An elderly gentleman with the most unique color of eyes that Carlisle had ever seen walked up behind him and said, "Please follow me, Mr. Lewis. He wishes to see you now."

No one had told Carlisle the name of the man who would decide if he was to become a part of the society and it hadn't really bothered him but he was curious. Was it someone he'd seen before? Someone famous? Who, exactly, had such power in this society of powerful and wealthy people?

Carlisle went back into a room that was to the side of the main meeting room, which had approximately sixty people in it, he guessed. Once inside, he was asked to take a seat.

From a door on the far side of that room, a person came in, a man he presumed by his height. He was quit tall, tall enough to be in the NBA, and it was hard to get a good look at him.

He sat down and began to talk in a very deep voice—Darth Vader deep—and Carlisle stared at him, trying to see what he looked like.

There was no introduction. The man just said, "Tell me your story, Mr. Lewis."

"It's quite a story. Do you have a starting point you'd like me to begin at?"

"Anything you feel is pertinent is good to know," the man said.

Carlisle pondered for a moment, wondering how to tell his story without taking up a crazy amount of time. Then, it just sort of poured out. He talked about high school, Disney College Program, Joan, the fascination with religions and cultures, and O.R.B., of course.

"…And that about summarizes it up to this point," Carlisle said, glancing down at his watch. He'd talked for about thirty minutes. The man had asked no questions or interrupted at all. In fact, he hadn't even cleared his throat and Carlisle wondered if he'd dozed off.

"Very well," he said. "Do you wish to be in this fellowship that you've been invited to join?"

"Yes," Carlisle said.

"Why?"

"It's good to be around motivated and like-minded people. I have the ability to teach certain things, as well as learn."

"Very well."

"Are you ready to join now?"

"Yes," Carlisle replied. He assumed they'd be heading back out to the main room and there'd be a ceremony of sorts. Apparently that was not the case.

A larger box was slid over to him, wooden and plain compared to the luxury of everything else around him.

Carlisle opened it up and saw a syringe inside of it.

"What is this about?" he asked, confused by seeing a needle. It was something he certainly wouldn't have expected.

He glanced again at the box and couldn't help but notice that the man had fingers that were very long and bony with very long, brittle and thick nails. It was a creepy looking hand.

"How do I know this is safe? What's it for?" Carlisle asked, feeling hesitant. He didn't love needles and the thought of injecting himself was disgusting.

"It's for your protection; something for us to know how to find you when we need you; when the fellowship needs to meet."

"And it's necessary?" Carlisle asked, raising an eyebrow.

"Quite," the odd man replied.

These people are the elite of the elite. If they've all done this, I can do it, too.

"Where do I inject it?"

"Into your forearm."

"I can do this myself?"

"If you prefer, someone else can do it for you."

"No, I'll do it," Carlisle replied. He wasn't sure why he felt he should but his senses told him that he had to overcome his hesitation alone.

With some instruction from the mysterious man in the shadows, Carlisle took the syringe and placed it by the beefy part of his hand, between his thumb and pointer finger, and taking a deep breath, he pressed down on the top of the syringe and a chip to know his whereabouts slowly slid into the area.

He cringed and it hurt but the blood that seeped out of his hand disturbed him more. A piece of gauze was slid across the desk for him to put on top of it and stop the bleeding. Then a band-aid to cover it until it stopped bleeding complete.

"So that's it?" Carlisle asked.

"Almost. Here is one more item for you, Mr. Lewis. It must be on you at all times. Do you understand?"

Carlisle looked at the small, square box that was now placed in front of him. It was ornate and gorgeous, having some creature on it that reminded him of an octopus in gold gilding. Really fascinating and really expensive looking.

He reached over and grabbed it, running his thumb over the ornate top, halfway expecting the gilding to come off, but it didn't. He opened it up and stared at the contents of the box. It was a ring.

It makes sense, he thought. *You always hear about rings being the mark of secret societies...The Skulls, things like that.*

Carlisle lifted the ring out of its slot in the box and held it in his fingertips for a moment, looking at it closely—as much as he could in the dimly lit room, anyway.

There was a deep red gem of some sort in the center of it that almost seemed to have something illuminating it from below that point and the ring itself looked to be forged from some metal he didn't really know what it was. It was sturdy, not a soft metal, and there were some small pictures carved into it. He couldn't make out the detail despite wanting to.

"Put it on," the man said calmly.

Carlisle nodded his head and slid the ring on. It was a perfect fit, almost like it was made just for him. How'd they get his finger size, though, to do that? He supposed that anything was possible.

He slid the ring on and felt it seal around his finger. He tried to tug it off but found that he couldn't. It was almost like it had instantly bonded with his body.

A vision flashed through his mind. That's right. Aerial has this same ring.

"Welcome, this ring is for your protection and to help identify you to other members of the fellowship. Not all will know who you are but the ring will let them realize what they can entrust you with," the man said. For the first time, he came out of the darkness and Carlisle couldn't hide his shock at what he saw. The man was not human, if even a man at all.

"Hi…uh…thank you," Carlisle sputtered.

"You are going to learn a great deal now, Mr. Lewis. I suggest you keep your questions contained to the walls of these rooms or in private conversations with the society's members."

"What's the name of the society?" Carlisle asked, realizing it to be a highly irrelevant question at that point.

"We are the High Royals," the man said. "And you, as a human, are known as The Light and I am a Royal."

"Oh," Carlisle said. As a human?

"Now, let's go find Aerial, shall we? I believe that he is the one best suited to explain things to you. You don't look like you're doing so well, Mr. Lewis. Rest assured, nearly everyone has been in your position, for a brief period of time anyway, and you'll get over it and move on once you understand better."

"Certainly," Carlisle said. He still didn't know this man…monster…whatever it was and he didn't care at that point. There was only one thought: *what the hell have I done and how can I get out of this?*

Carlisle walked out of the room and found Aerial to be quit close by the door. He stormed right over to him, not caring if it looked abrupt. "We need to talk—privately."

"Of course, Carlisle," Aerial said. "Let's go over here. There are no secrets here. We all are part of the same society now, a rather galactic one, at that."

Carlisle's jaw tensed. He saw no humor in this and no desire to treat it casually. "Are these demons that I'm surrounded by? Aliens, or what?" he asked, looking around and realizing that some of these 'men and women' seemed different.

"Demons and aliens is rather harsh but they are life forms from places other than Earth, alone. They've come from another dimension far from our own, somewhere deep in outer space; although, they've been living among us for many centuries."

"Is this some sort of invasion plan?"

"Oh goodness, no, Carlisle. Don't talk like a fool because I know you are not one. You wouldn't be here if you were."

"Why are they here, then?"

"The longevity of these demons, as you call them, is something that mortal men such as ourselves have a great deal to learn from. They've lived through centuries of rebellions and upheavals of life as they knew it but survived, becoming stronger as a result."

"You mean like immortal?"

"Perhaps, nothing is infinite—yet—but there are members here who are over a thousand years old. As humans, we are very fortunate that the High Royals have invited us into this society. They only want the best of the best with us. The people who are ambitious, motivated, innovative, successful, and can contribute something positive to society. It's not what you are born into here that matters. It is what you are willing to contribute. Not everyone is meant to contribute for a long period of time."

"And we just forget about them?"

"They are not invited, no, but you certainly realize that, Carlisle."

Carlisle thought about his mother and all his other friends. The thought that they weren't worthy made him feel guilty, like a traitor to human life.

"I see that look and know you're having remorse but I assure you, you are in a position that you want to be in and part of a group of beings that can change this entire universe for the better. Just as you were interested in one religion book, so are we—one ultimate race of beings from all types of backgrounds that contribute positively to the world and are not a burden on it."

"It's so inclusive. That's never what I wanted."

"It's inclusive of those who put forth effort in life. Those who don't...well."

For some odd reason, Carlisle thought of Ethan. If he'd included him in the website, would he have been invited into this world? He'd have to think about that later.

"I want out."

"You want to die?" Aerial asked matter-of-factly.

"No."

"Then you're in, Carlisle. Look, there's no way to hide. High Royals and members of this society are everywhere. You are a very public figure now and someone will always know where you are. You're fighting a moot point."

<u>Is Aerial truly a friend? Is this for my good, for the greater good?</u>

Seeing he had no choice at the moment, Carlisle accepted the fellowship although he didn't feel like a comrade to these people at that moment. He would keep his eyes and ears open to any weaknesses he could use to get out of it, though. It had been stupid of him to be lulled into it by a desire for power and prestige but now his eyes were wide open and he was alert to what was going on. The world would never be the same again. What he saw was reality but it seemed like a nightmare from where he was standing.

11

"My ambition won't allow me to stop."

Ethan's climb up to the ladder of success had been relatively quick but he was quickly finding out that staying on top was a completely different matter. Ethan Bryson was only a hot commodity if he kept pushing the limits, being creative with his quotes and being edgier each time he released a song or did an interview. He was starting to feel like he had lost a bit of himself along the way and was eager to get it back. Unfortunately, those thoughts only occurred in weak moments when he was stoned out of his mind. When he had all his faculties intact, there was only one thought that he was driven by: becoming more famous and powerful than Carlisle. He was consumed by it and would do anything to stop him.

With not having spoken with Carlisle for nearly two years, Ethan had found a new group of friends that were a bit more like him. Artists and songwriters that were trying to make their mark in the music world and become legends down the road. One of his favorite people he'd met was Rodrigo Maducci.

Rodrigo was an intense guy with wild, genius talent. He was a singer-songwriter, record producer, voice artist and choreographer. He was best known for his retro showmanship that usually included playing an electronic guitar and piano. His musical style was very wild range, including Reggae, R&B, Soul and Pop. Rodrigo had an emotionally intense voice despite his rather scrawny frame. He was really likable and all the tattoos he sported just lent to his unique image. He truly was a one of a kind.

"Hey man, I'm going to an after party, you want to come?" Rodrigo asked Ethan.

"Sure, why not," Ethan said. He was always up for a little more partying. He'd been kicking back, smoking some great pot backstage when Rodrigo had performed that night, and having a decent enough time. The two drew different crowds but were in sync when it came to personalities.

"Great, let's go."

The two got to the party and were greeted by some eager groupies inside who wanted to just have a brush or a one night stand with a famous musician. That was cool. Not everyone got in to those parties, though. There were also some girls who were being escorted out and protesting, "But we were invited."

It was a scene that Ethan had gotten used to over the past few years. He'd not had a serious girlfriend—one where he was exclusive, anyway—at all and he'd enjoyed a buffet of women nearly every night, sometimes they'd have a little group activity and other times, it would just be a wild one on one party. It was growing old, however, and now, he found that he wasn't the prime pick for these ladies either because he'd grown stagnant.

Ethan took a deep drag off the pipe that Rodrigo had handed to him.

"How do you keep doing it, man, having hit after hit? How are you so damn lucky?"

"It's not luck. It's the connections," he replied.

Ethan looked up at him and then quickly turned his head, seeing something odd to the side. He noticed this guy leaning against a counter, talking to this girl and when she turned her head, his tongue went out and it looked like a snake and behind his ears, it almost looked like there were gills.

This must be some seriously trippy weed, Ethan thought.

"What type of connections?"

"I have people looking out for me and helping ensure I'm successful," Rodrigo said, exhaling his pot into the mouth of a sexy diva as he kissed her.

"What? Like an agent?"

"No, you have an agent and they don't do everything, as you can tell. You're struggling but it doesn't have to be that way."

Rodrigo's words definitely attracted Ethan's attention. He leaned in and asked in a quiet tone, "What do you mean?"

"If you ever want to make it as big as Carlisle—or even bigger—you need to have the right network of people working for you. I'm not talking about just people in the music industry, I'm talking about people with real power across the world…fuck, across the universe."

"How do I get those connections?" Ethan asked.

"Do you really want to know?" Rodrigo asked. "It's not easy and there's no turning back once you decide to do it."

"I want to know," Ethan said.

I've never been so sure of wanting to know anything in my entire life.

"For starters, you've got to have passion and ambition man—not just for revenge but to be the best you can be, Ethan."

"I don't want revenge; I want justice. There's a difference."

"So there is, but this is what I mean," Rodrigo said, leaning even closer to Ethan. "If you're real and passionate about what you say then people will believe in you and feel it. That's what my music does and that's what that first release you ever had did. It was a song from the heart and written for your Momma. That's powerful shit, man. You have to dig deep into that place and find your drive. It comes from love, not hate. It comes from wanting to be a leader for those in need and surpassing those you envy by being better."

"Look, it doesn't matter what drives me, does it? I want those things and know that I can be a leader and get buck ass rich while doing it."

"It's about more than money. Someday money will be replaced with something else. What will you do then?"

"Figure it out," Ethan said. He had never been one to be in overly philosophical conversations and this was getting in the verge of being too intense but one thought kept screaming in his mind: surpass Carlisle!

"Follow me into the other room," Rodrigo said.

Ethan got up and the girls that were around them began to follow. It took only a simple gesture, raising his hand, for Rodrigo to indicate that they should stay. They pouted but they remained still, not willing to disobey his non-verbal command. Ethan was so jealous of things like that and he wanted that type of unspoken power so badly. If only he could make it to the next level of success…

Once in the room, Ethan watched Rodrigo grab a piece of paper and write something down. He handed the paper to Ethan.

"What's this?" Ethan asked.

"It's a date. You need to go to a third world country and buy a child there by this date. Once you've done that, give me a call and I'll advise you on the next step."

"How can I do that?"

"I'll get you some connections, Ethan, but you got to do this work yourself—show that you want it. It's not going to just happen for you or come easy. You got to put in the time. Understand?"

Ethan shook his head and was trying to put everything into perspective. He knew what was going on was likely illegal and shady but it would be worth it if he achieved his goals as a result.

One week later, Ethan was in Thailand, and standing in a dingy, dark alley with curious eyes peering out at him from dilapidated homes and making him feel awkward.

<u>They sense I'm up to no good. What if they tell the cops on me?</u>

His concerns didn't matter because he was drawn to achieving his heart's desire at that moment. He reached his hand in his pocket and felt the red matte lighter and then reached his other hand into his other pocket and pulled out a wad of crisp $100 bills.

He handed them over to the man who was standing there and he glanced down at them with mild curiosity.

"It's all there," Ethan said.

The man sneered but didn't say a word. Then he snapped his fingers.

From the shadows, a small boy, about five or six, came out and stared at Ethan with wide, frightened eyes. They were as dark as his dirty skin and hair. The mask of dirt couldn't hide the boy's fear, though.

"You ready to go?" Ethan asked. His voice sounded so strange to him, almost paternal or like he was a big brother. That was the plan, though. This was his younger brother. It didn't matter that they looked nothing alike.

The boy nodded.

The two took off walking and Ethan took him back to his hotel room with him. They went into the room and he tossed him some food that was on the dresser. "Be quiet while I make this call, okay?"

The boy didn't talk. He hadn't said a word at all.

"Yeah, Rodrigo, I got what I need. What next?"

* * *

The next stop for Ethan was Paris and he was so edgy, feeling comfortable with taking care of a small boy on the journey. It wasn't just because he'd bought him, either. People looked at him oddly and he felt paranoid.

Just remember, this is all worth it. Look how it's worked for Rodrigo.

Every time Ethan looked at the boy he stared back with his big, brown eyes and he seemed to understand what was happening better than Ethan did. He decided it was best to talk to him as little as possible; the less like a person the boy seemed, the less guilty he felt.

Ethan looked down at the piece of paper in his hand. The address read *1 Avenue du Colonel Henri Rol-Tanguy*. He was supposed to walk up to the front to pay admission and state that he needed two tickets to the *neuvième niveau*—ninth level.

Breathing in and gaining some courage, Ethan stood in line with the boy, having to wait over a half hour just to get the tickets to go stand in another line.

"Two tickets for *neuvième niveau*, please."

The young woman selling tickets looked up and appeared to be startled by what he'd asked.

Oh, shit, Ethan thought.

99

"That tour is starting immediately. The cost is 80€ each."

Ethan had never been to France before but he knew that was a lot of money. He slid it over to the woman and she took it, giving him two tickets and smiling. Then she turned her head and nodded to a young man who was standing behind her and told Ethan to follow him.

As Ethan and the boy followed the guy down the 130 steps that led into the catacombs there was no conversation. Distant tours could be heard and the sound of footsteps was all that Ethan could focus on. Three distinct sounds of footsteps. His palms were sweaty and despite the chilly air from going down into the ground, he felt so warm that he thought he might have a fever.

The guy who'd guided them down the stairs looked around and then he went to the side and unlocked a wooden door that blocked a vessel of the catacombs and motioned for Ethan and the boy to hurry in.

For the first time, the boy seemed resistant and Ethan had no choice but to grab his arm forcefully and shove him through the door. He was too young and frail to resist his brute effort.

The guy looked at Ethan and spoke for the first time. Thankfully it was in English. "Keep following this tunnel and you'll find that you will descend down to the ninth level."

Then he slammed the wooden door and locked it. He was on the other side of it and Ethan and the boy had only one direction to go—downward.

It was challenging to adjust his eyes to the light but Ethan finally did and instantly felt creeped out by the skeletons and bones that lined the walls of the catacombs. Over six million Parisians were buried in the catacombs, according to general information, but it was so creepy to be walking through the giant, underground graveyard. It was not something that Ethan cared for at all. He wasn't a cataphile like so many that snuck into the closed, secret vessels of the catacombs and meandered about.

This is all worth it. Don't forget. I have to become more famous than Carlisle and show him. In your dreams lies your destiny. Carlisle dreamed big and it worked. It can work for me, too.

A different sort of light was glowing ahead of Ethan and he found himself walking faster, eager to reach other humans aside from the small boy he was so fearful to talk to. Guilty, actually he was guilty because he knew that nothing good was going to happen to the young boy and he'd done nothing wrong. He was the victim of a family that sold him because they couldn't afford to feed him and a guy who would stop at nothing to reach success.

That's when a fraction of doubt entered Ethan's mind that he couldn't avoid or shove aside.

As Ethan stepped into the rounded area of the room where the light was coming from he saw a center sculpture of skulls that went from the floor to the ceiling and noticed that the entire floor was made up of femurs. It was an ideal setting for a horror movie but he was in a very real situation. The light was many neon lanterns. He wasn't sure why, but Ethan had assumed they'd be torches. Then he remembered something he'd learned in biology—there were probably gasses underground that made it impossible to light torches because the place would explode. In that case, it would make Ethan another deceased individual whose final resting place was the catacombs.

Rodrigo walked up and had a casual smile on his face but something in his eyes was very intense.

"Everything go okay?"

"I believe so," Ethan said.

The boy was behind Ethan and Rodrigo leaned his head around to get a look at him. Then he turned back to Ethan.

"Are you ready to let your dreams ignite your destiny?" Rodrigo asked.

His sentence was haunting to Ethan, who'd just been thinking similar words to those about Carlisle when he was making his way through the vessel of the catacomb to that room.

When he didn't answer, Rodrigo asked, "You okay?"

"Yeah…maybe, I think so," Ethan said in a jumbled reply.

"Are you sure you want to do this? There's no going back after you start."

"I don't know. It all seems a bit too cryptic," Ethan began. "What would happen to the boy if I decided not to?"

101

"Well, we can't have people knowing where and how to find this place. He knows a lot." Rodrigo said no more after that and Ethan was able to read between the lines: he'd have to die.

If the boy was going to die either way, Ethan might as well get what he truly wanted. It would be a waste of a life otherwise, right?

"I am ready to go. Tell me what to do."

Just then, Ethan heard a loud, piercing scream in the tunnel. It was a sound of absolute fear and he'd never heard anything like it before. It reminded him of a scene out of one of the Twilight movies that he'd seen, although he couldn't remember which one at that moment. His heart was pounding and racing so fast that it was muddling his thinking.

Not sure what to do, Ethan turned around and bolted toward the vessel which he'd entered through. A huge guy was there, stopping him, and in that instant, someone also grabbed the young boy.

"It's too late," the guy said. They were simple words and there was no discussion that was going to be had.

Rodrigo walked up to Ethan and talked quietly. "Knock it off, man. I've shared something substantial with you and if you keep acting out they're going to kill you. Is that what you want?"

"No," Ethan said.

He looked over and saw them taking the boy and they tied him down on the floor. There were four metal loops and ropes were strewn through them. It wasn't hard to tie down his wrists and his legs. Now the boy had tears streaming down his face and he kept saying, "Chhiá—no, Chhiá—no" repeatedly. He was begging for his life and he had good reason. A trickle of urine came out from underneath him and the top of his jeans showed that he'd peed his pants from the terror.

A group of six or seven people gathered around in a circle surrounding the boy and Rodrigo walked over, carrying a leather bound book in his hands. It wasn't a large book and the cover was flimsy, not solid like most leather bound books you'd find in a library. It was more like a journal.

"You shall read from this," Rodrigo said, flipping the book open to one particular page.

Looking down at the page, Ethan almost vomited. There were specks and smudges of blood on it. The words were foreign looking.

"I can't read this language," Ethan said. He knew it was a lame attempt to change the situation but he had to try.

"They are phonetically sounded out from the Serpent of Knowledge book of the Illuminati. Read them aloud and it will all begin."

"What will happen when I do?"

"You will be making a covenant with the master's of the Abyss. You'll be granted your wish and commit to the eternal source."

Ethan was amazed with how simple Rodrigo made it sound; like he was taking out a loan or something like that.

"Start reading," Rodrigo commanded.

Ethan looked at the words of the book and began reading them. They had a cadence and rhythm that wasn't unlike one of his rap songs but the message was darker, more urgent and mysterious. He felt as if he was summoning up demons from the bellows of the earth, that the entire ground may split open and unleash the fires of hell.

His voice was quiet, not liking the way it echoed against the walls in the silence of the catacombs.

"Louder!" Rodrigo commanded.

Ethan started to call out louder and his voice became clearer and more determined the longer he went. He felt empowered and he felt invincible. Each word gave him the courage and conviction that he would be the greatest and that Carlisle would be the one wallowing in his wastes, wishing he'd stuck with Ethan and not turned his back on their friendship. The anger and rage that were pent up within him began to unleash, making him clench the leather book tighter and say each word more forcefully. Although he couldn't read the language of the chant, something inside his mind told him what the words were in English. He knew what he was saying and he believed every word of it.

I surrender to the Abyss.
My covenant with the Abyss will guide me through.
I am loyal.
I shall use my gift from the darkness to help bring others to its light.
I am your servant and you are my master.
We are one.
My loyalty is absolute.
I am filled with your light and a student to you for life.
Plant me with the seeds of knowledge so I may reap the rewards of your protection.
Damn my enemies and those who think they are better than me.
Let me show them what true greatness is.

His body was shaking and he felt something surging through him that he couldn't quite explain. It was like adrenaline and he opened his eyes, trying to look around and everything was blurred. He squeezed his eyes shut and tried to open them again but when he did all he saw was darkness. There was no light on in that small chamber in the ninth level of the catacombs.

Ethan's legs went numb and he collapsed to the ground, feeling the coldness of the femurs on the floor press against his cheek. Loud screeches in the darkness became quieter until he heard nothing else.

12

"I've given it all I've got."

A gentle, salty breeze and bright light were what Ethan awoke to. He blinked his eyes a few times and rubbed his hands on his head. He felt like he was waking up with a wicked hangover.

<u>What the hell happened?</u>

The last thing Ethan remembered was going down into the catacombs with the boy. He froze and looked around.

"Where am I?" he mumbled. His mouth felt dry and his lips felt as if they were parchment.

"You're at one of my friend's beach houses in Dinard," Rodrigo said, walking over to Ethan.

Ethan tried to sit up but he felt too weak. "How did I get here? What happened last night?"

"You slept last night. You've been out for about a week," Rodrigo said.

Ethan bolted up. He didn't understand how that was possible. Then he froze, feeling something crawling around his stomach.

"What the hell did you do to me?" he asked in a panicked voice. "Why does my stomach hurt?"

"You'll be fine. It takes a bit to get used to but the worst of it is almost over."

"The worst of it?" Ethan mimicked.

A sudden burst of energy surged through him and Ethan lunged forward and tackled a caught off guard Rodrigo down.

"You son of a bitch. What did you do to me?" Ethan shouted and he smacked him with all the force he could across the jaw.

Rodrigo retaliated and wrapped his leg around Ethan's, putting it in a scissor kick and immediately gaining the upper hand by reversing the situation.

Ethan stared at him with wild eyes, flailing his arms, and unleashing all his anger—his fear—on Rodrigo.

He only stopped when he noticed that the cut he'd given Rodrigo's lip from when he punched him across the jaw had started to heal right there on the spot. Then there was a spark in his eye, it went very bright, then amber, and then it was gone.

"Calm down," Rodrigo said.

The second Rodrigo got up and started walking out of the room that Ethan was in he ran to the door and bolted it shut. Then he charged toward the bedroom window and opened it up, seeing the beautiful blue sea—the Dinard Sea.

It may have been breathtaking but Ethan was freaked out of his mind. He opened the window and climbed out, falling down about eight feet to the sandy ground below him. He landed with a thud and although he'd lost his wind, he got up and began to run and tried to breathe in so he could call for help.

There were people on the beach about a hundred yards up.

"Help! Please, I need help!" Ethan shouted into the wind and it carried his voice the other way. It was like the elements didn't want his voice to be heard.

He shouted louder, trying to run faster but he was awkward and immobile, tripping over his own feet.

"HELP!" He was now waving his arms in the air frantically but he couldn't get the attention of the people on the beach.

Ethan turned around to see if he was being followed and Rodrigo, along with two other guys were standing right there. The two guys grabbed him and locked his arms behind him, making it so he couldn't move at all. His fear had him feeling strong but he was no match for the two guys.

Rodrigo began laughing. "You're acting like a fool, man. I don't know what you think you're doing but it's going to stop—now."

Ethan spat out, hitting Rodrigo in the face and his laughter turned to an intense gaze. He slowly lifted up his hand and wiped the spit from his face and then reached it out and squeezed it around Ethan's throat.

"Don't ever do that again." His eyes gave that odd spark Ethan had seen in the bedroom and then returned to normal again.

"I didn't ask for any of this. What is this crazy shit you've done to me?" Ethan spat.

"Actually, you did ask for it and now you're on your way to getting exactly what you wanted. You didn't care about the price to others so why worry about your personal price? It's secondary to the amazing things that are going to exist for you now."

The two guys drug Ethan back into the beach house and into the living room.

Ethan watched Rodrigo's expressions as he calmly talked to him.

Rodrigo gave him a moment to soak everything in. "Are you ready to calm down? If you do, you'll be able to find the answers you seek a lot quicker."

Ethan nodded.

"Good. Now, why don't you come get something to eat and then we'll help you tap into what happened so you can remember every little detail."

Ethan saw the look on Rodrigo's face. He looked pleased in a twisted kind of way.

What am I going to remember?

Not able to avoid the feeling in his stomach, Ethan asked again. "Why do I feel like a worm is moving in my stomach?"

"You'll find out soon enough," Rodrigo said, laughing light heartedly at it.

It's not fucking funny, man, Ethan thought.

"Who are those guys?" Ethan asked, referring to the two guys that had dragged him back into the house and a group that was playing video games in the corner.

"Friends, members of the Illuminati."

"Illuminati?" Ethan scratched his head, trying to recall.

"That's what you are a part of now," Rodrigo said. "Look, I can see your edgy but it'll all come together soon. Then you'll deal with what you know and move on."

"What does that mean?" Ethan asked.

No one answered his question.

After a croissant sandwich and a cup of coffee, Ethan watched Rodrigo walk over to a chest of drawers and pull something out.

He came back and handed it over. It was a pipe.

"Ethan, this will help you remember everything," Rodrigo said.

"Is that weed or what?"

"Something a bit more powerful than that. It'll help you tap into your memories an extract them in vivid detail."

"What if I don't want to?"

"You'll want to. Everyone does. It's better to get it over with and know rather than have it eat at you and bug you. It'll interfere with your success if you do that. Aren't you ready to surpass Carlisle?"

Ethan nodded. He was ready for that and once again he found himself justifying what he'd done and finding a way to believe that it was for his greater good—therefore everyone's.

Not that young boy.

Ethan went for the red matte lighter in his pocket, as he'd always done, but stopped short of grabbing it to light the pipe. He didn't feel right using Momma's lighter to find out about this. Instead, he grabbed the lighter that Rodrigo had offered him.

He lit the pipe and inhaled deeply. Smoke filled his lungs and it tasted really smooth, almost like it had a touch of eucalyptus to it, and he held it in.

"Count backwards from twenty and you should be good," Rodrigo said.

Again, Ethan had no idea what he was talking about. He felt like everything being said was double talk.

20,19,18…..9,8……3,2……

Ethan was transported back to the night in the catacombs and was watching the scene unfold as if he was an observer in his own life.

I am reading the words on the pages, chanting the foreign language, yet I don't know what it means and I can feel my heart pounding faster with each word. I'm more empowered and I'm summoning something that seems so dark but I know it is going to deliver me what I desire most.

A slithering noise distracted me and I lost focus on the page and glanced over at the wall of the catacomb. Something was on there, sliding down and looking to have come out of the earth itself. What is it?

"Louder!" Rodrigo shouts.

I began to chant louder, more forcefully, stating what I want and saying the words which have great meaning to someone—or some thing—but mean nothing to me aside from the promise of surpassing Carlisle and extracting my revenge through success.

Again, I'm distracted by a slithering noise and I look up, seeing it just above my head. It looks like an octopus, about the size of a basketball. It's descending above me, almost like a spider on a strand of string from its web. It's body is black and there are white dots all over it. I see two heads. I don't understand.

"Keep reading," Rodrigo demands.

I obey, not knowing what else to do. My feelings are so jumbled and confusing.

I keep reading and now I feel the creature on my head. I don't stop, though. I can't. Something is compelling me to keep reading.

The tentacles slither into my mouth and I can't read any more. They are moving around and I feel vile rising in my throat. My lip begins to sting and my mouth goes numb and my eyes get blurry.

Then, as quickly as it came, the creature leaves, going back into the bones of the ceiling above me, back to its home.

I can hear Rodrigo saying, "Welcome to the Illuminati."

I stare at the boy and I begin to drool. I look at his eyes and they look so appealing to me. I breathe in and can almost smell his blood.

He's only two steps away from me at the most but I make it to him in a single step, almost like I floated over to him and my feet didn't even touch the ground.

I rip into the boy with my fingers, gouging his eyes out and eating them down. The taste, the texture, it's disgusting but I am drawn to it. Then, I take my pinkie finger, which has a long nail upon it and puncture his neck, leaning down and drinking the blood from it. His body is flailing but not for long.

The shock that I'm not satisfied is revealed.

I look around and know that I am not interested in anyone that is around me; they are linked to me and a part of me now.

Without saying a word, I sneak off, able to blend in with the walls of the catacombs and I go to its darkest vessels, waiting for the cataphiles that will sneak in there at night. When they come, I'll be waiting.

It doesn't take long and I find myself feasting for five days and nights on the eyes and blood of unsuspecting humans, feeling more alive than I ever have before. I am empowered and a grateful servant to the Serpent of Knowledge. This is my existence.

Every scream of terror in the darkness makes me feel so good. I briefly realize that it's the same sounds I heard when I was going into the ninth level of the catacombs. Now I know...now I know.

Ethan jumped up, his eyes wide and his hands squeezed so tightly that his knuckles were white. Rodrigo was staring at him, wearing that same smile that he'd seen a few times that day.

"What the hell happened? How could you let me do that to people?"

Rodrigo replied as if he was conducting a business meeting, focused on facts only. "I did nothing to you that you didn't seek out and ask for. Everything has a price and I know you know that."

"That octopus thing that went into my mouth? It bit me...or something. What did it do?"

"Octopuses don't have two heads, Ethan. That was a amphisbaena; two heads and it planted a very specific seed into you."

"A seed?"

"It's actually larva and its part of who you are now. Don't worry, though. You'll learn how to control it."

"What do you do to control it?" Ethan asked.

"Feed it, combined with learning how to control it."

Ethan shrugged his shoulders, wishing he could release some of the tension in there. "I am almost afraid to ask but how do you feed it?"

"The exact way you did the previous five days."

"What? How do you manage that without getting arrested for murder or anything like that?"

"Carefully but you'll find that it's most enjoyable to feed the larva living inside of you on bad people with bad intentions or those drawn to what we are. It may surprise you to realize that many people find it an honor and most are not given the opportunity to be anything more than a meal. You are in a position that is admired by many people that long for more power in their lives."

"And I'll never be able to get out?"

"Not alive."

Ethan sighed. He wasn't sure what was going on but he tried to focus on the odd feeling in his stomach and think about how he could control it and what he could do. He didn't want to be a killer.

Think, think, think.

He grabbed the lighter out of his pocket and flicked the flint wheel. Nothing ignited. He shook it and felt fluid in there and saw that the wick hadn't run out. Ethan shook it and tried again. Still nothing.

Ethan looked up and said, "Momma, I'm sorry but I can't turn back now."

Then he looked back down at the red matte lighter, his most cherished possession, and was going to try flicking the wheel again. Something stopped him. He didn't have the courage at that moment to think that his mother may have abandoned him for what he'd done. It would be too much—an unintended consequence he never would have thought of.

13

"You're only as good as the company you keep."

Carlisle wasn't doing well and although the High Royals had said it couldn't be done, he was trying to live his life anonymously and without any interaction with them. In his mind, these people were monsters that weren't from Earth, but according to Aerial they were so much more. He couldn't grasp it and honestly, he didn't want to.

Under a fake name, Carlisle had purchased a home in Charleston Park, Florida. It was as obscure and small of a town as you could imagine. Only there did he truly feel like he could get away and he'd created a disguise of a baseball hat, a Florida Gators shirt, large shades, and regular jeans—nothing extraordinary for the town that didn't have a very high average income. His only hope was that when he was there he didn't exist. So far, he'd been able to go for two months remaining under the radar and it felt like a miracle of sorts. Unfortunately, he had to go to Miami for business the next day and his obscure comfort would soon be replaced.

Flicking through the cable channels, Carlisle stumbled across an entertainment show that had his picture up front. He despised those types of shows but they did offer him a good indicator of what the pulse was about him in the world and that helped him plan his moves. Basically, he used the news like that to stay a step ahead of the game.

"Carlisle Lewis, was the pressure too much," the commentator said. "Sources say that he's trying to be off the radar. 'Bill, do you think that becoming a billionaire at such a young age was just too much for him?'"

"Are you kidding me? No," the man named Bill replied. "Rumor has it he's dating a few celebrities, models and actresses. Life has never been better. My sources tell me that he has a secret little love nest somewhere outside of Miami where he goes for some alone time with someone he may be getting serious with."

"Who?" the woman asked.

"That's the mystery. There are so many women around him all the time that it's hard to track down."

"Well," the woman said with a forced chuckle, "whoever she is, she's considered lucky by a lot of the female population in this world."

Then the camera flashed away and Carlisle flicked off the television set. He'd heard enough.

Carlisle got up and went over to his cupboard to get the bottle of scotch. He kept it hidden, less anyone come by because the bottle cost nearly half the price of the entire damn house he hid in trying to fake being normal. It was a sweet addiction but not so sweet that it could block out the eyes and mannerisms of all the High Royals and monsters that inhabited the Earth. Carlisle could point them out in an instant now although they were sly and subtle. A slight nod of the head, a touch of the ring, or a quick spark in their eyes that disappeared as quickly as it came. That was how you could tell who they were.

He gulped down the amber liquid. <u>Some honor to be a part of that.</u>

After a few more glasses, he began to pack and get everything coordinated for his trip to Miami. It would satisfy two purposes: business and letting him be seen to quiet the ridiculous rumors. Sometimes they were beneficial but not always.

Carlisle drove the newest Audi—one fully loaded with every option imaginable—to his garage in Fort Meyers airport, where he hopped on the private jet that was waiting for him to fly him to Miami.

The flight was smooth and while on the short jaunt, Carlisle transformed into the Carlisle the businessman that most people knew. A pressed shirt, business casual pants, and polished shoes. He looked hip, trendy, and relevant. Did he feel that way? Not really.

Once in Miami, his car service took him to the Mandarin Oriental, where he was going to be staying until his meeting the next day. He checked into his room, went up and unpacked, and then made his way down to the bar to have a drink.

No sooner did he sit down at the edge of the bar, hoping to be able to relax in the shadows and observe others, not be observed. Aerial walked in and walked right over to him.

"Hello, my friend, how are you fairing?"

Carlisle looked at Aerial, still not sure if he should consider him a friend. The man seemed quite happy with his billing with the High Royals. Why?

Aerial sat down, not waiting to be invited.

114

"I see them everywhere," Carlisle commented.

"Because they are everywhere."

"It bothers me that I never noticed before. I'm observant."

"They show themselves differently to those in the fellowship than they do to your average person."

"You say average like it's a dirty word."

"It kind of is, isn't it?" Aerial asked. "You've certainly aspired for more than average in your life. It wasn't because you were content."

"True."

The man calls it like it is.

"It does get better and easier. You'll discover the benefits when you stop thinking you can outrun or outsmart the High Royals. It has never happened and never will."

"No one ever has."

"No." Aerial's answer was definitive in nature.

"Tell me all about it. I want to know what's going on and understand. Don't hold anything back, either," Carlisle said, pounding his drink back. "I'm sick of trying to fill in the blanks for something that makes no fucking sense—defies reasoning."

"Fair enough," Aerial said. "Some time back, over a thousand years ago, there was a universal accord made that was designed to ensure that there were certain allies and friendly forces on every inhabited planet that was known. The one's who oversaw this named themselves the High Royals."

"Are any from Earth?"

"No but they are capable of being whomever they need to be in a given moment."

"So, they recruit people to serve their cause?"

"Yes, these can be humans, like us, or life forms from other planets."

"How do they get by under the radar?"

"Skills and abilities. Not all creatures adapt as poorly as humans. Some have other gifts, too. You've probably had sex with one and didn't even realize it."

Aerial laughed at his quip but Carlisle shook his head, feeling nauseated by the thought. He slammed down the drink that the bartender had brought over to him, realizing who he was by that time.

"Too much of that isn't going to be good for you," Aerial said. "Adapting will give you comfort more than a bottle ever will."

"Well, until that happens, I say 'cheers,'" Carlisle replied blandly.

"Why don't you come back to London with me and come to a party," Aerial said.

"What kind of party?"

"One where you can meet everyone and see it's not really as awkward or bizarre as you've allowed yourself to imagine it is. As the founder of One Religion Book , these beings wish to meet you, too."

"Beings…as in non-human."

"Beings encompasses everything that's alive for my purposes and for your purposes it should, too."

Carlisle thought about it and knew that the old saying was true: if you can't beat 'em, join 'em. Well, he'd technically joined them already and from what Aerial, a pretty smart man, said, you can't beat them.

"Sure, what the hell. I have business tomorrow and then I can get ready and go."

"I'll stick around in Miami until you're done and fly you to London on my private jet."

"I don't need a babysitter," Carlisle snapped.

"No, but you need someone to help you get through the rough period you're having."

"Did you have a rough period like this, Aerial?"

"No, I didn't. However, I was considerably older than you."

"With age comes wisdom, huh?"

"Indeed and compared to our new friends in the fellowship, I am but a child."

"That means I'm not even born yet," Carlisle said.

The irony of that thought struck him funny and he began to laugh. It grew louder and louder, causing heads to turn. More than anything, the laugh made him feel better—like he could breathe again.

* * *

Once Carlisle got into Aerial's private jet with him, he felt as if he was being liberated and began to feel a bit of excitement about what was happening. At minimal, he was thinking more clearly and realized that he couldn't just mope around and waste his life away because he'd thrown himself into a situation in which he wasn't informed enough. Aerial was insightful and he was bold—a revolutionary according to Forbes—so he had his act together. If it involved High Royals and beings from other planets and worlds, so be it.

"I have you set up to stay at Luton Hoo Hotel, where the party will be held. I think you'll find it to be an exquisite place."

"Not the same place where my introduction was held," Carlisle commented with curiosity.

"No, different. We utilize many places for different events within the fellowship. You'll learn them all over time and actually, believe it or not, look forward to attending them."

"That is hard to believe. Why would I look forward to it?"

"Because you're a problem solver and that's what we all do, solve problems and brainstorm ideas and solutions for a better universe."

"A galactic think tank."

Aerial laughed. "Exactly—a most fitting description."

"How can all this be kept secret at a hotel?"

"A member owns the Luton Hoo and all the rooms are reserved for guests of the party. It's rather simple."

Carlisle had to hand it to the High Royals for knowing how to get what they wanted and needed. That was a lot of money but he knew it was a mere pittance to the people he was about to meet.

The jet landed and a limousine was waiting to take both Carlisle and Aerial to the hotel that looked like a secluded mansion. When Carlisle walked in he was surprised to be greeted by someone who said, "Hello, Mr. Lewis. We are looking forward to you staying with us."

Carlisle smiled and looked at the person, sensing they were not any ordinary staff person of a hotel. They were part of the circle, serving in some beneficial capacity.

"Thank you. I'm looking forward to it, as well," Carlisle said.

Carlisle turned to Aerial. "Are you staying here?"

"Yes, I have a suite here that I actually own. You'll find a suit for tonight—as it's black tie—in your room. At 8 p.m. make your way toward the reception, which is in the Warren Weir area."

"See you then," Carlisle said.

He turned around and a gentleman was waiting with all his luggage, ready to take him to his room.

The rooms were amazing, old world charm with state of the art amenities. Truly incredible and for a brief moment, Carlisle thought that he could actually adapt to that style as opposed to the contemporary one he was naturally drawn to. Then he laughed and thought, *who are you kidding? They can change a whole lot but they can't change that.*

Warren Weir was inside the mansion and it was very eloquent and refined, plus very secure. After Carlisle handed a black, embossed card that Aerial had given him earlier and showed his ring, he walked into the venue and felt like he was walking in on a masquerade ball.

Everyone was in formal attire and beautiful women, as well as women who were likely beautiful in wherever they were from, were walking around, laughing and in pleasant conversations.

All the wait staff were woman, as you could tell from their perfect bodies that were definitely implant free, and they wore black sparkling g-strings that matched the black masks they wore over their eyes, revealing only their color. They were moving around gracefully and orderly, offering expensive cigars and perfectly shaped fruits such as apples, peaches, and grapes, plus beluga caviar and wines that accompanied its unique taste perfectly. And oddly enough—there was a woman walking around with a tray of short blunts to offer the guests.

Carlisle breathed in and was shocked to smell marijuana in the air. It was mixed with other scents, however, showing that it was hybrid marijuana. When he'd been in Hawaii many months back he'd had some mango marijuana and it really had smelled just like he was sniffing a mango candle. Amazing—and that was nothing compared to the amazing group of individuals that were before him.

It was easy to recognize a great many people and some of them shocked Carlisle. Aerial hadn't told him any names in specific, commenting that he'd be more amused to find out for himself. There were politicians, three leaders of countries, programmers, artists, many actors and actresses, plus a few business people that were considered the best of the best in the entire world—one's whose companies had introduced products to the market that changed the way people thought, acted, and what they expected to have in their lives each and every day as a result. To say they were 'trend setters' would be a severe understatement.

Carlisle took a glass of wine that was offered to him and was getting ready to say that he'd like a blunt when one was offered to him by someone else. It really did seem like people were reading his mind. It was just unsettling but he didn't care. A little smoke would be just the thing to take the edge off and allow him to get into the spirit of mingling with these people.

He lit up and enjoyed the smooth, mellow scent, which seemed to have a hint of cherry in it—like an old man's pipe might. Aerial was across the room and he was going to make his way over there. The two caught eye contact and Aerial nodded.

Carlisle started to make his way over there but he quickly got interrupted by people and beings introducing themselves, asking a question here and there, and wanting to learn more about their newest member—a man that had rushed onto the 'most notable' scene rather quickly.

Everyone was pleasant and nice—superficial in a way. Carlisle wasn't dumb enough to think that the niceties would fade away in a second if anything went askew. They knew how to network and schmooze but didn't take any shit from anyone he suspected.

Aerial had disappeared and Carlisle was growing impatient. He decided to explore the fascinating and beautiful mansion a bit further and see what he could find. His suspicions told him that the beings in front of him weren't the only interesting and unusual things around him.

There were many smaller, more intimate conversations taking place in the long corridors with marble flooring. Some would glance up and smile at Carlisle and he'd say, "Hi," and continue on, not wanting to interrupt the conversation.

He heard some animated noise coming from a room off to the right.

"Double or nothing," he heard a high, merry voice say.

"You're on," a gruff, deep voice responded.

Carlisle walked into the room and found that it was a gambling room. There was roulette, poker, and baccarat. He was immediately interested because he liked to gamble and thought it was a rather lively and fun way to relieve stress, meet some people, and explore how you could get the odds to work in your favor.

Two martini's later and another blunt down, Carlisle was laughing and talking with everyone, telling stories to them like he'd been their lifelong friends. He'd grown less reserved with his fame but he still kept relatively distant on his private thoughts until he knew people better.

A Canadian cabinet member from a distant planet said, "So, you're not in some small town near Miami having a romantic tryst with some unknown female?"

"You listen to that nonsense?" Carlisle asked.

"I listen to my wife, who happens to love that nonsense," he said.

Everyone busted out into laughter.

"That's probably why I don't have a wife," Carlisle said.

"Why bother when you can bed a dame a night," the man said.

Carlisle realized that it was his wife who was next to him and she said, "As if having me has ever stopped you from bedding someone if you desired them."

The two started laughing again and kissed.

Maybe that's some sort of bizarre foreplay, Carlisle thought.

Then everyone would get back to their card game—Pai Gow Poker at that time—and play another round and trash talk in between.

Perhaps it was beginner's luck but Carlisle was delighted that he was kicking ass and winning at everything he played. The minimum buy-ins for each round was $500 so he was cleaning up nicely, finding himself with a nice $50,000 profit at one point.

Carlisle had decided that he was getting a bit tired and it was time to move on. He was buzzed big time—from pot and proceeds.

"Why, hello there, old sport. You're really making a name for yourself," someone said.

Carlisle turned around and said, "You're damn right, I am. Who the fuck are you?"

The stranger laughed and nodded his head. "Excuse me, my friend."

He couldn't explain why but something about the exchange made Carlisle want to challenge this person. It made no sense and he knew he was impaired but there was no stopping him.

"I said, 'who the fuck are you?'"

There was no answer.

Carlisle called out. "Some actor or scientist; a he or a she. It's all good. I got love for ya."

"Well, well ... whatever, old sport, we'll meet again."

The stranger nodded his head and walked away, still smiling but he was a bit less amused looking that time.

Afterwards, Carlisle thought, *I hope I didn't offend him. I got a bit carried away.*

Then a swarm of women and female beings from other places swarmed him, each wanting to get a bit closer. He had no idea why but he loved it and was absorbing the attention from every type of female he could. It had been a long time since he'd gotten laid and maybe it would be the night to break that streak. His period of isolation had run its course.

<u>None of these women are the one for me.</u>

"I should find Aerial," he said out loud.

"I'm sorry, sir, I don't know where Mr. Kennedy is," a waitress said.

Carlisle hadn't realized he was talking out loud but when he looked at the curvaceous, highly sexual and arousing body on the waitress, he half wanted to take her up to his room. What would it be like to get it on with a woman wearing a mask? One whose face he'd never know but whose body he'd be unlikely to forget.

<u>I don't think I've ever been with a mystery woman in a mask.</u>

Then Carlisle wondered if it was okay to proposition the staff. He'd better ask Aerial.

"I'll find him, thanks," Carlisle said.

She turned and walked away and he admired her heart shaped ass, thinking she'd look great in some Apple Bottom Jeans.

Carlisle turned around and was greeted with a new surprise. A beautiful woman was standing all alone, looking at a portrait on the wall, and holding a champagne bottle in one hand and a flute in the other.

122

<u>She is incredible.</u>

Feeling lucky and no longer having problems with getting the women he wanted, Carlisle walked up to her. He soaked in her beautiful curly hair and light brown eyes.

"Hi, I'm Carlisle Lewis," he said, leaning in so his arm brushed against hers ever so slightly.

She turned around and gave him a once over. "You might think you're special but I think you're a prick."

<u>Whoa! Slow your row.</u>

"Excuse me. What?"

"I think you heard me," she challenged.

"I don't know who you think that I might be but I'm not a prick."

"You know what? You're right. You're not a prick. You're a douche bag that doesn't know shit about life so walk on and get away from me."

"Well, it was nice to meet you, uppity bitch," he said with slurred words. Then he grabbed his crotch and shot her the bird and walked away.

Something went whizzing by his head and Carlisle saw the champagne bottle through his peripheral.

"You're crazy!" he shouted, looking at her as if she was a psychotic lunatic, not a beautiful woman.

She laughed at his words but he turned to keep walking away. He walked a lot more quickly, though, and decided that he really needed to focus on one thing—finding Aerial.

Taking a peak into each room he went by, even when the door was closed, Carlisle found a great many things. Business leaders were making agreements; some people were resting or passed out from too much fun; some were doing cocaine; and there were lots of other things.

123

He walked into one room and stopped with the door open, very surprised at what he'd found. There was a room where a giant universal orgy of sorts was going on.

"Holy fuck ..." Carlisle couldn't even think of what else to say besides that.

He looked over and saw a white tuft of hair. It was Aerial. He was getting a hummer from some woman with a rather large mouth and three breasts.

I didn't know that Total Recall was based on a real movie. Carlisle couldn't help but remember the three breasted woman in the one district in that movie.

Aerial looked up and pointed his finger, indicating he needed a minute.

Carlisle didn't want to look like a pervert so he turned around and left the room, deciding to wait in the hallway. His mind was pretty damn curious about how aliens and humans got it on, though. Were the parts the same or did you like put it into some alien chicks ear or something? His mind was active with all sorts of crazy ideas.

Aerial walked out just about two minutes later.

"This place is incredible," Carlisle said.

There was no response.

"Is stuff like that," Carlisle said, pointing to the sex room, "common?"

"It's a complicated story; not one I'm willing to invest the time in sharing right now so if you don't mind, I think I'll get back to my fun."

Aerial winked and walked back into the room.

Suddenly a bell rung in the mansion and Aerial stopped.

"What's that for?" Carlisle asked.

"Follow me."

The two walked back into the main hall where the party had started and they turned their attention to the raised floor area in the front of the room.

124

"Can I have your attention, please," someone said from the front.

Then, much to Carlisle's shock, the man from the gambling room—the one he'd been kind of a dick to despite just kidding around—was standing up there.

"Welcome old and new guests. It's wonderful to see everyone. What a great evening it is, celebrating the uniting of our species and yours. May unity last forever and cheers to the evolution."

He raised his glass and the crowd called out, "Cheers," while raising their glasses, too. Then, just outside the open French doors to the veranda in back, fireworks started going off and everyone flooded that direction to get a better look.

Carlisle was dumbfounded. "Who is that?" he asked Aerial.

Aerial looked at him like, 'you've got to be kidding.' "That is Aiden Easton," he said, "the founder of MySpacious. I presume you've heard of him?"

"You're kidding! That's him."

He was floored by who he was and it suddenly made sense. Aiden was the first in the line of Internet people to bring people together and while there had been others, Carlisle was the second to be impactful.

"I was kind of a dick to him earlier, just kidding around, though."

"I somehow doubt he'll mind. He used to be an arrogant little prick, too."

"You're the second person to call me a prick tonight," Carlisle said.

"I doubt I'll be the last one in your lifetime, though," Aerial said.

The two men laughed and then Carlisle excused himself, wanting to go meet Aiden.

"Well, I was very surprised to find out who you were," Carlisle said. "I fear you caught me in a bit too much of a festive mood."

"No concerns here, Carlisle," Aiden said well heartedly. "This place is about the party; the connection and diversity—something I'm sure you appreciate."

"It's been a bit surreal but I'm getting into the swing of things."

"I knew you would."

"You did?" Carlisle asked. How would he know.

"We all know who to look for in this world, Carlisle. Don't look so surprised. Surely you have come to terms with what you've created by now."

"I have but what a long, strange trip it's been."

"And it keeps getting stranger, I'd imagine," Aiden added.

You've got that right.

Before Carlisle knew it, several hours had passed and he'd met someone whom he considered not only a mentor or someone he'd aspired to be like in the past but also someone who had the possibility to be a true friend. He needed a true, genuine friend and felt he was long overdue. Aerial was fantastic but with Aiden it was easy to see how much they both loved everything related to technology and the Internet and how it could bring people together.

It was finally time to call it an evening. The party was winding down and the first signs of dawn were appearing on the horizon.

"Do you golf?"

"No, never started and don't have the time to be very good."

"Well, we should give it a try. I suck but I find it to be a good challenge—me against the ball and the only thing standing in my way is my brain."

"Sounds good, Aiden."

Aiden handed Carlisle his card and said, "Call my secretary and let's coordinate a lunch. It would be great to brainstorm ideas we can do with our own money, not relying on investors."

"That would be fantastic," Carlisle said. It was an opportunity he'd tried to get many times when he was starting O.R.B. but had no success.

Then he walked away and while Carlisle hadn't noticed the woman sitting in the corner. He couldn't see her face but he did see a bit of a red dress. *Man, I hope it's not that woman who called me a douche bag,* he thought. He never did see her face as she left with Aiden and chose to run on the hopes that it was just another beauty in a red dress.

14

"If it comes down to waiting to be told or asking to be told, a wise man will ask."

It didn't take long for Carlisle to get used to his extended stay in London. He kept contact with his personal secretary back in Orlando but loved everything about the country—something he never would have thought when he was younger. Back then, all he assumed was that it was full of pasty faced, uptight people who didn't like to cut loose at all. Well, the party at Warren Weir had shot that theory out the window.

One of the things that Carlisle had dwelled on, almost like someone would dwell on the proper amount of time to wait to call a woman you were hot for, was how long to wait before calling Aiden for that lunch. If he followed what he wanted to do, he would have called the next day. He didn't, however, not wanting to appear too eager and like he had nothing else going on. So he waited a respectable week and one week later, he was meeting Aiden for lunch.

"This place is nice," Carlisle said, looking around the Bouchon Bistro with great appreciation. It had high ceilings—about forty feet he estimated—and soft golden colored walls with wainscoting. There was soft lighting and ornate flooring with perfectly spaced round table with crisp white tablecloths on them. All the furniture was mocha colored. It was a beautiful five star restaurant. Although Carlisle had eaten in many of them by that point, he was continuously fascinated with how incredible they were in their visual aesthetics. So much individuality and flair were in each and the style always seemed to be a perfect accompaniment to their menus.

"It's great to see you, Aiden," Carlisle said, walking over to the table where he was sitting. It was in the corner and a bit more private than the other tables.

"You, too, Carlisle. I trust you've been well."

"Excellent."

"Have you been back to the States?"

"No, I've been checking out some real estate here in England, as well as a few businesses that seem interesting."

"Substantially different business culture, isn't it?" Aiden commented.

Carlisle didn't get to answer because the wait staff came over.

"Mango iced tea for me," Aiden said.

"Water for me, please," Carlisle said.

"Make sure it's bottled," Aiden said.

Carlisle looked at him. He was a bit surprised. Why would the man care if he had bottled water or whatever type of water? Maybe bottled water was what people did in London.

Whatever. Who cares?

Then the waiter asked to take their orders and Aiden nodded to Carlisle to go first.

"I'll have the steak, baked potato, and ranch dressing on my salad," he said.

"No, don' order that," Aiden said.

He must have eaten here before. That's cool.

"I'll have the Chicken Marseille."

"I don't think you really would want that," Aiden said, looking sternly at him.

"What's going on? What would you recommend, Grand Master Aiden?" Carlisle asked, feeling a bit annoyed by it all.

"A salad."

"A salad? Are you serious? This is a five star restaurant and you think that I should order a salad?"

"Yes." That was the only response he got.

"Okay then," Carlisle said, looking at the waiter, "what salad do you recommend?"

The waiter actually looked at Aiden, who responded and added vinaigrette, not ranch dressing to the end of it.

After the waiter was gone, Aiden looked at Carlisle and said, "Here, take this pill."

He handed it over and Carlisle saw a pill that brought back haunting memories to him. It was the same color of green as the ecstasy had been that Joan had taken on that fateful night...the night that had indirectly brought him to that current moment.

"Why should I take this? I'm not used to putting things into my body that I am not familiar with," Carlisle said suspiciously. His mind was active with thoughts of the encounter that made him a part of the fellowship he was currently in and, of course, what happened to Joan. He didn't come as far as he had to keel over of a heart attack or from side effect.

"Relax, it'll help you."

"How?"

"You'll think more clearly, put things into perspective more effortlessly."

"There's a pill that does that?"

"Don't sound so surprised," Aiden said with a half-cocked grin.

"Why not use it for dementia, Alzheimers, or something like that."

"That wouldn't be very profitable, would it?"

"But if it could change the world, extend people's lives..."

Aiden stopped him. "We'd have a more over-populated universe than we do right now."

Damn, that's cold.

Carlisle grabbed the bottle of water that the waitress had set down in front of him and placed the pill on his tongue, swallowing it down with a gulp of water.

After the awkward moment of the pill and ordering the meal, Carlisle and Aiden broke out into easy conversation and for Carlisle, it was fascinating to hear all of the perspectives and beliefs of a man who had managed to change the way the world talked, thought, and interacted through his idea.

The two ate their salads and Aiden did a lot of the talking. Carlisle was glad to listen, too.

"Carlisle, when you think about life what comes to mind?"

"Well, I'm fortunate to have financial security but some day I'd like to have a wife and a family, take some time to really enjoy the people in my life."

"A common answer," Aiden said.

"Meaning?"

"From what I've learned and seen, people tend to do what they're told. They grow up, get a job, try to do something respectable and live the life that has been laid out by one person or another along the way. Maybe it was a parent, a teacher, a role model or perhaps it's just an expectation. That's pretty limited in scope. You've shown that you want to make some changes, O.R.B. is evidence of that but there's more, Carlisle."

"Okay," Carlisle said, nodding his head and leaning in. He felt as if he was about to hear the best kept secret in the world.

"It's so simple Carlisle, believe and Invest in yourself."

"Because every individual's creativity is priceless."

"There's so much that we can all do and most of the people that have changed the world are no smarter than almost everyone else. It's not about smarts as much as it is courage and ambition. You can change life by being innovative and putting your own ideas out there and showing people a different path, a different option. To be honest, that's what you did when you created O.R.B."

"And that becomes their norm," Carlisle added.

"Exactly," Aiden said, "it's messed up but that's the way it is. It's always better to be the pioneer and trail blazer than the one who plods down the path after it's beaten down and less exciting."

131

"I like the sound of that, Aiden."

"I knew you would."

Aiden turned his head and Carlisle's eyes followed to see what he was looking at. A woman in a red dress was walking to the table with a smile on her face, staring at Aiden with an obvious lusty desire.

<u>Shit. The woman from the party.</u>

The woman didn't seem to notice Carlisle. She put her hand on Aiden's shoulder and said, "Sorry I'm late. The flight landed late and traffic is a nightmare."

"No problems," Aiden said.

Then she turned to Carlisle and her casual, sexy look turned sour. "What is this douche bag doing here?"

"Now Marie, play nice and have a seat."

<u>So that's her name. Marie.</u>

Carlisle felt awkward, recalling the bottle being hurled at his head at the party a few weeks' back and honestly thinking he'd never have to see the woman again. It had been a bizarre situation and in his opinion, her nastiness toward him had been completely unwarranted.

Marie sat down and glanced at Carlisle again, looking at him like he was a contagious disease. "So, what is he doing here?" she said to Aiden. She spoke directly and boldly, clearly not in awe of his name or position the way most people would be. In an instant, Carlisle knew that she knew him well. He could tell.

"Carlisle wants to know the truth."

Marie let out a half-snort, showing her disgust.

Aiden turned to Carlisle. "I believe you want to know what's happening, don't you?"

"I'm pretty sure I know and I'm okay with it," Carlisle said.

132

"My friend, you have no idea what the truth is," Aiden replied.

Carlisle had no doubts that he'd made a horrible impression on Marie, although he had no idea how or why, but she didn't hide her thoughts and talked bluntly like he was not even present.

"This is a waste of time, Aiden. He is of no use to us. Why should he know and why do we need him?"

Aiden lifted his hand up and didn't say a word but it was enough to quiet Marie—from talking, anyway. She still shot laser beams that looked like they could knock anyone on their ass and immobilize them if she wanted them to.

"Carlisle, I am going on a business meeting next week. Would you like to come along?"

"Sure, that's one perk of being a billionaire. I can do whatever I want at the last minute," Carlisle said with a bit of a smarmy laugh. A huge part of him wanted to aggravate Marie more because she was being such a bitch to him. Was it nice? No, but he didn't care. He got under her skin for some reason, regardless of what he did, so why not have a little fun with it.

Neither Aiden nor Marie laughed at his callous joke and he suddenly felt a bit flushed and out of place. He changed his tone and asked, "So, where are we going?"

"The moon," he said. "We leave next week, as I said, and you'll have to meet me in Russia."

Carlisle didn't have a chance to answer before Aiden spoke again. "So, if you'll excuse me, I'm out of time. My secretary will send over the information you need to know to your room. Have a great day and thanks for the lunch."

"Thank you," Carlisle said. He came to his wits and stood up, shaking Aiden's hand and then he was left standing there alone.

As soon as Aiden and Marie were out the door, Carlisle sat back down and the waitress came over and smiled. "Anything else, sir?"

Carlisle realized that the bill hadn't been paid and said, "Just a scotch and the check, please."

133

"This goes directly on Mr. Easton's tab."

"Oh, thank you," Carlisle replied. He was only half listening because his mind kept screaming, "The moon! Going to the mother-fucking moon!"

<u>What would Joan think of this if she were alive?</u>

What a strange world it had become in a relatively short amount of time. Carlisle was drawn to it and fascinated but also a bit leery. It was hard enough to deal with humans, much less species he had no clue about.

Then things got crazy quickly. One week later, Carlisle was standing at an airport hangar that was the size of four football fields just over fifty miles outside of Moscow. His eyes were widened and he was staring at something that was more amazing than he'd ever imagined possible. He looked around and thought he must be on a movie set. It was surreal.

Next to him was Marie, who'd remained silent and aloof. Aiden was a few feet away and was watching Carlisle closely, gauging his reaction more than anything else.

"What is this?" Carlisle asked in awe. It was sleek and silver, looking like a giant rocket with insane wings on it.

As Carlisle's eyes perused the ship—make and model of the space ship—up and down, Aiden spoke, telling him a bit about it.

"This is called the Virgin Galactic," Aiden began.

"Virgin, like Sir Richard Branson's Virgin?"

"Yes, it's the prototype and hasn't been introduced to the market yet," Aiden continued.

"Wow, why?" Carlisle couldn't fathom holding back such a beautiful creation from the world. He also thought that this would have been an interesting stock to invest in.

"Cost and necessity, mostly," Aiden said. "You see, it's two million per seat. It'll be lower when it is eventually introduced to those in lesser income brackets but for now, we need to ensure that it's a billionaire's only opportunity."

"Why?"

"That is what suits are purposes," Aiden said. "I believe they're ready to board. Your luggage is already loaded."

"How long does a trip to the moon take?" Carlisle asked.

"With this technology, you're looking at a mere eight hours."

"Eight hours! Apollo took something like three days."

Aiden looked to Carlisle. "Things have advanced rather rapidly in such a short period of time." As an afterthought, he added, "And don't assume that there was not a more efficient means to travel to the moon back then. It's a matter of what's willing to be shared with government more often than not."

"This group is that powerful?"

"Powerful and purposeful," Aiden replied.

The group walked on to the plane and it was all Carlisle could do to move fast enough up the slight ramp that led to the cabin. Everything was state of the art, high tech, and truly revolutionary. That wasn't a surprise in and of itself, however, knowing it existed definitely was.

Once they were in their seats, Carlisle moved on to his next set of questions. He couldn't get them out fast enough, making him more excited than a child visiting Orlando—the theme park capital of the world—for the first time.

"And what is on the moon, Aiden?"

"There's a city. We call it Moon City and it is surrounded by the Moon Base. It's located on the dark side of the moon, leaving it hidden from sight for anyone who doesn't need to know about its existence."

I can't believe how many times I've stared at the moon and had no idea.

"Does it look like a city we'd see here on Earth?" Carlisle asked.

135

"Not much; it's built to adapt to the moon's geological structure, complimenting it and not being an eye soar like a lot of architecture that we are used to seeing here. It's really quite spectacular. I think you'll like it."

"Is it all enclosed or is there a way to walk outside?" Carlisle asked.

Aiden looked at him to see if he was serious. Carlisle justified himself. "Clearly nothing is impossible so don't look at me that way."

"Good point," Aiden said and then laughed.

Carlisle began to look out the window and when the Galactic took off, he couldn't even feel so much as a force working against him like you would in an airplane. It was a smooth, luxurious ride that just happened to take you to the moon. Within only a minute, Carlisle was staring out the window into the darkness of space. Although they were obviously going at as significant speed, he could see bits of debris in the vast atmosphere floating around and some of the stars and planets looked bigger than they did on the ground. Still, others in the distance looked as small as if he was still standing on the ground. In all his years of looking out at the night time sky when he was thinking about his future, he'd never really thought it would be possible to be going where he was. He never even wanted to, not drawn to the idea at all but there was no turning back now. He'd be one of a select few humans that had ever been on the moon at that point. It was so cool and yet he couldn't tell anyone about it.

It was hard to believe that it was even possible but Carlisle dozed off and the next thing he knew, he heard Marie saying, "Finally. I can't stand this flight."

"Yet, it's one that you'll be making quite a bit," Aiden said.

"Don't remind me," she grumbled.

Carlisle was becoming more fascinated with Marie. Who was this brooding beauty who seemed to think it was her against the world…or her and Aiden against the world?

"Just in time," Aiden said to Carlisle.

"I cannot even imagine what this is going to be like," Carlisle said.

"You won't have to imagine but for a minute more," Aiden said. "Look out the window over there and you'll get an overview of the base and the city."

Carlisle looked over and saw something that was challenging to even fully process. There was a giant building—kind of like a dome—and it reminded him of an eye ball. It was round and big in the center just like a pupil would be and then extended out in a swirling oval type pattern to the sides, reminding him of the white's of someone's eyes and also the "smoky eye" look of make-up that many women loved to wear.

The entire Moon City and Moon Base looked enclosed, which made Carlisle curious about one thing. "How are we going to land? It looks enclosed."

"There is a series of chambers to enter the dome without depressurizing it. We'll fly through one and then it's sealed. Then we enter into another and they seal that. Then the third one is the large landing area where we can get out and the ship will be inspected for contaminants."

"Contaminants?" Carlisle asked.

"Yes, we try to keep the environment pure, meaning that nothing aside from us are bringing particles into the moon's environment."

"Wow, I really am living in a sci-fi movie," Carlisle said. It was meant to be a thought but it came out loud.

"This is far more than some sci-fi futuristic novel. This is reality and this is the here and now. Today's way and tomorrow's future."

"And definitely designed by someone of higher intelligence," Carlisle added, referring back to the conversation at the restaurant.

"Yes," Aiden said.

The process to get into the Moon Base took about a half hour, with the amazing aircraft hovering between each chamber as it opened and closed. It was all so quiet, too, and you couldn't even hear a bit of engine noise.

When the door opened up and the ramp was extended, the three walked out. It was hard to believe that it was economical, even at two million a ticket, to only fly three people to the moon in a single trip.

<u>What does that really matter to me?</u>

A beautiful woman with crystal blue eyes walked up and greeted them. She wore a ruby red dot on her forehead that looked like a bindi but Carlisle sensed that it had nothing to do with social class and stature like it would in India.

Aiden saw Carlisle's curious glance. He leaned in and whispered, "The mark of a servant."

"Oh," was all Carlisle got out and then the servant began talking.

"Was your flight smooth, sir" she said, not offering a name but looking at Carlisle curiously. He could tell she wasn't a human but she looked more human than many of the beings he'd begun to meet.

"Yes," Aiden answered for the group.

"I shall show you to your quarters, Mr. Lewis," she said. "It's in the same wing as Mr. Easton and Ms. Saintvil."

Carlisle couldn't believe that she knew who he was and he smiled. Then he realized that Marie must be Ms. Saintvil. He'd never heard her last name or thought to ask.

<u>I'll have to remember to Google her name later and see if I can figure anything out.</u>

Then Aiden said, "Marie, look out for Carlisle and go around with him. I have a meeting to get to right away."

Marie rolled her eyes and said, "Fine," flatly.

The two followed the woman to the suite where Carlisle would be staying.

Marie turned to him and said, "You wait here and I'll be by to get you. Don't leave this room without me. Got it?"

Carlisle just saluted like Marie was a drill sergeant. Her face furrowed up and she made two fists, digging her fingernails into them.

<u>Why is she so tense? It's even worse here than it was that night at the party.</u>

His room was amazing; having a glass ceiling that showed the universe that existed outside of it, a round bed in the center that was soft and covered with custom sheets and blankets to fit its unique shape, and the entire one wall was filled with fish of all sorts, making it the largest aquarium he'd ever seen. It put the Georgia Aquarium in Atlanta to shame.

The corridors had been interesting and beautiful, too, having some unknown type of flooring on them that gleamed but not having any echo noise like a marble hallway would have when someone with heels or business shoes walked across it. On the walls were portraits of individuals—human and otherwise—that showed they were obviously very important people. A few of the pictures were very disturbing to Carlisle, almost giving him the chills because they looked more like a creature that would be in one of those cliché horror movies or maybe Predator for those Arnold fans.

Carlisle decided to take a quick shower and change from the flight. Then he sat down at the table and waited for Marie to come. Maybe she was dicking around with him and wasn't going to come back at all. It wouldn't have surprised him. She grew more icy to him instead of warming up to him like most people might. He didn't know her story but he could sense there was one. She had "girl with baggage" written all over her.

There was a knock on Carlisle's door and he went over to answer it.

He realized only then that there was no door knob.

"I don't know how to open it," he said.

Marie's voice came through on the other side. "Press the black button to your right two times."

Carlisle did and the door slid open, showing that Marie was now wearing a sapphire blue shirt and a pair of jeans that made her look absolutely stunning.

I'd be well served to keep my eyes off Aiden's girlfriend or even think of her as a sexual being at all, Carlisle thought. Those would be words to live by...not that Marie would ever give him a chance. That was clear to see.

The two walked down the hallway and Marie gave Carlisle some pointers on how to act and respond to the "unusual beings" he'd be seeing. He thought she was being a bit too militant until they came around one curve in the long corridor and saw a monster so hideous and vile that Carlisle couldn't take his eyes off it for the life of him.

The beast had two hoof-type feet, thick shell like armor around it's midriff and two arms with tentacles that looked like small snakes that were trying to break free from the eggs they were hatched from. The eyes were so dark and large, making them look like what Carlisle imagined a black hole might look like. There were marks all over the remainder of its face and body, which reminded him of either warts or like something was bubbling underneath the surface of their leathery skin.

"Do not stare at him, Carlisle," Marie whispered.

Carlisle didn't have time to respond to Marie's quiet warning.

"Come here human," the monster said.

"No," Carlisle said.

"He'll go," Marie offered. She stared at Carlisle and said, "You cannot refuse to go."

"Why?"

"Shut up and go…be careful."

Marie turned to the creature, talking with her eyes downcast. "This is Carlisle and he is here by invitation of Aiden."

The monster grunted and Carlisle began to walk behind him, which was a safer bet for him, and he turned around to see Marie staring at him with a helpless look upon her face. She didn't look worried for Carlisle very much, though. In fact, Carlisle thought he could read her thoughts: she seemed to expect that he'd do something to goof up. However, she began to walk slowly, remaining a safe distance behind. Knowing she was there made Carlisle feel better.

The English language the monster had initially spoken had changed. Suddenly his—its—dialect changed and it was talking in what must have been its native tongue.

Carlisle and he were sitting in a room that looked to be a dining area and the monster pointed to a chair and although it was reluctantly, Carlisle sat down. He didn't dare take his eyes off the monster now. Rude or not—he didn't trust it and was not going to turn his attention away from it for a single minute.

More words flowed from the monster's tongue, which looked like a hammer at the end of it. They were angry sounding words and also had a bit of condescension in them...or so it seemed to Carlisle.

"I'm sorry, I don't understand you."

The monster reverted to English. "You are only an ignorant human, not worthy to look at me but there you are, staring at me. I should beat you and place you in servitude."

Then the creature clacked its tongue, like how a bird might against the inside of its beak before talking, and called something out to a very timid looking creature of some sort in the corner.

Carlisle realized that creature was probably its servant; only it wasn't beautiful like the servant that had greeted them.

It scurried away and came back quickly with a large bowl in its two bony, spiny hands.

The servant handed over a bowl of something gooey and round. Carlisle looked at it and instantly thought he might puke. It was eyeballs.

"Get out of here!" the monster yelled and slapped the servant. Then it sat down.

It turned to Carlisle and asked, "Do you know what these are?"

"Eye balls," Carlisle said quietly.

"You're not so brave and assured now, are you? They aren't any eye balls, they are human eye balls. We eat them the way you might each chicken or steak. We love it." Then the monster leaned forward to stare closer at Carlisle and seemed to breathe in through the slits that were its nostrils.

Carlisle remained silent.

The monster banged its fist on the table and began to rant about how stupid humans were and something about toxic corn syrup. It was confusing to Carlisle, who had no perspective on what the beast could possibly be talking about. It continued on, also stating that humans allow them to put fluoride in their drinking water and it made them even more stupid. Also how humans flood the air and ground with chemicals that are unsafe. Then he added, "You're all cattle—worthless cattle—and there is no hope for your race. Morgs."

He probably shouldn't have done it but Carlisle felt like he did have to defend the human race in some way. He gave a weak, "There is hope for the human race. We are not dumb."

That was the wrong thing to say. It agitated the monster more and he continued to rant. "I eat five pounds of your species eye balls a day and drink gallons of your blood. You're stupid cattle going through life and waiting to be slaughtered. When your mothers die, we eat their eyes like you'd eat rice from a bowl." Then it muttered, "Morgs," again. Carlisle definitely got the connection. Humans and Morgs were the same thing.

Carlyle leaned forward and looked into the monster's eyes. "What the hell did you say?"

The monster was amazed that it had been questioned at all. "Did you just question me, human? I will kill you where you stand."

"Go ahead, give it a try. I'll take you out with me you ugly piece of worthless shit." Carlisle could feel the veins in his temples throbbing and his palms getting clammy from the instant anger and rage that he felt looking at the creature.

The monster stood up and roared, looking ready to pounce across the table and wipe Carlisle out in a single swipe.

Marie appeared from the shadows and jumped in between the two. "Stop! No! Please! He wasn't ready!" Her hands were spread out and the monster paused and turned to her.

"Fine, I'll kill you first!" it said.

"We are with Aiden Easton and under protection of the Council."

"Come with me," the monster said, grumbling. Marie's words were enough to stop it for the time being.

The two followed the monster out of the dining type area and down the hall, entering into a circular meeting room, in which there were chairs all around on various tiers and an area in the center where someone would take the stage to address the group as a whole.

142

With brute force, the monster shoved Carlisle and Marie into the center of the room and the one who'd been addressing the Council stated, "What's the meaning of this interruption?" in an emotionless tone. It was a voice that revealed they didn't want to hear anything emotional and only facts.

Carlisle noticed that the creature who spoke looked like many of them that had lined the walls on his way in—the one's he couldn't quite explain or figure out. Pterodactyl meets man, maybe.

"This human has disrespected me and must be punished for his ignorance," the monster belted out.

The monster isn't afraid to show emotions.

Everyone on the council was whispering and trying to figure out what was going on. Carlisle heard statements such as, "Is it true?" "Torture him" "Make an example out of him" and "Disgusting humans."

"Yes, it's true," the monster replied, saying it two times—once in its native tongue and once in English. "This disgusting human questioned me, stared me in the eyes, and showed no respect for my position as guard of the head of Council."

The monster definitely knew who Aiden was because it looked at him next and said, "Is he under your protection?"

"Yes," Aiden replied. "I shall keep him with me during the remainder of his stay here."

"Agreed," the members of the Council said. Then they looked to Aiden and one of them asked, "Is this the one you call Carlisle."

"Yes, that's him," Aiden said. "He's a vital asset to our research team and must come with us."

Carlisle was scared and upset, wanting to swear and call the bastards in front of him every name in the book. He didn't give a flying fuck who they were. No one treated him the way he'd been treated or threatened him without some sort of repercussion. He chose more wisely, deciding to put his head down like Marie had wanted and just listen.

143

The monster spoke directly to Aiden again. "You've killed ten thousand humans and you are a trusted human among our race. This Carlisle cannot be trusted and he should not come with you; he should be punished."

The council was debating the monster's words.

"What if he proved himself," Aiden offered.

Whoa, what does that mean? Carlisle thought.

"How?" the monster asked.

"Give him a test of courage. It might be worth a show, if nothing else."

The monster thought about it and his voice gave away his confidence that he'd get his wish of Carlisle just being punished and possibly dying.

"If he kills twenty Fires, he will gain our trust and courage."

"That is impossible for a human who has had no training," Aiden said.

The Council quickly spoke up. "That seems fair."

Aiden didn't skip a beat. "If you are going to have him going into the arena he will need a weapon to defend himself."

"Could he possibly have a blood saber, it might amuse us more." the head of the Council said to the others.

Carlisle looked toward Marie and asked in a whisper, "What's a fucking blood saber?"

"A sword to cut through any organic life as easy as you can cut through a piece of paper," she said.

"It is decided, Mr. Easton," the Council said in unison.

"How about if I kill a thousand humans as an offering to you. Could he have one," Aiden offered, gesturing to the monster. "I beg you, High Council."

144

Carlisle was dumbfounded, listening to an open murder plot being revealed and all to save him. It made no sense. Marie must have sensed it. "He really is trying to save you," she whispered to him.

In a loud voice, the Council said, "You have three months to prepare. You are dismissed."

Carlisle and Marie were escorted out of the room but the monster remained behind.

"What the hell just happened?"

Marie didn't answer directly but she said, "You'd better rest up because you are going to have a lot of training to do if you want to have any chance of success for this mission."

"And if I don't succeed?" Carlisle asked.

"You die. It's that simple."

Marie began to explain what the High Royal mentality was like. They were void of emotion, very intelligent, and saw things in terms of benefits, not personal desire. In short, she said, "They are the most sterile, dull professor you ever could have to the Nth degree. Only, instead of giving you an F if you piss them off, they kill you."

"Thanks for the comforting words," Carlisle said.

"They're meant to warn you, not comfort you. Don't mess around with these beings, Carlisle, because you can't win."

Carlisle's room came into sight and he went into it, glad to have a reprieve from what he'd termed "fucked up alien rules" and think about everything. He was so angry and wanted to smash something, or at least lash out. He couldn't do that, though, because some other life form wanted to eat his eye balls.

I've been deceived by Aerial and Aiden. Damn them. They should have disclosed all this crap before inviting me into their little fellowship.

Carlisle was not happy with his first hours on the moon. There was clearly no regard for human life there for the most part. And the killing…what type of culture had you kill your own to be revered by them? The High Royal culture, that's which one. They gave fellowship an entirely new meaning. He was going to find a way to get out of the shit he was in. It may take him a bit and he'd have to buy his time but he could play it smart...he'd been doing that his entire life.

15

"Never disrespect a man or monster in their own house."

No sooner had Carlisle settled in to his room and he heard a knock at the door again. His heart started to race. *What if that monster is here to get me and take out its own revenge?*

"Yes," he called out cautiously.

"It's me, Aiden, and Marie," a voice said.

Carlisle was so relieved that it was Aiden and he went over and pushed the black button twice, allowing them to come in.

The expression Aiden wore didn't match the composed tone of his voice. It made Carlisle's defensive instincts automatically rise.

"You have to be more careful," Aiden said in that same calm tone.

"Or what? You're going to kill me and give them my eye balls," Carlisle hissed, grabbing Aiden by the collar with more agility than he'd ever shown before. He'd always lost his temper a bit quickly but the last months the length of time it took to go from calm to enraged seemed to be no more than a nanosecond.

"Stop," Aiden said.

"Or what? What the hell did you do back there?"

"What did I do?" Aiden asked in amazement. "What did you do?"

Now Aiden lost his composure and he shoved Carlisle backward, putting his hand on his wrist and twisting it so he'd have to release his collar.

"What the hell happened with that monster and what have you signed me up for? I don't want any of this shit. I want to go back home."

"Well, that's not going to happen so be reasonable. If I didn't sign you up for what I did, that monster, as you put it—who happens to be the first body guard to the leader of the High Council at this time—would have killed you on the spot. I need you so I'm giving you a chance."

"I don't need any favors from *you*, Aiden."

Carlisle poked his finger into Aiden's chest and leaned in. His right hand was clenched in a fist and he couldn't hide the fact that he was debating whether to punch Aiden or shove him to the ground.

"Stop it!" Marie shouted, finally taking control of the situation. "What's done is done."

Then Marie said to Aiden, "I told you that you shouldn't have brought the douche bag with us. He's worthless and now we have all of this to deal with because of him."

"Shut up!" Both yelled it at the same time to her.

"Fine, you asses, do whatever you want. Duke it out. Be all manly but remember that this entire situation is only going to get worse if you two are fighting against each other right now. You'd better get a clue and get your act together. Good night."

Marie left and her words had left the two men speechless. Thankfully, they'd had enough impact and created enough silence that both of them managed to calm down.

"So, what is going on with this mission, Aiden? What is this really all about?"

"You'd better sit down for this," Aiden said.

Carlisle wanted to argue but it wasn't the time to do it. If anything, a bit of maturity had helped him learn that lesson a little. But when he lost it…

"Look, you may not like it and it may take time to accept it but the world is going to be over-populated by 2069. Not far beyond that, it'll not even be habitable anymore. We can't just stand by and allow that to happen. We have to preserve it for as long as we can and buy ourselves time to set up a new world—a place to start over with the best of the best."

"You talk just like that monster, not a human," Carlisle said. "Is that why I am here? To see this bullshit go down?"

"No, you are here because I want you to help me find another planet that our race can live on. Our future depends on it."

Carlisle was confused by the answer and couldn't see where his skill set even played into the equation. Then it came to him; Carlisle was meant to be more like Aiden. "So, you killed ten thousand people?"

"We'll talk about that more later on, but for now, keep a low profile. We're going to leave in the morning and be heading to Canada for your training."

"And you'll explain on the way? I have eight hours to kill—no pun intended."

"In short, Marie and I had to kill people to earn their trust and we've done that. We've worked hard to keep it and I plan to keep it."

"Why is their trust important?"

"To keep us alive. That includes you, Carlisle."

"How come that guy wants me as a servant? What's up with that?"

"All humans will be servants to these guys. Most of us aren't smart enough and believe it or not, there are some that know and don't care. Lazy…traitors…cowards…you name it."

"I still don't get why you invited me to the moon," Carlisle said.

"To see things for yourself and see if you think like Marie and I, or like most other humans. I need your help and if we don't find a new planet, we are either going to be wiped out or servants to the High Royals forever. Personally, I prefer death."

"Then why suck up to them?"

"It'll make the mission easier. It's as simple as that. And, I am not a quitter. I beat people at their games."

Carlisle lingered on Aiden's last words. Nothing about any of this could be called simple by his definition. What a crazy few days it had been. London. Russia—albeit briefly, the moon, and now Canada for training. For the first time ever, Carlisle thought that starting O.R.B. might have actually been more of a curse. However, he knew that was hesitation speaking after a little bit. He wouldn't trade what he had now for everything—especially a life of servitude.

* * *

Aiden's cabin, which is how it had been described to Carlisle, was awe inspiring. The place had to be about eight thousand square feet and all of the outdoor pools and water features surrounded by rolling hills and a few mountains were breathtaking. It was a place that anyone would be thrilled to call home—if they didn't like being around anyone else, that is—and it was Aiden's 'cabin.' Well, if that was cabin living, Carlisle was all for it. He'd take it.

"What do you think?" Aiden asked, obviously taking great pride in his little Canadian retreat.

"It's beautiful…breathtaking," Carlisle voiced, not able to hide his appreciation.

"I'll show you the training facilities now," Aiden began, "of course, all the outside terrain is also used for training."

"Great, can't wait."

Once again, Carlisle was awed into silence. The training facilities were high tech all the way and the equipment seemed to be the ones that they might use to train an Army Ranger or Seal Team member. It was equipped with everything that anyone had ever heard of when it came to tools for training someone to really become an assassin, plus a slew of things that were not easy to describe because they were not available to any military organization—yet.

Always a step ahead of the rest of the world, Carlisle thought.

"So, am I going to have a trainer or what?" Carlisle asked.

"Two, in fact—us," Aiden replied.

"Marie and you?"

"Don't look so scared. I can't kill you—unfortunately," Marie said. She turned around and although he couldn't see it, Carlisle guessed she was probably rolling her eyes at him and mumbling, "Douche bag," her term of 'endearment' for him.

Aiden laughed and gave Carlisle a friendly pat on the back. "You have to learn to control your emotions and not take things so personally. You are the master of your mind, not other people's words and actions."

"Yes, sensei," Carlisle replied with a cocky grin.

"Okay, for the next week you have a very basic schedule. Take the pills we give you without question, eat salads, do push-ups in the morning, afternoon, and night, run and work on your core strength and work the shit out of the various obstacle courses."

"All that for an entire week?" Carlisle asked. "We only have three months."

"Trust me, it's just as hard to conquer those things mentally as it is anything else. We are our own worst enemies in many ways," Aiden said. Then he stared at a sword in the corner and reached over and pinched his fingers together like he was taking something off of it. Maybe he was but it was too small for Carlisle to see. He observed it briefly and then flicked it in the air.

True to his words, Aiden proved to Carlisle that it was very hard to do things that were considered dull and tedious. Every one of his muscles hurt and he could barely move sometimes. It was so mentally exhausting—even more so than physically—and Carlisle had never been so grateful for the little bit of time he'd spent with his personal trainer. If it hadn't been for him the task could have been too much.

The only thing that stopped the pain for even a brief period of time was a small blue pill. "What is this?" Carlisle asked.

"Silphium."

"What's it do?"

"Stops pain, helps in healing, among other things."

"How come I've never heard of it?"

"The plant to make it is thought to be extinct but Marie has found a way to cultivate it for our uses."

Carlisle was impressed with Marie's talents but glad to hear that there was something to help his sore muscles.

"I'm grateful that you don't subscribe to the 'no pain, no gain' theory."

"We overlook pain, as it is a nuisance," Aiden replied quite seriously.

Carlisle broke out into a wide smile and wanted to laugh about it but his face hurt too much to even attempt it. He was that sore.

Finally, the second week came, which consisted of sword training with Marie.

At first, Carlisle felt really awkward trying to slice a woman with a sword. He wasn't chauvinistic or anything but his mother and step-father had always raised him to understand that it was not okay to strike a woman—ever. Yet, there he was, ready to unleash the beast slayer on Marie.

"Knock it off. The Fires are not going to be kind to you. They want to kill you and feast on your eye balls, not to mention drink your blood. Pretend I'm a Fire and I'm going to kill you."

Carlisle went up to Marie, swinging his sword full range and hesitated just short of striking her. It was completely unnecessary because her excellent swordsmanship had already ensured she had blocked his attempt.

"Your eyes give away your moves and what you're going to do. Focus on me, using your peripheral for everything else. Don't ever hesitate before a strike or it'll be your last strike attempt ever."

"Is everyone going to have swords that I encounter?" Carlisle asked.

"They'll have worse. They'll have the knowledge and power of the book behind them."

"What book, Marie?"

"The Serpent of Knowledge," she replied.

The entire time they had these talks they circled each other and entered into combat.

"Is it good to get your opponent in a monologue?" Carlisle asked.

"It can work on the new Fires but experienced ones will not fall for it. Use your judgment."

Overall, it didn't take long to see that Marie was a completely different person with the sword. She was so experienced, relaxed and actually pleasant when she was pretending to assassinate Carlisle.

<u>Should I take this personally?</u>

What Carlisle didn't know about was that the night before, Marie and Aiden had been having a conversation about how Carlisle needed an extra push. He didn't have a killer instinct and they had to spark him to realize that it was truly going to take someone else's death to save his life. The decision had been to see if he could astral project. That specific skill wasn't telepathy or anything as simple as that; it meant accurately hurling bombs at people—Fires, in that instance—from a distance and leaving no trace or explanation as to where they came from. It was like trying to figure out why a meteor seemed to target a certain house from the universe above—it just did. Of course, on occasion it did have some guidance from a being who could control it. The person who could astral project could leave their body and roam about like a ghost or they could actually go to the astral plane, a very complex grid of networks that took the mind matter of a person to other planets and places, such as the moon. This ability allowed for the opportunity to wipe out opponents without being seen but it was tricky to get back. You could be lost in the astral plane forever, never returning to your human shell, if you didn't know what you were doing. It had happened before and would likely happen again. Marie and Aiden couldn't risk that happening to Carlisle so while they needed an aggressive strategy, they needed to be smart about it.

In efforts to learn more about the 'academic aspect' of training, Marie had begun jogging with Carlisle every day so she could share bits of insight with him that just might help him and save his life.

"We still have a lot of work to do on your stamina if you're going to succeed with this thing. You can have all the skills in the world but if you can't go the distance you will lose."

"I'm working on my stamina," Carlisle replied, puffing his cheeks out for extra oxygen.

"Breathe slowly and from deep down at all times to reserve your supply. The environment is different up there," Marie said, pointing to the sky. "You have to control it from within."

"It sounds so spiritual."

"Spiritual practices about breathing have a lot of wisdom behind them. Call it what you like but remain as focused on your stamina as you are on the sword. You know, you really are a natural with the sword," Marie said as she bolted ahead of Carlisle, forcing him to sprint six miles into the run to catch up to her.

"What do you mean?"

"With the sword. Some people understand how to connect with a weapon much easier than others. You do that and that is good because it won't take you twenty years to reach the skills you need to reach within just a few short months."

"To kill the Fires?"

Carlisle had just started understanding the Fires better and he felt kind of bad for them but if it came to a matter of life and death, he'd take their death and his life first and foremost. The Fires were the people who killed humans just to feed without any logical purpose. They couldn't survive long periods of time without eating human eye balls and drinking their blood. Their real threat was how they put everything that the High Royals were doing in jeopardy. The situation was made worse by the fact that they were wealthy, successful individuals who happened to be reckless and not prone to any decorum at all. If these people wanted to do something, they just did it and didn't think through the consequences. The fellowship had business minded ingenuity in it and that was what helped them stand apart—slightly superior according to them—compared to the Fires. Anyone who was a Fire was someone who'd never had the slightest possibility of making it into the fellowship and fewer diplomatic meetings with the High Royals, much less input in the High Council. Clearly, Aiden was an impressive human to have made it as far as he had. However, everyone reported to the High Royals in some manner, making everyone intricately linked.

Marie sprinted ahead again and this time Carlisle was ready. He caught up to her quickly and wasn't too winded to ask what was on his mind.

"I Googled you, Marie. Your father was Bruce Saintvil, wasn't he?"

154

Carlisle saw her briefly hesitate and falter but she regained he composure quickly.

"Yes, but that's not too hard to find out."

"He was a great chemist and died mysteriously."

"Yes, I'm a great chemist, too. My entire family is chemists. So what?" Her voice was getting slightly defensive but it wasn't angry. To Carlisle it seemed more like she was determining if she wanted to talk about it.

"Is his death what got you to this point, Marie?"

She nodded her head, indicating Carlisle was correct. "The High Royals killed my father because he had stumbled across Silphium when he was looking for a way to give humans a chance against the monsters and beings that want to kill us."

"People like the Fires," Carlisle added.

"Yes, as well as many other kinds of beings. Anyway, the High Royals found out and wiped out all the plants—or so they think—and then killed my father, considering him a threat because of his research. What they don't know is that I am restarting his research and I'm still working on it, creating something called Qeres, which is an ancient Egyptian perfume that uses Silphium in it. It is harmless to humans and works as a defense for us. It is also able to counter demons and monsters, rendering them defenseless and providing the opportunity to destroy them."

"You'd be dead if they found out," Carlisle said, feeling panicked at the thought.

"Yes, but they won't," Marie said. She turned to him and added, "I will get my revenge on them some day and meeting Aiden has helped with that. We've worked well as a team and made a lot of progress; which is why I can't afford to have you goof this up by not doing your best or taking this seriously."

Carlisle finally understood Marie a bit better and it all made sense.

"What can I do to become better at the sword?" he asked.

"You're good and quite gifted at it, I'll admit, but you will never be prepared in two months, which is all the time we have left. Aiden and I have something else in mind."

155

"What's that?" Carlisle asked, wondering how much more he could take.

"It's called astral projection and it's a way that you can trap and kill twenty Fires all at the same time."

"Why not just do that from the start. It sounds the easiest."

"Astral projection is hard and challenging, requiring complete focus and concentration, as well as skills to use the bomb without blowing yourself up. Not to mention you can enter into the astral plane or float around like a ghost here on earth."

"Blowing me up is definitely counterproductive but having an out of body experience sounds too scary for me and un-fucking-believable. It's hard to take all of this in just to save my life, but I'm not going to stress out." Carlisle said.

Marie turned to him and stared at him briefly and then burst out into laughter. It was the first genuine laugh he'd ever heard escape her lips since he'd met her.

"Well, we'll find out. Aiden's waiting for you to take over this new phase of your training, hand to hand combat, garbling and being aware."

"Will we still work the sword?"

"Yes, Carlisle. Your training has just intensified. Be prepared."

Carlisle was definitely going to be prepared.

What Aiden began to teach him was complicated stuff, making Carlisle feel like he was a super hero or some other supernatural being.

"First, you need to sense what is around you at all times without growing distracted. Distraction is a weakness," Aiden said.

"Okay, how do I finesse that?"

"This is how," Aiden replied. He tossed Carlisle a blindfold and told him to put it on. Then he instructed him. "Noises and sounds are going to be coming at you from all around. It's up to you to determine which ones are legitimate threats to you and which are just background noise that's meaningless. This is called 'awareness' and it is critical."

For the next two days Carlisle tried to practice his awareness and felt like he was not improving at all. Aiden remained calm and talked him through what he had to change and adjust, showing him footage afterward. The sounds that went into the training room around him were so haunting though: wolves howling at the moon, people screaming as if they were taking their last breath, the sounds of soft footprints on the ground, branches breaking, and bodies being drug across the ground, too. Sometimes it would be just one sound and other times there would be many.

Finally, on the third day, Carlisle thought he'd found a pattern or logic behind it. It was the quiet sounds that you had to watch out for most because they were up close. All of the loud sounds came from a distance and it was easy to pinpoint their location.

Yes!

Carlisle made it through an entire half hour session intact and without getting killed by a mythical Fire. It was a great success.

"Wonderful," Aiden said. "Now it's time to move on to astral projection, which will be considerably more challenging. The first thing you need to understand is what happens during this is called the awaken state. You are better in this state than at any other time. For me, my strength doubles and my hands move more quickly and agilely. For Marie, she can stay awake for longer than anyone I've ever met, making her most dangerous with her bombs and swords—which I know you've discovered that she rather loves."

"Excellent," Carlisle said, sounding intrigued with every part of astral projecting.

"As a warning, you'll see Marie and I in this state to learn it yourself. You will know when we are—when anyone is—astral projecting because of our eyes. They become a shiny, metallic silver."

"Like the moon servants eyes?" Carlisle asked.

"No, you'll know when you eventually see it."

Within an hour of lessons, Carlisle's euphoria at getting down awareness to some extent had evaporated and he felt an extreme headache growing as he worked with astral projection.

His mood darkened and it only got worse after his sword session with Marie, who told him in no uncertain terms that, "you're worse today than you've ever been. Get the hell out of my sight."

Carlisle took it personally and became so mad, pacing around and wanting to unleash his inner beast on somebody or something. Every rule they'd emphasized had went out the door.

He shook it off to a bad day but it happened for the next seven days, making him so irate and agitated. He didn't want to fail but they were asking him to do something he was clearly not prepared to do.

He stormed into Aiden's office and screamed, "I can't do this shit. Kill the Fires yourself and find your planet yourself. I'm out. If I die, I die. My head hurts, my body hurts, and frankly, this is just all too fucked up for me to deal with."

"Your reactions are normal and expected. You can do this, Carlisle. We have one month left and it will work."

"So that's it? No debate…just ignore what I said?" Carlisle asked.

"Yes, that's it. We don't have time for this," Aiden said. Then he turned around and grabbed a case from his desk. "Take a look at this," he said, sliding the box over for Carlisle to grab.

Carlisle opened the case and saw a pair of futuristic sneakers that had definitely been jacked up a bit. They were cool and innovative, he smiled, thinking of how the pair of shoes would have been his ticket to popularity when he was young. He was famous now but they were still exciting. They were black and had red and silver details in them and were out of this world…his last words—out of this world—made Carlisle grin widely.

"What are these about? Can I try them on?"

"Yes, they're not activated and loaded yet."

"Activated and loaded?"

"Exactly. They are called GRAILS and they are more than just shoes; they are your lifeline and best defense to beat the Fires in your upcoming battle."

"Shoes are going to help me win a battle?" Carlisle questioned. The doubt in his voice couldn't be hidden.

"These sure will," Aiden said. He went on to explain how they worked. Carlisle had one on his foot and Aiden held the other. One button made them inflate and wrap protectively around his ankle for support and to ensure they couldn't be stolen by anyone.

Man, everyone would want to shoe-jack me if they knew what these could do, Carlisle thought.

Aiden went on to explain that in the heel the bombs that he'd use with his astral projection to kill the Fires were located. They would go off by pressing a button on a watch he was wearing. The key would be to press the button without a Fire realizing it and having a chance to respond and therefore, cause the effort to fail.

At the front of the shoes was a small laser beam. "It can't kill but if by some odd chance you are ever a prisoner, it can help you escape," Aiden said.

"Assuming they don't take the shoes," Carlisle added.

"Exactly. The good thing is that no one else, aside from us, knows they exist."

"Did you invent them?"

"Marie and I...she makes the bombs and I designed the rest based off of experiences I've had."

"You mean killing Fires?" Carlisle asked.

Aiden nodded.

Carlisle looked at the shoes and just loved them. Just holding the shoes made him feel more powerful, like he could win. Was it psychological or were the shoes really that much of an advantage? He wasn't sure but he was glad to feel confident because that feeling had been eluding him for the past months, making them more challenging than they needed to be.

"I have one request," Carlisle said.

"What's that?" Aiden looked at him and tapped his fingers on his desk.

"Can I have one thing customized?"

"Sure, I suppose, so long as it doesn't compromise the true purpose of the GRAILS."

"Can we get an eye at the end of the souls, along with the double infinity sign? I always liked that sign. Oh, and the O.R.B. emblem in silver on the shoe?"

Aiden smiled. "Very clever...I don't see any reason why we can't do that. I'll have to double check with Marie first to ensure it doesn't impede the bomb's ejection abilities."

Carlisle was really pleased. He'd also been thinking about what would happen if the shoe would malfunction. It'd blow him up.

Well, better to be blown up than have some freaky Fire or monster eat me alive.

16

"Climbing so high I can almost touch the sky."

Just as Rodrigo had promised, Ethan's life took an amazing turn for the better. He began to climb back up the ladder of success that he'd started to descend from and life was good—one big party and he was loving it.

The new album, which had risen to number one in sales by its second week out, led to a great tour circuit where Ethan was being greeted with loud, thunderous applause and chants for more at every venue.

"You are all amazing. Without you, I'm nothing," he said.

Everyone would cheer more. And the women in the first row, who were all lovely and voluptuous per Ethan's efforts via body guards and show promoters, would toss something on stage or their phone number, hoping the great Ethan Bryson would invite them backstage for some one-on-one time, or maybe even some two-on-one or three-on-one. A great many people would do anything for Ethan just to be a part of his day.

The downside to his fame was that before he could get wild at an after show party, Ethan had to take a trip to the woods or some other isolated place nearby and eat.

"I wish I could find one so I can go back and get laid," Ethan would say, laughing casually. "The woman in the front row just to the right was fine. Did you see her?"

"I sure did, man, and I've already enjoyed her," his friend said.

Ethan turned around, shaking his head. He knew that meant that his friend had already taken her, feasting on her eye balls and drinking her blood. No wonder he had so much energy.

"You're being too reckless, man. You've got to play it cool. We can't have a string of missing persons and unsolved murders following the concert around from city to city. Be smarter," Ethan said.

So, oddly enough, Ethan had finally grown up and started to think about what he was doing. He didn't want to get busted for murder and knew that if by some slight chance he ended up in a holding cell in a jail that no one in that cell would make it to see the morning, or the cops working the shift. And if that happened…regardless of it being his fault or not…Ethan would be killed on the spot to stop the madness. Or, those that liked to hunt and kill guys like him would track him down. He wasn't going to allow that to happen either and be the pawn in their game. They were a bunch of haters in his mind, jealous of what he'd been offered.

A group of teenagers camping in the woods appeared in the distance. They had a fire lit and some music going.

Ethan walked across the forest floor, not making a sound, and his two friends stayed behind him.

He walked in. "Hey, how's it going?"

"Holy shit, man! You scared the crap out of me," one of the guys said, taking a hit from a joint.

Then he peered closer at Ethan. "Hey, aren't you …"

He never had a chance to finish his sentence. Ethan said, "Yes, I am," and in the next second, he was puncturing the neck of the guy and draining his blood. His friends screamed but only for a second because Ethan's friends had taken their feast on them. They'd never seen it coming, which is what made it all so effective.

"They were good. The younger ones always taste better, don't you think?" Ethan's friend commented.

"They're all great and they all keep us living the good life," Ethan said.

"This method you came up with is great…smart."

Ethan smiled and nodded. He'd put more efforts into figuring out this new transformation in him and how to optimize it than he'd ever done with anything else in his life, aside from picking up women at Vista. He'd become stronger, faster, and more successful than a great many others in his new posse. His sights were set on becoming as good as Rodrigo, who was even better than Ethan, having an extra year with the seed in him.

For the next month, Ethan enjoyed everything life had brought him and he was looking forward to connecting with Rodrigo. They'd be playing the same venue for a festival and have a chance to catch up on what had been happening. They were also going to be doing a photo shoot together for a Rolling Stone special on the hottest music talents out there.

Drake, you got nothing on me, baby, Ethan thought.

* * *

Sitting in a private room off the suite of Rodrigo's hotel, Ethan and he were enjoying what Rodrigo termed 'pre-dinner.'

They were in the UK and had just wrapped up performing at the Glastonbury Festival. It had been another great experience, making the fan base for both sky rocket. They'd surpassed the States and were now on the International Fast track.

"So, any new skills developing?" Rodrigo asked.

"Getting quicker, man, so watch out," Ethan joked. "Also been able to start seeing through walls, which is pretty good for finding me some dinner more easily and discreetly."

"How do you like hunting?"

"Love it. Have a great system and I've really mastered not leaving a trace. It would be nice to do it solo sometimes but having the guys around is a good safe guard, I guess."

"Any revenge hunts or have you been sticking with unknowns?" Rodrigo asked.

"Unknowns but if Carlisle crossed my path, I'd take him down in a second. The fucker wouldn't know what hit him and that would be the end of him."

"It's tough for guys like us to be billionaires, art is never appreciated as much as business in a financial sense, but I have an opportunity for you that may help that happen. Interested?"

"What is it?" Ethan asked. "I'm definitely interested but you know that, Rodrigo. Otherwise, you wouldn't have brought it up."

"True."

"There's a tournament out there that's for our kind. If you win the tournament you'll win a billion dollar purse. It's not easy and it takes a lot of discipline and practice."

163

"I'm in," Ethan said without thinking twice about it.

Within a few months time my skills will be mad; no one will be able to beat me.

"I see that confident look in your eyes but you have a lot more training to do to stand a chance at this tournament. You've never fought anything like what you would there."

"What do you mean?"

"Well, there's no way to put this delicately. It's pretty out there; especially the first time you hear about it," Rodrigo prefaced.

"Give it to me straight, man. I can take it." Ethan didn't think that much could surprise him any longer.

"Our kind report to a group called the High Royals. They are kind of like the tracking system, monitoring everything going on."

"High Royals? Where are they, here in the UK?"

"Not exactly, they are on the dark side of the moon."

"The moon," Ethan said, looking at Rodrigo with doubt. "Stop messing with me man."

"I'm not. The tournament takes place in Brazil and there's no first, second place, or anything like that during this tournament."

"What is there?"

"Win or die."

"Win or die? Would I have to fight people like us?"

"Yeah, otherwise it wouldn't be much of a competition. The usual entrants are mostly premier athletes, Olympians, strong men, people like that."

"They won't have anything on me," Ethan replied cockily.

"They do if you underestimate them. There are some seriously skilled people and you don't know what they got until they're delivering it."

"Well, whatever it takes, count me in. What are the details?"

Rodrigo smiled, shaking his head. "There's a one hundred twenty-five million buy-in to enter the competition. There are only eight contenders allowed; only one walks out."

"And you think I can be that one?" Ethan asked, suddenly feeling suspicious.

"With some training, yes."

"Why aren't you joining?"

Rodrigo shook his head at Ethan. "Not my thing, man. Besides, I've already won one of those competitions once—and doing one of them was enough for me."

"What should I do to prepare and how long do I have?"

"It's in two months. Train and eat as much as you can so your larva is stronger than your opponents and you'll stand a chance."

Ethan was more than happy to go out and hunt, eat, and train as much as he could with his tour schedule over the next few months. He had finally arrived at the opportunity he'd been craving for so many years now. He was going to be richer than Carlisle and there wasn't a damn thing the guy would be able to do about it when he got to confront him—then kill him.

It was a smooth landing into Galeão International Airport in Rio and Ethan was feeling the energy surging through him, eager to get to the fight and give his best efforts. The thought that he might die had only entered his mind once but was brushed away by thoughts of besting Carlisle financially. It fed the fuel inside of him almost as much as the larva did.

I can just imagine that bastard's face when he finds out I'm richer than him…and I didn't need him to do it.

A black, stretch H2 limo with tinted windows was waiting at the airport and Ethan hustled into the limousine. In no time at all, murmurs that he was playing a surprise concert somewhere in Rio surfaced and that information plant had been intentional. Nobody knew where he was really going and he stared out the window, eating a few eye balls that he'd collected before the flight and placed in a small, leather pouch. He also found a carafe of blood in the limousine, courtesy of Rodrigo, and was drinking on that. When it came time for the fight he would be ready.

Traveling down winding roads that went further up into the mountains which was eventually getting narrower as they went, the limo finally pulled over and Ethan got out, walking over to a Hummer, where Rodrigo was waiting, along with a driver, for him.

The three made their way through the jungles and came upon a clearing that was surrounded by tall trees that looked to be some sort of palm tree. They were enormous and the place was just about as secluded as you could hope it to be.

This is great, no one will hear their screams…except for me, Ethan thought.

He hopped out of the Hummer and walked into the clearing and found seven other people standing there. He was surprised to find that two of them were women. He'd assumed that he'd be up against men but he knew that the powers he had were greater than any specific gender and a well trained woman was certainly as deadly as a man.

An unusual looking person—who didn't even look human—walked into the center of the clearing from the side and looked around at all eight contenders.

"We are all here now and the tournament may begin. This is a one winner walks away with it all tournament. As for the losers, you will be cloned and reintroduced to your life within a week. I trust you've all given yourself a free passage for the next week."

The dark, almost lifeless eyes, of the one talking looked around at everyone.

Ethan had cleared out the week but quite honestly, he planned on doing that surprise concert that he'd made sure had captured momentum. He wasn't going to lose. He could not lose—there was no other option.

The line-up of who would fight was announced. Ethan would be in the second fight against a woman, who they called Temptra. She was tall, leggy, curvaceous, and wore a pair of tight shorts, a tank top, and was barefoot. Ethan had on a pair of shorts, no shirt, and some shoes. Everyone was allowed to wear what they felt most comfortable in but there were no weapons of any sort allowed to be used.

It's going to be crazy taking out a woman but I will do what I need to do.

166

The first fight didn't seem like much of a fight at all. This white guy, some athlete that was calling himself Zone, took care of another guy in about five minutes. He was skilled and Ethan watched closely, trying to find a weakness in him. It was hard to find one, though. He'd have to be careful if he ended up having to fight him.

Now it was Ethan's turn to have a go at Temptra.

There was a gong that was rung to announce the start of the matches and as soon as it was hit, its deep sound bouncing off the tall trees that surrounded the fight ring, Ethan and Temptra started to circle each other.

They looked like two lions trying to take control of the pride and each was trying to act casual but had their hands in a position where they could act fast if necessary. Ethan could hear her breathing and the pattern to it. Could she hear his?

He decided to use that to his advantage and he focused as they teased, moving in and out in quick, swift motions, and he realized that he was attuned to her heartbeat. Every time she moved forward, her heartbeat would speed up. That was perfect.

Temptra moved forward and Ethan jumped up, landing right in front of her and his hand went to her neck, pressing his pinky finger into it to start draining her blood.

She retaliated swiftly, dropping down and sweeping one of her legs around to knock him down to the ground. She landed on top of him quicker than a jaguar pouncing and hissed at him, showing fangs that were every bit as capable of puncturing Ethan's neck as his sharp nail was hers.

As she leaned down to bite him, believing she had a clear shot, Ethan closed his eyes, channeling his strength and then he opened them, staring at her chest and into it, just like he peered through walls, and his hand quickly came up and he plunged it into her chest, grabbing her heart with his hand. He yanked it out and she was temporarily frozen, giving him time to slide out from under her.

Ethan jumped up and Temptra stared up at him, not alive but not dead despite him holding her heart in his hand.

She gasped and he smiled at her, taking a bite of her heart as her brain finally told her body that it was dead—game over. Ethan walked over to her and knelt down, sticking his hands

167

in between her teeth as she lay there close to death. In one swift motion, he ripped her head off and then held it up in the air. Another fire was dead and Ethan was one step closer to his goal.

In an intimidation move, Ethan looked around at everyone in the ring and held the head up, blood trickling down his arm and crusted around his mouth. He screamed out like a warrior announcing their battle cry. Then, as quickly as it had happened, he walked over to the side to take in the next fight and see what weaknesses he could find in those opponents. Ethan was also aware that all eyes were on him. It was good…perfect, actually.

The line-up of who would be fighting again was announced. Ethan was up against a professional lightweight boxer called Warren Jones .Ethan had assessed his opponent from his previous win .Ethan thought that he was given a break because the fighter was a lightweight boxer, but that was hardly the case. The gong was rung to announce the start of the match. The two men dashed at each other. Ethan quickly tried to spear his heart using the same trick as his last opponent .Jones dodged the strike swiftly and quickly hit Ethan with a fierce series punches knocking him to the ground. Jones used his fancy foot work and backed away cocky of the attack he used on Ethan. Jones extended his hand and taunted Ethan to come on.

After five minutes of fighting hand to hand, blow to blow. Ethan thought he couldn't afford to keep this up. As Jones swung for a right hook Ethan grabbed his arm flipped him to the ground .Ethan still had his opponents arm locked, he quickly stood on one knee and pushed down his opponents arm breaking it.

Thank god for all the street fights Carlisle and I had when we were younger.

Ethan jumped on top of his opponent and began jabbing his hand like a spear into the neck of his opponent and ripped his head off to end the match.

Four men and the two women had fallen now and the last two remaining were Ethan and the one who called himself Zone. Throughout Zone's battles, Ethan had studied him closely, seeing no flaws but he was also distracted by something familiar about him. Sure, he was a famous athlete but that wasn't it. It was something more personal. If he could figure it out, he might find his advantage.

The one running the fights turned to Ethan and Zone, commenting, "Here's the purse for whomever takes this match." They pointed to a tree to the right of the two, who were facing each other, and a palette lowered from between the branches on two thick chains, revealing piles of money totaling a billion dollars on it. It was a distracting sight and Ethan quickly reminded himself not to worry about that; it'd be there for him when he had done what he set out to do.

The gong went off.

Zone was clearly as attuned to his opponents' actions, searching for weaknesses, as Ethan was. Just like he had in the other matches, he decided to be a bit more vocal, talking and trying to taunt and get Ethan to lose his cool so he could heal his wounds from his previous matches.

"You're nothing…you couldn't get laid even with a billion dollars, you freak."

Ethan had grown accustomed to shoving words like that aside. He had barely heard them at all in his life since high school.

Wait! Since high school. Ethan stared at the guy in front of him and a wicked smile came across his face.

"Why its Jason Young from high school …how about that."

"Who…" Jason never finished because in that moment, Jason Young a/k/a Zone, had lost focus. Ethan had snapped his neck and ripped the larva out of his stomach. Ethan punctured his carotid artery with his sharp nail, lunging in and drinking the blood of the jock that both he and Carlisle had hated with a passion in high school, the one that always got the girl and degraded them every chance he could. "Sweet justice," Ethan said, wiping his mouth and walking away.

Rodrigo, the one running the fight, and a few others were all that remained, and as Ethan looked at all of them, one by one, with the most pleased, sadistic grin on his face, they began to clap, chanting his name. It felt so good to Ethan, better than seeing his name on the first lighted marquee had ever felt.

"That was awesome, man…the best I've ever seen," Rodrigo said.

"Thanks."

"Who was that guy?" he asked.

"His name was Jason Young, a real prick in high school. I didn't figure it out until he said something during the fight."

"You dominated, man. How did you do it?"

169

Ethan gave a brief recap about finding the weaknesses in his opponents with his new abilities and it was impressive for Rodrigo to hear about. For the very first time in his life, he felt that he was smarter than Carlisle Lewis and he couldn't wait to show the world. It was almost more exciting than being as rich as him, now, which Ethan was.

As he'd hoped to do, Ethan held an impromptu concert to help the impoverished areas of Brazil, donated a cool million dollars, and then was off to his destination—the moon. Meeting the higher-ups was an added bonus, something very few people got to do. He smiled: you win the Super Bowl and you go to Disney World, you win a fight like this and you go to the moon.

17

"When you play with fire you're likely to get burned."

Three months had passed and Carlisle was headed back to the moon with Aiden and Marie. He had mixed feelings about it. A part of him was eager to help the two in the plan, now that they understood it better, and he'd realized that he was quite compelled by Marie's desire to avenge her father's brutal death, all from accusations of being a traitor to the High Royals. The disappointing part of it all was that he hadn't mastered astral projecting and they were not going to allow him to attempt it during his efforts to kill the twenty Fires. He'd have to rely on his awareness, shoe bombs, his sword skills, and the hand to hand combat. Thankfully his endurance had increased quite a bit, making it acceptable but still lackluster compared to either Marie or Aiden's.

Back when the insane deal had been made, Aiden had agreed to kill a thousand humans to offer to the High Royals for payment, leaving Carlisle with the task of killing twenty Fires. It wasn't an easy feat.

They were at the hangar in Canada, waiting to get to Russia, where they'd board the Virgin Galactic and head off toward the dark side of the moon.

A white utility van pulled up and a man, dressed all in black, got out and walked over to Aiden with two silver briefcases, one in each hand.

"Here you go, sir," was all he said and then he walked away.

Carlisle glanced over and he felt his stomach flip just a bit.

"Is that what I think it is?"

Aiden looked at Carlisle and didn't respond. Instead, he set the briefcases down and opened them up. Eyeballs of all sizes showing irises of all colors were exposed. "Two thousand eyeballs," he said casually.

"One thousand lives lost."

"Not ones with potential," Aiden said, as if that justified everything.

Unlike his first trip to the moon, Carlisle was a bit more somber and tense with this trip. Marie gave him the rundown of what to expect.

"You have some advantages with the awareness and the shoe bombs if you use them properly. The bombs are in the heels of the shoes, as you know, and to activate them you'll press this button on this watch. Left button is for left shoe bomb; right button is for right shoe bomb."

Carlisle sighed, feeling out of his element and league more than he had in years.

"Pay attention, this is important," Marie said. Her voice sounded a bit harsh and in a gentler tone, she added, "You'll be good. You've trained hard for this."

"But the astral projecting," Carlisle countered.

"Was never a guarantee. Don't worry about it."

Finally, the moon was in sight just ahead and it was time to get off the space ship and be escorted to his room. Carlisle would be glad to have a minute of privacy.

A servant was there waiting, a different one than before, and she took the two briefcases first thing and walked away with them.

Marie went off in a different direction and Aiden and Carlisle began the walk down the hallways that would lead to their quarters.

"Carlisle, I've said it before but it bears repeating—you must stay alive."

"I know," Carlisle said. Then he changed the subject. "Hey, I've been wondering how you and Marie met."

"That's quite the topic jump," Aiden said, "but okay, then. We met because of her father, a man I greatly admired. When I first came into my substantial wealth, I hacked into some data files and found a man getting eaten by monsters, slowly and torturously. It was sickening but it aroused my curiosity. Who was this man? Well, it wasn't hard to find out that it was Bruce Saintvil. To make a long story short, I'd been invited to the moon for the first time. I got here and met Marie. I could see that she was fearless and intense. Then I found out her last name. It got me thinking and I was afraid to approach it but knew I had to," Aiden said. He sounded sadder than Carlisle had ever heard him sound before—more emotional. He continued on. "Well, I showed Marie the video and she said it was her father. From there…well, we made sure

172

Marie was able to retrieve all her father's research and we teamed up to create plan where we could continue what her father had done and tackle this giant problem—a problem that most people don't know exists right now."

"Wow," Carlisle said. Inadequate words but the only ones he could think of.

Aiden quickly looked around, as if realizing where he was, and said, "Enough of that, Carlisle. This isn't the place to be discussing it. There are eyes and ears everywhere."

"Well, eyes anyway," Carlisle replied, trying to make light of the situation.

It worked. Aiden laughed. "You have one weird sense of humor, but so do I. That's the way it is with technology guys like us, I guess."

They were now in front of Carlisle's corridor. "So, when does this fight start?"

"Tomorrow, the High Royals' head guards will escort Marie, you, and I to the arena. From there, it's all in your capable hands."

* * *

With a blood saber in hand, Carlisle marched into the arena, staring around at everyone and wondering just how effective he was going to be. This was all so new to him…monsters, aliens, and, of course, the training that was critical to either dying or staying alive—which he definitely preferred.

A firm, robotic sounding voice was talking over a sound system and it said, "Carlisle Lewis."

Carlisle looked around and sensed many eager eyes on him, hovering from above and staring curiously at the human being whom most of them knew minimal about, other than that he'd pissed off the body guard for one of the High Royals.

He glanced over to Aiden and Marie, who were looking at him encouragingly and he gulped, as they couldn't hide their concern. It showed in their stiff posture and tense faces.

A light humming noise resonated through the arena and before his eyes, as if he was hallucinating, a building appeared that looked like Woolworth Building in New York City. It was very distinct, having many jagged, beautiful points and peaks on the outside. Then, a second

173

later, he found himself standing inside of the hologram building. It was physically there and he could feel the floor below him but he didn't understand how he'd gotten in there.

Faint footsteps sounded from the stairs over to his right and he glanced over, wondering if they were really there or just sounds being filtered into the arena. Remember, you are in an arena and the rest is an illusion…part of the game.

Carlisle decided that he should head toward the stairs and check things out. He began to walk up them slowly, pleased that his GRAILS were so quiet, making him feel stealth-like. Although they'd practiced complete control, Carlisle could feel his heart racing just a bit and his pulse quickening as he walked up the stairs, constantly looking around to see if anyone was watching him or had suddenly appeared. He couldn't rule any possibility out—even if it made no sense in his logical mind.

As Carlisle's foot landed on the second floor, he looked down at the first level and saw many people running around, some looking frantic and some looking more like predators. Instinctually, he glanced up and saw the same thing happening on the third floor. Why was no one near him? He didn't understand and his instincts told him that most of what he was seeing was not real, only an illusion meant to distract him. It didn't seem logical that he'd be able to walk out of the hologram building so he decided to go up to the third floor.

Moving more swiftly this time, feeling the need to be more urgent in his actions, Carlisle made his way to the third floor and as his foot landed on it the semi-transparent yet solid floor, the watch on his wrist started to vibrate, making him jump.

Fuck, did I accidentally set off a bomb?

He had no idea but the thought was unnerving. As quickly as it entered his mind it was pushed aside. He touched the screen, which was glowing a pale green, and Marie's clear, distinct, and authoritative voice came through it.

"Listen up," she began, "I'm going to be your eyes and ears for this. Got it? Remember what you've learned and you will make it through this."

Carlisle nodded his head and realized that Marie couldn't hear that. "Okay," he whispered, too hesitant to talk out loud.

"I want you to hide right now. Look around and see what places you can hide in that will keep your back side covered and still give you the ability to see what may be coming your way."

Carlisle looked around saw a large credenza pressed against a wall in the corner. It had doors on it and he ran over to it and opened it up, ready to tackle anything that may jump out at him. No one was there and he slid into the credenza and closed the doors, peering through the mesh screen. The thought that it seemed like it was planted there for him to hide in didn't elude him and he hoped that he wasn't putting himself in a trap. Marie said she was looking out for him but still…

Two heads peered on the top of the flight of stairs and they were attached to two huge, muscular bodies. Just looking at them unnerved Carlisle.

"There are two people on the floor," he said.

"I see them. They are Fires—human form," Marie said.

"Can I get them?"

"No, you have to get all twenty together at the same time," she replied.

"But…"

She cut him off in an urgent whisper. "No but. You only have one chance and you need them all together to use the shoe bomb effectively. Got it?"

"Yes," Carlisle said, shoving aside his pride for her advice, which was considerably more knowledgeable in these areas than anything he had to offer.

"You need to sneak out of there and take the elevator shaft, not the stairs."

"The shaft," he repeated. It made sense because taking the elevator would alert his presence to everyone on every floor. There was so much to consider and take in.

The two Fires on the third floor went into a room and Carlisle snuck out of the credenza, making his way toward the elevator doors. He put his fingers in between the two doors and tried to pry them open. They wouldn't budge.

"The blood saber," Marie whispered.

175

Carlisle looked down and realized that he didn't have his head in the game the way he should. He couldn't count on Marie and Aiden to win this fight for him. He had to be all in or the results would not be good.

I have to live and see this through.

The blood saber fit in between the doors and its strong, steel blade was good enough that it didn't bend at all as Carlisle leveraged his weight against it and the doors slid open. Then he used his fingers to make them open up just enough that he could get in and climb up the elevator shaft to the fifth floor. He climbed the sturdy, steel cables like they were a climbing rope in a gym and although it burnt his arms he didn't let it stop him from doing what he had to do. "In it to win it," he kept mumbling.

"I'm here," Carlisle said.

"Okay, there are nine of them on the sixth floor. You need to go there and plant the floor bomb and then make your way up to the ninth floor to activate it."

Carlisle turned around and found a monster standing there. It had appeared out of nowhere and he realized that he was going to be completely vulnerable until he succeeded.

The monster grabbed Carlisle and he felt it applying pressure to his neck. In that split second, all the words and warning of how to handle Fires flooded into his mind and Carlisle was able to lift the saber up just enough to spear the leg of the monster, making its grip loosen.

Carlisle took his free hand and put it on top of the six fingers of the monster's claw-like hand and twisted back, making the monster completely release him from its grip. He could smell the monsters stench, reminding him of damp moth balls and old swamp water mixed together. It was so pungent that his eyes watered and stung, making his vision blurry. He gained some distance between them and then without hesitating, he did what he'd been trained to do—stab the Fire in the stomach, followed by cutting off its head.

The blood saber swished through the air in one fluent move, connecting with the thick, short neck of the monster and its head rolled to the side, landing just before the stairwell, where it teetered back and forth, eventually deciding to take a roll down the flight of stairs.

"So much for being inconspicuous," Carlisle said aloud, trying to make a joke of the situation. If he didn't, he'd go numb, realizing that human or not, he'd just killed a living being.

"Good work, now keep moving," Marie said.

There's no way I could kill two of them at one time with just my skills and a sword, Carlisle thought.

Realizing how resilient and skilled Fires were, Carlisle said a quick mental thank you to Marie for having the ability to create weapons to help him even out the odds. He'd never felt at such a disadvantage before.

With his vision still slightly blurry from the stench of the monster, Carlisle focused on the stairs as he climbed them, half feeling like he was on a bad trip. He kept repeating his task in his thoughts: plant the bomb.

His luck ran out because the Fires all stormed in on him, not allowing him to go to make it to the sixth floor. Each of their heads looked like doubles, making it seem like there were twice as many. Focus…remember there isn't.

"I have to plant the bomb here," Carlisle said into his watch as he stumbled back down to the fifth floor.

There was no response.

He released the bomb from the bottom of the soul of his GRAIL and kicked it across the floor. With all the commotion and the Fires coming at him, none of them noticed what he'd done. Now he stared ahead, realizing that he had to make it from where he was to the elevator shaft. It was about thirty feet and there were sixteen monsters coming at him, ready to shred him, drink his blood, and then eat his eyeballs.

"Augh!" Carlisle shouted, sending adrenaline surging through his body. Why be quiet? They all knew he was standing right there.

Pulling his blood saber out of the holder on his side, he began swinging it back and forth, shouting like a mad man to keep himself pumped up and cause a moment of hesitation, if nothing else, in the Fires that were swarming in on him like bees to their queen. "I killed one of you with this and I'll get you all," he said, hoping they'd focus on the saber, thereby reducing their chances of seeing the bomb.

Grunts, groans, and the foul smell of the monsters penetrated the air in the hologram building. Did they really smell that way? Carlisle had no idea and regardless, he had to get out of there.

Swishing and leaning his head forward like a bull on the rampage, he busted through four of the monsters to be greeted by seven more standing before him, tall and erect, with their hands out, ready to pierce every major artery he had—there trick to subdue someone skilled in dealing with them.

With the saber in his right hand, Carlisle used his left hand to block the arms, delivering forceful forearm blocks to their arms, giving him that split second to get a step further. Then, quicker than a flash, he moved his saber to his left hand and began to use the arm techniques with his right. He wasn't sure why he could do it because he'd never been ambidextrous but Carlisle had discovered that he could fight equally well on both sides, which was a significant advantage in the situation he was in during that moment. It took more than a single injury to make him weaker and vulnerable.

He realized that the monsters ahead of him had come in from behind, trying to sneak up on him and subdue him that way but they'd run out of time, leaping over their fallen fellow Fires but not able to catch Carlisle, who was extremely agile and flexible, able to contort his body in response to the claws, arms, and leg sweeps that were coming his way.

Just a foot from the elevator shaft he dove forward, his slim physique flying through the two doors and he began to fall downward, finally grabbing the steel cable and coming to an abrupt halt, which sent an instant wave of pain into his shoulder.

"Block it out," he said through gritted teeth.

Estimating that he was nearly by the third floor, Carlisle jumped down and landed on top of the car of the elevator and reached over to press the red button on the left with his hand. He hesitated for a second, wanting to make sure that it was indeed the left shoe bomb that he'd removed. So much had happened so quickly and while he was focused, he didn't feel certain.

He'd felt and had remembered correctly. He pressed the button and a loud explosion was felt. It was intense enough to make the air move slightly and it felt like even the holographic building was swaying from it.

Okay, Carlisle assessed, I've gotten seventeen Fires I believe. That means that three are still around somewhere but where.

"Marie...update," he said. She'd been quiet, waiting with baited breath just as much as everyone watching the spectacular death.

"Eighth floor."

"Three left?"

"You got it."

Carlisle made his way up to the eighth floor, taking the stairs and not the elevator shaft. They knew he was in there now because of all the commotion from the blast. He was more of a sitting duck there than out in the open.

Feeling winded but still holding his own, Carlisle made his way up to the eighth floor and took his time to recapture his breath. He hoped that he could see the three, roll the bomb out, run like hell, and then detonate. Such wasn't meant to be the case.

Of course, this isn't going to be easy.

He walked onto the floor with his saber out, staring over to the closed elevator shaft and trying to see if he could get there and escape down it and toss the bomb as he did before. It was not a plan that looked feasible and his gut instincts told him that this was the moment to show that his skills were equal to his ability to plant a bomb. If he didn't, he'd never have a reprieve and would always be sought out by those who wanted revenge. He had to earn respect just the way Aiden had.

He walked up slowly to the Fires, who were looking at each other and then at him. He could tell they were giving some sort of signal to each other on how they could work together to bring him down.

Carlisle put the blood saber into his sheath and decided that he'd be able to handle an attack where they were surrounding him best with his arms and legs. He breathed in, taking in his surroundings and being aware of every little item around—both what may help him and what may hurt him.

The Fires were impatient. One of them grunted and came toward Carlisle with thundering steps, making it seem like it weighed many hundreds of pounds, and it swung at Carlisle. He ducked and the punch didn't make it but a punch did connect from the monster's

179

other hand as it smashed into his ribs, making Carlisle lose his breath. Then another blow that connected to Carlisle's face. Leaving half of his face numb from the impact.

"Legs first if you can," Marie said through the speaker.

At the oddest time possible, Carlisle's thoughts drifted to a realization: only he could hear Marie, not the Fires. He didn't know how it was possible but it was good that it was.

Another Fire came toward him from the side and Carlisle delivered a forceful, quick side kick that smashed into its stomach, making it fly back and land on the ground with a forceful thud.

Knowing he had a second to act, Carlisle took the blood saber and smashed it down forcefully across the neck of the beast, decapitating it. That would have to do until he could stab the stomach.

An angry grunt came from behind him and Carlisle felt the limb of one of the monster's putting him into a choke hold, to which he replied with dropping his body and flipping the monster over his back despite being about twice as heavy, and when it landed on its back, Carlisle was right there, spearing its stomach and slicing its head in one perfect motion.

He turned around and saw the last standing Fire stomping toward him, looking determined to succeed where every other one had failed. Carlisle pretended that he was going to run from him and that he was wounded. He made his way over to where the only half finished off Fire was and quickly speared its stomach, which put to rest its flailing limbs. It was the alien version of a chicken with its head cut off.

Then he crouched down, breathing in and could sense that the monster was about a step behind him. He reached down to his shoe and put something in his hand and then turned around, jumping up into the air and kneeing the monster under its chin with his leg, which made its mouth open as it screamed out in pain…maybe obscenities. It was hard to tell but it wasn't happy.

The monster put its head back down and Carlisle moved forward, punching it in the mouth. Sharp teeth shredded the top of his hand as his fist went into the monsters mouth and opened up. Then he pulled it back out, getting shredded more.

A loud cough came from the monster and it shook its head, trying to process what had happened. It left Carlisle just enough time to sprint toward the stairs and run down a flight of stairs and then press the right, red button on his watch.

The muffled explosion sounded out and that was it. There were no more Fires. Carlisle had shoved the bomb in the monster's mouth without it even realizing it. He had won.

"Holy fuck, I won!" He couldn't help but shout it in a mixture of shock and disbelief as he ran down the flights of stairs and out of the holograph building, which disappeared as soon as he exited it.

A crowd of shocked individuals were staring at him from their seats around the arena. It was easy to spot where the High Court was seated, as it was enclosed and more elaborate than the other seats.

"You challenged me and I won!" Carlisle shouted, staring each and every ugly being right in their beady little eyes. "Twenty Fires have died."

There was complete silence in the arena and Carlisle stared around, showing no fear. Then everything went black.

18

"Even victories have a price."

Carlisle's eyes were so heavy and he could barely open them up. No matter how hard he tried they refused to listen. He was ready to call out for help but his mouth was so dry that he felt like it was glued shut.

He remained still and tried to focus on what he had to do, taking in the sounds around him to figure out where he was and what had happened. Images of the fights he'd gone through against the Fires flashed in his mind but he couldn't remember much else.

A slight sob came from the left of him and Carlisle finally found a way to open his eyes, just a bit. He glanced over and saw that it was Aiden.

"Aiden," he said so quietly that he wondered if it was even audible.

Aiden looked over and jumped up, quickly wiping his eyes as he did.

"Here's some water," he said.

"What's wrong?" Carlisle asked.

"It's Marie," he said, releasing another sob.

"What happened? What's wrong?" Carlisle asked, finding a stronger voice after the sip of water. He couldn't sit up but he turned his head.

"For helping you, they beat her."

"What do you mean?" Carlisle asked. He was trying to keep up but his own head hurt like hell and his body ached badly. It was hard to focus.

"The bombs. They didn't know she could make them or had them. Well, she paid a price."

"She shouldn't have…"

Aiden jumped up and leaned over Carlisle. "Don't you dare say it," he shouted, pointing at him. "She did what she had to do and don't demean it by saying she shouldn't have done what she had to do. There was no other way. She knew it and I knew it."

"You knew she'd get in trouble for it," Carlisle commented. "What did they do to her?"

"Eighteen lashes on her back, making me watch each and everyone. Damn it, I would have traded places with her in an instant but they wouldn't let me. Those screams have tortured me. Her screams…Knowing we couldn't jeopardize our plans…so brave despite it…fuck…fuck."

"We'll figure it out," Carlisle said. They were completely inapt words for the situation but he didn't know what to say. There were no words of solace that he could offer and it caused him to reflect back on the pain he'd endured after Joan had died. He didn't know if this was worse or better but it was clearly excruciating to Aiden, and to Carlisle, too. Despite their rocky start, he'd really grown fond of Marie.

"We have to escape from here," Aiden said simply. It was crystal clear and there were no muffled sounding words from his stuffy nose or muddled thoughts.

"How are we going to do that?" Carlisle asked.

"We'll find a way and they'll never find us once we do."

"How will we find this new place to live if they're watching us closely?"

"It's going to take about a year but it will happen," Aiden said. "We just have to die first."

"Die?" Carlisle said with his mouth gaping open.

Aiden nodded his head yes, got up, and left.

* * *

With the haunting words that Aiden said weighing heavily on his mind Carlisle went about the process of healing. The technology and abilities of the High Royals to heal were

183

amazing, making them seem almost god-like. They sure carried a "God complex" like what many doctors did.

It had been three days since he'd fought the Fires and he hadn't seen Marie yet and he wanted to desperately. He had so much to say to her face. His thoughts had been driving him mad.

Aiden was resistant at first but finally took Carlisle to see Marie. When the two walked into the room Carlisle immediately walked over to Marie, who was lying on her stomach, staring out of a window out into outer space as if all the answers she sought existed there.

She turned her head and there was no fiery spirit in her eyes like there usually was. "Hi," she said softly.

"Hi, how are you doing?"

"Coming along, which is definitely perplexing to *them*."

"How are you recovering from that? It seems like it should have killed you."

"The pills," she answered simply.

"Well, how did you get them?"

"Never leave home without them," she said with a slight smirk.

"I'm glad you know how to make them…and, thank you for all you've done for me, Marie."

"You're welcome."

Aiden had been quiet the entire time but he finally spoke up. "We get to leave for earth in three days."

"We get to leave?" Carlisle asked. He was surprised. "Aren't we prisoners?"

"We don't have to be on the moon to be their prisoners," Aiden said.

Carlisle nodded, understanding exactly what Aiden meant. The High Court and the High Royals reach was far and wide, further than any human could ever fathom.

The day came where they went back home and for the most part, the instructions were to act as if they were strangers until further, specific instructions. Carlisle reverted back to his billionaire playboy self, trying to do anything he could to be distracted from the reality of what existed in the world and what he was destined to eventually do.

One day, Carlisle received word that billionaire Aiden Easton had died of pancreatic cancer. No one had realized he was sick despite there being rumors that he was struggling with his health.

Two months later, Carlisle received a letter from Carla Saintvil, stating that Marie had died in a car accident, a bizarre explosion that left no remains of her body. A funeral announcement and the details of the ceremony were included.

Carlisle's time still hadn't come yet, however, and he was eager to show those he loved just how important they were to him and to say goodbye in his special way. He had to be discreet or the High Court would have no problem ordering their murders or sending some Fires to eliminate them. That was a fate Carlisle was not willing to have his mother and step-father suffer.

Wearing the gold tie that had meant so much to him over the years, Carlisle went to visit them and spend some quality time with them, as the boy they knew growing up, not the billionaire that the world thought they knew. It was a special time and Carlisle sensed how his mother and step-father sensed something was going on.

"Are you going to be okay, baby?" his mother asked.

"Yes Mom. I love you."

"I love you, too."

Carlisle hugged his mother, then his step-father and walked away. He had instructions to go to Canada to Aiden's cabin. It was there that he would wait. And it was there that someone sent him a mysterious packet, along with a video of something that they believed he would 'find of interest' happening on the moon.

He read the letter first:

185

Ethan is on the moon and he is training hard. He's a Fire and he has a lot of favor with the High Court and High Royals, who know about his former relationship with you, Carlisle. He's working on a research team and has learned the language of the High Royals, showing that he is someone whom they are beginning to trust. He is aware of your fight and has seen the tape. As you know, revenge on you is something he has sought out for a long time. First by becoming a billionaire; and, now by becoming the one thing that can destroy you. Be alert and aware ...

That was all the information that the letter contained. Carlisle turned to the minute disc and put it into his computer, waited a few seconds for it to load and then witnessed something most startling on it.

Ethan was walking on the Moon Base and he came across a creature that almost blended in with the surface of the moon itself. It looked almost like an octopus, black with white speckles and many tentacles. It was moving slowly. Then the video flashed to Ethan walking in some corridor—some place that was unknown to Carlisle—and he stumbled across a room. He walks into it and there's total darkness but suddenly audio came on the video, making Carlisle jump. He would know the sound anywhere. It was Ethan's voice.

He asked something in the language of the High Royals.

A High Royal walked up to him and grabbed him by the throat and shoved him out of the room. He shouted something else and slammed the door.

How strange, Carlisle thought. *Clearly this means something. What?*

A week had passed .Carlisle got to researching, discovering that the odd creature on the moon was something called the Lilith Seed. Then with some light enhancement technology, he brightened the video just enough to realize that the room that Ethan had been walking through was filled with the Lilith Seed creatures and there was some large, foreign machine toward the back of the room.

This is key to something but what?

Carlisle decided to give his brain a rest and he turned on the television and saw his picture. He turned it up to listen. A reporter was saying, "Carlisle Elias Lewis has been murdered. Allegedly, his private doctor administered him with improper medication which lead

186

him to have a cardiac arrest in his pool...." The words faded as he saw a picture of his family attending his funeral.

There was no way to describe seeing yourself die on television but Carlisle didn't have time to dwell on the thoughts about it because there was a knock at the cabin door. He got up and walked over, feeling tense.

"Yes," he said, staring at two men in black suits with black sunglasses on and a black SUV parked in front of the cabin.

"It's time for your trip, Mr. Lewis, come with us please."

There was nothing that Carlisle needed to take. He walked out the door and followed them, finding himself arriving at a familiar place. Yes, it appeared that he was boarding the Virgin Galactic once again and heading off to the moon.

Part Two

19

"Sometimes we run into people's fists in the craziest places."

There were five other beings on the flight to the moon, two human and three of different origins, although Carlisle didn't know where. It was a quiet ride, Carlisle lost in thought. He'd been growing stir crazy in Canada but he wasn't sure that he was ready for what was to come. So, it was a long, quiet flight with him distracted at the images of his mother's sadness in those pictures of his funeral.

The three level clearing process to enter Moon City seemed to take forever but finally the Virgin Galactic landed and the door opened, revealing the extended ramp that they could exit from.

Carlisle got off first, looking around and immediately taking note of the beautiful, crystal blue eyed servant with the ruby red dot on her forehead. She was waiting for him and had a serene smile on her face. Despite not being human, she was clearly beautiful in her own way, as were all the servants on the moon. They were like perfect beings, just not human beings.

"How was your flight, Mr. Lewis?"

"Fine, thank you."

"I'll take you to your room," she said.

"There's no need. I remember where it is," he said.

"You have new quarters, Mr. Lewis. Follow me."

Carlisle didn't really have any more attachment to his moon room than he would a hotel room so he shrugged and followed the servant. She pressed a few buttons and the door slid open and Carlisle walked in and she walked away.

Around the corner were three people: Aiden, Marie, and Ethan. It left Carlisle speechless.

<u>What the hell is going on?</u>

Ethan walked right up to Carlisle and extended his hand out and Carlisle couldn't even talk. He reached his hand back but found out that he was receiving a swift sucker punch to the jaw, not a handshake.

"Ouch…what the fuck!" Carlisle said, immediately feeling aggravated.

"Thought you'd left me behind, huh," Ethan said, this time moving forward and giving a swift forearm hit to Carlisle's ribs.

Carlisle didn't hesitate and he charged toward Ethan, ready to show him that he had some skills, too. He put Ethan's hand in a lock but Ethan retaliated with a drop and sweep, sending Carlisle flying back.

"Enough already," Aiden suddenly said, stepping up and stopping the fight. "You are not two children anymore with a score to settle."

Ethan listened to Aiden but got up and glared at him before storming out of the room.

Never one to not try to get the last word in, Carlisle shouted out after him. "It's nice to see you, too, man."

Ethan turned around one last time and made a small lunge forward but just flipped Carlisle off and then turned back around.

"What the hell was he here for?" Carlisle asked immediately, feeling more agitated than he had since the day he'd had to fight the twenty Fires.

"This is where we'll be getting the technology we need to take the trip and discover what we need to find," Aiden said.

"How are we going to do that secretively? This entire place is clearly on camera; I got some footage myself of that asshole that just punched me finding some freaky shit."

"Yes, I made sure you got that, knowing that your curiosity would keep you occupied. It can get rather stir crazy at the cabin alone, only training, researching, and watching television. So, how was your death?"

Carlisle raised his lip and showed that he wasn't going to dignify it with an answer.

190

"Just trying to lighten the mood," Aiden said, putting his hands up in the air but his face revealed a mischievous smile.

"How is Ethan here?" Carlisle asked, still stunned to see him in person. He hadn't seen him in person since that court date so long ago when Carlisle had prevailed in the law suit.

"He's a Fire but he's also a billionaire now due to a battle he was in," Marie said.

Carlisle noticed that Marie had a fond expression on her face when she said it.

Does she like that shit? Unbelievable.

"Let's get down to business because we don't have much time," Aiden said. "We are going to be going to talk with the Council today so you need to get dressed and be presentable."

"And don't be arrogant," Marie added.

"That may be hard," Carlisle said, a smile breaking out on his face.

Marie was quite serious, though. "Well, it's important that you keep your composure, got it?"

"I got it. We've gone through too much now to have me goof it up with a bit of ego."

"Ah, with age comes wisdom," Aiden said.

An hour later, a servant was escorting Carlisle, Aiden, and Marie into the High Council's meeting room. This was only the second time that Carlisle had been in there but it was less intimidating this time because only two Royals were standing in there, along with one strange figure. There was no shock and awe about seeing such an odd variety of powerful, intense life-forms like there'd been the first time.

"You have a half hour to state your case," the one High Royal said, remaining standing and staring at all three of them with a certain look of disdain upon its unique face. The bony peak that extended off the back of its skull was longer and larger than most, making it look as if it could make its head tilt backward at any moment.

"By the year 2069 the Earth will no longer be inhabitable because of the increase and unrestraint of $\sum CO^2$, population growth, self-destruction of the humans, and the contagions that exist on the planet itself. Our research has proven this and that data has been forwarded to your undersecretaries," Aiden said confidently.

Carlisle listened closely as Aiden went into business mode. There were very few men in the world as good at business mode as he was.

"Waging a war is not an option because it would become a wasteland. Eventually, we will need to find a new place to live or we will become extinct."

Aiden paused and looked at the Council members to gauge their reaction. It didn't seem to bother them one bit that there may be no humans in the future.

Putting his hands out in front of him, Aiden made his plea. "You have been chosen to lead your race. Your ship has all the technology you will need on your mission, your captain is High royal Faust, a highly reputable and notable Royal."

The strange, unknown figure stepped up and Carlisle looked at him. That must be Captain Faust.

"The second in command is High Royal Cadmus," Aiden continued. As he spoke, Carlisle took in his sight, too. He had snuck into the room from another entrance just before his name had been called. "And, as per our discussions, I would be the third ranking member of the exploration space ship."

"Yes, we are aware of all these things," one of the High Royals said. "We've decided to let you go, despite what happened last year." The High Royal looked at Carlisle and then to Marie. The fight with the Fires was apparently as close to an unforgivable sin as you could get on the moon. "However," they continued, "we will be sending along one of our researchers, too."

Ethan walked into the room next and Carlisle couldn't hide the annoyance on his face. At that moment, he felt as if he was being presented with the biggest challenge of his life. That was saying a lot all things considered.

"You're dismissed. Details for your departure will come when needed," the High Royal said.

Aiden nodded, as did Marie, and Carlisle followed suit after he received a friendly nudge from Aiden's right elbow.

Later that day, Carlisle knew he had to find Ethan and try to smooth things over. It was the right thing to do and he couldn't afford to have their personal tension and friction jeopardize the mission. That wouldn't be fair to anyone.

20

"Just when you believe you've seen it all; something new and more amazing comes along."

Carlisle set out to find Ethan on the Moon Base. He needed to resolve matters because there was no way he was going to go into a different galaxy or dimension with the guy being so hostile toward him. It would jeopardize the mission and make it miserable, too. Neither was an option Carlisle was willing to accept.

It didn't take long to track Ethan down. He was in a large domed room that was all glass and sitting right at the edge of it, staring out of it at Earth.

"Mind if I sit down?" Carlisle asked.

"Go ahead, I don't mind," Ethan said, not bothering to turn his head.

"What do you think of everything happening?"

Ethan shrugged his shoulders, not saying a word.

"All the money in the world and we can't even enjoy it. Pretty crazy."

Carlisle hadn't meant to anger Ethan by bringing up money but he clearly did. The vacant look that Ethan had on his face turned serious and angry. It was a look that Carlisle had seen many times in his life, even if he hadn't in the past few years.

"More money, more problems, I guess," Carlisle continued.

"I don't know if you're trying to provoke me but you'd better watch it, fucker," Ethan spat. "You're a back stabbing piece of shit. You took all the money and didn't give a rat's ass."

"You're doing fine," Carlisle justified, "and besides, the judges sided with me."

"I can't stand you, Carlisle. If it wasn't for the situation we're in I'd rip your arms off and beat you until you died, eat your eyeballs, and drink you're blood."

"You're a Fire?" Carlisle asked. It was an odd question but he couldn't think of anything else to say.

Ethan ignored his words and Carlisle felt the need to get back to the reason why Ethan clearly hated him.

"I did all the leg work for that idea, Ethan, and you know it. I invested the resources and did the tough part. You walked around partying, spreading the word, piggybacking off of my efforts. An idea doesn't mean you get half the wealth."

Ethan stood up and began to point his finger just an inch from Carlisle's face. Carlisle didn't blink or avert his gaze. "You left the only friend you ever had, when I needed your help the most .I kept pushing you to do it .I even helped you with the name and you got a billion dollars! If I wouldn't have took you to that Brazilian girl's apartment you would have never. I couldn't even help my ....oh god... You backstabbing son of a..."

Carlisle stared at Ethan, seeing his eyes turning red. He jumped up and took a few steps backward, uncertain of what Ethan may do if he lost control.

"That's right, fucker," Ethan hissed, "I'm evolved; I'm better than you." Then he turned around to a table that was next to him and smashed his fist down on it, splitting it into two and sending slivers of wood flying from the force of his punch. Then he walked away, leaving Carlisle in shock.

Carlisle made his way back to his room, thinking about what had just happened and how much had changed from the fun days of his youth. Despite some of the hassles there had been a lot of fun. The past years had been so busy that he hadn't had time to think about it but now ...

He lied down on his bed and drifted off to sleep with all the vivid images of his youth and the fun he had. Then it turned ugly and he found himself forced to stare and watch the High Royals eat his parents and feast on their flesh, glancing at him with satisfied grins. He wanted to move but he couldn't; he was afraid to and he was embarrassed by it. His throat felt constricted and he kept swallowing, trying to find a way to clear it so the words would come out.

"Stop!" He finally screamed it and lunged forward, trying to stop the High Royal that was closest to him.

Then Carlisle froze, realizing that he was strangling his pillow and that it had all been a dream. He was sweating so badly and his t-shirt and boxers were stuck to his body, his sheets soaking wet. He got up and glanced at the clock. It was early morning.

Sleep wasn't going to come again so Carlisle took a cold shower to calm down and then made his way down to eat some quick breakfast and then go to the room where they were preparing for launch. He had to do something—anything—to get the chilling dream out of his mind.

It was no surprise to see that Marie and Aiden were already there, preparing for the launch. He walked by another room and saw Ethan in there, hanging out with two High Royals and the strange figure he'd seen the day before—the crew.

Carlisle didn't know if Aiden knew that Ethan was a Fire but he was going to make sure he did. With any luck, he'd find a way to get it so he wasn't on the mission. Whatever research he can do hardly seems worth it if he unleashed his best, could it?

When Carlisle was within ear shot, Aiden quietly said, "They can see through walls, you know."

"I don't have a good feeling about this, Ethan's a Fire."

"Don't worry about that. Focus on the task at hand. I've spoken to him and he's an okay guy."

"One who wants to kill me," Carlisle protested.

Aiden stopped and looked at Carlisle. "Look, we spoke and he told me his side of the story. He's an okay guy."

"Don't get me wrong, Aiden. I just feel like it's my fault that he's one of them now…that I somehow pushed him to it," Carlisle countered.

"He made the choices that led him to this place. Like all things, we take the benefits we can and eliminate the threats when necessary. That is not necessary right now."

"But…" Carlisle countered.

Aiden didn't let him finish. "But nothing, no need to feel sorry for him."

The two began to walk away toward the platform that led to the ship, which was gold and grey, another unique vessel in this mysterious world Carlisle found himself living in. After making the walk up the long ascending platform, Aiden and Carlisle boarded into an elevator, or at least what looked like it was an elevator from Carlisle's perspective, and the door shut.

A low, buzzing noise started to sound and blue rays shot out of the sides of the elevator and moved up and down their bodies.

"What's it doing?" Carlisle asked, feeling a bit leery.

"Scanning our bodies."

"Kind of trippy. Will it do this every time we enter?"

Aiden laughed. "Yes, it has to recognize that we are good, meaning that we haven't been infested or altered internally in any way that the ship doesn't recognize. Also, we need to be decontaminated as we re-enter the ship from our excursions on our search."

"I've never seen anything like it before," Carlisle said, more to himself, really.

"Of course not, it's hardly something capable of being made by a human."

"What do they need us for at all?" Carlisle asked. The thought had just popped into his head. After all, they ate humans and degraded them constantly. Why keep them around?

"We have one thing they don't understand—how we awaken."

"They can't do that?"

"No."

The box started to move upward and it was a smooth, quiet ride that almost made it feel like they were not moving at all. If not for the red, pulsing lights moving up and down Carlisle would have had no clue. It was smooth—like a Ferrari on the Audobon.

Finally, the doors opened and they revealed a large room, a cockpit of sorts, and Marie was standing there, looking at a bunch of instrumentation that seemed like it would need someone in NASA to interpret.

Marie leaned over and punched in a code on a keyboard. Green lights lit up everywhere her fingertips touched and as the last code was entered, a holographic control panel appeared out of nowhere directly in front of her. Carlisle looked down and saw that she was standing on some pad.

That must be a sensory pad; something to make this all work. He was fascinated and mesmerized just like any person would be seeing something that was so high tech that they would never believe that it *really* existed without visual evidence.

A soft, gentile voice that didn't fit the machismo of the ship sounded out—apparently out of thin air—and said, "Hello, my name is Watson. How may I assist you, Marie Saintvil?"

Marie responded like she was talking face to face with someone. "Watson, show me the ship's layout and its features."

Within two seconds, a holographic image of the ship was in front of Marie and it was talking about the ship's features, turning the green color of the holographic lines into a bright blue hue as it discussed that certain area.

"Amazing," Carlisle said out loud. "Watson's probably smarter than most humans."

"Definitely has access to all things it learns," Marie said, "using all its memory, not just a fraction of it the way the human brain does. Without Watson, this likely wouldn't be possible."

"Indeed," Aiden agreed. He put his hand on his back and patted it before walking closer to Marie. Carlisle followed.

Through watching Marie interact with the hologram and the voice, Carlisle learned where the sleeping quarters were, the eating area, the restrooms, and the gravity conditioning room. He was pretty sure he knew what that was and it was an exciting thought.

"Come on," Aiden said, "Marie will brief us later. Let's look around ourselves."

Carlisle had no problems doing that. He was fascinated with every single aspect of the ship and wanted to absorb it all firsthand.

As they walked about the ship, which had many corridors that were marked by numbers, High Royal symbols and letters to keep them straight, Carlisle was pleased to have Aiden share some specific insight about the ship with him.

"The ship has a robotics room, which you'll want to get familiar with and be comfortable with."

"Why?" Carlisle asked.

"It'll perform suit upgrades, quality checks, and make sure that every precaution necessary is being taken to ensure your safety."

"What type of suit? Like an astronaut's suit?"

"Similar concept, I suppose, but these are considerably more advanced. They are customized to work efficiently for every type of terrain and atmosphere we encounter, regardless of the galaxy or dimension we enter."

"Okay, geometry was never my strongest subject. What does that mean, exactly?"

"Dimensions are very different, depending on where you are and can have different qualities. All of them are ones we can be awakened in; however, some may be two dimensional, others three, and some four."

"Are there any with a higher number than four?"

"Not that have been discovered yet," Aiden said. Carlisle had been joking but the answer he received was quite matter-of-factual.

Aiden looked down at his watch. "It's time for us to go. I have someone for you to meet."

"I thought I'd met or seen everyone on this mission."

"We have one more. His name is Christopher Blackwell. Marie and I don't know much about him so we'll have to watch him closely."

"Chosen by the Council?" Carlisle questioned.

Aiden nodded his head, relaying that was his hunch. "An unexpected change. Either way, until we know more about him we'll be alert. He's clearly important to be here on such short notice and with so little red tape."

As an afterthought, Aiden added, "Carlisle, I want you to stay away from him until we find out more about him."

"No problem," Carlisle said. It wasn't a big deal to him.

"What's up with the other two Royal's?"

"I'll tell you later. We've got to go because it's time to get this ship launched."

They walked back to the room that Carlisle took to be the cockpit, for lack of a better term, and they all took their seats and prepared for launch. Carlisle looked over at the latest addition to the crew, Christopher Blackwell, and was immediately fascinated by what his story might be. He was very pale with black hair and the same piercing blue eyes that the servants of the moon had. By Earth standards, he would be considered part of the Goth craze but by the universal standards, he could be anything at all. What that was remained to be seen.

21

"Every man needs to have that day where they awaken and understand."

From the few minutes that Carlisle and Aiden had left the control room of the ship it had grown in intensity and action. In the background an alarm was sounding off at a loud enough frequency that you had to pay attention to it.

"What's up with the alarm?" Carlisle asked.

"It's what they use to prepare all the ships systems and get everyone into place," Aiden said. He opened his mouth to say something else but wasn't given the chance.

"Attention everyone!"

All eyes turned to the source of the command.

The hideous monster known as Faust was staring into everyone's eyes and without saying another word to show it, he got the attention he demanded.

Faust began to pace about and Carlisle couldn't help but stare at him, taking in all his grotesque details. His muscles seemed to be on the outside of his skin and it looked like he'd been burnt badly but it seemed to be more of a protective shell, a hard exterior to match a seemingly hard beast. He was everything that a kid's nightmares would be made of from Carlisle's perspective.

"I am your Captain, Faust, 29th ranking General of the legion. We are about to embark on a critical mission—one of more importance than any of our species has ever faced …"

Carlisle noticed that his second in command, Cadmus if he recalled correctly, followed exactly two steps behind Faust and seemed to know exactly when he was going to turn and do everything. It was a miracle they didn't collide or trip over each other.

Faust continued. "… This mission will be successful, as per my expectations as well as the orders of the High Council." He paused and looked around, focusing on Carlisle and then

Aiden and Marie. "If there is any insubordination of any sort I will have no problems killing the insubordinate myself. Is that understood?"

Carlisle had no idea if he was literally supposed to answer that question so he followed Aiden and Marie's lead and remained silent. Faust walked around, looking at everyone more closely and Carlisle could smell the monster's peculiar scent. It was kind of musky but also a bit charred as if its flesh had been burnt.

Faust stopped in front of Carlisle and leaned in, whispering in his ear. "Once this mission is completed and we're successful, you and I are going to have a little one on one talk, human."

The two looked into each other's eyes briefly and then Faust walked away, calling out, "Prepare for launch."

Aiden grabbed Carlisle's arm and guided them toward their seats. "Keep your temper in check—your life depends on it," he cautioned.

Carlisle nodded. It was shocking that the monster that threatened to eat his eye balls when he first arrived at the moon seemed tame and harmless compared to Faust. The man…it…whatever you wanted to call it was seriously a seriously freaky looking badass.

The seats were large and when Carlisle sat into it, it suddenly changed shapes, adjusting itself to his exact body size. It was startling at first and felt too confined but there was nothing that could be done about it and if Carlisle was going to cause trouble it sure wasn't going to be about a seat. On the other half of the command room Ethan took a seat and did his best to ignore Carlisle.

"Sequence beginning," a female computer voice said. "10, 9, 8…3, 2, 1…launch."

Blue lights started to circle around the command room, appearing out of thin air and they moved quicker and quicker, simulating a strobe light of sorts. Carlisle closed his eyes, feeling like they were going to make him sick. He could tell that they were moving but much like in the elevator, it would have been hard to notice if you really weren't paying attention. When he finally opened his eyes, he looked up and saw a bright moon ahead of him.

"What's that, Aiden?"

"A moon in the next solar system."

"We've already went into another solar system?" Carlisle asked. "Now I'm really confused."

"Time works differently up here," Aiden replied. "You'll get used to it after six months."

"Six months? What do you mean?"

"That's how long it'll take us to travel to Planet 05141984, our destination…in time that you're used to."

"That is a long time," Carlisle said. His biggest concern was wondering if Ethan and he could make it on the same ship for that long.

The nauseous feeling that Carlisle had upon launch had subsided and he no longer felt like he was going to get sick. He began looking around at all the amazing things that could be seen from the windows of the ship. There were bits of debris, more stars than he'd ever thought possible, and in the distance, earth's solar system could be seen.

Ah, yes, earths solar system. I hope that dream of my parents wasn't real.

"What's that over there?" Carlisle asked, pointing to the right.

"That is a black hole," Marie said. It seemed odd to finally hear her voice for Carlisle because she'd been so quiet and focused that entire morning.

"Is that where we go through?" Carlisle asked.

Marie rolled her eyes briefly and then stopped herself. "I forget you're new to all this. No, we don't go through there because if we entered into a black hole we'd have no idea where we'd end up and the ship would get damaged without the proper shields. We need to focus on specific targets that we've been mapping out and studying for many years."

"Hey Marie, don't black holes suck you in or something like that?"

"It could, but not a ship like this. This ship is equipped to handle unique explorations and the vast challenges of our expansive universe."

"So, do they know the answer to the big universe question up here?" Carlisle asked.

"What do you mean?" Marie asked.

"Do you know where the universe ends?"

"No but we don't need to know that; it's irrelevant for this mission," Marie said quite frankly. Carlisle glanced at her and could tell she meant it, too.

Aiden cleared everyone to get out of their seats and went over to talk to Carlisle.

"We have six months and a lot of work to do," Aiden whispered and said, taking control of the conversation. "Our past attempts to get you to astral project have been highly unsuccessful and you have to master it by the time this ship lands. You're going to have to be very focused and pay attention."

Carlisle looked at Cadmus and Faust, making Aiden grab his arm and add, "Focused on us, not them right now."

"Okay, I'm not a kid. I got it, good behavior and focus," Carlisle said. He'd never liked getting told what to do and that had never changed despite all the mad changes that had taken place in his life.

"For now, let's rest until we get there," Aiden said.

"That's a good idea. We want you well rested," Faust said.

Carlisle couldn't help but notice that everything the High Royal commander said sounded like it had a double meaning.

Faust began making a series of commands and pressed some buttons and from what he said, Carlisle could tell he was putting the ship on an auto pilot of sorts. Then everyone moved to a different room that was at the end of the corridor to the left of the command room and each person or beast put their hands on a sensory pad and from above, a chamber of some sort slowly descended from the ceiling and they got in. It was just big enough for you to lie in and stretch out but there was not room for anything more.

Carlisle sought out eye contact with Aiden or Marie to find out what was happening, exactly. He didn't like feeling like he didn't know what was happening and for someone who'd typically been one of the smartest guys in the room he suddenly felt a bit dumb, quite out of place.

"These are newly upgraded hyperbaric chambers, they will put you in stasis state while you sleep." Aiden said, "it's time to take these." Aiden handed Carlisle some pills and said, "Swallow."

"What are they for?"

"To sustain nutrition," Aiden said, "now, we've got to get going. See you in awhile."

That was odd? What does that mean? Carlisle thought. Well, there was no time to dwell on it now. Carlisle nodded and got into the pod and a door shut around him. The temperature was perfect and the mattress was very comfortable. It made it seem a bit less small because it was so comfortable.

With no concept of time, Carlisle laid in the chamber and fell in a deep sleep. The thought about his parents began to wonder in his head. What would they say about this? Were they doing okay now that they believed him to be dead? And, of course, what would they say if they realized he was a billion miles away in a space ship trying to find the next Earth?

The most pressing concern he had was how he was going to master astral projecting and understand the entire astral plane thing he'd heard about. It was hard for him to fully grasp it.

A voice began calling out to Carlisle and he looked around but he couldn't find it. "Open your eyes, Carlisle. You can do it."

He blinked, not sure what was happening. The voice repeated itself but Carlisle couldn't find it. He kept blinking. "My eyes are open; who is this?"

The voice grew a bit more intense and it said, "Open your eyes, douche bag."

"Marie?"

"Who the hell else?"

Aiden's voice could be heard next. "Knock it off, Marie. Remember he's new to this."

Then Aiden spoke directly to Carlisle, although he couldn't determine where his voice was coming from. "Okay Carlisle, listen up, remember the training back at the cabin in Canada.

Remember what we taught you about learning astral projection and allowing your psyche to travel to different places. That's what's happening at this time."

"My eyes are open but I can't see you," Carlisle said again, not liking that sensation.

Marie said, "Picture yourself opening your eyes, Carlisle."

He tried but couldn't do it and panic set in and he felt like he was being suffocated.

"Calm down, Carlisle," Marie continued, "listen to my voice and come toward it. Take it step by step, nice and slow. You're doing good."

"Open your eyes, Carlisle," Aiden said again. "Picture yourself opening your eyes and you can do this. You're ready."

Determination set in and Carlisle focused hard on opening his eyes and walking. A blurry vision of Marie and Aiden came into sight for him and he felt as if he needed glasses. They were so distorted but they were there. *Thank God I'm not blind,* he thought.

As he adjusted, Carlisle saw that Aiden and Marie looked more like ghosts than anything else. They were blue shades and their eyes looked to be a silvery grey metallic. They were also floating like they were ghosts or some paranormal creature, too. Neither was wearing clothes but it was like their private parts were sort of filtered out, not even showing nipple on either…only the outline of breasts on Marie.

"What happened to you guys?" Carlisle asked. He looked down and saw that he was in the exact same state.

"This is what happens when our pineal glands are cleansed and activated. This is astral projecting, Carlisle."

"And the Silphium helped with this?"

"You got it," Marie said.

"I feel dizzy." Carlisle dropped to his knee, or what would be his knee in a solid mass form, and held still, hesitant to move. "It's like I'm on a Gravitron machine at a fair."

Aiden laughed a bit. "That's natural, Carlisle. Your pineal gland has never awaken before and it's trying to figure things out. It has to get in tuned with you activating it."

"How come you didn't tell me this is what we were going to be doing?" Carlisle asked.

"You would have over-thought things and it wouldn't have happened," Marie replied.

"How long did it take me to do this?"

"Quite a while. Month and half to be exact, Carlisle."

"Month and half? How could I have gone without food for a month?" Carlisle asked.

"The pills sustain nutrition and the chamber has your body in a complete stasis remember," Aiden began, "but the pills also stimulate your pineal gland and give it a chance to be as healthy as possible to astral project with fewer risks."

"Why did you have me stop taking the pills then, Aiden?"

"Well, Carlisle, they are like a steroid and we didn't need you to have this ability any time before now. It wouldn't have been wise…or necessary."

"Did they help me survive the fights with the twenty Fires?" Carlisle wondered.

"I think so," Marie said, "it upped your intelligence and awareness to get pretty innovative in taking care of those Fires."

Carlisle couldn't see Marie's eyes the way he was used to seeing them but something in her voice made him believe that she was thinking of her punishment of the whippings for helping him in that fight. It had impacted her more greatly than either her, or Aiden, let on.

"Can all humans astral project?" Carlisle asked.

"Yes, but the High Royals don't allow for it for most of us."

"How do they control that?"

Aiden's form glowed in front of Carlisle but he could see his hands moving as if he was giving a business presentation, making him very identifiable. "They control humans by putting a chemical into our water and food. 89% of everything we eat and drink is filled with this chemical."

"So, there must be some consequences to doing thing this," Carlisle said, his analytical mind kicking in.

Marie glanced at Aiden and then turned to him. "There are to our physical beings. For every year we astral project we lose two years of our lives. It could be a bit more or less depending on the amount of training and discipline you've done and how you finesse it."

"Is it possible to lose my human shell forever? Am I looking at your souls, my soul?"

"We take precautions to not lose our soul and there is a link. You can see it more strongly with Aiden and I because we are more practiced." Marie turned herself slightly and Carlisle noticed a flickering light by the base of her neck, almost like a bolt of lightning.

"I didn't see that before," Carlisle said, feeling confused and disoriented again.

"You must also practice Awareness when you are Awake. That'll help."

"Can I go anywhere in this state?" Carlisle asked.

"Yes, but it takes a lot of practice. Teleportation is a very advanced skill, one that even Aiden and I haven't mastered completely. It's a last resort—always. Basically, it's like a muscle and the more you exercise it the longer you can maintain it."

"Okay," Carlisle said. "Can the High Royals do this, too?"

"Not that we know of, which is why they control it in humans," Aiden said. "Since they come from another dimension we believe that it is not possible for them to achieve this."

"What about a Fire?"

"You mean Ethan?"

Carlisle nodded.

"No, Fires cannot do this. The larva inside of them feeds off their pineal gland and every time they are hurt they rely on the larva to heal them. In the process of this exchange they lose a bit of their soul, it becomes weaker," Aiden said.

"Until they have no soul left," Carlisle commented.

"I want to show you something," Marie said, extending her hand out to Carlisle.

"Trust her," Aiden added.

Carlisle did as was asked and as soon as he felt the connection with Marie's hand he felt as if he was being lit up—he was the light bulb and she was the power source. It was so strange.

"Think about the space around us," Marie continued, "everything is going to start to fade now, as if someone was dimming the lights until there was complete darkness. Do you feel it?"

Carlisle could only nod his head because he's been temporarily rendered silent, not sure how to take it all in. Then the area faded back and an endless blue land could be seen and above were billions of stars.

"This is the astral plane. In order to awaken and unlock your body to its full potential, you have to concentrate here."

This place is so amazing.

"How do I do it?" Carlisle asked.

"Follow my lead," Marie said. She knelt down and closed her eyes. Carlisle did the same.
Then Marie continued talking. "You need to focus, like you're staring at an apple or something small and specific. Once you have that visual honed in, you are going to picture yourself back in your body."

Then a loud humming noise started to echo in Carlisle's mind and a piercing pain penetrated his temples—or where they would be. He curled himself up in a fetal position trying to get the pain to stop but it wouldn't. He was growing dizzier.

Marie and Aiden were above him.

"What's happening?' Carlisle asked, his voice quiet but full of panic.

"Your body is still stabilizing. It needs to rest. You're not strong enough."

Then everything went dark and the pain subsided.

22

"Idle time is like an invitation to invite the demons in."

It had been hard to believe that Carlisle and the others had been on the ship for almost six months already. Each and every day Carlisle still found a way to be amazed at the ship's intelligence, too, thinking that if most humans were half as intelligent as Watson seemed to be that the world he'd grown up in would have been considerably different. However, he also realized that a world that didn't include any have and have-nots based on their individual efforts would be rather dull. He'd joined the society Aerial introduced him to because he liked being a have and rising up from the ashes like a phoenix from poverty. That seemed like eons ago, not five years ago.

As much as possible, Carlisle practiced his astral projecting with the help of Aiden and Marie. Aiden was more patient with him than Marie.

"Who teaches you two these things to keep you advancing?" Carlisle asked one day, feeling desperate to not be the only one who needed a teacher.

Marie started to answer but Aiden cut her off. "We taught each other. What we can do is limitless but we have to keep conditioning ourselves, pushing the inner most parts of our brains and bodies. Things can get tricky when months seem like years."

That was strange; feels like he's hiding something. What?

One big problem that Carlisle had and he sensed Marie and Aiden had, too, was how bad his headaches were after he astral projected. They didn't seem to lessen over time and, in fact, the more agile and gifted Carlisle became when projecting, the worse the headache would be when he left his awakened state. It was a concern, one that none of them talked about because they didn't want to portray weaknesses to Faust, Cadmus, and on a personal level, Carlisle didn't want to do that in front of Ethan, either.

Carlisle had been making an effort to make amends with Ethan but it had been a slow process. He couldn't help but reflect on his role in the destroyed friendship either. He'd done what any logical business person would do but now that he was a bit older and had way too much time to think about "things," Carlisle knew that he hadn't really handled the situation the best he could.

One day, after recovering from a headache he'd gotten while meditating in the astral plane to make his body stronger, more fit, Carlisle decided to go over to Ethan's hyperbaric chamber and see if they could maybe—just maybe—talk things through.

"Hey, how you holding up?" Carlisle asked.

Ethan looked at him oddly. "Great." He said nothing else.

"It's hard to imagine that we could have ended up here. Even seven years ago it would have seemed impossible, huh?"

"Yeah."

Carlisle kept asking questions and Ethan's patience ran out. "Is there something that you need, Carlisle?"

"No, just wanted to talk, man."

"Well, I'm busy," Ethan said. He turned around and Carlisle walked away.

I am going to get that thing out of him and help Ethan return to his normal self, Carlisle thought. He was positive that Ethan would have given him a chance to show he was sorry if he wasn't injected with the larva and a Fire.

Walking around, trying to avoid Christopher Blackwell, who never spoke to Carlisle but didn't hesitate to show that he was assessing him closely, Carlisle stumbled upon Marie, who was very engrossed in something on the ship. She was in a large room that he'd never been in before. He walked in and coughed, announcing his presence.

"You really are obsessed with studying this ship," Carlisle said jokingly.

"It's unbelievable—the most innovative piece of equipment I've ever seen," Marie said, staring at something.

"What's this room all about?" Carlisle asked.

"You won't even believe it," Marie said, not turning her head.

"Try me."

"This is a cloning room," she said.

"And they just let you walk into it?" Carlisle asked, most fascinated with that over anything else about it.

"Well, I asked permission but before I did, I'd walked through the walls to get into it."

"You what?"

"Astral projection benefit; you're obviously not quite there yet. Takes a lot of time to understand fully. You might get lost"

"I guess you certainly kick my ass on that benefit."

Marie laughed. "I kick your ass in almost everything."

"True…can't dispute that."

Marie continued talking but didn't look up. "I remember when I was a child, a High Royal showed me something like this. I didn't get it and thought it was odd but my father was in its favor and it thought I might be fascinated with it."

"The High Royal was correct."

"Well, I'm off," Carlisle said, not wanting to disturb her further.

"Okay…by the way, Carlisle, we have been on the ship for nearly a six months and we'll be landing soon."

That was great news for Carlisle because he was starting to get too stir crazy despite all that he'd been learning and the expansive size of the ship itself.

* * *

Aiden had been rather suspicious and quiet, making Carlisle very curious about it. Perhaps the isolation was wearing on him, too. Marie didn't seem to think it was out of the ordinary, however, and told Carlisle to worry about his own training, not what Aiden was up to.

213

One night when the three were astral projecting, Aiden shared what he'd learned the day before with Marie and Carlisle.

"I projected and went into the command center when Faust was meeting with the Royal Council earlier. I had a feeling something was up and had to be certain," Aiden said.

"What did you discover?" Marie asked.

"He said that they plan on experimenting with the two humans," Aiden said.

"Which two? There are four of us on here, right?"

"Technically four and a half if you count Christopher," Marie said. She was being rather light hearted despite what Aiden said and Carlisle quickly found out why. "We know that they wouldn't be interested in Aiden, or me either, Carlisle."

"That means …"

"You and Ethan," Aiden said.

"Well, what did they say?"

"They talked about a beacon coming from Planet 05141984 and Faust mentioned that the objective had worked and we were able to leave Earth's galaxy with the humans, making it ideal to start the experiment."

Carlisle was trying to stay calm, as per all the instructions had told him to do when projecting, but he was anxious.

"And then what?"

"I don't know. The conversation ended. Faust sensed something," Aiden said.

"But he didn't see you, did he?" Marie asked.

"No, but I went back to my body the second I suspected something and saw him just a short time later."

Carlisle realized that if he ever did what Aiden did he wouldn't be so fortunate because his headaches always wiped him out. Their determination to get him past that made a lot more sense after hearing about what happened to Aiden.

Everyone went back to their bodies quickly, knowing they had things to do and couldn't' be discovered out of their bodies.

Carlisle went to find Ethan right away; wanting to give him a warning about what he suspected may be true. He found him in the training room.

"Can I talk to you?"

"Free world," Ethan said. He was at the punching bag and his hits became more aggressive and rapid. Carlisle was pretty positive that his old friend was picturing his face on that bag and the thought of Ethan connecting with his face made him cringe. He packed a big punch with his new skills.

"I'm not perfect you know but I do try," Carlisle said, unsure of where else to start his conversation. Ethan punched the bag harder. "A person getting out the hood wasn't logical and two people getting out the hood was mission impossible."

Ethan smirked.

"So, you're rapping now and boxing," Carlisle said, stating the obvious. "You have always been smart, Ethan, and I apologize for how it all went down. You were my brother—are my brother—and if you hate me, you do, but I'll always have your back. It took me a while to learn that money is not worth a true friendship."

Ethan kept punching the bag, going rapid fire on it and not missing a solid connection no matter how hard the heavy bag started to swing.

Carlisle waited for him to say something and eventually said, "Well ..."

"Well what?" Ethan said. "You done?"

"Yeah, I'm done."

"Okay then."

215

Carlisle left and went to the control room, where he saw Faust and Cadmus and they seemed tense about whatever was going on, making Carlisle immediately tense. They were not prone to showing any sort of emotion whatsoever but from afar he'd learned to read their body language just a bit—every living being had it, regardless of where they came from.

"Get everyone in here now," Faust ordered as Aiden left.

An announcement went out over the system and Carlisle was already standing there waiting. For once, they didn't even seem to notice him or pay attention. It was only when everyone was in the room that they seemed to even notice.

"We are going to be departing the ship at thirteen hundred hours and starting our search," Faust began, "Our scan analysis had indicated that there is a temple on this planet; one that we had not known about until recently. Some beacon is going off that we don't understand so we'll need to be cautious and more alert than ever." Faust scanned the room, focusing on Marie and Aiden, and Cadmus followed suit, looking to see a sign that they may not be surprised.

Faust glared at each and every one of them and then continued talking and giving instructions. "Everyone will take samples and research the terrain. We'll be here for approximately one year, as that's how much time it will take to survey everything that is required to make an assessment. All actions are to go through me and be approved by me. All testing results and briefs of daily activities will be submitted to me prior to the dinner hour every night…or, you'll become my dinner."

Cadmus took over talking. "After this, we shall all report to the robotics room to have our suits customized for the journey in the smaller vessel to land on the planet and then the Survival Oculus's will collect samples as we all make our way toward the temple to investigate its origins and how it appeared without our prior knowledge."

"Any questions?" Faust concluded. No one asked any. Almost as if it was an afterthought, he turned to Aiden, and asked, "Is this temple something that you've known about?"

"No," Aiden said simply but Carlisle had a feeling that he knew something.

Why is this temple so important anyway?

"Any questions?" Faust asked.

Carlisle did what he seldom did, he asked one to Faust. "How do we know how to operate the Survival Oculus androids? I haven't been trained on them."

"They are quite intelligent, highly capable of functioning without your commands. In fact, it is you that will likely benefit from their protection and presence so there is no need to worry."

Faust just said more to me than he has this entire past six months, Carlisle thought.

"Thank you," Carlisle said.

Everyone was silent.

Then everyone was dismissed and went to prepare for disembarking from the ship and going onto the mysterious, planet.

For Carlisle, the entire past six months had seemed more of a concept than a reality and he found a million questions running through his curious mind now that it was time to actually go out and walk on a planet. He suspected he probably felt the same way that Neil Armstrong and his crew did the first time they walked on the moon.

"How long will we be out there?" Carlisle asked Marie.

"Hard to say; could be days, could be weeks. We'll be fine."

"What about food and water?"

"The Survival Oculus's can do a lot, convert most liquids to drinking water and we'll be dining on food capsules to keep nutrients in us and not make us feel starving the entire time."

"That's crazy," Carlisle said. "What about sleep?"

"You'll always sleep in your suit and you're never to unlatch it or take it off."

Carlisle thought of two things immediately: the bathroom and body odor. It must have shown on its face.

"The suits will take care of practically everything, including those things. It has filters that control body temperature, making odor a non-issue and the capsules you will take for nutrition don't have any waste in them, therefore no...well, you know."

Carlisle nodded. He was happy to go off of the 'well, you know' because he really didn't feel compelled to have a conversation about bodily waste with Marie.

They were in the robotics room getting fitted for their suits and Carlisle discovered something else that they'd all be using, too, as part of their equipment.

"Wow, these are fly," Carlisle said, looking at the glasses. They were titanium on the frame and sides with reflective, transparent lenses, and small sensors all around their frame."

"They are called Oculus X5Js," Aiden said.

"Kind of like Google glasses," Carlisle said.

"Those were the basic intro prototype for these. Google glasses have nothing on what these babies can do."

Marie stepped in and continued explaining to Carlisle. "You see, the atmosphere where we are going isn't so much like Earth's that we can handle it without these special glasses. Until your eyes adjust to the planet they will make it so you're less vulnerable, able to process everything with fewer hassles." Then Marie turned to Ethan. "Since you're a Fire you don't need these, Ethan. Your eyes automatically adjust."

He nodded and smiled at Marie. It was a smile that Carlisle knew well. He was playing her, navigating in. Didn't he realize that she and Aiden were a couple? Of course, that had never been said but Carlisle had just assumed from the way they acted and behaved around each other.

"It's time to leave," Cadmus said, walking into the robotics room.

Everyone walked like they were robots, following him to the smaller ship that would take them to land on the surface of the new planet. Carlisle thought about movies such as Land of the Lost and wondered what, if anything, they may encounter on this planet. A temple seemed lackluster by all means unless it turned into an Indiana Jones adventure.

23

"Normalcy is almost always an illusion."

Looking out at everything that surrounded them, Carlisle thought he was going to be sick. Everything was awful and he wanted to turn back around and go onto the smaller ship that had taken them to the planet's surface. *If this is what this world looks like, I'll pass*, he thought.

"Get your glasses on," Marie said. Carlisle looked to her and nodded, realizing he'd forgotten to put the Oculus X5Js on.

He quickly put them on and looked around again. A smile came across his face and he nodded his head in approval. The view before him now was more like it. Nothing was blurry and as crystal clear as could be in front of him he saw an amazing, lush forest. He felt as if he was walking into a rainforest somewhere in South America. Well, this wasn't South America but it was amazingly beautiful and vibrant. The colors were outstanding and the shades of greens, blues, reds, and yellows were similar but much brighter than what he'd known his entire life. Despite there being no blazing sun shining on the terrain, it, as well as the botany, looked like it was all lit up from the inside. It glowed outward—as if its very flesh was made of neon.

"This is incredible," Carlisle said.

"Make sure you keep those glasses on. They will help you familiarize yourself more quickly and learn what you need to know at a more rapid pace. The signals they send to your brain stay in your preferential memory bank."

"No excuses about I didn't know or I forgot, huh," Carlisle said.

"You got it douche bag," Marie said. She had a huge smile on her face and Carlisle's less than charming term of endearment from her had stuck with Marie…but at least the edge was off of it and you could tell that she actually did like him.

A gust of wind swept down over Carlisle and everyone else must have noticed it, as well. They looked up and Marie pointed to something. It had just landed on top of one of the tall trees and it was the most bizarre looking thing that Carlisle had ever seen, as far as a creature went. It looked to be a bird but it was more the size of what a megalodon shark would be like—and he knew because he loved watching Shark Week on Discovery. Its beak alone was about the size of an albatross and its claws as big as the steel stakes to hold down a seriously big building.

"Is it dangerous do you think?" Carlisle asked.

"Don't know," Aiden said. "Let's just avoid it."

That sounds easier to say than do, Carlisle thought.

Walking was a different sensation than it was than walking on Earth, too. Carlisle realized that he couldn't feel the ground below him and it gave the sensation that he was floating, yet he realized he definitely wasn't when he accidentally kicked a rock in front of him, sending a searing pain that traveled through the shoes of his suit.

They also came upon a pond and Carlisle stopped to look at it because the Survival Oculus that he was responsible for began to collect some water samples. The water was a light pink color with small yellow bubbles in it and it also looked to be thicker than the water on Earth, like it was Mountain Dew or something like that.

As the oculus collected and assessed its samples, Carlisle stared at something that was swerving in the water. It looked like a snake but when it went to the shore about twenty feet away from him it had all sorts of small legs on it and then it looked more like a centipede. Well, whatever it was, it became the mega bird's meal and that was the end of it. The bird flew off with its body dangling from its beak until it was out of sight.

"It's time to move on," Cadmus said suddenly.

Everyone followed orders and they began moving down the lake's bank until they were in a more open area where there were a few random trees on it with black circles hanging from them.

"What are those?" Carlisle asked.

"Baranji Fruit," Cadmus replied.

His oculus had an arm that began extending out, traveling up about twenty feet to reach the lowest branches where the fruit was dangling from. It began to pluck the fruit and Cadmus motioned for Carlisle to come and collect it all in a mesh bag that was part of the camping gear.

220

As Carlisle did that, Marie and the others took samples of flowers, soil, and even the creepy, crawly, rather large insects that were flying and crawling about.

Aiden had been rather quiet and on high alert, wanting to hear everything that Cadmus and Faust may say to each other. They seemed to realize this because they spoke in the native High Royal language, which Aiden only knew snippets of. It was a highly complex language and he knew that it had over one thousand characters and sounds in it. It made all other languages every known to man look like a breeze.

Carlisle watched Aiden as he pulled Ethan aside. He went up next to the two, wanting to know what was happening.

"What did they say, Ethan?" Carlisle asked.

If that language is so complicated how come Ethan knows it, maybe being a fire helped him learn something. Carlisle wondered. It wasn't to be mean but he wasn't a guy to apply himself to that type of thing.

"Not much but we are being followed. They don't want anyone to know."

"Why?" Marie said, looking surprised.

"Well, they are afraid you'll turn around and they'll be discovered, causing problems. And…they are afraid that some of you will try to play hero or warrior, causing us more problems." When Ethan said that part he looked at Carlisle.

"I'm not about to do that," Carlisle said, thinking Ethan was being a jackass. He doubted that's even what Faust and Cadmus said. Hopefully he wouldn't be more hell bent on yanking Carlisle's chain than being serious about the mission.

"Now boys, play nice," Marie said. She smiled at the two of them but again Carlisle noticed that there was something interesting happening between Ethan and her.

"There's the temple. It must be where the beacon they mentioned is coming from," Aiden said.

Everyone looked and saw a temple in the distance with mighty points and peaks on it. Even in the odd light you could see that it was made of colorful stones and was definitely made by something other than nature.

Three beeps sounded out and a flash of blue light shot straight up into the sky, making everyone jump up. The oculus's began going crazy, trying to assess what was going on and everyone was looking in every direction.

"Do you …" Faust began.

His voice was interrupted by a loud roaring noise that also sounded as ferocious as a thousand warriors giving a call to battle. Then there was a moment of silence—an eerie silence like someone would have in the eye of the storm—then five more roars sounded out and the number of roars kept multiplying. They were coming from all around, too, and in that moment, everyone knew that they were surrounded but they had no idea by what.

The ground started shaking and Faust screamed out, "Run to the temple—now!"

Everyone began moving but they were met with immediate resistance. Large insects with heads and manes like lions, wings like a dragon, and legs with pincers the size of motorcycles on them began to swarm in. Some were in the air and some were in the ground. They kept roaring and hissing, knowing their positions perfectly and what to do to take down the intruders.

Having no time to evaluate a plan, Faust began to fire at the creatures that looked like they came straight out of mythology book. Cadmus followed and as those guys fired, everyone else used their weapons to fend off the creatures. For Carlisle, it was the ultimate test of the skills he'd developed in training and using the fully loaded gun to increase his odds of coming out of the situation intact.

A creature swarmed down on him, making the most piercing roar, and Carlisle shot at them with rapid fire but his inexperience in combat left him without any ammunition and still plenty of creatures that wanted to see him die. Looking down to the ground, he noticed large tree roots and he ducked as a creature swooped in on him, grabbing the root and swinging it around like a staff, warding them off and dazing them as much as he could as they kept trying to sneak closer to the temple.

They were all in a circle, defending outward with their backs to each other. No insect could get in the circle unless one of them broke the formation. Hopefully that wouldn't happen.

Then the shots started to slow down and Carlisle turned his head to see what was happening. They'd run out of ammo and it was in that moment he got to witness the true power of the High Royals on the battle field. They were clearly more than just authoritarians. Faust and Cadmus began showing some mad skills.

Faust and Cadmus lunged toward the creatures, diving into them and stopping them as quickly as if the creatures had hit a stone wall. Large teeth were bared, snarling at the creatures and they attacked them rapidly, using their teeth to instantly wound them and their fingers as the daggers that sent them to their death. Ethan was doing the same thing, too, but he didn't seem to have the instincts of their moves down, although he definitely had similar strength. Limbs were being severed from bodies and the mighty looking wings of the creatures were snapped in half as Faust and Cadmus met their enemies and fought fearlessly.

Carlisle and the others, including a very curious and calm Christopher, were in the middle, watching everything. There was nothing any of them could do against such creatures, as they hadn't the strength or weapons to defend themselves. The roots had only been effective as a staff because of the other weapons, Carlisle realized and he wasn't about to try his luck with just that against the creatures. Their roars started to die down as they fell one by one but the ones left remaining were strong and fierce, certainly fearless. They were clearly ready to fight until death, just as much so as it was clear that Faust and Cadmus felt the same way.

Everyone had bits of blood on them and their suits had holes from the fights and battles they'd ensued. Faust began to bark out orders through their communication devices about what he wanted everyone to do. "Ethan, Cadmus, and I will create a diversion. Run to the temple as fast as you can, stopping for nothing or no one."

Carlisle started to dash toward the temple and Aiden was behind him, followed by Marie and Ethan.

A loud gasp sounded through the communicators and Carlisle turned around and saw one of the creatures taking Marie down. He turned around to go back to her—to hell with the warning—but Ethan was there. He leapt about twenty feet and jumped on the creatures back, using his strength to have it go backward and release Marie.

"Take me on, fucker!" Ethan screamed. His screams were a combination of what was necessary to handle the magnitude of it and a genuine warrior mentality that believed he was invincible and could conquer all.

With the type of intensity that comes from an array of emotions that include both mental and physical awareness, Ethan shredded the creature and plunged his hand into its chest, pulling out something that was throbbing—perhaps a heart but it was hard to tell. It was thick and black, moving in an odd rhythm, like it was rippling water not a heartbeat.

"Run!" Ethan shouted to Marie.

She held her hand out to help Ethan up but he sprung up and next to her immediately.

They began running and Faust gasped into the communicator. They turned around and saw that he was being swarmed in on by the creatures. There were two in the air and two on the ground. Each had a part of him and he was not in a position to easily defend himself. He couldn't release from their grasp or use anything for leverage to help him.

Cadmus ran up to him and tried to help but he wasn't able to do anything. The creatures were large and angrier than ever, therefore, they were more ferocious.

"Get to the temple. Run!" Cadmus commanded.

Aiden, Carlisle, Marie, Ethan, and Christopher began running toward the temple, obeying the orders but it was so hard to do. The sounds of injury and maybe death were coming into their communicators and it was distracting. They kept turning around, wanting to make sure that they were not being followed by the creatures and to hopefully see Faust and Cadmus catching up.

"This is enough of this shit," Aiden said, quickly turning back around and going toward Faust and Cadmus.

A creature swooped down on the remaining ones and Ethan and Marie went right to avoid it but kept running. They were all getting separated. Was it a sound strategy that would confuse the creatures or were they sending themselves to the slaughter by becoming more weak? Carlisle wasn't sure but he didn't know what else he could do.

Not sure what else to do, Carlisle kept running and he suddenly heard branches breaking and footsteps behind him, catching up to him rapidly. He turned around and saw that Aiden had Cadmus on his back.

"Keep running!" Aiden screamed this out and maneuvered on the bumpy, root-laden path like he wasn't carrying a heavy, large creature on his back.

"There's an opening!" Carlisle screamed, pointing ahead to a hole in the side of the temple.

They ran into the temple and the noise stopped. It was illuminated slightly in there from the glowing rocks but no creatures came in. Everyone was breathing hard and staring straight ahead.

"We've got to go find Ethan and Marie," Carlisle said between his heavy breathes.

"Faust first," Cadmus said, not showing that the gaping wounds and sticky green blood that came from them was bothering me.

"He's probably dead. Ethan and Marie escaped," Carlisle said.

In that instant, Cadmus was up and pressing his arm against Carlisle, sending him flying back into the cave and staying right by him, choking him from the pressure of his arm across the throat.

"We save Faust," Cadmus hissed.

Aiden and Christopher stood back. Aiden tried to get Carlisle's attention and shake his head that he should stop but Carlisle was instantly enraged, reinvigorated with anger and at that moment he chose not to exercise any control over his emotions.

"Let's get this straight, insubordinate, the High Royals don't need you but Aiden seems to. You don't call the shots and if you talk to me that way again I will not hesitate to eliminate you."

"Fuck you!" Carlisle said, shoving back with all his strength. It did nothing more than make Cadmus temporarily totter.

"Carlisle, stop!" Aiden finally screamed, running up next to him.

Aiden's tone got Carlisle's attention.

"We will not question Cadmus's demands or leadership," Aiden said with authority and a very recognizable tone of caution.

Cadmus turned to Aiden. "Keep him in line," and then turned back to Carlisle. "He just saved your life."

"What's next?" Aiden asked.

"If we don't rescue Faust the ship will explode. That must be done first and foremost."

"Explode?" Carlisle said and when Aiden shot him a dirty look he shut up again.

"It's a safeguard. I'll message Christopher and have him send a retrieval ship to us at this location."

Carlisle looked over at Christopher, who was standing there and his face showed he thought Cadmus was a fucking idiot.

"That is an android; experimental, but we thought it would be necessary. Blackwell's still on the ship."

"Clever," Aiden said, definitely intrigued by it. "Explains the excess quietness."

Cadmus spoke in the High Royal tongue and gave his commands to someone—presumably the real Christopher—and then turned back.

"We have approximately one hour," he said. Then he began sniffing around, acting like he was a tracking dog. "Someone's been here...recently before us."

"Who?" Carlisle asked.

"Or what...it's an unfamiliar sensation and it's more of a mental energy than it is a physical presence," Cadmus said.

Carlisle knew that everything was made up of energy but he'd never considered that the High Royals, or Cadmus, at least, would have the ability to sense a presence. It made him wonder just how much Cadmus may know about him from his thoughts. It took a mere look from Cadmus to see that he likely new plenty—especially what was running through his mind at that given moment.

Aiden walked up to Cadmus. "Permission to contact Marie and get clarification on Ethan and her status."

Cadmus nodded his head but didn't say a word.

24

"Instinct is also a powerful weapon."

Marie and Ethan's efforts to escape the creatures had taken them to a cave that they'd found behind a waterfall. They'd initially hoped that the creatures wouldn't enter into the water; that it would make it so they couldn't fly—something common in many winged creatures. They'd gotten part of their wish granted because the creatures didn't follow them; however, they could be heard roaring outside and it was obvious they were swarming the area, knowing that Ethan and Marie would eventually have to leave.

It took Marie glancing at Ethan one time to realize that he needed help. She began frantically looking for something in her pouch to clean his wounds. He had gaping wounds on his arms, legs, and one on his neck. She leaned over him and began to frantically look for something to help clean the wounds. Finding an abandoned shell from some animal, she picked it up and headed out toward the waterfall.

"Don't," Ethan called out weakly.

"We have to clean the wounds," Marie said.

"I can heal myself, Marie. Benefit of being a Fire. You need to stay safe and worry about your oculus. It has damage, too. Fix that first."

Marie began to protest and Ethan whispered, "Please."

Marie and Ethan's eyes locked for a moment before the sound of Aiden's voice came through her glasses. "Marie! Marie! Can you hear me?"

It was really loud in the cave from the waterfall and Marie shouted out, "Yes."

"Are you okay?"

"I am. Ethan's hurt but we're doing good. We're behind the waterfall in a cave. The creatures are swarming outside but they won't enter through the water. Right now, anyway."

"Once we make sure we're stabilized we'll come and get you."

"Okay, but hurry. Ethan's badly hurt and losing a lot of blood. He needs attention that I can't give him."

"And you're Surveillance Oculus?" Aiden asked.

"Damaged but repairable."

"Hold tight until we get there," Aiden said. Then his voice was gone and Marie turned her attention back to Ethan.

She sat down next to him, unsure of what else she could do. She didn't have what she needed to save him. "Why didn't you run? You could have gotten away but you turned around."

"I just did. Don't make me regret it," he said, coughing violently and oozing blood from the corner of his mouth.

"Fine, maybe I should leave you here," Marie said casually. Her words would indicate she didn't care but her eyes had a different message.

"Maybe you should," Ethan said. He turned away.

"Ethan, why don't you like Carlisle? I know he can be a bit of a douche bag but he seems to mean well."

"You've got that right. Honestly, I'm so used to disliking him that it's probably more of a habit than anything else. I've wanted revenge on him for so long."

"About O.R.B.?"

"Yeah, but it's not really the website as much as it is a betrayal by someone who was my best friend. We were brothers, tried and true, and I never thought he'd stab me in the back and leave me hanging during the time I needed him most." Ethan began coughing and Marie reached over and squeezed his hand to calm him down.

"I understand completely, douche bag," she said and laughed softly.

Ethan started laughing, too, and before the two knew it, they were talking casually about a great many things. Each opened up to each other more than they had up to that point.

Wriggling to get up on his elbows, Ethan sat up as much as he could and took one hand to pull Marie closer in. Ever so slowly and softly, he kissed her on the lips. "I've wanted to do that for a long time."

"Why'd you wait so long then?" Marie said, kissing him back.

For the next minutes, the two were lost in each other and Planet 05141984 didn't exist in their thoughts. They were hidden in their own intimate spot, a secluded paradise and there were only the two of them.

"Marie! Marie! Copy," Aiden called out.

"Copy," Marie said, not able to wipe the grin off her face.

"We're outside of the waterfall but will need you to come out."

"Ethan's weak. I need you to..."

Ethan interrupted. "I can make it out." He mustered up his strength and stood up, almost toppling over onto Marie. She sprung up in a second flat and put his arm around her neck to support him.

"We're on our way out."

The two walked out and Marie looked around, realizing that everything was too quiet. Where had the creatures gone? Surely they hadn't just given up. She surveyed the area to find where Aiden might be and finally saw them standing on a small cliff about a hundred yards away. She waved and they began to run toward Ethan and her, Carlisle leading the way.

He ran over the rocks, moving quickly and assuredly to meet them as quickly as possible. Once he got there and grabbed Ethan, Marie turned around to run back into the cave.

"What are you doing?" Aiden called out.

"I have to get the Surveillance Oculus," she shouted.

A loud roar came from above and three of the creatures were circling around the waterfall, starting to descend downward to their potential prey.

229

"You run and get it. I'll ward them off," Aiden ordered.

Cadmus shouted out a command to Carlisle to get back to the ship with Ethan while they got Marie back.

Carlisle nodded, half wondering if they were trying to kill him. Thankfully they'd restocked his ammo and he'd learned a valuable lesson from firing too rapidly when they'd first encountered the creatures.

Try to count your ammo and stay calm.

The blood was flowing freely out of Ethan and it attracted many curious creatures. Birds like vultures flew from above, hoping to see the two bodies collapse so they could have an easy feast.

"Hang in there," Carlisle said to Ethan. He looked to Ethan, who could only nod his head.

Ethan's body was becoming more like dead weight and they kept tripping as they ran but every time they fell, Carlisle would get them back up as quickly as he could. His weapon was in his left hand and his right hand held onto Ethan's, helping to support him.

"We're almost there, brother" Carlisle said. He turned his head and saw something swooping down at him through the corner of his eye. Without even having to look directly at it or break his pace, he fired and hit one of the creatures, who gave a mighty last roar as it spiraled down toward the ground, bouncing off the thick branches of the trees that separated it from the ground.

Voices sounded from the background and due to their ability to run at a quicker pace, Cadmus, Aiden, and Marie caught up to them. The ship was in sight and the creatures were starting to flock around it, two even sitting on top of it as they waited for everyone to arrive.

"How are we going to get past them?" Marie screamed.

"Leave that to me," Cadmus said. He released a small canister from his side, one that Carlisle had thought was a water flask, and pressed a button on it, counting down from three to one and then threw it up over the ship and it clinked on it between the two creatures and began to emit a strong gas at a very rapid rate.

230

The creatures screeched in horror and began to fly. Cadmus shot the fleeing creatures to ensure they wouldn't follow or attack. It was very erratic and they couldn't get their bearings straight, or so it seemed from below.

Then the ramp to the ship lowered and the group of five ran into it and it rose back up immediately.

Everyone was breathing hard, feeling slightly victorious from escaping the creatures but also knowing that they had to head back out onto the planet to rescue Faust. That was a mission that couldn't wait for them to rejuvenate or catch their breath. They had to dig from deep within and make it happen.

Marie took Ethan to the medical room. "After I drop him off I'm going to go make a few surprises for our retrieval mission. I have a feeling we'll need them," she called out behind her.

Aiden, Carlisle, and Cadmus went into the control room, where Christopher was standing. "Any indications of where Faust may be?"

"We believe we've pinpointed his location," Christopher said. "Watson, pull up Faust coordinates."

Watson made a hologram appear out of thin air with the geographical terrain and map of the area between the ship and where they believed Faust was.

"It looks like a straight shot but quite a bit uphill," Aiden said.

"Yes but with some severe temperature variations along the way," Cadmus said, pointing to some green spots that seemed to be pulsating.

"Like steam holes?" Aiden asked.

"Possibly. We cannot say for certain but our suits should be acceptable for any temperature they are, no matter how severe," Cadmus said.

Carlisle tried to process his words. "And if they're not?"

"Well, we either are stuck here if Faust dies and the ship blows up or else we have to risk it. There's just one choice," Cadmus replied.

231

"Let's go," Carlisle said, taking a picture of the terrain with his glasses so he could reference it if necessary.

They ran to the armory, where everyone picked their weapons. Aiden and Carlisle pulled up a computer screen that went over the inventory to decide which ones would be best to use. Aiden chose an assault rifle and a flame thrower, while Carlisle chose dual guns and a sub machine gun.

"This should do it, combined with my blood saber I'll be ready for whatever shit this planet throws my way," Carlisle said.

"I don't doubt it," Aiden said with a coy smile. "Let's get to the robotics room now and get suited up. Marie should be in there by now."

Marie was in the robotics room and Carlisle was amazed by how fast and smartly she worked on their new suits. They were exoskeleton armor, which was tougher and thicker than any other know material, all while being lightweight. Carlisle mused that it didn't feel like he had anything else on but was so well protected. Too bad they couldn't wear it all the time. It seemed logical.

"The bombs are in the feet and there's also a jet pack that you'll have to be able to conquer whatever you find up high or down low."

"It's good to have options," Carlisle said, laughing. It was a nervous laugh because his heart was racing like crazy but he really was pumped up to show these creatures and the mother fuckin' planet they'd landed on that they would not best him.

While Carlisle did the final adjustments to his exoskeleton suit, he overheard Marie lean in to Aiden to ask him a question. "Why are we helping with this retrieval mission? Do you really think this ship will blow?"

"I don't know for certain but we can't risk it on this hostile planet. Plus, they're searching for something and I want to know what it is. Until we get more information, we'll go with the flow and keep them alive," Aiden replied.

"It's time to go," Cadmus said, walking into the room. Carlisle hadn't even realized he'd disappeared until he reappeared.

Four warriors, as well as a group of Survival Oculus androids that Marie had programmed to operate weapons, walked out onto Planet 05141984 again, ready and armed to make the estimated twenty minute trek to where they believed Faust was being held.

25

"A warrior knows no defeat."

An eerie sound came from the cliffs of the mountains where the beasts chanted and howled to the sky. The noises could be heard from below as the rescue mission commenced. No one spoke and everyone was on high alert, wanting to make sure that they could hear anything that might be happening.

Carlisle looked around, his eyes quickly and constantly assessing the ground, the trees around him, and the rocks on the sides of the path they were taking. They almost looked like they had faces in them and he was reminded of villains that were made out of rock and suddenly attacked unsuspecting people.

He shook his head, trying to get the thought out of his mind. He was determined to show the High Royals and everyone else that he could conquer. His lessons had been learned and he had it in him to do what was necessary to survive. No one was going to bring him down—no one!

A weird sound that sounded like a slow leak in a tire began to sound out. It was hard to tell where it was coming from but when Carlisle looked down he saw an odd sight. There was a tree that was moving from some sort of breeze. Only the air was stagnant.

"Watch out!" Carlisle yelled, breaking the piercing silence.

Everyone stopped and turned around, weapons drawn and trying to figure out what he was shouting about. "The ground, it's going to blow!"

Carlisle ran forward and shoved both Cadmus and Aiden out of the way. Marie was out of reach from him and she turned, her eyes wide open, and then something went flying over Carlisle's head right toward her. It was Ethan.

Ethan wrapped Marie in his arms and went flying off to the side, where they landed forcefully against the rocks that lined the pathway. Just as they hit, the ground erupted and a loud, hissing burst of steam went flying straight up, making the air immediately humid and foggy.

"How are we going to see?" Aiden said.

"Our senses," Carlisle said, knowing how he needed to rely on his awareness to make it through this.

Once everything was deemed to be under control for that second, Cadmus turned to Ethan and hissed, "What are you doing here? You should be healing."

"I'm good," Ethan said, turning away.

At first Carlisle couldn't figure out why he'd healed so quickly and then he remembered—Fires could heal themselves quickly because of the larva but each time they did, they became a bit less human.

There was a new sound that was coming closer to the rescue crew next. It sounded like something was being dragged on the ground and they all looked down, trying to focus below the fog that was still lingering.

Something touched Carlisle's leg and he looked down to see something huge and round slithering past him. That's a fucking snake! It's head was past Carlisle and it clearly wasn't interested in the rescue party for a snack because it ignored them all.

"Watch out, it's some sort of Snake," Carlisle whispered, hoping that everyone could hear him from their communicators in the helmets of their exoskeleton suits.

"I see it," Aiden said, "it's heading up the hill. Let's follow it."

"It's responding to the howls of the creatures up on that cliff," Marie replied.

"Let's use it to get us to Faust and then kill it as soon as possible," Cadmus said.

Everyone followed the snake and stayed only a few feet behind it. It was about thirty feet long from their estimates and about two feet in girth. It was almost like a mutant, having two tongues that constantly flitted out to smell and detect what was around it—or in this case, what was waiting for it.

Climbing up the cliff was more challenging than anyone had anticipated. The rocks were loose and they kept toppling down and making it challenging for them to remain anonymous. So far no creatures had come after them so it seemed that they were safe. None of them were about to assume that was correct, though. They couldn't take any chances or make any false assumptions because they wanted to make it out of there alive…and with Faust.

The howls that had been in the distance before suddenly became very loud, making it seem like Carlisle's ear drums would burst. He was getting ready to pull his sub machine gun when he suddenly heard a rocket being launched from just behind him. It whizzed past his head and he turned around to see what the hell was happening.

There was Marie standing with a bazooka and she'd sent the rocket into the snake that was up ahead, sending fragments of its flesh flying everywhere and the main part of its torso flew into the air and off the cliff, landing with a forceful thud in the ocean below; one that sent drops of pink water flying up onto the cliff. Their presence was definitely known and it was show time.

The creatures started to roar, letting all of them within hearing distance know that there was trouble. Everyone pulled out their weapons and prepared. Carlisle ran into a cave that was on top of the cliff and quickly assessed six creatures in there, all hovering around Faust in a protective manner, and popping out their talons as their preliminary line of defense.

Faust was in chains and he was staring at Carlisle, assessing him critically despite the rather compromising situation he found himself in.

Breathing in, Carlisle looked to the side of the cave wall and ran over to it as quickly as he could, running halfway up it and launching off of it, doing a half body twist in the air and coming down with a forceful thud with his blood saber, severing one of the creature's heads. His right hand was holding the semi-automatic still and he aimed it as he landed on two feet, kneeling on the ground toward the head of another creature, pressing the trigger so the bullet flew out of his barrel and in between the eyes of that creature. It almost seemed to move slow motion and he could see the bullet doing as he commanded it to in his mind. In another swift motion, Carlisle severed the chains that were binding Faust's wrists so he could move.

The two quick deaths of their companions left the four remaining creatures dazed for a brief second but it was only a second. They began to walk toward Carlisle, trying to enclose him in a circle so they could attack from all angles.

"I don't think so!" he shouted, dropping the sub machine gun and pulling out the dual guns from their holsters at his side. He began to travel in a circle, shooting at the creatures and shouting for Faust to duck and crawl out of the cave to the others.

Flames were coming from the outside of the cave and Carlisle looked back, seeing Aiden blasting them away. There was something gaseous in the cave, though, and the rocks started on fire, releasing a green, glowing flame that sizzled.

"What are though's flames?" Carlisle asked.

"Barithium gas. Get the hell out of there, douche bag!" Marie shouted.

Carlisle backed up but hadn't gotten all four of the remaining creatures. He was trapped between them and the flames that Aiden was firing off from the flame thrower.

The suit can handle a lot of heat, he thought, remembering what he'd been told. It was his only choice and it gave him an idea.

"Come and get me," Carlisle shouted to the two creatures, who were coming at him quickly.

"Faust, get behind me," Carlisle ordered the High Royal and he listened, not having any other choice.

As the creatures came closer, Carlisle kept inching nearer to the flames, egging them on to come and get him.

"I'm sending Faust out, Aiden. When I count to three you need to stop the flames out there and quickly fire into the cave. Got it?"

"Got it but hurry. I am almost on empty," Aiden said.

"1, 2...3!" Faust dove out of the cave and Aiden rolled to the ground in a ball, protecting himself from the flames. In an instant, the flames connected with the creatures and they started to catch on fire, smelling like scorched feathers, fur, and flesh. Their shrieks lasted for only a few moments and then all was quiet.

"Get the hell out of there, Carlisle," Marie ordered.

He got out of there just as the top of the cave collapsed in, burying the charred remains of the creatures of the cave.

Carlisle got out and looked at Faust. "Here, you take this back to the cargo ship." He whipped off his jet pack and Faust put it on and took off, moving with masterful precision.

"Faust is on his way back," Cadmus said, advising Christopher, who was in his spot at command central on the ship.

Although Faust was on his way back to the ship, there were still four people up there, fighting off the slew of creatures that didn't seem to ever stop coming to attack.

"How many of these bastards are on this planet?" Ethan asked, as his body got smashed into a set of rocks by one. Their talons were stuck in his chest and you could hear his ribs cracking as he landed. He gasped, barely able to move.

As the words came out, another creature flew straight down, spiraling down like an arrow that had been shot high into the sky and was returning to the ground, and it bit Ethan's leg, taking a huge gouge out of it and sending blood spurting in every direction.

"Ugh!" Ethan screamed.

Shots were being fired from everywhere and Carlisle was aware that they had to get moving quickly because they were all running out of ammo. The bazooka was tossed aside, he lost the sub machine gun in the cave of fire which collapse, and Aiden's flame thrower had lost all its juice.

Carlisle couldn't get to Ethan but he shouted out, "Here," and tossed him one of his guns. He still had one and his saber that he could use.

Ethan emptied out the clip and dropped three additional creatures.

Carlisle ran over to him and helped him get up, he started to make his way down the hill with him.

"You guys cover us until you're out of ammo and then take the jet packs back. We have to go by foot. Faust has my pack."

The packs weren't big enough to hold more weight than the person who wore the exoskeleton so they weren't an option for Carlisle and Ethan. Carlisle was fortunate to have a suit on but Ethan had just gone out with minimal protection, not having been fitted for one by Marie.

Making their way back down the path, another one of the heat spots burst and made it foggy again.

"Can you see through this?" Carlisle asked Ethan.

"I can," Ethan said.

"Okay, you let me know if anything is in front of us. If it is, all I have left is two shots and one bomb. We have to use them wisely."

"We're out of ammo and heading out," Aiden said. "The Survival Oculus's will ride it out to the end and then self destruct, leaving the final surprise."

"We're halfway there. Keep a look-out for us," Carlisle said.

Running as quickly as he could, Ethan managed to keep up despite the gaping wound in his leg and the severe loss of blood. He definitely was a step closer to not being human. It was easy to tell.

Cadmus was suddenly hovering over them on his rocket pack and he paused for a moment, staring at Carlisle curiously. Carlisle looked back at him and it seemed like an awkward pause that took an eternity despite the madness.

Why did he stare at me like that? Carlisle didn't have time to contemplate it but it made him uncomfortable.

Finally, the ship was in sight again and standing at the top of the ramp as it was lowered was Faust. Marie, Aiden, and Cadmus quickly threw off their jet packs on the ramp and then ran to help Carlisle and Ethan onto the ship. The ramp closed and everyone collapsed on the inside, exhausted and once again, Ethan was in need of emergency medical attention to repair his wounds. He'd stripped his soul two times in one day.

"Damn, that was something," Carlisle said. "Whew! We did it!"

"You were amazing, Carlisle," Marie said, breathing heavily.

"Don't think that I owe you anything for what you've done, human," Faust said. The commander walked away, leaving Carlisle standing there with his mouth agape.

239

He was ready to call out when he felt Aiden's hand on his arm. "Don't do it. It's not worth it and we can't have problems. Got it?"

Carlisle looked at Aiden and nodded, seeing that it was more than a friendly suggestion to keep the peace. It was more of an order.

26

"It's nice to know that not everyone is out to kill the human race."

Carlisle was left with Aiden and Marie since both Faust and Cadmus had went to the control room. The only thing that everyone seemed to be in agreement on was that they wanted to get off that planet as quick as possible. But where would they go?

"I'm getting a bad feeling about this," Carlisle said. "How could all this advanced technology not pick up on those creatures?"

"I agree. I'm not sure but we know that they don't mind if any humans die, myself included," Aiden said.

"And what about Ethan? Is he going to be all messed up in the head now?" Carlisle asked. "I'm having a hard time processing this Fire thing."

"He'll appear the same to you, as he has that ability, but each time he has to heal it's a bit more intensive."

"So are there larvae on this ship or something for these cases? And, if so, isn't that dangerous?"

"Ethan recovers in a water pod. Since the larva is in him his recovery process is different," Aiden said.

"And definitely quicker," Marie added. "I am going to go check on him."

She walked off and Carlisle looked at Aiden, who had a frown on his face. "You alright?" Carlisle asked.

Aiden nodded his head. "I'm going to go astral project and see what I can find out from Faust and Cadmus," he said abruptly. He walked away, leaving Carlisle alone.

Carlisle decided to go to his quarters and write in his journal. He'd been tracking everything that happened in that journal just in case he'd ever need to reference back or someone wouldn't believe him if he had to tell them. He knew he wouldn't have believed his story just a few years ago.

After writing in his journal and hiding it—or so he hoped—Carlisle just laid on his bed and hoped to get some sleep. His body was exhausted and his head ached slightly, the headaches never completely disappearing now that he'd begun experiencing astral projecting and being in the astral plane. It was his greatest challenge by far and that was saying something considering he'd become a monster slayer and a warrior of sorts.

When Carlisle awoke he saw that about four hours had passed. He was curious to see what Aiden may have found out and went to pay him a visit.

He knocked on his door and Aiden called out for him to enter.

"How did you know it was me?"

"Every knock is different. It's easy to tell if you just pay attention."

Carlisle nodded his head, impressed as always with the sense of awareness that Aiden and Marie had about everything. It made him wonder why Aiden didn't want to just admit that it seemed Marie and Ethan had some sort of special connection going. Awareness about relationships was clearly a different thing than awareness of surroundings.

"What did you need?" Aiden asked. "I came by earlier but you were sleeping."

"I was just wondering if you found anything out from Faust and Cadmus about their plans."

"They're up to something," Aiden began. He sat down in a chair and folded his hands in front of him and leaned forward so he could talk without his mouth being seen by any possibly hidden cameras. "They've found a new planet that we're going to be heading to—Planet 01291954. Once there, if there's intelligent life we're to remain alive. If not, well …"

Carlisle nodded his head. "It just doesn't make sense."

"To me, either, but just go along with what they say and don't let on. It'll be hard for you but I'm counting on you, got it, Carlisle?"

"I won't let you down, even if I'd like to wipe that snarky royal attitude right off their mugs," Carlisle said.

"You and me both," Aiden said, laughing.

"Even if I'm not going to be projecting?" Carlisle asked.

"You just never know when you may have to in a place that isn't the safety of this ship."

"Did they say anything else, Aiden?"

"They mentioned that in that temple Cadmus's body was scanned by something that was curious as to its make-up and intelligence."

"I didn't notice anything like that," Carlisle replied.

"Me either but I could tell he was attuned to something and it was odd enough to him that he only gave us partial disclosure. I can't imagine what it was, though. Well, you best get back to your room and be as rested as you can be for anything. Make sure you keep taking the pills to keep your nutrients up."

Carlisle got up and walked out. He realized that the thought of that wasn't as unnerving as it would have been just a few months ago. He'd come a long way and he knew that there was a long way to go but he was going to make it out of the situation all the better for it. He'd survive regardless of what they brought at him. In his opinion he had no other choice.

On the way back to the room, Carlisle walked by the medical room and saw Marie sitting in there talking with Ethan, who was now sitting in a chair. They were laughing and Carlisle couldn't help but notice her finger gently tracing a pattern on the top of Ethan's hand. It forced Carlisle to look at Ethan and assess him: was he still a man? And, most importantly, could Carlisle really be friends with a Fire? After all, he'd had to kill twenty of them just a few years ago to prove something to the High Royals.

As his hand began to punch in the code for his room, Carlisle heard an announcement sound out over Watson that said everyone was to report to the command room. He cancelled his room code and walked down to the room, waiting for everyone else to show up.

Aiden came in about a minute after him and two minutes later, both Marie and Ethan entered. Cadmus and Faust were standing in the center of the room and Christopher was standing in the shadows behind them, not wanting to be a part of the presentation but certainly all ears.

"We have our new assignment," Faust said. "We are going to be moving on to Planet 01291954."

Carlisle noticed Marie looking at Aiden. She hadn't known about this the way Carlisle did from their conversation. She was looking for some sign of information in his eyes but she didn't' receive it.

Cadmus continued. "This planet is made up of 70% water, making it similar to Earth in that regard; it's water that our tests show can be drank by humans. We'll be arriving tomorrow and then we'll head out to explore. You're dismissed."

The group may have been dismissed but that didn't stop the questions from rolling off of Marie, Aiden, and Carlisle's tongues. Ethan, on the other hand, seemed to be quite comfortable trusting the High Royals completely.

Another day came and the ship landed, sending everyone out on another mission except for Christopher and especially Ethan, who Faust had personally commanded to stay behind that day. He wasn't dumb enough to ignore the commander's order.

"Let's hope this is a bit friendlier than what we encountered yesterday," Marie said.

"We'll see," Carlisle said, "but if it isn't, I'm ready." He patted his reloaded dual guns and blood saber, smiling confidently.

"Yeah, just what we need—Billy the Kid in outer space."

"Sounds like a cool sci-fi movie if you ask me," Carlisle spouted off back.

"Hey you two, save the bickering for later this is serious, we don't know what's out there." Aiden said.

"Okay, Dad," Marie said cockily. Carlisle glanced over and saw that Aiden's fists were pulled tight.

"There's another temple on this planet," Faust said casually as they were walking on the planet.

244

Marie had been watching her oculus android collect samples then she suddenly stopped, looking at Faust oddly. Why would he just say that now? She glanced at Carlisle and Aiden, seeing that they both wore the same curious expression she did.

They began walking toward the temple and Planet 01291954 was definitely different than Planet 05141984. It was calm and serene, so tranquil and very beautiful. There were no deformed bugs or giant creatures roaring and swooping down at them to kill them.

"This is almost freakier," Carlisle said laughing. He was never the one to enjoy silence in tenser situations.

"Be quiet, human, and listen," Faust commanded, sneering at him.

Carlisle's mouth opened, ready to say something but Aiden punched his arm and indicated he'd better be silent.

Everyone walked around, trying to find possible danger amongst the beauty. There were so many shades of blues on this planet, each one gorgeous and something that an artist would long to capture on canvass if they so desired.

You could hear Cadmus and Faust sniffing the air, looking for signs of life. The sound was irritating to Carlisle, making him think of a rat. It was kind of fitting because he sensed they were rats. He'd been around enough of them during his lifetime to know.

"Is anyone here?" Marie called out. She wasn't silenced the way that Carlisle had been, though.

There was no answer and they walked around a bend. Marie had been in front and she stopped walking and stared at what was in front of her with an awestruck expression. There was a temple standing in the distance. Surrounding it were mountains made of grayish blue stone and light blue sands that swirled in a way that they looked almost iridescent.

"This is so beautiful," Marie said. "I've never seen anything like it before. It looks brand new, doesn't it? I don't know how that could be because this place seems deserted."

Aiden glanced at Cadmus and Faust after Marie made her comment. The two gave each other a knowing look.

"What do you think, Commander Faust?" Carlisle asked, wanting to test the waters just a bit. He didn't care if it bothered Aiden. This was his mission, too, and if he was so important to it his voice should be heard. He wasn't some petulant child.

Carlisle turned to Faust for an answer and the commander said, "Let's go into the temple."

He's just going to ignore me? What a jackass!

They all walked closer to the temple and upon closer inspection it looked to be much older than what Marie had initially thought. It was still in remarkable condition, however, and ornate carvings were all around it, making it a museum piece that most curators would pay handsomely to secure.

"So amazing," Aiden said, looking around.

"Not as amazing as the inside," Carlisle said. He'd walked in through the giant arched door and was standing in a room that was brighter and more sparking than anything he'd ever seen before. "I think this room is solid gold…and I'm not kidding."

"This must be worth billions," Carlisle said, his eyes lighting up. Gold would always do that to a kid from a rough 'hood.

"Yes, but it isn't our billions," Aiden said cautiously.

Marie stepped in. "I don't think he was implying…"

Carlisle cut her off. "Oh yes I was. What does a barren planet need gold for?"

"It's obviously not barren. How else would this be built?" Marie asked, shaking her head.

"Pay attention and stop your arguing," Faust growled. He turned to everyone and his eyes grew wide.

Everyone turned to what he was looking at and saw a giant ball of light flying at them. Just like that, the light penetrated Faust and Cadmus and they froze in place, unable to move or even blink. Then the light continued to move and it flowed right through Aiden, Marie, and Carlisle.

Their hands seemed to float off the triggers of their weapons and their silence was one of intrigue, each looking as relaxed as if they'd just gotten an hour long massage. They all looked around but didn't see anything. Where had the light come from?

Carlisle looked at Aiden and Marie. Their pupils had turned white and he glanced over at a golden wall and saw two white lights reflecting in his eyes. They'd turned white, too.

From the corner of the room, a creature was standing there that had a catlike head but a human looking body that was twice as tall as any of the three staring at it. It was looking curiously at Carlisle, Marie, and Aiden.

"Welcome," it said in a soothing, almost hypnotic tone.

"Who are you?" Faust asked. Apparently they could still talk despite not being able to move.

"I go by many different names," the catlike human said. "Some call me Ephira, while others call me Felinxia."

"Which do you prefer?" Faust asked, showing great respect to the creature that he certainly never showed to a human, or any other being for that matter.

"Felinxia will be fine," she answered, still talking in a silky voice.

"Why have you called out to us?" Faust asked next.

"We approached you many ages ago, hoping this day would come," Felinxia said.

"What is it that we can do for you?"

"We are a neutral race that travels to different galaxies and dimensions in search of technology that will help us in our pursuits," Felinxia began. "We trade for these things, offering one thing for another, ensuring we all benefit from our agreements."

"We've traveled for many light years to meet you. I am not the leader of my race. Before we can trade I will have to consult with my Council and then I can return."

"I understand, may you go in peace," Felinxia replied.

The freeze was removed from Faust and Cadmus. Faust bowed and walked away, taking steps backward like she was a queen…perhaps she was.

Carlisle had an uneasy feeling and he saw that Aiden felt the same way.

They all left the temple, more confused than when they'd entered into it. Carlisle looked to Cadmus and asked, "Why did we leave?"

"Don't you dare question the captain's judgment, human," he snapped.

"Ugh," Aiden said softly.

"What is it?" Marie asked him.

"I don't know," Aiden said, shaking his head, "just a jolt, I guess."

Carlisle knew Aiden was lying and he flashed through the images in his mind and was pretty sure he'd seen some light hit Aiden when leaving the temple. What was it and why did it focus on him?

"What's happening to the ground," Marie said.

As they walked back toward the ship the soft sands were starting to get very hard, as if they were turning to concrete below their feet.

"That's far enough. You're not going back to that ship," Aiden said to Faust. He drew his weapon and when Faust turned around he was completely surprised.

"What did you say, human?" he asked, trying to maintain his composure.

"You heard me. Why don't you explain why you are really here, you bastard."

27

"Sometimes it boils down to a good, old fashioned fight. Are you willing to risk it all to fight for what you believe to be right?"

In an instant, the tables had turned and both Marie and Carlisle found themselves in an altercation that they'd anticipated but hadn't really felt would go down that day, at that very moment, on Planet 01291954. It wasn't challenging for either of them to point their weapons at the High Royals who'd always degraded them. As for Marie, she still had a personal vendetta against them for the whipping she'd received after helping Carlisle kill the Fires in the challenge.

"Talk!" Aiden demanded.

"I hate humans. You're always looking for hand-outs and now it's time to pay for what we've given you," Faust said, not hiding his hatred at all.

"What do you mean?" Aiden asked, shoving the butt of his gun into his chest. Faust was about a foot taller than Aiden but he wasn't going to back down.

Cadmus began to say something but Marie smacked him with the butt of her bazooka and it quieted him down right away.

"You humans are subservient to us. It's not what we can do for you; this is about what you can do for us and nothing is going to stop it, certainly not any of you."

Everyone was quiet for a moment, not sure what to say and how to assess Faust's statements and abrupt change of attitude. Faust decided to speak again since everyone was focused on him. "Of course, it would have been preferable to wait for the Council's instructions but this sudden turn of events means that I'll have to take control myself and do what's in the best interests of the Council."

"What is it that you've done for humans as a 'hand-out,' as you put it?" Marie asked.

"I shall grant you your answer but keep in mind, it's the last thing you'll ever do," Faust said. He smiled this time, looking absolutely delighted at the fact that the humans would finally be dead and out of his way.

Faust pressed a button on the band he wore on his wrist and an image flashed up in front of them. It was three dimensional and in color. An unfamiliar voice was talking while the characters in the image acted out the scenes—it was like watching a documentary.

Long ago we came to your Earth from another dimension to save it from the atrocity it had become. Despite your unique and abundant planet, it needed to be saved. We learned of this when we intercepted a signal that was trying to reach your Earth from another galaxy, one which we estimated to be several light years away.

At that time, the Council sent a scouting troop to investigate that signal. Before the mission was completed it was aborted. The scouting troop informed the Council that the ship was scanned and some unknown force pushed the scouting vessel back to the Milky Way Galaxy, Earth's home.

Such technology was too advanced for us to comprehend and we could not figure out what was trying to reach the humans, an obviously inferior species, and why. We needed to ensure it wasn't a threat to us.

We continued to monitor the signal and it kept growing stronger. There was only one option left—to send out another search party. We did and again, they were sent back and a barrier was discovered around your galaxy. Nothing could come in and nothing could go out.

Since we knew it was trying to reach your species we sent our servants to adapt and live among you and once trained deploy them to the beacon, but once again, the ship never reached out of the solar system. The barrier tightened and closed in, as if something out there knew we were trying to tamper with your species. That was a direct threat to us and our way of life, much less our plans.

Not knowing what we were up against, we have treated this species as a foe while trying to befriend it so we could expand colonization of your race, making you subservient to us and the servants to replace those on the moon as they become extinct.

We chose two subjects in which to experiment on: Aiden Easton and Marie Saintvil and called our experiment Project Genesis. Marie was chosen because a High Royal took a liking to her for some unknown reason and had been a friend of her fathers, a prodigy among humans, we all admit.

The dimensional image shut down and Marie and Aiden stared where their miniature likenesses had been just moments before.

"So, as you can see, you will not be returning to Earth. You are too much of a threat to your kind…and ours," Faust concluded.

The cockiness couldn't be hidden from Carlisle's voice. "So, you're saying that this is it, huh?"

"If I need to break it down for you human, I shall. Yes, I am saying that this is it for you," Faust said, "and I'll be more than glad to be rid of you, in particular."

"The show is over," Cadmus added, "that's how you humans like to phrase things, if I am not mistaken."

"So now what?" Aiden asked, shrugging his shoulders. "Are you going to make a deal with them or destroy them?"

"That's not my decision to make," Faust said, showing his loyalty to the High Council, "but I feel confident that they will see them as the threat they are."

"Why concern yourself with it, anyway? Either way, you're not going back to Earth— ever," Cadmus said. He started to laugh.

"Like hell we aren't," Marie blurted out. "The Council must be real cocky to send you two to finish us off."

"Oh, there are more but the two of us are more than capable," Faust replied.

"Now!" Aiden shouted.

Carlisle and Marie knew what he meant.

Aiden closed his eyes and opened them again a second later, revealing a metallic silver iris and then Carlisle did the same, pumping himself up by pounding his fist into his palm and then blinking, revealing the silver eyes.

"Are you kidding me?" Faust said with a grin on his ugly face. He was practically salivating with eagerness.

Faust's heavy body moved toward the three with surprisingly quick speed. Cadmus was right behind him and the two didn't hesitate, revealing that they had confidently maneuvered in many skirmishes in the past and were a formidable force that had no fear, much less respect, for humans.

Aiden charged forward, meeting Faust halfway and fists began to fly so quickly they were almost in a blur. Faust's large fist connected with Aiden's face and then the other fist connected to his ribs, making him hunch over in pain. Then Aiden retaliated with an uppercut that managed to provide an impact despite Faust's strong torso.

"You're not going to win, you son of a bitch," Aiden said.

Faust smacked him again and as Carlisle heard the crunch he thought that it sounded like a piece of steel smashing into a chain link fence. He began to circle behind Faust, wanting to get him from behind but Cadmus had turned his attention on Marie and lashed out at her. Marie pulled out her saber and quickly started to slash her way trying for a connection to her opponent's skin. She noticed him dodging with great speed avoiding her attempts to land a critical blow. Cadmus quickly countered an attacked .She saw him coming and was able to angle her body to avoid receiving the full fury of his long nailed swipe. She ended up with a scratch on her arm followed by a punch to the face leaving Marie on one knee.

"Why don't you take on me?" Carlisle snickered to Cadmus, drawing a glance from him.

"I can handle both of you low life's," Cadmus hissed, taking two giant steps and going face to face with Carlisle.

Carlisle had his blood saber out he was trying to quickly assess the situation and what he'd learned about Cadmus's weaknesses the past year while making sure he didn't get distracted. It wasn't easy but his training had paid off.

"Stick to the plan we discussed in the astral plane," Aiden called out.

Damn, I wish I could kill Faust, the bastard, Carlisle thought. That would be his ideal plan. He didn't feel certain that the ship was going to blow up if Faust died but it was a chance that he couldn't take.

Carlisle thought the plan seemed more logical in the astral plane but there, in the present, kicking everyone's ass as quickly as possible was a preferable alternative.

252

Drawing his blood saber, Carlisle shouted to Marie, "Help Aiden, I've got this ugly bastard."

Carlisle's skills were swift, accurate, and calculated. His steady hand and complete control were a surprise to Cadmus. "Impressive but you're still no match, Carlisle."

Stay focused. He's trying to distract you. Carlisle could tell a player when he saw one and from a different planet or not, Cadmus was trying to be a player.

"Let's just see who comes out of this for the better," Carlisle said.

He began circling around Cadmus, assessing the High Royal's moves and mannerisms. He took one small dart outward with the blood saber to see if it would distract him. It didn't.

Cadmus laughed and when he did his head tilted back slightly. Carlisle took the blood saber and slashed across his chest. It happened so fast that Cadmus had to look down and see what had just happened. Deep, blue colored blood began to trickle down his chest and he took one hand and wiped it.

"Enough playing, boy," Cadmus said.

He came at Carlisle, not fearful of the saber getting him and within a second, Cadmus's body was pressed against Carlisle's and the monster was moving Carlisle backward and he almost lost his footing. When his arm swung out it was greeted with a block that stopped the saber from connecting with Cadmus again.

Again, Cadmus laughed. Carlisle needed to gain some separation in order to strike out at Cadmus again without accidentally connecting with his leg while doing it. Through his peripheral, Carlisle assessed what was around him that he could use to his advantage. He saw something that made him smile.

Carlisle darted to the right and tried to duck under Cadmus's arm. With the creature being so tall it should have been fairly easy but Cadmus wrapped his arm around Carlisle's waist, sending him flying backward. It hurt like hell but Carlisle thought, *that's right, fucker.*

Cadmus charged Carlisle and he responded by putting his feet up and shoving back with all the might he had against Cadmus's already wounded chest. It didn't slow the monster down a lot but it did allow for enough separation for Carlisle to grab a rock that was next to him and smash it into the side of Cadmus's face. His jaw became unhinged and he shook his head, locking it back into place.

By that time, Carlisle was on his feet and holding out his blood saber. He broke out into a sprint to cover the short distance between him and his target, preparing to swipe the saber across Cadmus's right arm.

Cadmus got out of the way easily. "You're slow."

Carlisle wasn't slow, though. He'd flipped in the air and was coming down and sliced the tendon on the backside of Cadmus's shoulder, making his arm practically useless. It was barely dangling there.

"I may be slow but you're having some problems now," Carlisle said, grinning wildly.

Cadmus glanced at his arm, which was no longer able to move and then Carlisle quickly finished it off, slicing clear through it and the arm flopped to the ground, twitching as if it were alive for a few seconds. Cadmus could only stare at it in shock.

He reached to his side and took out the gun that he'd had holstered and pointed it at Carlisle and shot, sending a golden bullet spiraling through the air. It hit Carlisle's arm, only grazing it, and his arm immediately began to sting.

"See how that treats you," Cadmus said.

Carlisle knew the bullet had some sort of toxin on it and he focused on slowing his blood flow so it wouldn't spread while moving toward Cadmus, who kept firing but was now missing, dealing with an extreme amount of blood loss.

"This is for trying to kill us," Carlisle said, raising his blood saber over his head and striking down on the arm that was holding the gun, removing it from Cadmus's torso with little effort. The gun dropped to the ground and Cadmus was left standing there, refusing to go down despite having no arms in which to defend himself.

"Go ahead, get it done with," Cadmus said.

"I'm not going to let you off that easy."

Carlisle began to tell the High Royal just where he'd went wrong and how monsters with no hearts could ever possibly understand the integrity of the human spirit. He kept talking and while he did so, he sliced off each leg of Cadmus, who still wouldn't die. The monster kept eye contact with him the entire time, staring at him coldly and without an ounce of emotion. It occurred to Carlisle that Cadmus spoke with poisoned words but really couldn't process them in the same emotional capacity as a human.

"I will return and save everyone" Carlisle added and with one final swipe, he severed off Cadmus's head.

"One down, one to go," Carlisle said, he smirked in triumph. The adrenaline was surging through him now and he'd forgotten about the toxin on the bullet, tapping into something that came from a place stronger than any poison. It was that place inside of him that knew how to tap into infinite resources of energy—it was his inner warrior and it was ready to come out and make an introduction to Faust.

Marie and Aiden were working against Faust, finding a match that was equal to their combined skills. Carlisle saw them struggling and hurried to them, hoping to be able to surprise Faust from behind.

Carlisle moved in and as he did, Marie swung her gun toward his knees forcefully but missed. Faust turned around and his arm was already going full swing, connecting with her with the same velocity a whip would have as it was being cracked on the ground.

"I'll deal with you later," Faust sneered, seeing Carlisle there. "Time to deal with you."

Faust glanced over the top of Carlisle's head, something easy for him to do and paused for a moment, seeing Cadmus dismembered and he snarled, showing as close as he could to an emotional attachment to his friend and confidante.

"Hold on, there," Aiden jumped in, "we still have matters to tend to, Faust."

Carlisle gritted his teeth, angered that the beaten and battered Aiden had done that. He was clearly hurt and going down fast, losing in the battle. Marie was dazed from Faust unleashing his full strength on her and of no help.

"Damn it, Aiden! Let me do this," Carlisle shouted.

Faust had him by the neck, squeezing it. Aiden's face was turning blue and his eyes bulging from lack of oxygen. His hands were up in an effort to pry loose Faust's talon-like grip. He was at the losing end of the battle and wouldn't be able to take it much more.

Carlisle ran up behind him and speared the blood saber into his backside, which would have been the kidneys on a human, and Faust turned his head around, barely loosening his grip.

"This is you and me, Faust, no one else. Let's finish this now." Carlisle lunged at him again with the saber, this time going for his eye and Faust had no choice but to release Aiden from his grip.

"Gladly," Faust said to Carlisle.

The two began to move back and forth, Carlisle delivering swipes with the blood saber that Faust seemed to predict easily and avoid. Then Faust would move in, his limbs a blur from his speed, and Carlisle found a way to predict his moves, tilting just to the side and then bringing his knee up, slamming it into the torso of Faust. With the High Royal's hard exterior, the knee strikes didn't have a lot of penetration but they were enough to slow him down, giving a valuable second of vulnerability.

Faust delivered swift retaliation, smashing his elbow into Carlisle's shoulder blade. Carlisle was shocked to feel the blood saber drop to the ground, all feeling lost in his arm from the impact. As he reached down to get it, Faust kicked him in the ribs hard and he fell down.

Lying on his stomach, Carlisle reached out with his arm to retrieve the blood saber and as he felt it in his hands he rolled on his back just in time to put his feet up and thrust Faust backward as he was coming down on him with the butt of his weapon, which was aimed for right in between Carlisle's eyes.

Carlisle pierced the blood saber into his stomach but it didn't stop Faust; it only enraged the High Royal as he kept going, seeming to grow stronger and quicker from the challenge.

Bang! Bang! Bang! Bang!

Shots rung out and Faust's eyes widened temporarily and he turned around. Carlisle had time to roll out of reach from him and noticed Marie pressed against the wall, holding a sub machine gun. She'd planted bullets into him.

Then Aiden came out of nowhere and tackled him down, finding one last burst of energy. Faust suddenly realized that three battered humans were still a force to be reckoned with and he tried to get up and run away.

"Don't let him get to the ship!" Marie called.

Carlisle ran forward and took a flying leap into the air to try and gain the lost distance on Faust, landing on his back. It didn't knock Faust over but when he whipped his body around, trying to release Carlisle's grip, Marie was running up to him. Carlisle tossed her the blood saber and she caught it in mid-air and pierced it into Faust's stomach. She twisted it and then yanked it out.

With Faust stopped, Carlisle jumped off his back and Marie snapped, she just repeatedly continued stabbing Faust over and over in the stomach.

Aiden couldn't stop her and Carlisle maybe could have but didn't want to.

Faust began talking calmly and his eyes started to turn blacker, making it so there was no white showing in them at all. "For my goddess, Lilith. My race will find you and you will be judged. In the end you will surrender and face your judgment, ignorant humans. You cannot win."

"Well, we beat you," Carlisle said, flying into Faust, who was now hunched over as he was drawing his last breaths and smashing into his throat with an intense kick that collapsed his throat and sent him to his knees once and for all.

"It's all over," Faust said. He touched his wrist band. Then his eyes grew wide for a moment and closed. His body was still and he'd died.

"We've got to get to Christopher and the ship…fast," Aiden said, coming up from behind. He was not able to talk loudly and you could see his entire throat was bruised in the shape of Faust's hands.

Carlisle and Marie helped support Aiden, who'd fared worse than they had in the encounter, and they moved toward the ship. The words didn't need to be spoken for them to realize that they may have ran out of time and just written their death sentence by allowing Faust to die.

28

"There's often an unspoken battle that exists between a single second and a lost opportunity."

Running into an unknown destiny, Carlisle, Aiden, and Marie charged up the ramp of the ship, uncertain if it was good or bad that it had remained open. They knew right where they had to be and that the quicker they got there, the better.

Making their way down the long corridor, leaving bloody footprints from their beatings as evidence of their path, the three walked into the control room calmly, knowing that there was no need to be hasty at that moment—a collective mind was their best asset.

They saw Christopher standing in front of a control panel that had been opened by Watson and staring down at it, starting to initiate the destruction sequence.

"Christopher, stop," Aiden said in a soft voice—one that didn't reflect the urgency of the moment. "We can't let you do that."

Christopher turned around and the face that greeted the three of them left Carlisle wondering if he was looking back at a human or what he was exactly. It was hard to describe but it left him realizing that Christopher likely didn't care if he died right along with everyone else on the ship.

"Let's deactivate the bomb," Marie said, walking forward. "I can help you do it."

Christopher looked at her with his piercing blue eyes and there were no waves of emotion in them. "I have to do what I was commanded to do" he said in a gentle voice.

The next moment, Christopher was covered in a blue shield which made him freeze in mid-motion, leaving Carlisle, Aiden, and Marie confused. They looked around and Carlisle turned around, seeing the creature with a tesseract standing there, staring at them.

"How did you do that?" Marie asked, not able to understand.

"We have many things we can do; advancements that are beyond most races abilities to process," the voice said. It was soft, almost feminine, but had a masculine authority to it, as well, that made it very confusing to process. The sound was more of an 'it,' for lack of a better word.

"Why did you call us here from Earth?" Aiden asked, wanting to buy time. It was good that Christopher was frozen, as it gave some time for thought. "There has to be a reason.

"Many cycles ago, a disease broke out on our planet that we could not cure despite our perceived intelligence. The leaders of our world thought of an idea to save our race. We decided to trade our technology with other intelligent life forms in order for hopes of finding a cure for our race from complete extinction. Until one day after traveling from an exchange from a race from a nearby galaxy .One of our leaders met a unique life form .This intelligent life form communicated with him and stated that your race was the image of him and within you there is a cure. We sent probes trying to search through this vast universe to find you .We decided hope was lost until we stumbled upon your dimension. We decided to come to you but we could not enter fully in your dimension and if we attempted to travel to your galaxy we would soon start to die in time to reach it .Since you live in a third dimensional world and ours is a seventh dimensional one. "

That answers my curiosity about more than four dimensional, Carlisle thought. Still, something wasn't making sense to him and they didn't have a lot of time to sort through who was the real enemy. It seemed like it might be Christopher, but was it really?

"How can you see everything on Planet 01291954 then?" Marie asked.

"What you see before you is only a part of our being," the creature explained, looking translucent as the veins of life that flowed through it could be seen from the outside. "We can never go lower than the fifth dimension without any consequence, the tesseract will keep us protected but only for a short period of time .It also allows us to communicate with you."

"I don't see how we can help you?" Aiden said.

Carlisle looked at him and recognized his expressions. He was fishing for information and his intuition was on high alert.

"The ones you've brought with you," the creature said, pointing to Christopher and obviously referring to both Faust and Cadmus, "are four dimensional creatures. We've scanned their bodies and probed their minds. They are an insidious species, not compatible with our needs. They've tried to send altered humans but their blood was not compatible when we scanned their ship, making it necessary for us to keep our shields raised .We also placed a barrier

259

around your solar system to shield out any more threats to protect your species .This technology also protected our dying race for many cycles but now ..."

The creature was quiet and Carlisle looked at Aiden and Marie to see if they had any hints on their face as to what the creature was talking about. He didn't trust that he had it.

"And when we neared your shield you were able to scan us and see something different," Marie said.

"Yes, we saw purity in your blood so we allowed you to pass."

"We've been tricked to coming here," Aiden said. "So now what?"

"We need you to travel with us so we can find a cure for our race."

"What? You expect us to be your guinea pigs?" Carlisle spat.

"We prefer your cooperation but you may term it however you see fit," the creature said, looking at Carlisle as if it was scanning his body at that very moment.

"And if we don't wish to help?" Carlisle asked.

"You have no choice in the matter," the creature replied.

"We are not coming with you to be your test subjects," Aiden said adamantly.

Carlisle could sense when he was on the losing end of a discussion. They were clearly at a disadvantage and he knew two things: he didn't want to die and he didn't want to be a test subject.

"Wait, I have an idea," Carlisle offered.

Marie and Aiden looked at him with angry eyes. He nodded his head slightly and mouthed, "Trust me."

"What is this idea?" the creature asked. "You are the one they call Carlisle, yes?"

"Yes," Carlisle replied. "This ship has excellent technology, including a cloning machine. Do you have anything like that?"

"No, what does this machine do?" the creature asked.

"If you were to take our blood you could make copies of us with the technology. That may be the key to saving your race."

"Excuse me a moment," Aiden said to the creature. He went over and grabbed Carlisle's arm, turning him around and pulling him off to the side. Marie went over there, too.

"I'm not so sure about this, Carlisle. Think about it…we could end up creating a bigger monster than any of us can slay."

"What options do we have? Christopher's frozen right now, none of us can barely stand because we've been so beaten up. We're at a severe disadvantage. There's no other compromise."

"He's right," Marie said.

They turned around and the creature was staring at them calmly, expectantly.

"Would you be willing to try this?" Aiden asked it. "We'll create these clones for you."

"But we do have some conditions," Carlisle stated next.

"We are not unreasonable beings," the creature said. "What conditions?"

"We need to update our ship's technology to ensure that we have the speed and protection from any unknown threats so we can make it back to Earth. Plus, we need the ability to scan things and communicate with other species and the facilities to remove the creatures from Ethan's body without killing him, as well as the bomb from Christopher's body to ensure that none of us blow up," Carlisle said.

"These are reasonable requests and will be granted as we proceed with this cloning and see if it works," the creature said. "However, I should caution you; if the cloning doesn't work we will use you as our test subjects."

"That's fair enough," Carlisle said.

"Well," Marie interrupted, "let's get to work, starting with that bomb. From what I've learned about these things, there's likely enough power in that bomb to not only blow up this ship but half of this planet, too."

The creature nodded. "You should be able to move the subject without incident, as he cannot move until I have released the shield freeze on him. May I observe during this procedure?"

Marie nodded.

Nobody wanted to leave anyone alone with the creatures just yet so they collectively went to the medical unit, wheeling Christopher in on a stretcher that he was strapped down on. Ethan appeared out of nowhere and walked in, too, making everyone temporarily uneasy.

"You should get out of here," Carlisle said to him, not feeling much sympathy for the guy who was on the ship to kill him.

"He's fine," Marie said, defending Ethan, "let him be and let's all focus on the bomb, okay?"

"Carlisle, Ethan was here on orders from Cadmus and Faust. They're out of the way and he's the least of our problems," Aiden said, pointing his finger for added emphasis.

A short time later, Marie was removing the bomb from Christopher's stomach, looking at it with fascination. It was a small sphere that was a shiny, black metallic.

"That small object is capable of such destruction?" the creature asked, observing from a respectable distance.

"Yes," Marie said, slightly turning her head, "it's complex molecular structure makes it most lethal. It's compacted and something that can only be mad in a zero gravity room with the most advanced technologies made in an anti-gravity matter to assist in its creation. It's quite amazing, really, but it's something we need to deactivate."

"You can do that?" Carlisle asked, feeling a trickle of sweat go down his temple as he stared at it.

"Yes," Marie said and sooner rather than later.

Aiden peered over the open stomach of Christopher. "Hey, what's that?" he said, pointing down.

"The Larva," Ethan called out from the distance. "I can smell it."

"He's a Fire?" Carlisle asked.

"Not of human descent, though," Ethan said.

"Let's remove it," Marie said.

They began to remove the larva and all the machines went off, showing that Christopher would die without it in him.

"How can this be?" Aiden asked.

"I don't know. Do we kill him?"

"Yes!" Carlisle expressed.

"We don't kill without a good reason and while we aren't sure if we can trust him, we may need him for something. We just don't know yet," Marie said, shrugging her shoulders.

"Okay, leave it in him."

"Explain this larva to me," the creature said, looking at Ethan, who clearly had a very solid understanding of it.

As Ethan explained the creature asked, "May we have yours for study?"

"No, I'm keeping mine," Ethan said, which made Carlisle's suspicions be raised again despite Aiden's willingness to believe him.

"You don't want to be human again?" Carlisle said.

"I am human and I shall keep my body as it is," Ethan replied.

"Carlisle, enough," Marie said angrily. "You're going back to being a douche bag again and causing new problems. We have enough to deal with."

"Fine," Carlisle said, storming away.

In his quarters, steaming about everything going on and how out of control he was with his own destiny, Carlisle paced back and forth, grabbing his weapons and practicing, doing exercises and anything he could to calm himself down.

"Is it helping?" Aiden asked.

"I didn't even notice you came in," Carlisle said, barely turning his head.

"You've got to remember that Ethan doesn't have a soul that's fully in-tact anymore. With the larva he's actually less human."

"Don't you see the way he looks at Marie and she does at him?"

"There's nothing going on there," Aiden said.

His expression changed after he said that, though, and he left Carlisle's room again. One thing that hadn't left Carlisle over all this time was his abilities to judge when people were talking smack and he didn't believe for a single minute that Aiden really believed that there was nothing unusual about Marie and Ethan's relationship.

29

"The frontier of discovery is never ending...and constantly evolving."

Carlisle and Marie had needed the least amount of medical attention and therefore, they had offered to give their blood to the creature on Planet 01291954 first so they could honor the agreement. Overall, it was a small price to pay for the technology that their ship would be receiving in exchange.

"I can't believe this ship," Marie said, looking around at everything. "This is beyond anything that I could ever have imagined. If only my dad could see this ..." She stopped talking, spiraling into thoughts of her father and how he'd been needlessly killed.

"The tesseract and the scanning technology that they've given us is incredible. The tesseract literally absorbs every bit of information it sees around it and doesn't seem to ever forget."

"It educates and breaks down everything even down to our human responses and emotions, which is exciting but makes me nervous, too," Marie said.

"Why?"

"I don't know. It just does," Marie said, yawning loudly.

"You're exhausted. Why don't you go get some rest," Aiden offered. "The ship will be waiting for you."

Marie opened her mouth but didn't say a word.

"It won't pain you to admit I'm right; go on," Aiden encouraged.

"Maybe—just for an hour, though, I'm eager to explore the nano technology further and understand it better."

"It reminds me of sand," Carlisle said, walking into the room as Marie was leaving.

"It may resemble sand but it's capable of a whole lot more than any sand I've ever seen before," Marie said.

"Well, I'm off. See you in an hour."

Marie walked out and Carlisle was left with Aiden, reviewing everything about the ship that they could muster. Standing in the corner, still void of emotion but at least without a bomb, was Christopher.

"I don't like it how he always seems to be listening," Carlisle whispered.

"You might as well talk out loud. He can hear you, as his senses are hypersensitive to everything," Aiden said.

"Hey Christopher, why are you always listening?" Carlisle called out. He was feeling a bit agitated, not comfortable with his blood being part of a cloning machine and the creatures on Planet 01291954's testing. Yes, it had been his idea but it still didn't settle well with him.

"Listening to you is hardly a joy for me. It's simply…unavoidable," Christopher replied in a robotic voice that matched his emotionless face.

"Leave it be, Carlisle," Aiden cautioned, "I know you're on edge. We all are but we have to stay focused. Do something productive, okay?"

"I know, I know you're right," Carlisle offered. "Maybe I'll go back to school and see if I like it better this time."

To that very day, thoughts of school made Carlisle cringe. He'd loved it that he'd gotten as far as he had without having to go to some fancy college and waste his life behind a desk all day long.

Carlisle looked through the vast libraries of information that the tesseract provided him access to and decided to read up on the ship's features. He knew Marie and Aiden knew a whole lot about it but what if… He didn't want to finish his thought but he knew that he had to be as self sufficient as possible.

Some of the creatures of the planet entered into the control room, staring down at something that was on their tesseract and looking around.

One of them asked, "Where is the female?"

"Resting, why?" Aiden asked.

"We need her now."

"Did you discover something?" he asked.

They didn't answer his question and only said, "Bring her at once please."

Aiden went to get Marie and she came rushing into the room, having no idea what was going on that they'd need her. Everyone was tense and felt instantly uneasy.

"Yes, what it is?" Marie asked.

"Your tests showed an interesting conclusion; another being is inside of you."

"What do you mean?" Marie scratched her head, not able to understand what they were talking about.

"I believe humans call it pregnancy."

"Pregnant? I can't be pregnant," Marie retorted. "Let me see that."

She looked at the image they were showing on the tesseract. It was of her body and sure enough, right there in her womb, was a warmer image, very small in size that showed it had life to it.

"I don't understand," she mumbled, nearly falling over.

In a split second, Ethan was there, arriving out of thin air—or so it seemed—and he helped her sit down.

"Pregnant? How?" Aiden asked.

Marie looked to Ethan and then Aiden got it in that moment. His eyes turned a metallic silver and anger quickly crossed his face.

"What the fuck …" Aiden shouted and he began to pace around the room. "Pregnant, and from a Fire. Fuck!"

"I didn't think it was possible," Marie began. "Plus, I've still been taking the Silphium, it's a natural birth control. I've been researching it, on the side. How could I have not known?"

Aiden stormed out of the room, swearing the entire way. His voice could be heard for a long way.

The creatures stared between Ethan and Marie. The one who'd initially spoken said, "Come with us. We must perform some tests."

"No!" Ethan said, jumping in between the two.

"There's no choice in the matter," the creature said, "We must collect data."

"I'll let you experiment with my larva in exchange for leaving Marie alone," Ethan countered.

The creatures looked at each other and one of them nodded. "We accept."

Marie and Carlisle realized that's really what they'd been interested in and they had kind of been played.

"But you're not removing it," Ethan said.

"We do not need the full larva, as we've already checked its compatibility. It can be cloned. We will also enhances its genetic code so it cannot consume your life as quickly and you will have your full conscious control over it."

"How can you do that?" Carlisle asked but he already knew the answer before the question escaped his lips. "Christopher."

* * *

With everyone disbursed to their rooms and the mood on the ship very heavy, Carlisle knew that they had to do something quickly and leave the planet. Had they given the creatures enough for them to feel comfortable letting them go? He wasn't sure but they really didn't have a choice any longer.

Carlisle went into the control room and accessed one of the computers, reading about all of the things the new, enhanced ship could do. The biggest thing it said it could do was actually not implode upon entering a black hole due to some protective force field that could come up around it. That seemed hard to grasp but Carlisle had already seen a lifetime's worth of what he'd previously have termed impossible happen before his very eyes. Of course, it didn't solve the problem of ending up in an unknown place at the other end of the black hole, either.

By the next day, Carlisle had come up with a hopeful plan. He tracked Aiden down and unfortunately found him in the middle of a very intimate argument with Marie. He was where he shouldn't be but he had nowhere to go without being noticed.

"This was not the plan; you can't have that child, Marie."

"What do you care, Aiden? This child is a rare gift."

"Everything we've built, all that we've planned, its contingent upon us as a team."

"We may be a team but I need more than that. I need someone who cares for me and loves me, too," Marie said.

"I do care for you deeply and I've been with you thick and thin…unlike *him*."

"Do you love me?" Marie challenged, not hiding how irritating those supposedly magical words were to her. "Since when?"

"Since always," Aiden said, rubbing his hands through his hair.

"Why can't you say it you never told me that before?"

"I have a history about that word. One I'm not ready to explain yet .I just assumed you knew. " Aiden said.

"You're an idiot then," Marie said.

A hand reached out and touched Carlisle's shoulder, making him jump. He turned around and saw Christopher standing there with a haunting smile on his pale, iridescent face.

Well, Carlisle's cover was blown and he walked into the room, facing Marie and Aiden, who were trying to wash away their mutual anger and frustration at each other.

"What is it?" Aiden asked.

"I think it's time for us to go and get back to Earth. Do you think they'll allow us to leave without troubles? We've fulfilled our end of the deal." Carlisle looked to Aiden and then Marie.

"We still need the other human's blood," another unknown voice said.

Carlisle turned around and saw that one of the creatures was looming over him and pointing toward Aiden.

"Well, you're not getting it. That was their deal, not mine," Aiden said, crossing his arms.

"I'll give you a bit more," Carlisle offered.

"Wait! I have a better idea," Marie said.

"We know that I'm with child and it's of interest to all of us to return home. Back on Earth, we can tell our leaders of your technology enhancements and have more comeback for an exchange for more technology .There will be more blood supplies for your testing plus get the information on a different type of cloning technology I have access to."

Aiden glared again and at the worst time possible, Ethan came into the room.

Aiden lunged at him and growled, trying to throw a fist at him but he had no chance against Ethan. Ethan was fully healed and Aiden was struggling to recover from the brutal fight against Faust and Cadmus. He hadn't stood a chance.

Ethan just snickered at him and walked away. "If I only have one more fight in my life, it's sure not going to be a half dead jealous human that I go up against."

What is that supposed to mean? Carlisle thought. He hoped it wasn't him that Ethan was referring to. Despite it all, he still couldn't imagine him and Ethan coming to blows in a stay alive or die match.

30

"You can never go back home and find it exactly as you left it."

Christopher, Ethan, and Marie were in the control room of the ship waiting for everyone else to show up so they could prepare for launch. It hadn't been easy but everything had been settled for the "short" trip to Earth, which really meant about four months when you factored in the time continuum of the galaxies. It did shave two months off due to the ship's superior performance and function.

"This was such a beautiful but yet peculiar planet," Ethan commented, looking out the huge windows at the blue sands and temple of the place that they'd been on for the past week. "Kind of peculiar that we offered so much up about ourselves and know nothing about them, not even what they call their race."

Christopher nodded, the closest he tended to get to a conversation. It seemed obvious that Ethan and he didn't consider each other a threat. Everyone else was somebody on high alert…except perhaps Marie now that she was pregnant and had a protective Ethan hovering over her.

Aiden and Carlisle walked in and the tension suddenly grew thicker without a word even being spoken.

"Ethan, why don't you go sit down and stay out of the way so we can get this ship up and out of here before anything else happens," Aiden said dismissively.

Ethan turned around, his fist clenched, and Carlisle thought, *here we go,* but Marie placed her hand on his and squeezed it softly, nodding for him to just listen to Aiden.

Carlisle overheard her say, "It's not worth it."

Aiden walked over and looked around at everything suspiciously. "This is different? What's going on?" He looked to Marie and then to Christopher. It was obvious he no longer trusted her, either.

"It's fine. The rest of the upgrades have been completed and this is what it is. Remember, this adapts to suit the needs of the direction we're traveling. The gold and black

271

provides the right exterior, interior, and data for a trip to Earth. If you wouldn't have been so pissed off at me the last few days you would have read about it and known that," Marie said.

"Whatever," Aiden said.

"Child," Marie mumbled.

"Okay everyone. We all want the same thing here—to get off this planet and back to Earth, right? Let's work together. Everyone's getting what they want."

Carlisle glanced at Aiden after he said that, realizing that Aiden really wasn't getting the one thing he clearly wanted—Marie. What did he expect, though? He should have told her he loved her if he wanted her. Instead, he'd left a trail of stories about trysts with other women throughout the years and certainly in the social media stratosphere.

"Carlisle, you do surveillance on the planet as we're leaving. See if anything unusual happens or anyone follows us," Aiden began. He turned to Marie and said, "You keep track of all the ship's data and see if you see anything that we should be alarmed."

Aiden looked around and added, "I'll just take care of everything else."

"I can do something; I know this system as well as any of you," Ethan offered.

"If you really want to help, jump off the fuckin' ship and stay here," Aiden said.

For the first time that he could recall, Carlisle had to pull Ethan aside and remind him to keep his temper in check. "You're not helping. Just deal with it and stay focused, Aiden."

"10, 9, 8..." the updated Watson 2.0 began, "...3, 2, 1."

The ship lifted and took off, leaving Planet 01291954 lingering below it as it rose straight up in the air. The blue sands seem to move around below them, swirling like a blue sand storm, and then they settled down abruptly and the ship catapulted into space, moving faster than anything anyone on the ship had ever experienced before. Yet, they hadn't even buckled themselves in or felt the impact.

"Amazing," Carlisle said.

"Hey guys, spotted something," Marie said. "As we took off, the temple on the planet took off, too, going in a complete opposite direction."

They rushed over and Marie played back the imaging on the screen in front of her. "This blue blur, that's it."

"Where's it going?" Carlisle asked.

"No clue. We know where we're headed and that's the priority," Aiden said.

"I've got to check. We have to be sure," Marie said, standing up to Aiden more than working by his side.

She grabbed the tesseract with both hands and began to ask.

This was the one question the tesseract couldn't answer. However, it gave the exact coordinates to make it on an autopilot to the Milky Way Galaxy and to Earth, leaving the five inhabitants of the ship to figure out the details of the looming question: what next?

"Do you believe it's truthful that they can't enter into the Earth because of the dimension?" Carlisle asked.

"It makes scientific sense," Marie said, "however, we had a deal."

"One that we are going to break. We aren't going back there and we'll just have to start over on our own for a planet to replace Earth."

"They'll kill you all," Christopher said.

"You never talk and that's what you say when you decide to?" Carlisle said, rolling his eyes. "Just leave if you can't be helpful, or at least be quiet."

It was surprising to Carlisle that Christopher did leave. As soon as he was out the door and Carlisle was sure he wasn't lurking around a corner, he continued. He turned to Aiden and said, "We need to get some input and resources from Aerial. Who else can help us?"

"It may be too late for him to. He's powerful but he's not a High Royal," Aiden said.

273

"Well, how about landing the ship on Earth and letting people see it; know what exists and what's going to happen?" Carlisle offered.

"That is the most asinine thing I've ever heard," Marie spat. "What will that do other than create complete chaos?"

"Plus these guys control all the rich and powerful. They'd lock us away and we'd rot away there until they came to kill us," Ethan added.

Carlisle looked to Aiden for his response to Ethan's words, which were logical to him, and saw Aiden nod his head. He agreed although he wasn't going to verbally acknowledge it.

"We could use the bomb they implanted in Christopher and detonate it on the moon, eliminating the problem," Aiden said.

"I'm no master scientist like you two," Carlisle said to Marie and Aiden, "but wouldn't debris from the moon plummet to Earth and cause a whole lot of destruction, ruining it faster than it's being destroyed already?"

"Bad idea, for sure," Marie said. "We've saved the bomb and I'm uneasy about it but it may come in handy at some point—just not for that."

"What then?" Ethan asked.

"Just give it up and return to the moon, admit defeat," Christopher said.

"You would say that; you're their servant…nothing more," Carlisle said.

"That would mean that Ethan is, too, right?"

Everyone looked at Ethan and he stared back at them vacantly, playing the ultimate poker face. Marie's gaze lingered there just a bit longer than the others and Carlisle caught it. He wondered if she was worried.

"None of these ideas are leading to a viable plan," Aiden said, slamming his fist on the top of a control panel.

"Wait," Ethan said.

Everyone turned to him and he paused, giving a dramatic effect of sorts as a result. "What if we clone everyone?"

"What?" Marie asked.

"That is not a good idea. I've already stated that I will not be cloned and I sure as shit am not changing my story here," Aiden spat.

"It's a brilliant idea," Carlisle said, "If we can hack and retrieve everyone's genetic code and take their DNA we can clone them."

"Hack genetic codes?" Aiden questioned. "Carlisle, this is bigger than your little high school gig of amateur hacker."

"I'm telling you, with the proper diversion it'll work."

"And maybe that is where we use a bomb," Marie began, "maybe I can make a bomb powerful enough to make an explosion on the Moon Base that distracts everyone long enough for you to pull off the ultimate hack on Earth."

Aiden clapped his hands together, starting to feel the excitement from the plan. "The only blood bank I can think of that would have that many files of DNA would be Cord Blood Corp, the world's largest depository."

"It's perfect!" Carlisle put his hand out toward Ethan and without thinking about it, just like during days long past, they gave each other a solid high five.

The next five hours were spent creating the first draft of a plan, one that would likely be revised and tweaked over the months in flight, but eventually pulled off. It was the ultimate plan that should lead to the ultimate results. Their technology was beyond human comprehension and their determination was motivated by a desire to save the human race itself.

* * *

Curious, eager, and in the mood to not be under the scornful eye of Aiden, Marie was in the robotics room, tinkering around and configuring some ideas about how to create a bomb that would serve their purpose for saving Earth.

Ethan walked in. "Hey beautiful."

"Hi," she said, looking up and smiling, and then putting her head back down.

"So, you liked my ideas today. Kind of hot," he said, wrapping his arms around her.

"Somewhat," she said, smiling coyly at him. She did stop working though and stared at Ethan, showing that their chemistry was undeniable.

It wasn't challenging for Ethan to pick Marie up gently by the waist and set her down on the table. He pressed in closer to her and began to kiss her softly, stroking her long, soft hair with his hand.

"Mmm," Marie mumbled.

"Feels good, doesn't it?" Ethan whispered in her ear, gently blowing on it.

There was a knock on the wall by the entrance to the room. Marie turned her head and Ethan quickly turned around.

"Thank god that's not Aiden," Marie said.

It was Christopher.

"There you are, Ethan. Did you still want to lift weights?"

"Oh yeah, I forgot about that. Just a second," Ethan said.

Marie turned her head back to Ethan and he planted a deep, sultry kiss on her, making her pull away. She didn't say anything but she looked like 'what the...' She wasn't the only one, either. Christopher had that same look on his face. He shook his head, turned around, and walked out of the room.

Ethan ran out of the room and followed Christopher down the hall, pleased with the response he'd gotten and full of questions.

"So, has anyone been asking questions about our relationship?"

"No," Christopher said, looking at Ethan like he was crazy.

"Good, not a word, do you understand?"

"Everyone knows she's pregnant," Christopher said, "what else is there to say?" He looked at Ethan and saw that his eyes were red. It would have scared most people but Christopher just looked back at him with his own type of warning, showing that he wasn't someone that could be intimidated, either.

31

"Isolation and a sense of helplessness often go hand in hand."

Carlisle was quickly finding out that even the most decked out ship in the universe couldn't stop the boredom from setting in after repeated days of the same activities taking place. He was going stir crazy and those nasty thoughts such as "is this really worth it" kept entering his mind. He couldn't do anything to lose them. Writing in his journal hadn't helped the way he thought it would but the journal did prove to be beneficial in another unexpected way. Carlisle was determined to leave evidence of his story and journey behind for future generations to read. Everything he was doing could not be in vain. Of course, no one would ever come to know it if the human race became extinct.

"I've got to get rid of this insane energy," Carlisle said aloud, jumping up from his small desk and hiding his journal. He looked around and decided that he needed to get to the training room and pound out some serious physical energy. It was keeping him pent up and if he were to be really honest, he was horny and had no way to find a woman's touch as they navigated through the universe with no end in sight.

The training room was a great place, one of Carlisle's favorites and he loved how he could keep improving his weaponry skills and simulate fights with multiple creatures at the same time. The simulator was awesome that way, bringing up real holographic images of various creatures—known and unknown—and forcing Carlisle to assess their strengths, weaknesses, and possible vulnerabilities.

He warmed up and went right to the simulator, set to kick some holographic ass, and in short time, he was in the groove, killing the opponents or maiming them, as well as growing ever more comfortable with how he could master any weapon placed in his hands. That day it was a blood saber with a twist—small, piercing needs that extended out of its sides and sliced the unlucky opponent, leaving a lethal toxin on their exterior that burnt badly—even for those tough exteriors like what High Royals had.

Sweating and feeling great, Carlisle completed his third round of simulator training, getting a higher score than he ever had before.

"Damn! You've got some skills," someone said from behind him.

Carlisle turned around and saw Ethan there. "Yeah, it's a work in progress. You certainly have some skills, too, from what I hear."

Ethan tilted his head ever so slightly and a cocky grin spread across his face. "I was pretty motivated, that's for sure."

"I have a feeling I know why," Carlisle said, laughing. That moment was the first time since seeing Ethan again where he wasn't sporting that look that said he wanted to kill him. It was progress.

"I don't feel like killing you as much as I did at one time. It was the very reason that I entered that tournament and made sure I won it, becoming a billionaire and going to the moon. You were supposed to be my next biggest fight," Ethan said bluntly.

"Times have changed…somehow, I don't think those things are happening on the Moon City the way they once were; we're fugitives on the run, man."

"With a high powered ship," Ethan added.

"I just want this all to end and to give humans a chance to survive, maybe learn a bit if we're fortunate. What are you hoping to gain now, especially since you're going to be a father?" Carlisle asked.

"I'm not really sure. It was as much a surprise to me as it was everyone else."

Carlisle chuckled. "Not Aiden, I suspect. He was literally blindsided by the news."

Ethan shrugged. "I'm not into missing opportunities anymore."

"So, how did you end up as a Fire, anyway?" Carlisle asked. He'd been curious, waiting for the right time to ask.

Ethan's face turned a bit sour and he walked over to a punching bag and smashed it with his fist, sending its bottom into the steel wall behind it and leaving a small dent from the impact. "Rodrigo, you know him, I assume?"

"Yeah, he has pretty good music."

"That's because he tells you he does, you know."

"What do you mean?"

"I've become increasingly more aware of just about everything. When I was working out the other day with Christopher one of Rodrigo's songs came on and he has all this subliminal shit in them. That shit really works."

"Messages to buy his songs? Hard to believe no one else has noticed yet."

"It's not easy to pick up on; most people wouldn't but it's there. *Money rules you, hear me*…things like that."

"Do you have that in your music?"

"No and I don't plan on it. The words should speak for themselves, not get all trippy like that," Ethan said. "I have one motivation with that guy."

"What's that?"

"To kill that mother fucker the first chance I get. Without his suggestion I wouldn't have had any of this happen."

"Some good's come of it, right? I mean, you have Marie and you're going to have a baby."

"That's not how I wanted those things," Ethan said, his voice rising a bit. He stared into Carlisle's eyes, a flicker of red shining through. "Is that how you'd want a family and girlfriend?"

Carlisle shook his head no.

"Anyway…"

A message sounded out over the system, asking for Carlisle and Ethan to meet with everyone in the control room.

"What now?" Carlisle asked.

They walked down to the control room and Carlisle felt good about their conversation. He'd made a commitment to give everyone a chance and while he didn't share that with everyone it was important to him. It was the right thing to do and he did want to make good on how he'd dogged Ethan all those years ago, despite dogging him not being his intention.

"What's up?" Carlisle asked.

Aiden turned and looked at him and you could see that he was surprised to see Carlisle and Ethan standing next to each other in a friendly manner. He shook his head and Carlisle watched as he turned his gaze to Marie and Christopher, who were standing next to each other and just staring straight ahead.

"We still have a lot of time on this ship and we're all going a bit stir crazy, I think," Aiden began. "I have an idea."

"What's that?" Carlisle asked. "It seems like Ethan and I are the only two who don't know from the looks on your face."

"We got onto the subject and that's why I called you down here," Aiden said.

Carlisle could see that he was determined to take control as the leader of the ship, perhaps fearful that too many chiefs would lead to too many problems. It made sense and while Carlisle was aware that he wasn't the official leader, he had a sense that his intentions were perhaps the most humble out of anyone's; no motivations to be king of the universe, just a good part of it.

Aiden continued talking. "I think we need to go into the pods for the next months until it's time to land. This ship is about five times faster than the previous; it's made a huge difference."

"There's too much left to do," Carlisle began, "I don't like it."

"Well, I don't know. I've managed to make a smaller form of the bomb we extracted from Christopher already and have a hundred set," Marie started.

"We still have a lot to learn, though, training to do…"

Aiden put his hand out. "Well, let's vote on it," he said, cutting Carlisle off.

"Sounds fair enough by me," Marie said.

281

"Me too," Ethan said.

"I'm with Ethan," Christopher said. It wasn't the time to bring up that he mentioned only one name, not the team. Carlisle was beginning to think that Christopher didn't want anyone to trust him that was his preference.

"Okay, let's vote," Aiden said. "All those who want to go into the pods until a week before landing raise your hand."

Carlisle looked around as one, two, three, and then four hands went up into the air. He was the only one against the plan.

"Sorry Carlisle," Marie said. She patted his shoulder and he moved it away.

"I don't see why I can't just do my thing while you guys do that," Carlisle said.

"We can't operate that way; you know it," Aiden said. "It's been decided. We'll commence the plan in an hour."

Carlisle wasn't ready to surrender quite so easily, though. "Marie," he said, turning to her, "you realize that you're going to be very pregnant in four months. What if it's not good for the baby?"

"I know what you're trying to do but I'm more than capable of ensuring the maturation process isn't impeded by this, Carlisle. You'll have to do better."

How about you and Ethan not getting to hang out together? Aha! That was it, Carlisle realized. Everyone had their own reasons and there was a good chance that Aiden and Christopher both liked the thought of Marie and Ethan not being able to grow closer.

"One last thing," Aiden added, "no visiting the plane during this one. It's not necessary and we need to save all the energy we have for when we get to Earth and try to pull off the greatest heist the universe has ever seen."

Then it was time for last minute details, a last minute briefing, programming the ship, and everyone retired, knowing that they'd be brought to consciousness when they were within a week of landing on Earth.

32

"Sent to destination no return, but we still came back!"

Awake and alert, staring out of the massive windows of the ship, Carlisle watched as he re-entered the Milky Way Galaxy. It had been a long time, nearly a year and a half since he'd been there and it made the vast area feel more like home than anything he'd experienced in quite some time.

"Okay everyone, here's your wardrobe," Marie said, handing the four guys suits to wear. They weren't space suits and there was nothing special about them in that sense but they were definitely made from the finest Italian silk and power suits that were only worn by powerful people.

"Look at you," Carlisle said with a smile. He looked at Marie's belly and while it wasn't sticking out very far it was protruding enough that it was apparent a baby was growing in her otherwise slender torso.

"Yeah, pretty neat," she said with a glowing smile.

Carlisle looked to Ethan and he was smiling, too, even walking up and putting his hand on her stomach. "I can feel its heartbeat," he added.

Aiden even seemed okay with everything, not showing any signs of emotional duress. Perhaps the hiatus did him good despite it only seeming like a night, not months, when you were in the pod.

A beep started emitting from one of the consoles.

"What's that?" Marie asked, running over. She looked down and then looked back up. By that time, everyone was around her.

"What do you see?" Aiden asked.

She pointed out the window into the distance. "In that direction, there are four ships coming right toward us; three seem quite small and one is rather large."

"Friend or foe?" Carlisle asked.

"We'll find out," Aiden said.

Christopher looked down at the console and then looked out. "I know what they are."

"Speak," Aiden commanded.

"They are lethal, made by High Royals and I can assure you that they have nothing good for our well being on their command list," Christopher said, void of all emotion.

"They want to obliterate us?" Marie asked.

Christopher nodded his head. "Maybe, I don't know much about them."

They all watched, unsure how to proceed as the four ships came closer to them. They began circling their ship, making everyone wonder what was going on.

"If they wanted to fire they would have done it by now, right?" Carlisle asked.

"I think they want to communicate," Christopher said.

"Let's find their frequency," Aiden said.

Marie did all this quickly and it felt like time was frozen, waiting to see what happened next.

A voice came through on the radio that had the familiar non-emotional cadence of how a High Royal spoke. "You are commanded to land on Moon Base."

Aiden looked and knew that was the last place they could go. What could he do?

"How about sending a carrier?" Carlisle offered.

"That might work but we'll have to be set to evacuate in a different direction at the same time."

"Are we close enough?" Marie asked.

"I think so."

"We're sending down a cargo to meet you," Aiden said into the radio.

They went to the cargo and manned the auto pilot to go to the moon and then Marie and Christopher prepared two other cargo ships for Ethan, Carlisle, and Aiden to use.

"One ship will be empty again, another decoy, and that'll head to Russia. We'll be heading to Canada toward Cord Blood Corp," Aiden commanded.

They launched the cargo carrier that was headed to the moon first, watching it get escorted by the smaller ships that had been circling them.

"Okay, now!" Aiden said.

They launched from their ship and auto launched the decoy, heading to Earth in a flash, hoping that if they were to be detected it wouldn't be too quickly and that even the High Royals wouldn't have the balls to blatantly attack them on Earth in daylight.

It was a race for safety and while they were going as quickly as they could, having to do relatively little during the wait, they all watched the monitor as it showed the decoy cargo ship getting set to land on the moon.

"It's landing now," Marie said, her voice echoing through the radio on a different frequency than what was being used with the vessel that was watching the main ship.

The small blip of the vessel on the screen suddenly grew larger.

"It's gone," Marie said, "blown to smithereens."

"Shit!" Aiden said. "We need to make sure we eject as quickly as possible when we land or risk being toast."

Full speed ahead, like shooting stars, the two cargo ships blasted into the Earth's atmosphere and headed toward their destinations. A decoy was on its way to self-destruct Russia and the other was headed to the land on the outskirts of Cord Blood Corp in Canada.

"We've been spotted by intelligence, American and Russian both, I think," Marie called out.

Trails of flames were in the air, all headed toward the cargo ships and showing that they were tactile missiles, set to obliterate and destroy the foreign objects in the sky.

"Damn it," Carlisle said, looking and feeling completely crazy. No amount of weapons training he had could help him diver this.

"The green button with the three arrows—press it!" Marie yelled out.

Ethan looked at the navigation counsel in front of them and saw what she was talking about and then pressed it like Marie had commanded. A thin, green luminescent shield rose around the cargo ship, deflecting the rockets off in a different course.

Jets came into sight next and they all watched them, feeling like they were players inside a video game.

Then, as quickly as it had started, it was over and they were in a field that was one mile away from the blood bank they were to enter into. The landing was gentle despite the madness in the atmosphere above the Earth.

No one wasted a second talking or celebrating, not wanting to be blown to bits, and they hit the eject button for the cargo vessel and ran out the door into the woods that were nearby as quickly as they could.

With barely any trees between them and the cargo ship, it exploded, sending a huge mushroom cloud into the air.

Carlisle, Ethan, and Aiden instinctually put up their arms to block any debris and stop the brightness and then they looked over at each other and burst out into maniacal laughter.

"Un-fucking-believable," Carlisle said.

"Now, let's get out of here before the po-po and every government agency in the world is swarming around us," Ethan said.

The three men began walking through the woods toward their destination, still perfectly polished in their business attire. They walked through the forest like it was a casual, noon hour stroll.

"I never thought this is how it'd be going down the next time I walked Earth," Carlisle said. "I'd kiss the ground if I didn't have this suit on."

"So, what's the next stage of our plan, hacker boy?" Ethan asked.

The three began to talk about the logistics of what they had to do, knowing that Ethan had the ability to ward anyone off who might want to hurt them quickly. Hopefully he didn't have to kill too much. Then again, Carlisle was also aware that he hadn't fed in quite some time and that, in and of itself, was unnerving. He also sensed that Aiden could care less who all died, so long as he didn't.

33

"Blood that saves; blood that kills."

At the edge of the woods there was a small, plain wooden box sitting there. It had obviously recently been placed there and Aiden walked over to it.

"Good, some supplies," he said casually. He opened up the box and began taking the contents out. There was large briefcases, guns, grenades, bullet proof vests and other devices that definitely looked like they could cause damage and, of course Carlisle's Grail shoes alongside with some of the bombs that were quickly becoming Marie's signature were also there.

"Who dropped this off?" Carlisle asked.

"I programed Watson to make a phone call when we reached earths solar system" Aiden said.

Carlisle wondered how Aiden had planned Watson to communicate with anyone to get those things there on such short notice. Then he realized…Aiden is a well thought of strategist .It would be a huge mistake if anyone ever crossed his path.

Equipped like soldiers, looking like Wall Street brokers with briefcases, the three made their way toward the front doors of Cord Blood Corp., smiling and ready to inflict some damage.

Before entering, Aiden reminded them, "We will have ten minutes max before police arrive. Keep that in mind. Don't waste time."

"And there's likely to be cameras so don't look at them directly," Ethan added.

A security guard was standing by the center doors of the building and he gave the three a thorough once over and nodded his head.

"Good day," Aiden said, smiling and he walked in through the front door, acting as if he belonged there, adjusting his suit as he strode past him.

They walked up to the receptionist desk. "Here for Mr. Arman," Aiden said.

The receptionist looked up and smiled. "Your name, sir."

"Easton," Aiden said.

"Just a minute, Mr. Easton," the receptionist said. She put her head down and Aiden pointed to the right, where there was a locked door that required a scanner. He motioned with his head and Carlisle walked that way quickly, followed by Ethan, who was his back-up.

"I'm sorry," the receptionist said, "you're not on…" Her words were stopped short by a small vile of gas that Aiden had opened up in front of her, making her head slump down, her hand still on the phone's receiver.

Aiden ran toward the secured door and got there just as Carlisle and Ethan got it open. They slid into the hallway and Ethan pointed to a room two doors up on the right. "In there."

"How do you know that?" Carlisle asked.

"A little gift."

They tried to bust the door down, which had a triple layer protective lock on it, and it wouldn't budge.

"We don't have time!" Carlisle shouted, standing back and shooting his gun at the hinges, making them loose. Ethan kicked the door in then and as he did, alarms started to go off.

"We'll stop whomever and you do your thing," Aiden said to Carlisle.

As the sirens blared, security guards came scrambling down the hallways, weapons drawn and when they saw what was there to greet them, they paused, clearly showing that they were not used to having any sort of real gun battle.

"Stop! Hands in the air," one of them shouted.

"Really, how cliché," Ethan said. He leapt toward the one who said that and in short measure, immobilized him.

One of the guards started to shoot and Aiden had no choice other than to shoot him to ensure he stayed out of the way.

289

For a relatively quiet place, guard after guard started to show up out of nowhere. It was like they were coming from the walls and the ones that were showing up had considerably more skills than the ones that they'd already taken down.

Aiden and Ethan were shooting in every direction, Ethan feasting when he had the moment to do so, and the sirens were still blaring loudly.

"How's it going?" Aiden called out.

"Almost there," Carlisle called out. "There's two systems though—get your ass in here if you can, Aiden."

"I got this," Ethan said with a sadistic grin.

Aiden charged into the room and you could hear Ethan unleashing a fury that was more powerful than what any creature seemed capable of doing alone. Every creature didn't have the abilities to kill and heal like a Fire, though. It made for a fearless fighter.

Aiden went to work on getting the codes to get into the vault where the blood types were stored while Carlisle downloaded the data base on the small, high capacity flash drive he had removed from his shoe.

"I've got the codes, now I have to go down the hall to get the samples," Aiden said.

"I'll keep going, fuck! I have about a minute left…I'll meet you there," Carlisle said. His eyes didn't leave the screen and his fingers were going so quickly that they were almost in a blur, his mind seeing what he was doing from a different perspective, a more enlightened Carlisle. It was almost like he had two minds working for him in unison, each helping the other and remembering every small detail.

"Done!" Carlisle shouted and he got up and ran into the hallway, nearly tripping over all the dead bodies.

He looked at Ethan and saw blood on his face and spattered all over the suit. There was no time to process the gruesomeness of the scene more. They had to get to Aiden.

They ran into the room where the vault was and found Aiden taking the last few samples. "This is all we have time for. We've got to get out of here," Carlisle called.

In the hallway the three saw the SWAT team had arrived and they were penetrating the hallways like stealth ninjas.

"Fuck! Hurry to the roof," Aiden shouted.

"What then?"

"A helicopter will get us," Aiden said. Then he pressed a button on the watch he was wearing.

Another voice came out to all three earpieces that Carlisle, Aiden, and Ethan had on. It was Marie. "How's it going? We are running into some problems up here."

"On our way to the roof," Aiden said.

The communication device went dead.

Looking back behind them as they ran up the sterile, echoing steps of the stairwell, Carlisle heard someone burst through the door on the first floor. Without hesitation, he reached into the inner pocket of his suit and pulled out a grenade, released the pin, and pressed a red button, activating the neurotransmitter. "This'll buy us some time."

The grenade exploded and screams could be heard and although they were already four floors up, bits of charred flesh splattered their suits and the walls around them, making the stairwell a splattered red painting of death and destruction.

In slow motion afterward, the stairs below Aiden, Ethan, and Carlisle began crumbling. "Move faster or we're screwed!"

Finally, the doors showing that they were on the roof level showed themselves. Having no time for anything else, Ethan ran ahead and busted through the door, sending it flying and when he turned around, he saw that Carlisle was right at the edge of it and one of Aiden's hands was holding on to the edge, his body dangling over the stairless opening.

Carlisle reached down and Aiden swung up his one hand, which was still clutching the suitcase, and it landed with a heavy thud on the roof.

"Take my hand," Carlisle shouted and Aiden grabbed it with the hand that was holding the suitcase and in a single, forceful pull, his body slid onto the roof. He was panting and breathing, his face scratched up and his temple bleeding.

"There's the chopper," Ethan said.

Barely able to talk, Aiden panted, "That's not ours."

The chopper had a police emblem on the side of it and the pilot looked down at the three battered men in business suits and his face froze.

"You seeing a ghost?" Aiden called.

One of them leaned out of the side of the chopper, high powered rifle pointed right at the three and Ethan quickly dodged out of the way.

"Where is it? We are sitting ducks" Carlisle asked.

"There it is," Ethan said, just rounding the tall building over to the right.

Sure enough, Ethan had heard it. The helicopter was coming full force and it was firing at the police chopper with someone manning a machine gun. The police pilot was injured and started to land the chopper.

The three got on the helicopter, which hovered above the roof and lowered a ladder for them to climb. Once inside, they breathed a sigh of relief and then Aiden tried to make contact with Marie again.

"Marie, come in…Christopher," Aiden called out.

There was no response, the signal was dead.

34

"It's not always easy to keep working the plan when emotions become your boss."

Christopher and Marie found themselves in the odd situation of working with each other and having to toss aside any speculation about what their true intentions may be. They were calm, calculating, and trying to keep things under control.

"See if you can get any additional information on what we're up against and I'll keep an eye on the shields," Marie said.

Unfortunately, Christopher and Marie were in limbo, waiting to hear from Aiden and the others about their status so they could know how to commence down to Earth afterward.

"The shields are at 91% and declining by 2% a minute," Marie said. "Damn it, where are those guys."

Marie tried to reach out to Aiden and there was no answer.

"It seems they were able to disrupt our transmissions or hijack our frequency."

"How do I fix it then?" Marie spat. She wanted to stay in control but she was worried about a bunch of things at that time, including the baby in her stomach.

"You cannot but that's why we have a predetermined plan, correct?" Christopher asked.

Marie didn't answer but she knew he was right. Internally she was shouting, "Forget the plan!"

The ship shook unexpectedly and a loud, piercing noise that sounded like an angry bird started to screech out "breach" repeatedly.

In that single moment of offensive attack from the High Royals ship, the shield reduced to 57% percent and began to spiral downward rapidly.

"If it hits 20% we have to go," Christopher said, "there won't be any time left."

"I'm not leaving them there."

293

"It's our orders," he replied.

"Don't you have any decency?" Marie asked, her eyes wide and feeling a greater sense of panic than she'd ever felt before.

"No, I do not. I know what I am meant to do and what I should do, nothing more and nothing less." Christopher's answer was truthful and matter-of-fact; the kind of thing that would normally get him belted by Marie, who wasn't equipped for that particular mentality at that moment.

"I'm going to get them. I don't care what anyone says," Marie said.

"You shouldn't do that."

Marie flipped Christopher off and then started to run out of the control room to get to the last smaller vessel that was remaining on board the large ship. She never knew what hit her but a dart went right into her neck and she dropped to the ground.

"Sorry, but the High Royals cannot get this ship and you cannot leave, either," he said.

He carried her to a stasis pod and then went back to the control room, preparing to take off and follow through on the command Aiden had given. It was fortunate that it happened to coincide with his plans.

* * *

"What's wrong?" Marie asked, looking at Christopher with a keen eye.

"You don't remember me," he said, putting his head down and showing something close to emotion, or at least an emotional connection.

"You look familiar but I'm not sure how I should know you."

"You've met me twice before, Marie. When you were a child"

Marie looked at Christopher and thought about it. Her eyes sparked, showing an inkling of remembrance. "Our fathers were best friends," she said softly.

"Yes, Lucius was a High Royal and your father's friend. He always talked highly of your father and you, too, wanting to work to help free your species from the High Royals."

Marie smiled.

Christopher continued. "That's why I was made; a genetic mutation made from the genes of Picasso and Caesar, my father's attempts to mix our species together to make one superior one."

"That doesn't sound that bad; it was done with a good intention," Marie said, putting her hand out to touch Christopher's arm.

He retracted from her touch and said, "I'm a hybrid; the ninth clone and the only successful one. I'm supposed to teach the human race to be better, how to survive."

"And the High Royals found out about you," Marie said, "and then ..."

"They killed your father and imprisoned mine, each for the crimes they perceived they'd done."

"I'm so sorry; I know how hard it is to lose someone you love, someone you admire."

"He was the only being I ever felt capable of loving as a father, as family. Now I live in fear, knowing that I'll be dead if they ever find out what I really am. I cannot allow that to happen."

"Your secret is safe with me," Marie said.

"I know, that's why I knew it was time to tell you," Christopher said.

You can say we're family ...

Marie jumped up, nearly hitting her head on the top of the stasis pod.

How did I get in here? She thought and touched her head. Then she remembered.

"Christopher," she whispered.

"Yes, it's true," a voice said. She turned to look and saw him standing at the entrance to her pod.

"That wasn't a dream?"

He shook his head no and then said, "We have a lot of work to do."

He walked away and Marie looked down at her stomach, patted it, and then got up, making her way to the control room to see what had happened since she'd been out. How long had she been out? She didn't even know…perhaps a few hours, maybe a few days.

35

"There comes a point in many people's lives when they have to evaluate one question: where do I go from here?"

Despite pulling off a great heist, Aiden, Ethan, and Carlisle could hardly celebrate, as they didn't know what was happening with Marie and Christopher. Then there was the surprising lack of a plan at that moment. Yes, they knew things could go awry but losing communication wasn't something they thought possible. The technology was just too advanced. It left the unspoken question: were Marie and Christopher alive or dead?

"How about your cabin?" Carlisle asked.

"That place has been removed; too much going on there and too many prying eyes," Aiden said. He put his head down and Carlisle could only imagine how sick that must have made Aiden feel. He'd never had time to really grow attached to any of his homes. They were beautiful and made from everything he wanted, desired, but they didn't really have a human connection inside the walls, something he was realizing he wanted more with each passing day.

Aiden called out to the pilot of the helicopter. "Drop us down at 43.7020° N, 79.4014°W."

The pilot nodded, adjusted his navigation system and turned the helicopter in a different direction, heading to where he was ordered.

"Are they going to be able to track down this thing?" Ethan asked.

"No, it has some rather sophisticated advancements, makes a Stealth jet look like a child's toy," Aiden said.

"You must know where we are going to be going, Aiden, where?" Carlisle asked.

"Safe house just outside of Toronto. From there, we'll be able to make contact with Marie and get reconnected."

The rest of the ride was smooth and when they landed in a clearing in the middle of the woods, Carlisle thought, *who has the time to search out these crazy ass spots?*

Within minutes, the three were walking through the woods again but this time they'd changed and had a whole supply of goods that they may require should they encounter trouble.

"Feeling like Rambo," Carlisle said laughing.

"Hopefully the early episodes, not when Stallone's an old man," Aiden said.

"How far is the walk?" Ethan said. He'd been rather quiet, absorbed in thoughts. Carlisle understood from his facial expressions that he wasn't thinking about anything too pleasant, either. He had a cynicism to him that couldn't be easily hidden.

"An hour," Aiden said. He looked down at his watch, which had a compass feature in it and started to veer to the right slightly. "We won't miss it when we get there."

When they got there, Carlisle knew exactly what Aiden meant. It wasn't glamorous by any means. It was a decrepit, old hunting cabin with a rusted tin roof on it. The front door hung by a single hinge and Carlisle was quite certain that if all three of them stepped onto the small porch at one time they'd fall through and crush any remaining integrity in the old boards.

Then, on the inside, another surprise was there. In the midst of the dingy, musky atmosphere sat a polished and poised Aerial.

"Damn, I'm glad to see you," Aiden said.

"You definitely have a bit of a predicament, don't you," Aerial said, laughing. "Carlisle, you're looking well."

Ethan looked back and forth between them and said, "Hey, I have to go take a leak. I'll be back."

He turned and walked out, leaving the three behind.

"Our transportation will be here in two minutes. I can't wait to get out of this shithole, either."

298

"Definitely not a place anyone would expect to find any of us in," Carlisle began, "even if we were still alive to them."

"The rumors are already circulating on the internet based on the police seeing you in the helicopter. You'll have to be more cautious," Aerial warned.

"Well, we'll be out of site now. Back to Canada and then finding a way to connect with Marie and Christopher," Aiden said. Then, almost painfully, he asked, "Have you heard anything about them?"

"They're good; under control for the moment," Aerial said.

"Oh, thank god!" Aiden said, breathing in a huge sigh of relief.

Aerial's phone buzzed and he pulled it out of his suit jacket. "Time to go."

"I'll get Ethan," Carlisle said, walking outside.

A black Hummer pulled up, loaded with armored plates and its windows were tinted. The driver of it didn't get out.

A minute later, Carlisle said he couldn't find him anywhere. Yelling for him wasn't an option, either, as you never knew who or what you may run across.

"What the hell are we going to do?" Carlisle asked. "We can't just leave him."

"I'm afraid we have no choice," Aiden said.

"Is that fact or preference?" Carlisle asked, looking at him oddly. He wasn't judging him but he knew Aiden's life would be easier with no Ethan in it.

"Fact," Aerial said. "Carlisle, these plans need to be followed."

"I just don't want him to do something dumb. He said …" Carlisle stopped talking mid-sentence and said, "Fuck! Do we have access to the internet somewhere here?"

"What's going on?" Aiden asked, walking over to him.

"I think I know where Ethan is heading—it's wherever Rodrigo is."

"The singer?" Aiden asked.

"Yes, the one who turned Ethan on to becoming a Fire."

"Well, that explains a lot," Aiden said but his face didn't look surprised.

Of course, Carlisle thought, *he'd know who all these people are since he's a killer of Fires.*

"Chicago," Aerial said.

"He's becoming a problem that needs to be addressed" Aiden said

"Well, that's where we need to go. Ethan has good intentions but a temper and…"Carlisle said.

Aiden finished. "And that means he could leave a trail."

"Yes!"

"I'm getting too involved in this mess of events .I'll drop you off in town and have one of my pilots prepare a jet for you so you can use to travel. After that you're on your own," Aerial said. "You two are playing a dangerous game and I cannot be associated with it."

"Don't worry about it, man," Carlisle said, "I completely get it. None of this is what I thought it would be—at all."

Aerial didn't answer and Carlisle had a sneaking suspicion that it was exactly what he'd expected it would be. There would be time to deal with that later.

In a small town, about a half hour out of Toronto, Aiden and Carlisle strolled into town. They tried to act casual and the only thing that helped them pull it off was the fact that it was a tourist town and had a fair amount of traffic.

"There," Aiden said, pointing to a small family, a husband, wife, and young son, getting out of a small RV just ahead. "Let's go."

"It's a family," Carlisle said, an immediate red flag being raised in his mind. "That's messed up."

"We don't have time," Aiden said. He was not about to enter into a debate.

Aiden ran up to the family and said, "We need this." He pushed them aside, grabbed the keys from the father's hand, and tried to get in.

"No," the father said, too timid to resist but wanting to stand his ground.

"What's going on?" the mother asked.

The son's eyes were wide and he went and wrapped his arms around his mother's waist, watching it all unfold.

The dad peered at the two closer. "Hey, aren't you two…"

"Yes we are. Change of plans," Aiden said, pulling out a gun and commanding them to get into the RV.

They got in the RV and the son trying to be brave but his lip was quivering and his mother was holding him close, while the father tried to stay in front of them, ready to protect them with his life.

"We're not going to hurt you if you cooperate," Carlisle said. "It'll be okay."

"I don't understand. You two are supposed to be dead?"

"That's a long story…a real long story," Carlisle said, trying to be friendly and assure them that everything will be okay.

"Stop asking questions!" Aiden barked out the words and showed that he'd stop at nothing to keep his secret and get to where he wanted to go.

"Aiden, chill, they're cooperating and not going to try anything stupid," Carlisle said. Then he turned to the family and said, "Right?" They simply shook their head.

Aiden rushed off toward the Toronto airport and there were many moments of silence, with questions smattered in between.

"What are you going to do with us after you get where you're going?" the father asked.

"Let you go but you cannot tell anyone about this or else …" The end of the sentence was left hanging, leaving it to the imagination. It was too much for the small boy, though, who began to cry.

"Don't worry. You're all going to be fine. We all want the same thing," Carlisle said, staring at the family with a gun pointed at them. Aiden drove and that was his thing but he was glad to be holding the gun instead of Aiden because he was fairly confident he would have no reason to shoot the poor, innocent family.

"Just drop us off by the road," the mother offered.

"Can't do that. This is your rental and they'll be able to track us down if we did that. We need you to drive away after you drop us off," Carlisle said.

"Where are we going?" the father asked.

"You'll know when we get there. Now I want all of you to shut up!" Aiden shouted the words and everyone listened. Carlisle was quiet, too, trying to use kind expressions to show the people that although he was pointing a gun at them he didn't want a tragic ending.

He did notice the young boy staring down at his shoes. Ah yes, the GRAILS.

Finally the airport exit was up ahead. It seemed to take forever even though it was only forty-five minutes.

Aiden went past the first checkpoint and pulled into the back of a parking lot that was located between the private hangars and the main terminals.

"This is it," he said, looking back. "Here's 10K. You can NOT tell anyone about this, got it?"

"Yes," the father said.

"Come on, Carlisle."

"Just a second," Carlisle said.

302

He reached down and started to take off his GRAILS. He looked at the small boy. "This has to stay quiet and I know we've scared you but it's important…for all of us. I'm going to give you these. They won't fit yet but they're pretty cool. They can even make you fly. What I really need for you to do is to take this," Carlisle said, clicking on the soul of his shoe. A USB stick popped out with O.R.B. written on it.

"What is it?"

"It's my story. You'll know when the time is right to share it with people, got it?"

The boy nodded.

Carlisle slid on another pair of shoes from his bag and hopped out of the RV.

"What were you doing?" Aiden asked suspiciously.

"Just reassuring them. They're good people…and we are, too, even though it sure as shit didn't look like it."

"Desperate times. Desperate measures," Aiden said.

An hour later, they were on one of Aerial's private jets, making a very important journey. Two people that were supposed to be dead needed to go stop someone that the world also thought was dead from making a very public scene. Yes, life as a dead person was getting more complicated than it ever could have when they were considered 'alive and well.'

36

"Blaming someone for what you've become doesn't change who you are."

Ethan was walking through a Toronto suburb, clicking on the red matte lighter that still helped him clear his thoughts and stay connected to his mother, who he knew would be so sad at the choices he'd made in the past years, as well as the one he had made and was on his way to.

With his distinguished looks Ethan supposed it was only a matter of time before someone recognized him.

"Hey, aren't you..." someone asked, staring at Ethan in awe. "I thought you were dead."

"I'm very much alive."

"Can I get a picture of us together?" the guy asked.

"Sure," Ethan said turning around. The only flash the guy saw, however, was Ethan's fist coming at his face, unleashing a powerful punch to the jaw that sent the guy reeling backward and blood splattering all over the sidewalk.

"Nice to meet you," Ethan said, leaning down to grab his keys. The guy's eyes were opened and reflecting in them was the red gleam of Ethan's eyes. He would have taken the guys eyeballs and drank his blood if they weren't out in the open.

Ethan hopped into the car and began to make his way to Chicago, a journey that would take about a day and a half of straight driving. It was a good thing he didn't require much sleep.

Finally without watchful eyes or restrictions, Ethan was able to indulge and feast his way to Chicago, wanting to have as much energy as he could for when he confronted Rodrigo. His face was on the news, people assuming that some doppelganger was out there on a killing streak, playing off their likeness. He couldn't help but smile at how twisted it was. He also realized that there would be some people looking for him that knew how to find him and also had an idea of how to control him. Then there were also thoughts of Marie...damn, he knew in his heart of hearts that their child, whatever it may be, was probably better off without him around it.

Chicago's silhouette was in the distance and Ethan knew right where to go. He was so attuned to his desire to get to Rodrigo he could practically smell him. He walked up to the club where Rodrigo was set to do an 'impromptu performance,' something his agent was masterful at arranging, and saw one of his bodyguards there guarding the VIP entrance.

"Hey, how you doing?" Ethan asked.

"Ethan," the bodyguard said, instantly on alert. "No wait…the lunatic they're saying looks like him. He's dead."

Ethan started laughing and unleashed on the bodyguard instantly, beating him to a pulp and tossing his body against a dumpster that was a few feet away.

"I'll show myself in," he said.

Even in the noisy environment of the club scene the disturbance that Ethan had caused didn't go unnoticed. He walked down the back hallway of the club, knowing that the bulky bodyguards would guide him in the direction he needed to go to get to Rodrigo.

"I suggest you turn around," one bodyguard said in a deep, calm voice.

Bam! Ethan palmed him under the nose, sending him down to his knees, eyes stinging and clutching his oozing nose.

He kept walking.

Another one came. Another one went down.

A large opening came and a DJ could be heard talking to the crowd, who was getting more animated and just as he said, "Rodrigo Maducci," Ethan entered the room and saw him starting to walk on stage.

Rodrigo turned around and saw Ethan, walked to the side of the stage and took off running through a side door.

Ethan charged through the crowd—a very confuse crowd—and toward that door and out into the alleyway.

Two guys were standing there, holding Baretta BU9s in their hands, and their fingers on the trigger. Ethan stared at them, his eyes red and glowing like embers would in the darkness of the night, and there was a car door slamming to the right.

305

Ethan looked and saw Rodrigo getting into the car and before the door was even shut, the driver was pressing down on the accelerator. He started to run and the shots rang out. A second later, an intense burning was in Ethan's left shoulder and on the calf of his right leg. He fell down, shocked from the sting and unable to catch the car. He stared as its taillights disappeared as it rounded the corner and merged into the busy Chicago traffic.

Lying there by his feet was a piece of paper. He grabbed it and stared at it, reading it via the lone light in the alley he was sitting in. It read:

Paris. 1 Day. You know where.

"Gladly," Ethan mumbled. He turned around and saw the two bastards who'd shot him from behind and got up, limping toward them. The one called out, "I'll shoot you again, fucker, if you don't stop."

However, that guy and the other one still had no idea that Ethan could make a single leap, like a panther on the prowl, and pounce the two over, shredding them to pieces in an instant. They didn't have time to do anything and Ethan was out of there before a crowd emerged from the club. Everyone he walked by cleared a path and he could hear murmurs of his name. He had no problems letting them think what they wanted to.

Meanwhile, Carlisle and Aiden had just arrived in Chicago and were walking through the security checkpoints since they'd been on a Canadian flight. They heard a name on the news and couldn't help but turn their heads.

"Well known musical artist Rodrigo Maducci has been in an altercation tonight. There's no word if he was hurt, as his security detail was able to get him out in time. However, the real mystery lies in the eye witness accounts, which state that supposedly deceased musician, Ethan Bryson was the one seeking Maducci out. More details to follow as this investigation unfolds."

"So, what now?" Aiden said.

"Ethan told me that when Rodrigo helped him become a Fire that they did it at the Catacombs," Carlisle said.

"Paris, huh?"

The two walked right up to the ticket counter, knowing that the situation had just grown more intense. They had to find Ethan before he caused more damage than what could be repaired.

When Carlisle and Aiden were at the ticket counter the attendant smiled and said, "You know…you two remind me of…oh, never mind." She looked at their IDs with aliases on them, booked their flight, and sent them on their way.

* * *

Making his way down into the Catacombs for the second time was an entirely different experience for Ethan. The screams and darkness of it all didn't startle him at all; in fact, he felt comforted by it, knowing that he was among his own. It had been a long time since Rodrigo and him were face to face. It would prove to be an interesting experience, regardless of how it turned out.

In the distance, a small candle was lit and it grew brighter as Ethan got closer.

"If you want to see me, come closer," a voice called out. Ethan recognized it as Rodrigo's but didn't give him the courtesy of a response. Everything he wanted to say was going to take place face to face.

Rodrigo called again and his voice echoed, bouncing off the walls.

He's moving; trying to trick me. Well, I have a few tricks of my own, Ethan thought.

He sensed Rodrigo on the other side of one of the walls in the Catacombs and he stopped walking, listening quietly. He heard the slight shuffle of feet and moved forward, so silently that it didn't seem like his feet were even touching the ground.

Taking a quick peak around the corner, Ethan saw three of Rodrigo's men standing there. They were each staring in one direction and the one that was staring at Ethan slowly nudged the guy to his left.

The three heads turned.

"Looking for me?" Ethan said.

The guy on the right took a giant leap and landed right in front of Ethan, thinking he could just pounce on him and immobilize him while the other two severed his head and speared his guts. Well, he had another thing coming.

Ethan's hand went out into the air and his pointed nail punctured the artery in his neck. Blood began to spurt out of the side of it and the guy's legs dangled on the ground. As the other two charged over to help, Ethan threw his body into them and they toppled over. Before they could even move, Ethan was on top of them and he was ripping out their guts and snapped their necks, grabbing their own short knives to decapitate them afterward.

"You're going to have to do better. It's just you and me, Rodrigo," Ethan called out.

"I'm glad you're here," Rodrigo called and in a second flat, he was standing right in front of Ethan, just about two feet away. His arms were crossed and his grin was confident, even cocky.

"Why me? Why all this?" Ethan asked, wanting to get to the point. He didn't have much time.

"It was part of the plan; what needed to be done. You were chosen by powers higher than you or I to receive the Lilith seed and to go to that tournament."

"For what? Certainly not for fame," Ethan said.

Rodrigo gave a sadistic laugh and shook his head. "We are decent musicians but the power isn't in our talents as much as the message, now is it?"

"What the fuck you mean?" Ethan said.

"Have you ever listened to your own recordings?"

Ethan didn't answer, not sure where Rodrigo was going with it.

"The label puts them in afterward; your music has the exact same thing brother. It's what keeps the cause funded and gives us special Fires the ability to go wherever we want and do whatever we want without getting busted. However, you've fucked up the plan."

"Which was what, Rodrigo?"

"To kill Carlisle, Aiden and Marie."

"Well, I'm my own boss, no one else," Ethan said. "So, now that your plan is ruined it's time to carry out mine."

Rodrigo still laughed, not backing down or showing any hesitation about his ability to defend himself against Ethan.

Ethan charged at him, saying, "I'm going to rip your head off and blow you up in this Catacomb—erase your existence from this Earth."

"What about the world?" Rodrigo said.

Ethan didn't care what he said. Rage was his fuel and revenge was his mission. He wrapped his arms around Rodrigo's torso and the two went flying backward, falling to the ground. Rodrigo was punching at his ribs, puncturing them with his nail, and Ethan poked his fingers in Rodrigo's eyes, only pulling away when he began to bite on his palm.

Then Rodrigo was on top, laughing as he looked down at Ethan, choking him with one hand. Ethan couldn't loosen his grip and he reached down next to him, feeling a skull that they'd tripped over when they fell and smashed it into the side of Rodrigo's head. He slumped to the side but immediately stood up and stared at Ethan, a sneer on his face.

"What the…" Ethan didn't understand why Rodrigo was growing stronger the more they struggled.

"Priceless, you think you're 'all that' but you aren't anything more than what you've been allowed to believe—guided to accept—all these years, Ethan."

Everything was changing and Ethan didn't understand it. Before his very eyes, Rodrigo the human turned into a form he knew all too well. It was that of a High Royal but in human size with long horns poking out of his forehead like a ram and a long tail coming from the back of his spine.

"I don't get it," Ethan said. He stepped back and suddenly realized that the tables were turned and what he'd set out to do was a bit different than expected.

"Well, if I'm going down, let it be in a blaze of glory," Ethan mumbled. Then he charged toward Rodrigo, giving every bit of effort he had saved up to topple over the guy and slaughter him regardless of who he was or what he became.

With blow for blow being delivered, Rodrigo was not tiring and it became clear to Ethan that he had to find a different tactic other than physical strength. He knew that he'd grown stronger mentally against the commands of the High Royals, making him not as much a servant to them as they believed him to be. Then again…if they'd ever suspected it before they had nothing to speculate upon any longer.

Rodrigo's tail began to thrash around, moving back and forth as it made a 'whoosh' sound in the stagnant air of the Catacomb. Ethan managed to avoid it but he was walking backward slowly as he did and he realized he was pinned against a wall.

Smash. The tail connected with Ethan's face and he toppled backward, smashing his head into the stone wall and his body went limp, lying on the ground like a piece of cooked spaghetti.

Ethan was blinking, trying to focus, and Rodrigo paced back and forth in front of him. "They'll be here in four hours to get you. I have to keep you alive but they didn't' say how alive."

Rodrigo laughed, not revealing what he planned on doing.

Then his head whipped around and Ethan turned and saw two bricks flying through the darkness at him. It was unexpected and Rodrigo paused, remaining motionless for a fraction of a second but it was enough for Carlisle to deliver a full-out flying side kick into his hard torso and sending the Human High Royal toppling backward.

Ethan took advantage and wrapped up Rodrigo's legs and the creature toppled to the ground in a big heap that sounded like a boulder falling off a mountain. Then Aiden moved forward, hacking away at Rodrigo with an axe, one that had 'fire emergency' written across its handle in French, English, and Spanish.

Rolling out of the way, Ethan stood up and began to kick at Rodrigo over and over, unleashing his fear and anger.

Carlisle was trying to get up off Rodrigo and felt his claw-like hand wrap around his throat. He was squeezing so hard that Carlisle thought his eyeballs might just pop out for the monster on their own.

Reaching to his side, he tried to grab his gun as he watched the High Royal's mouth open wide in anticipation of biting his face off. Just as Carlisle pulled his gun out of the back side of his waist where it was tucked just under his jeans, the handle of the axe smashed into Rodrigo's mouth so hard that his grip loosened.

Carlisle rolled off and saw Ethan holding the axe. Aiden was helping him up and the two stood back and Ethan unleashed his fury on the entity that had changed his life forever, selling him a false bill of goods—to his way of thinking.

Everything went silent except for the sound of heavy breathing.

"We have to go," Aiden said to Carlisle.

Carlisle walked up to Ethan and took the axe from his hands. "Come on, man, we've got to get out of here."

They began to walk out of the Catacombs on high alert but quiet. There was nothing to be said at that moment.

A slight crackling noise came from Aiden's body then and he suddenly said, "Yes, Marie."

Everyone stopped walking to listen to half of the conversation going on between the ear piece Aiden was wearing and Marie from the other end.

"Yes...he's alive...twenty minutes. See you then." Aiden stopped talking and turned to the two and said, "We've got to hurry and get out of here. It's our one shot."

They all ran up the winding layers of the Catacombs and ended up in the graveyard.

"South gate," Aiden said.

They went over there and blending in with the spooky darkness was the outline of a vessel. It was their cargo ship, which gave them a one way ticket out of there with no delays.

37

"Coming to terms with the inevitable happens eventually. It's really a matter of choosing the easy route or the more challenging alternative."

Running aboard the small vessel, the small set of steps into it slid up and the door closed immediately. Everyone charged into the control room and Marie looked at them, startled.

"We look worse than we are," Ethan said, trying to assure her.

Carlisle looked at Ethan, who he knew was as bad as he looked, and noticed that he had an abundance of love in his eyes at that moment. He really did care for Marie but something was wrong...

"We don't have much time," Marie said. "The shields are still weak on the main ship and if we don't get into the Earth's orbit quickly and find a way to out maneuver those High Royals we're S-O-L."

"Please don't tell me Christopher's manning that thing alone," Aiden said.

"Yes, and I trust him."

"Boy, you seem to trust all the wrong people, these days" Aiden snapped.

"Seriously everyone; this isn't the time," Carlisle said. "Marie, how long until we reach the ship?"

"Top speed, about three hours," she said.

"Why don't you rest and let Aiden take the helm. You look exhausted," Carlisle suggested.

She opened her mouth, ready to unleash on him but a yawn came out instead of a yell.

"Fine," she said and she walked out and into another chamber that was lined with cots attached to the walls for short rests; it was not a big enough ship to have chambers for stasis pods.

All was silent.

Eventually the ship came into sight and Christopher helped them re-enter into it without hassles and they began to slowly raise their weak defense shields.

"Do you think they know about the damage?" Carlisle asked Christopher.

"Of course, they know everything," he replied.

"I'll be back in a bit," Carlisle said. Since there was no need for a response, Christopher didn't give one.

Carlisle walked away and toward his chamber, ready to catch a bit of rest himself. It had been an exhaustive few days and although small, blue pills and other devices helped him keep going; he was still a human who needed sleep and rest to function at his best.

Now in his quarters and kickin' back, Carlisle slowly drifted off to sleep. It didn't last long. Loud voices came from the hallway and they were just outside his door. It was Aiden and Marie and they were having a heated talk, one that Carlisle didn't have to strain his ears to hear.

"I just don't get how you could have done it. And, you actually plan on keeping that thing?"

"It's not a thing; it's a baby and yes, it's a gift, one that no one would have thought possible, and I will be keeping it."

"You're not ready to raise a child, you don't know what it'll grow up into," Aiden countered.

"And neither do you," Marie said. "It's not like you have to be the father. This baby has one—Ethan."

There were no words in response to that but a loud smash of something against the wall. Carlisle guessed that Aiden had smashed his fist on the wall. Then everything went silent.

There was silence and then Marie screamed again, "Aiden! Stop it!"

Carlisle ran out of his room and down the hall and saw Aiden standing there, blood trickling down his face from a split lip and Ethan's hand clenched in a fist.

"Stop it, you guys, this isn't going to help…or change anything," Carlisle said, running up.

"You'd better watch it," Aiden said, pointing at Ethan. "Remember, you're the one who brought me back here, anyway. If you didn't want me around, why'd you do it?"

"You jeopardized our mission. The missions integrity comes first and foremost," Aiden said, controlling his words but you could hear them quavering from his pent up anger.

"You're all heart, aren't you? No wonder why she came running to my arms." Ethan's words were like an accelerant on a flame—ready to inflame and ignite a second explosion.

"Ethan, come on, let's go work it off, man," Carlisle said calmly.

Ethan turned to him and paused for a moment, then nodded his head. The two walked silently to the training room and once they were in there, Carlisle started a conversation.

"You know, you have to realize that this is tough on Aiden. He was blindsided. He had no idea that you two had anything going on," Carlisle said.

"It didn't seem like he had dibs on her or cared…for more than a piece of ass, anyway."

"You really like her, don't you?"

Ethan nodded, acknowledging Carlisle was right. "It was easy to grow close to her when everyone was in their pods; we'd talk and I got to know her pretty well."

"Well, that's obvious," Carlisle said, letting out an abrupt chuckle.

"It's some heavy shit, man, like it or not, I'm not sure I'm ready for it."

"I'd suppose it is a strain when you know you're going to be a father," Carlisle said.

"She wants this child but I'm not so sure."

"Well, Marie is. She's probably let you know that and she's definitely let Aiden know that. She's driving the ship, literally and figuratively."

314

Silence filled the space between the two again until Carlisle broke it. "Look Ethan, what I'm saying is that we all have a tough situation we're in here. No one knows what's going to go down and we have to work together, not against each other...make sense?"

"Yeah, Makes sense," Ethan said.

Carlisle left the training room a few moments later and breathed in heavily, going to find Aiden and hopefully have a successful conversation with him, too. He felt like he'd gotten through to Ethan but time would tell.

38

"It's easier to go into the unknown if you know you're a free man."

Marie woke up and her stomach was cramping. She felt something hot and warm and reached down with her hand slowly, sitting up as she did so. When she looked at her fingers she paled. They were red. She was bleeding.

There was only one person she felt she could trust to help her with this situation—Christopher. She called out to him on the communicator next to her bed and a short while later he was entering her room.

"The baby's coming…I need your help," Marie said, wincing as she spoke each word.

Christopher walked over and had no panic in his voice. "I'll get the tessseract and be right back."

Marie nodded and laid her head back on her pillow, pressing back with each cramp and biting her lip. Sweat was pouring off her face and every pore, making her entire body clammy. She breathed and tried to remain calm but she was panicked. While she was no expert at child birth she knew that what was happening was not normal—what should be expected. Plus, it was about six weeks' early. Maybe it was associated with the Lilith seed, but she didn't know for certain.

Christopher came back in and behind him was Aiden, Ethan, and Carlisle. He said, "No, only me."

Ethan began protesting but Marie screamed and that shut him right up. Christopher went in and shut the door.

For the next four hours, a hybrid human/High Royal and a woman, afraid and uncertain, worked through everything that was necessary to deliver a baby. It was a boy and it cried, it was all there and absolutely beautiful.

"What will you name it?" Christopher asked.

"Honestly, I don't know yet. I'd like to name it after my father but I guess I have to consult 'the father' first, huh?"

Christopher nodded, not seeing the weak joke in her words.

"For now, we need to get this little guy down to the medical room and scan him and make sure he's healthy and okay," Marie said, trying to get up. She didn't get far, though, because she was tired and weak.

"I'll do that," Christopher said calmly.

"I want to be there," Marie demanded, "I have to know he's alright."

"And what about you? You need to be alright, too. Just rest and I'll be back as quickly as possible, okay?"

Marie finally conceded and Christopher walked out of the door to her room and toward the medical room. Ethan ran up to Christopher and looked down at the small child but saw its strength. It was an amazing feeling to him and out of all the things he'd experienced he couldn't recall anything quite like it. And…it was part him.

"Can I watch?" Ethan asked Christopher.

Christopher nodded and the two walked into the medical room together. A half hour later, they walked back out and the baby was lying in a sterile bin filled with soft sheets on wheels—a makeshift bassinette. A surveillance oculus android followed to inform any one on the ship of any alerts or changes with the new baby. They went down the hall back to Marie, who'd been bothering them constantly on the communicator while the child was out of her sight.

They walked into the room, wheeling the baby. Ethan smiling and Christopher as calm as always, and Ethan ran up and kissed Marie's head, "Good job, baby. He's perfect."

"What should we name him?" Marie asked.

"Whatever you want," Ethan replied.

"You need to get assessed, Marie," Christopher said. "Ethan and the oculus can stay with the child."

Marie turned to Ethan. "You okay doing that?"

317

"We'll find out," Ethan said.

Christopher guided Marie to the medical room. She'd insisted on walking and Ethan sat down. He was looking at the baby and he couldn't take his eyes off the little guy with his silky smooth, wavy hair. His eyes were still closed, not revealing what color they were or might be.

There was a knock on the door and Ethan looked up as Aiden walked in. He immediately tensed up, feeling protective.

"I...uh...sorry to bug you. Carlisle needs you for a minute," Aiden said. "He's in the training room."

Ethan looked at the oculus and stated "record". A small red light let up on the oculus. Then Ethan looked to his son and back. "I guess it's okay; he's sleeping and it'll only be a minute."

Ethan walked out of the room and ran down to the training room. Carlisle was working out and he looked up and quit what he was doing, calling out, "Congratulations Ethan."

"Thanks. Aiden said you needed me?" Ethan questioned.

"I'd mentioned going to find you later and see the baby," Carlisle said. "Aiden must have misunderstood me."

"You want to come see him now?" Ethan offered. "I'd better get back there or Marie's likely to kick my ass if she returns before me."

"She doing okay?"

"Yeah, Christopher's a decent doctor—and nurse," Ethan said, laughing. "Who would have thought?"

"Not me," Carlisle said.

They walked out of the training room and down to Marie's room and got into the room and walked over to the baby. A second later, Marie was there, too.

"How is he?"

"Sleeping peacefully," Ethan said but he stopped in midsentence.

Carlisle and Ethan looked down and Ethan said, "Fuck! Christopher."

He was shaking and Marie ran up and stared down at her small son. He was blue and not breathing, lying still. She was shaking him, tapping his small cheeks, and leaned down to breath into his mouth.

"I'm sorry, Marie," Christopher said. He put his hand on her arm and tried to get her away from the dead child but she flailed, resisting. Finally she had to admit what was obvious.

"What happened? I don't understand," she said, dropping to her knees and instantly beginning to weep.

"I'm not sure," Christopher said, immediately going to the tesseract to reference something…anything.

"Wait, where is the oculus?"

"I know," Ethan said, his eyes began to grow red.

He ran out of the room and charged into the control room. Aiden was sitting by the controls and staring out the window into space. His gaze was in the general direction of the High Royal ships that suddenly had them surrounded.

"You son of a bitch!" Ethan shouted out and charged up to Aiden, grabbing him by the neck and whipping him out of the chair.

"What?" Aiden said, staring him in the eyes. He didn't wait for Ethan's response. He raised his knee up and shoved it forcefully into Ethan's gut, making him reel backward and release his grip.

"You killed him, you sick son of a bitch," Ethan said, jumping back up and lunging at him, slamming his body into the rim that surrounded the control panels of the ship's shield system.

The two started going back and forth, each using every skill and bit of strength they had to unleash their hatred for each other.

319

Meanwhile, Marie was pale and confused. "Where did he go?"

"I don't know," Carlisle said. Then he realized. "He went to find Aiden."

"Oh no, we've got to find them," Marie said.

"Why?"

"You guys don't understand Aiden like I do. He won't stop until he kills Ethan," Marie said, starting to walk.

"And Ethan won't stop until he kills Aiden, either," Carlisle added.

"I'll run ahead," Carlisle said, "Christopher, you help Marie since I know she won't stay back."

Everyone briefly glanced at the lifeless body of the baby and Carlisle couldn't blame anyone for not wanting to witness such a sad, painful sight.

When Carlisle got into the room he saw blood everywhere, damaged equipment, and two men still trying to best the other despite looking like they were ready to die at any given moment. Aiden clearly had the upper hand, though, and he quite literally had one hand to use. His right arm was broke, dangling and a bone could be seen sticking out of his shirt.

"Stop it! What the hell," Carlisle said, running in between the two. "Neither of you can come out of this good. Calm down."

"He's a fucking murderer!" Ethan shouted, barely able to stand from all the blood he'd lost.

"You can't just assume that. We don't know what happened yet. Where is the damn android? Maybe it knows" Carlisle said.

"Oh, I know," Ethan said.

"You weren't even sure you wanted to be a father," Aiden said. "Maybe the android short circuited when it was on alert and killed the boy. When I left it was alone with the child."

"I never told you that it would go on alert." Ethan said. He looked at Carlisle and Carlisle hadn't told Aiden that either.

"Where'd you hear that?" Carlisle said.

"I overheard Christopher programing the oculus" Aiden said.

Marie walked in and said, "Stop it! That's enough." Her voice was strong but there were tears stinging her eyes. Christopher was by her side and said he'd be back in a minute.

He left and Carlisle tried to calm everyone down while Marie went over to the equipment to see how damaged it was and so she could raise the shields again.

Then Christopher came back.

"Where'd you go?" Aiden asked.

"To move the body," Christopher said.

Carlisle looked at Christopher and while he couldn't explain why he was certain, his intuition told him that Christopher wasn't being completely honest.

"Is there something else?" Carlisle asked.

"No," Christopher said.

"You're lying," Carlisle said, walking up to him and going about an inch from his face. "What's going on?"

"I'm not supposed to say," Christopher said.

Carlisle hadn't noticed until now that it was a metallic robotic leach on the back of Christopher's left ear. Almost as if it possessed Christopher.

"Oh no!" Marie shouted.

Everyone turned around as a large ship bumped into the side of theirs. The High Royals were attacking. Marie turned to Christopher. "You knew about this?"

"I wasn't supposed to say anything," he said plainly.

"Still following their orders, huh?" she said, glaring and turning back around. "All defense shields are down. We are screwed."

"No, we'll figure it out," Carlisle said, stepping up to the plate. He didn't have time to deal with Aiden and Ethan, who'd made themselves ineffective to be any help at all. As for Christopher, who knew what the hell was going on with him .It was too late to deal with him at this point. The ship was under attack.

"Marie, this is up to us and we've got to do this together," Carlisle said. "Can we get to a cargo ship and escape that way?"

"Too risky, we're likely to be blasted."

The communicators grew loud and static was emitting through them for a few seconds. Then everything became clear and the voice of the High Royal that had spoken with them before came through.

"They've jacked our frequency," Carlisle said.

"Listen now," the High Royal said, "you are going to surrender to us peacefully and turn this ship over or you shall die. There's no negotiation and no other options."

"No," Carlisle said. He offered nothing else and there was silence on the other end.

Marie turned to him and said, "Look at the situation here, Carlisle. Those two are beat up, I'm in rough shape, and somehow they made Christopher compelled to obey them. We need to surrender and go from there before we all die."

"She's right," Aiden called out.

Carlisle looked around at everyone and was in disbelief. "We haven't done all we've done for this," he said, pointing to the large vessel which was hovering so close that they could see the High Royal who was talking to them. It was the bastard that Carlisle had first met when he'd landed on the moon—the one who had a clear dislike of humans—all humans.

"Be logical," Marie said.

"Fuck being logical. None of this shit is logical. You guys wrapped me up into this shitty world and said you needed me. I am not going to the moon to face any of the only two fates they'll offer—quick death or torture and death. I would rather die trying to be a free man or finding that place where we can start a new civilization for humans."

"Let's vote," Aiden said.

Well, the vote sucked for Carlisle. Only Ethan and he were on the same page. Everyone else said they should surrender to the High Royals and formulate a new plan from there. They'd figure it out.

His voice may have been stifled at that moment but his spirit had not been.

"We are going to land on the Moon Base," Marie said.

"Wise choice," the High Royal responded. "This little game has gone on long enough."

"Surrendering to these guys is fucking ridiculous," Carlisle said, "they don't respect us; they don't even want us alive."

"Well, if you want us to stay alive keep your head," Aiden said, gritting his teeth.

"Enough talk about death!" Marie shouted this out and her hands were shaking. She breathed in, recomposing herself, and prepared to take the ship out of hover mode and take the three hour journey to the Moon Base.

Christopher quietly said, "I'm sorry, Marie. I know it must be hard that he's gone."

She looked at him with vacant eyes and said, "His name was Connor—for the record."

Christopher nodded.

The ship began to move and Carlisle was sitting next to Marie. Her and Christopher were whispering something to each other and Carlisle could have cared less what it was. He had his chance and he slowly leaned over, finding the hyper-drive jet activator, and the ship lurched, making everyone's body's shake forward.

Marie and Christopher turned around, stunned. Aiden broke the silence.

"No! What the fuck have you done!"

Carlisle's eyes turned silver. Channeling his strength from the astral plane

Carlisle said, "The right thing."

The ship took off, averting the direction of the moon and heading toward a great void that lied beyond the moon.

Laser beams and astral cannons were flying by them in a matter of seconds, some directly hitting the ship and others missing or simply grazing. It was staying on course and Carlisle channeled into everything he'd researched and read up on when it came to navigating the ship.

Marie moved in, trying to shut down the jet, and Carlisle turned in front of her blocking her way, "If you doubted we'd be dead before you know we'll be dead now."

"You douche bag," Marie mumbled but she didn't stop him.

She turned around and went over to Ethan and Aiden. Ethan was passed out and Aiden was struggling to get out of his seat and attempt to go knock Carlisle on his ass but Marie stopped him.

Then, just as a large astral bomb cracked the large window in front of the control panels, the ship entered the black hole, plunging into it and then there was an explosion. All that could be seen was a bright white anomaly in the darkest skies of the universe. That ship wouldn't be landing on the Moon Base—ever. Destination unknown.

Epilogue

O.R.B.
Dark Seeds

Carlisle and the other survivors roamed the planet they'd landed on, battered and bruised; no one was sure of where they were or what was to come. Yes, they had survived for the moment...but for how long?

Staring down at his hands and legs, Carlisle knew that he had to do something and that all too familiar anger swept over his emotions quickly. "I'm going to kill every one of those prick bastards," he shouted, kicking a bit of debris from the ship that was by his foot. Yet, he also knew that it had been nothing short of some divine intervention that they'd landed with life intact. Had the tesseract saved them? Time would tell.

In the distance, Marie and Ethan were kneeling down, staring at something. Carlisle walked over and saw them looking down at the small, lifeless body of their child. "This child will have a proper burial," Marie said.

No one argued and there were no words to comfort them in their time of grief—a time that had come now that they knew they were not prisoners of the High Royals.

With a tourniquet on, Aiden did what he could, and Christopher and Carlisle began gathering vines, leaves, and peculiar woods from the trees on the mysterious planet to make a coffin.

In the distance, you could hear the crashing waves of the silver ocean that they'd landed near. It shimmered with such beauty in a time of such sadness, making it almost too much to bear. Even the glasses that they wore couldn't tame its radiance.

Marie and Ethan called everyone over and as they all stood there, a wave of anger swept over Carlisle as he stared at the dead child. "I am going to find a way to go back and kill them for what they've done."

Marie turned and looked at him, not saying a word. Her eyes had no expressions and although she was alive and breathing, her eyes seemed as dead as her child's. Then she turned back to what she was doing and just kept going, Ethan at her side showing more support and tenderness than he'd ever shown before—that Carlisle could recall, anyway.

It was time to put off the inevitable and Ethan and Marie each carried one part of the small coffin they'd created and walked toward the ocean, placing it by its edge. They paused for a second and stared down at it while everyone else watched from a respectable distance behind the two. Marie pulled something out from the pocket of her tattered and scratched suit and leaned down. With a single click that echoed louder than a thunder bolt at that moment, she started the casket on fire and then she and Ethan pushed it out to the ocean.

Carlisle and the others watched as it floated out to the ocean until it couldn't be seen any longer, aside from a small trail of smoke. Marie turned around and walked away, not looking at anyone in particular, although everyone was looking at her. As soon as she'd passed the last person standing there a single tear fell, rolling down her cheek and onto the ground.